Masquerade

"No matter what *you* may believe, women are not all mindless ninnies," Cat snapped. She looked up and realized he was standing far too close. "And not all women are panting for your caresses, either, your grace. Gad, what arrogance you must have to think that every simpering miss is waiting to fall at your feet!"

"So you are not one of those, all of whom are manufactured by my . . . enormous arrogance?" Ransom asked, his lips curled in amused skepticism. "I see. Well, I certainly have no desire to force my presence where it is unwelcome."

He turned to go and, with conflicting emotions, she followed him silently to within a few steps of the parlor doors, then nearly collided with him when he turned suddenly.

"But first I have a desire to make a liar out of you, Miss Amberly," he whispered . . .

Heart's Masquerade

DEBORAH SIMMONS

AVON BOOKS  NEW YORK

HEART'S MASQUERADE is an original publication of Avon Books.
This work has never before appeared in book form. This work is a novel.
Any similarity to actual persons or events is purely coincidental.

AVON BOOKS
A division of
The Hearst Corporation
1350 Avenue of the Americas
New York, New York 10019

Copyright © 1989 by Deborah Siegenthal
Published by arrangement with the author
Library of Congress Catalog Card Number: 89-91199
ISBN: 0-380-75851-2

Special Printing: June 1993
First Avon Books Printing: October 1989

AVON TRADEMARK REG. U.S. PAT. OFF. AND IN OTHER COUNTRIES, MARCA
REGISTRADA, HECHO EN U.S.A.

Printed in the U.S.A.

RA 10 9 8 7 6 5 4 3 2

Chapter 1

Catherine Amberly felt her horse shy nervously at a rustling in the dry leaves underneath the great oaks.

"Easy, Jackson," she whispered to the animal. She was riding the great hulking beast for the first time, her own horse having been sold, but she was surprised at his jittery behavior. She was an expert rider who normally handled even strange horses with ease. Against her will, Catherine felt a measure of the animal's disquiet transferred to herself as she heard the noise again, and she was not relieved to recognize the sounds that heralded another rider.

It could be the groom or another servant sent to fetch her, Catherine thought, but immediately discarded the idea. For where among the acres of Wellshire Manor would they know to find her? Unless she had been followed . . .

The answer was swift in coming as the sounds grew suddenly nearer, and she sucked in a breath before a black gelding appeared along the path.

"Oh, Edward, you startled me!" Catherine exclaimed. Although she tried to keep her voice light, it sounded strained even to her own ears, and her heart pounded uncontrollably as fear tingled up the back of her neck.

"Sorry, cousin dear," Edward Moore said with his most insincere smile as he edged closer.

Tightening her grip on the reins as Jackson backed away, skittish at the presence of another horse, Catherine felt a stab of irritation at her mount for demanding her attention when she needed all her concentration to deal with her cousin. Taking an unsteady breath, she looked across the few feet that separated the two horses and raised her eyes to the man she suspected of murdering her stepfather.

Catherine was as fair as Edward was dark. Her golden hair fell about her shoulders in a glorious, shiny mane, and her pink cheeks glowed unfashionably. But it was her eyes that drew attention. An unusual sea green similar to those of more than one feline, they had earned her the nickname Cat. Although they had sparkled with happiness and, more often than not, mischief, for most of her sixteen years, now her eyes were devoid of luster as they regarded her cousin.

Edward's heavy-lidded black eyes, close-cropped black hair, and full lips gave a sensual cast to his face that was not lost on the female population, but Cat had never found him appealing. She thought his skin too pale and his dark eyes too menacing. She found his behavior objectionable and as false as a misplayed note, for Cat suspected the smooth polish of his manners disguised a core so rotten that he had killed his own uncle without remorse.

Still, she was not ready to accuse her cousin, especially when they were alone in a deserted stretch of forest, so she struggled for an innocuous subject of conversation. Before she could speak, however, Edward's voice, thick with loathing, broke the stillness. "I congratulate you, cousin. You are a better rider than I expected. I see that you handle the stallion well—but then you are full of surprises, aren't you?"

Her eyes never leaving Edward's face, Cat tried inconspicuously to ease her horse away from her cousin as he continued talking, his mouth twisted into a leering smile. "This sudden interest in your stepfather's death, for example. I never expected a little thing like you to cause me such trouble. And it's too bad. I would have liked to get to know you more . . . intimately, but I've no time now for such fun. I want this to be neat and tidy."

"What are you talking about?" Cat asked with only partly feigned surprise as she struggled to hold her horse.

"A poacher's stray bullet killing both Lord Pembroke and his stepdaughter would be stretching credulity, wouldn't you say? That's why I'm so glad I got you that horse. Yes, that will be just the thing. A riding accident. And she broke her pretty little neck . . ." Edward laughed aloud as Cat urged Jackson toward the edge of the woods.

"It will do you no good, really," Edward said as he watched her maneuvers. "Even you, dear cousin, can't handle that nervous brute among the trees. You see, he doesn't like enclosed spaces, and he especially dislikes loud noises." Edward's grin widened as he began to pull a gun from his cloak.

Cat barely glimpsed the pistol before she kicked in her heels, sending the horse bolting through the trees. Desperately hoping to reach the open fields before Edward could fire, she urged the animal into a gallop. She'd made it to the border of the forest when the shot rang out, ricocheting off a tree close behind her. Jackson reared, his forelegs pawing the air. Ducking close to avoid tree limbs, Cat struggled with the reins as the stallion tossed and pranced, then suddenly they broke through the remaining woods and flew onto the pasturelands, Edward close on their heels.

Counting on her cousin's poor horsemanship to

hold him back, Cat struck out for the road and the village, where, she hoped, she would not be murdered in broad daylight. She was thankful for her years of riding as she watched Edward fall behind. Although the village lay some distance ahead, the road came into view, revealing a lone rider who Cat prayed would deter Edward from his pursuit. She held on for dear life as Jackson, still frothing with fright, raced down the hill. Fighting to keep the horse along the beaten track, she shouted for help.

Either her words reached the horseman or he simply deduced from her flying hair and billowing skirts as she clung to the horse's neck that her mount was a runaway, for she soon heard the other horse charging along beside her and she felt Jackson finally slow, his sides heaving.

As the horse was brought to a halt, Cat's heart, nearly bursting, stopped its painful racing and she opened her mouth to speak, but the world suddenly seemed clouded in gray. With embarrassing certainty, Cat, who viewed swooning females as idiots, knew that she was about to join their ranks, and without even catching a good look at the stranger who had come to her aid, she fainted dead away into his arms.

When she opened her eyes again, Cat's lashes fluttered across her line of vision, and it was a moment before the world came into focus. As her senses returned, she looked back at the hill she had raced down and saw, at the top, the silhouette of her cousin Edward, still astride his horse. Watching from beneath lowered lids, she let out a deep breath and shuddered with relief when she saw him disappear.

"Are you hurt?" Velvety-rich masculine tones warmed her ear, and Cat opened her eyes wide, only to catch her breath again. Poised barely inches above her was the most handsome face she had ever seen.

Dark brown eyes, the color of the deepest forest, returned her gaze, and as she stared, one dark brow rose in question. His cheeks were finely molded and cleanly shaven, yet his full lower lip lent a warmth and sensuality to his otherwise classic features. Cat's eyes, having moved to his mouth, tarried there while her breath lodged in her throat, for she had never been this close to a man's mouth, and it drew her irresistibly toward him.

"Are you hurt?" he repeated. Cat caught an undertone of amusement in his voice, and her eyes flew to his in embarrassment.

"No. I'm fine. Thank you, sir!" She was loath to relinquish her position in arms that felt so strong and safe around her, but she forced herself to sit up, aware that she had lingered too long in the stranger's embrace. "I'll be fine now," she said. "I appreciate your help, sir."

"What is your name, little one?" he asked, a slow grin warming his features.

"Catherine Amberly."

"Well, Miss Amberly, I refuse to let you get back on that monstrous beast, which you should not have been riding in the first place. Why don't I see you home?"

"Oh, no! If you would just take me into the village, Mister . . . ?"

"Du Prey. Ransom Du Prey," he supplied. "I think that will suit us both. Get on in front of me and we'll lead your horse along."

Though Jackson seemed calm now, Cat nodded in agreement and settled herself in front of her rescuer. She did feel comfortable, as though she fit perfectly against the hard chest, the top of her head nodding against his wide shoulder. A sheltered and solitary life had little prepared her for conversation with men, especially a being as wonderful and handsome as this one, so for a few minutes they rode in silence. Then Cat, eager for the sound of her hero's voice, asked him where he was bound.

"I've a ship at Barton Quay," he answered.

"Do you? What is her name? What is she?" Cat gasped in delight.

"The *Reckless* is a privateer," he answered, amused at her enthusiasm. "With a commission to take French and Spanish ships."

Cat thrilled at his words. A life at sea had always held an allure for her, and it seemed intensely unfair that only men were allowed to partake of such adventures. "And what do *you* do?" she asked.

Although Cat was genuinely interested in his answer, she longed, too, to hear the sound of his voice again. Deep and rich, it seemed to envelop her, and combined with the warmth of his chest against her back, it worked a lovely spell upon her, sending the oddest, though not unpleasant, tingles throughout her body.

"Well, I'm the captain, so I do a little of everything, though I'm sure you would hear arguments from some quarters on that score," Ransom said dryly. "I sail tomorrow for the West Indies."

"The West Indies!" The words set off bells in Cat's head, for her mother's sister Amelia lived on a plantation in Barbados. When Aunt Amelia's husband had succumbed to fever, she had stayed on there, a decision Cat's stepfather had denounced as "quite mad" and in keeping with her "foolish nature." Although she could barely recall her aunt, Cat sporadically received letters from the lady, urging her to visit. That had been impossible when her stepfather was alive and disapproved of such a trip, but now . . . Cat peppered Ransom with questions, her thoughts whirling until she was dizzy with the boldness of the scheme that was forming in her mind.

"Oh, but it must be wonderful to go to sea." She

sighed as they entered the village of Coxley, for even as she prepared to leave his side, Cat felt a strange pull, as though her body, possessed of a will of its own, longed to remain snug against him. She forced herself to lean forward, away from him, ignoring the warm chest that seemed to beckon her back. Although aware that everyone in the village would soon know Lord Pembroke's daughter was riding with a strange man, she was far too excited to care. After directing her rescuer to the inn, she thanked him profusely for his help as he dismounted and lifted her to the ground.

"You are more than welcome, little one," Ransom said. "It has been an unusual ride. I don't often discuss sailing with lovely little girls." At his words, Cat blushed a rosy red, but as Jim, the inn's stable-boy, held the two horses' reins, she rushed inside without a backward glance at her hero.

Ransom watched her skip up the steps, light as a feather, her golden hair windswept and tumbling down her back, and smiled at the idiotic pang he felt at parting from her. At first he had been annoyed when called upon to rescue a swooning female, yet he had been forced to admire the flawless features of the child he held in his arms.

Relieved that he did not have to alter his route, Ransom had not been averse to spending a few more moments with his winsome young charge. And what an entertaining trip it had been! The youngster was like a breath of fresh air as, bubbling with excitement, she pestered him with questions. How sad that such an engaging girl would grow into a woman—becoming either a drawing room bore or a sly, deceiving creature.

Ransom caught himself staring almost wistfully after the child and gave himself a mental shake. She couldn't be more than sixteen, he reminded himself, and he had never been attracted to chits barely out of the schoolroom. How his friends would laugh to learn that the world-weary Du Prey, duke of Morcester, had been drawn to a wide-eyed innocent!

With a grimace, Ransom firmly dismissed the child from his thoughts. Retrieving the reins from Jim, he mounted his horse and headed on to Barton, leaving the inn yard behind. By the time he departed the tiny village, the incident with Miss Amberly was buried deep within his memory, where it would lie forgotten for many a day.

Chapter 2

66 Well, if it isn't little Miss Amberly! We haven't seen you in some time. We've missed your smile."

Through the dim light inside the inn, Cat glanced fondly at the elderly owner of the village's one hostelry. "It's nice to see you again, Mr. Tyber," she said. Although she genuinely liked the old innkeeper, he was not known for his brevity, and Cat dreaded a lengthy chat. The very real fear that Edward would reappear and kill her danced in the pit of her stomach.

Cat knew that her cousin, in his new position as baron of Wellshire, could drag her forcibly from the premises, and no one would raise a hand to stop him. Even if she could convince someone that Edward had murdered her stepfather to gain his wealth and title, and had tried to kill her as well only a short while ago, she knew no one who had the power to help her. Her only hope lay in a quick escape. A daring plan began to form in her mind . . .

"I've had a little trouble with my horse," Cat told Mr. Tyber nervously. "Do you mind if I rest here before going home?"

"Certainly not, Miss Amberly. You go freshen up in the front room. How about a little mutton pie?"

"Yes, that would be lovely! No! Well, why don't

you wrap it up for me, and I'll eat it on the way home?''

"Certainly, Miss Amberly.''

Pie in hand, Cat climbed the stairs, only to exit down the rear steps to the rooms where she knew Jenny, the serving girl, and Jim slept. Rummaging through the tiny hole in the wall where Jim bedded down, she found what she was looking for: boy's clothing that just might fit her. In its place she left a coin, part of her precious hoard of pin money collected before her stepfather's death.

Once safely ensconced in the front room, her mutton pie tucked away and the door locked behind her, she dressed in Jim's shirt, baggy pants, and patched coat and bundled up a spare set of pilfered clothing. Everything was a little large, but the looseness was all the better to disguise her sex. Besides, Cat reasoned, she would grow into them.

She looked critically at the golden waves of hair reaching to her waist and, grimacing at her impending loss, hacked them off mercilessly with the shears she had borrowed from Jenny's room. Her first attempt at barbering was atrocious, but more clipping and cutting improved her appearance to the point where she looked merely ragged instead of ridiculous. To complete her costume, she pulled a large cap down over her forehead to shade her features.

Holding her breath, Cat gazed into a milky mirror over the washstand and was delighted with her new identity; she did not look at all like the young girl she had been a moment before. She took off the hat and squinted at her face. The nose was, perhaps, a little too pert and the cheeks too rosy, but even without the cap she looked like a somewhat grubby boy. Well, good, she thought, quickly suppressing a twinge of disappointment at the ease with which she had achieved her disguise. Then she collected her shorn hair and original clothing, and again sneaked down the back staircase and, keeping to the shadows, slipped away from the inn. She didn't dare fetch her horse from the stable for fear that Jim, the stableboy, would see her wearing his clothes.

Avoiding the main road where Edward might be watching, Cat followed the alleys and byways, heading for the road to Barton, a far distance from the village. As she passed one tiny alleyway, she disposed of her cut hair and girl's clothing in a heap of refuse, then hesitated as she fought the impulse to say good-bye to her dearest friend.

Budd, who had been her family's estate handyman until Edward had cruelly turned him out, had been a surrogate father to Cat as she grew up motherless and often alone in her stepfather's household. Cat smiled for the first time in weeks as she remembered the night long ago when, as a little girl, she had sought the warmth and comfort of the manor's kitchens during a storm. Budd, a kindly old sailor, had seated her in a chair by the great fireplace, tucked a blanket around her, and settled down beside her with a pipe. Scoffing at the weather that raged outside, he began to describe a typhoon that had tossed one of his great seafaring vessels like a cork upon the waves. By the time his tale was told, Cat was asleep, dreaming of the sea.

The friendship that sprang up that night between the solitary little girl and the lonely old sailor had grown over the years. Cat had soon declared her intention to sail the seas, too, when she grew older, and the aged man had indulged her by teaching her everything he knew. What a blow it was when she grew old enough to realize she could never be a sailor!

Cat's wistful smile spread into a mischievous grin at the knowledge that her long-dormant dream of a seafaring life was close to realization. Her heart beat just a little faster with anticipation, though she knew her old mentor would never approve of her scheme.

Budd had entertained her with his tales of storms and battles, pirates and fantastic underwater creatures; he had shared his knowledge with her until she knew each part of a ship and every knot in a rope, but, in the end, he told her she had no place at sea. Her future was as a lady, Budd advised, while Cat groaned in disappointment.

Looking again down Cherington Lane, where Budd had said he would be living with a "lady friend," since he now had no home of his own, Cat knew that Budd would try to stop her from going. He would insist she stay with him. But Budd's would be the first place Edward would look for her, and Cat knew her friend was no match for Edward. With a firm shake of her head, she moved from the lane, sending a silent farewell to her old friend. Then, turning again toward Barton, she took her first steps toward a future away from the family estate and tiny village that had encompassed her entire world.

When she reached Barton near dawn, Cat was bone-weary from the hours she'd spent on the road and wary, not of her cousin, but of the infamous gangs of pressmen who periodically roamed the coastal towns and cities in search of bodies to fill England's naval vessels. Her plans for going to sea did not involve being forced to join the navy, where conditions were known to be deplorable. No, Cat did not want to fight Napoleon; she simply wanted to work her way to Barbados on a decent ship, and she hoped Captain Du Prey would provide that opportunity.

She found him standing at the end of the quay, one foot on some rocks tumbling near the edge, a long cloak thrown back, and his eyes on the breaking dawn. For a moment she hesitated, wondering fearfully if he could possibly recognize her as the young girl from the day before. But she could not turn back now, and taking a deep breath, she walked toward him. Still, she had forgotten in the span of a night how utterly handsome he was, and her surprise made her stop again before reaching him.

The sun lighting his face seemed to caress his features: the dark brows over deep-set eyes, the classic nose, the full lower lip, and the waves of thick, dark hair brushed back from his face by the breeze. He was blessed with a youthful countenance, which made his age difficult to determine, yet his bearing told Cat he was no green youth. He held himself with complete self-assurance, as though nothing could touch him, no troubles or squabbles or storms at sea. Here was a man Cat instinctively knew others would follow.

"I sincerely hope, for your sake, you are not intent upon picking my pocket." Cat almost jumped at the words, for the captain's eyes never strayed from the horizon, nor did he stir from his position.

"Certainly not!" Cat replied indignantly. At her response, the handsome face turned, and with an eyebrow cocked sardonically, he looked her up and down.

Annoyed to feel herself blushing, Cat straightened her shoulders and looked directly into the chocolate-brown eyes that surveyed her with such disdain. "You are the captain of that ship, sir?" she asked, pointing to the *Reckless*.

"I am," he answered, a curious mixture of pride and self-mockery in his voice.

Cat's body tensed with the realization that her life depended on the next few minutes. Sending up a brief prayer of entreaty, she took a deep breath and plunged ahead. "Well, sir, I would like to offer my services. I would make a good cabin boy, sir. I can read and write and I know my mathematics. I could keep your books . . . and I know just about everything about sailing," Cat rushed on. "And I do ever so much want to go to sea."

The eyebrow cocked even higher as the captain regarded her in surprise. "Have you ever crewed a ship before?" he asked.

"No, sir, but I . . ."

"Then, pray tell, how did you come by all this wisdom?"

"My—my grandfather, sir. He was a sailor. Taught me everything he knew, he did," Cat answered, studying the toes of her boots and trying desperately to look and sound less like herself and more like Jim, who would be dumbfounded to learn that anyone was holding him up as a model of behavior.

"I see . . . and you live with this legendary seaman, I assume?"

"Well, not anymore sir," Cat said as she looked earnestly up at him, warming to her tale. "You see, he lost his work and sent me out to earn my own way."

"How old are you?"

"Thirteen, sir," she lied, "but I can work hard, truly I can. Oh, please, sir, do take me. You won't be sorry, I promise you!" Cat held her breath while the object of her entreaties gazed back to the horizon, considering her request.

As he watched the colors of the dawn unfold over the water, Ransom pondered the youth's petition. More than likely he was being pursued by the authorities—or worse—over some bad business, and that explained his sudden desire to go to sea. Ransom's first inclination was to brush off the scrawny youngster, but there was something about the lad, perhaps the way those earnest green eyes met his own, that made him change his mind. If Ransom's years at sea had taught him anything, it was to trust his instincts. "All right." He sighed. "Just cease your constant chatter, boy, and don't be a bother to me or I'll throw you to the sharks."

Afraid to open her mouth, Cat simply nodded, her eyes sparkling as she fairly skipped along beside Ransom all the way to the ship. They stopped before the *Reckless*, and Cat gazed in awe at the giant vessel that loomed high above them, its masts stretching into the pale sky. Even at this early hour, Cat could see the dark figures of men moving purposefully aboard, and her heart soared nearly as high as the crow's nest as she smiled at the sight.

Cat's reverie was broken by the sound of Captain Du Prey's deep voice, raised in casual dismissal. "Bosun, this child fancies himself to be my cabin boy. Take care of him, will you?" he told a short, stocky fellow, and then left Cat to study her shipmate.

Bosun—who despite his name was the first mate—was older than the captain, with flecks of white in his wild black hair and a scar that began at the edge of one bushy eyebrow and ran all the way down his cheek, making him look thoroughly ferocious. He nodded at the captain's words without even glancing in Cat's direction as he oversaw the transfer of a sailor, seemingly unconscious, from the quay to the ship.

Cat watched in fascination as they rigged the prone man into the block and tackle, a system of pulleys used to haul people aboard, and she smiled when she recognized the type of knot, a bowline, that was used to secure the rope around him.

"The damn fool drank too much! Let it be a warning to you, lad," Bosun growled, pointing at the still prostrate man as they hoisted him aboard.

"Yes, sir!" Cat piped up, grinning widely, much too excited to be intimidated by the fellow. Wellshire, Edward and his crimes, and even dear Budd were forgotten as her childhood ambition of going to sea became reality, and she spared no worries for the captain or the wild-looking man before her.

"Are you waiting for God himself to ask you aboard?" Bosun's voice broke into her thoughts, and with an indrawn breath, Cat scrambled happily up the plank. As her feet touched the solid wood of the ship's deck, she nearly hugged herself in happiness, her thoughts on the life of adventure that loomed ahead.

Chapter 3

Cat's first week at sea passed in a blur as she ran errands, scrambled up the ratlines, and helped hoist the sails and the anchor. Initially, all was confusion as she familiarized herself with the ship, for as Cat discovered, it was one thing to know the parts of a model, another to know where the bow lay when in the dimness belowdecks. Still, she learned quickly, and although a few turns around Wellshire's duck pond had not prepared her for the reel and roll of the deck beneath her feet, Cat soon gained her sea legs, leaping up among the masts or down into the bowels of the vessel as though she'd been born to sail.

"Well, boy, I'd say you're a right little sailor," Bosun said, slapping Cat heartily on the back after watching her week of work. "Now that you know your way around the deck, you can see to the captain's cabin. Off with you!"

Cat beamed with pride at Bosun's praise and, eager for less tiring labor, she raced to the main hatchway before Bosun could change his mind. Cat liked the captain's neat and spacious masculine quarters, with its books, navigational tools, and maps. Sunlight from the diamond-shaped windowpanes bathed the room in a warm glow, illuminating the massive bed and large sea chest as she looked around the room. The cabin smelled good, too, Cat thought. Instead of the reek of damp wood, unwashed bodies, and stale air belowdecks, here she breathed traces of tobacco, books, salt air, and the captain's cologne.

Cat had barely seen Ransom since boarding, her only contact brief periods of fetch and carry when she brought him a steaming cup of coffee at dawn and waited on him at mealtimes. Maybe things would be different now, she thought, hoping for a chance to talk with him as she did on the way to Coxley when they'd nearly struck up a friendship. And now she would really have a chance to prove herself, she thought as she rubbed her hands together in contemplation of giving the cabin the most thorough cleaning it had ever known.

When she finished scrubbing down the walls and the floor, the pungent odor of lye soap pervaded the air, but it, too, was a good smell, she thought as it chased the mustiness from the corners and lent a fresh, clean scent to the room. Her work completed, Cat found herself with some free time before supper and took the opportunity to write a letter to Budd.

"I don't know when this will reach you," she began, "but I hope you are not worried about me. I am safe aboard a ship and doing well. It is quite as you said it should be, except for a few details you omitted: namely, the water, the food and the smell. The water tastes like the metal it is stored in, the food is awful (even though they say we have been eating well since leaving port) and the smell is foul. I guess one simply grows accustomed. You would be quite proud of me as I am a real sailor. That is what the first mate said today. With love to you, Cat."

The letter was brief, but she only wanted to set his mind at ease and dared not say too much. Smiling ruefully, she added "Cabin Boy" to her signature. She did not want Budd to think she was lodged with the crew, where it was overcrowded, dark, and damp, and the air truly unwholesome. It never occurred to her that Budd might not be reassured to know she was sleeping in the captain's cabin, for Cat was well pleased with the hammock strung up for her in a corner of the room.

She folded the letter, then opened it again, wondering whether she should explain the reason for her sudden departure from Wellshire. She did not want Budd to think she was foolhardy, running off to sea like an irresponsible child, but neither did she want to worry him needlessly with tales of Edward's treachery. She frowned, hoping Budd would not think her a coward for flying from the different circumstances at her childhood home, but, oh, how things had changed!

Although Cat had grown up under the cold and often disapproving eye of her stepfather, Lord Pembroke, he was the only father she had ever known, and she had loved him. She'd had the servants, too, many of whom became like family to her, and she'd had the run of Wellshire Manor. She'd loved fishing and boating around the duck pond and exploring and riding the acres of grounds. And so to Cat, unaware of her lack of family or friends, it was an idyllic childhood.

Oh, once in a while her stepfather would lecture her on her lack of maidenly accomplishments, and Edward's mother, Margaret, would be summoned to the house to teach her proper decorum. But Margaret was a poor relation, bitter over her lot in life, and even Lord Pembroke would soon tire of her shrewish ways, leaving Cat once more to her own devices.

Edward, who was even more mean-spirited than his mother, was, thankfully, rarely along for these visits. In fact, thinking back, Cat was not sure exactly what Edward had been up to until he had suddenly appeared at Wellshire after Margaret's death, sporting a sheen of fine manners that completely charmed her stepfather. Soon, Lord Pembroke was talking of grooming Edward as his heir since the title would pass to him eventually, and Edward was at his side, ingratiating himself daily . . . until the accident.

A poacher's stray bullet had felled her stepfather, the authorities said, but Cat was not satisfied, and apparently Edward had got wind of her suspicions. She shook her head in grief and anger, remembering the way he had casually admitted his guilt before implementing his scheme to do away with her, too. Apparently, he had been too impatient to wait for the title and was now too greedy to share the estate's wealth. Edward had moved quickly, and now he was enjoying her stepfather's property and position with no one to stop him. The thought galled Cat so that her fist closed around the letter, nearly crumpling the paper.

"Cat!"

Cat almost jumped at the sound of her name, her bright eyes fastening on the tall figure of Ransom striding through the cabin door. "Here, captain," she said, putting the letter away and noting again how handsome he looked. Some dark brown locks carelessly brushed his forehead, and his open white shirt revealed dark curls dampened with sweat on his chest as he walked to the middle of the room and stopped abruptly, a puzzled expression on his face.

"Good God, what's that smell?" he asked.

"Soap, sir. I scrubbed down the cabin," Cat answered, surprised by his incredulous look. "I found some in the stores, soap, that is, sir. I hope it's all right," she finished lamely.

He broke into a grin, displaying even white teeth.

"All right? By God, it's almost civilized." He laughed, then sat down on the edge of the bed and stripped off his shirt. "Well, I'm for a bath. How about you, Cat?"

"No, thank you, sir," Cat answered, darting her eyes away from the muscles of his bare back.

"Perhaps I phrased that incorrectly," Ransom said, removing his boots. "You have not had a bath since boarding this vessel, correct?"

"No, sir, but . . ."

"And you are definitely beginning to stink," he interrupted. "Although there are men on board who smell worse than you do, I don't share my cabin with them. Therefore, you *will* take a bath; that's an order. You can use the tub when I'm finished. Now, run along and fetch me some water. Get the cook to help you."

Cat hurried to do Ransom's bidding, her mind working all the while on how to avoid the bath. She could barely lift the wooden buckets of heated salt water and was out of breath when she entered the room, a grumbling cook at her heels. "Fer God's sake, will ya hurry?" the fat fellow, called Hale, complained with disgust, pushing past her. Outweighing Cat several times over, he lifted his buckets easily, emptying them into a brass tub that now stood in the center of the cabin. Then he was gone, pushing past Cat to return to his domain.

Cat moved over to the tub more slowly while nervously eyeing the captain, who was laying clean clothes on the bed. The difficult task of lifting each unwieldy bucket to the side of the tub required her full attention, but when the last was emptied, she glanced back at her captain, only to find him stripping off his pants. She turned to fly from the room, but his voice stopped her in her tracks.

"Hold, lad, I won't be long; you'll want yours before the water cools."

Cat steeled her shoulders, took a deep breath, and turned around for her first look at a man. Her breathing stopped as she saw him step into the tub. He was beautiful: tall and lean, flat-stomached, wide-shouldered, his whole body firm muscle and his skin a warm golden color, and there where his tan ended . . . She quickly averted her eyes and busied herself putting out clean towels for him as she listened to the splashes of his bath. But every now and again she discreetly glanced at his finely muscled back as he lathered, and the picture of him naked was branded on her brain forever.

When he was finished, Cat willed the blushes to leave her face and began laying out her own clean clothes: the other threadbare shirt and pants she had taken from the stableboy.

"Well, lad, it's all yours," Ransom said, and Cat could hear him toweling off, although she studiously avoided looking his way.

"I'll be wanting my privacy, sir, if it's all the same to you," she mumbled.

The captain burst out laughing, looking at her from under the towel he was running roughly over his hair. "What's this? Have you something I've not seen?"

"Yes, sir," Cat answered coolly, her green eyes wide and sparkling as she finally turned toward him. Looking him straight in the eye, she said, "Scars, sir. Birth scars. A horrible sight, they are. I'm quite conscious of them," she added, hanging her head in apparent shame.

"Hmmm . . . well, have it your way then, lad," Ransom said gruffly, running a hand through his wet curls. He donned his breeches and boots and, grabbing a shirt, opened the cabin door. But before leaving he turned and scrutinized Cat, who earnestly looked up into his face, and his eyes narrowed. "If I find you didn't wash, my lad, I'll toss you in the ocean for your bath, make no mistake," he threatened, then was gone.

Cat listened for his receding footsteps, then shoved a heavy chair against the door just to be sure. She furtively stripped off her clothes, leaving in place the strip of cloth that wound around her chest, tightly binding her breasts. If Ransom reappeared, she could claim some chest injury while hoping that he looked no closer, Cat decided, and with a nervous sigh, she stepped into the tub.

The water felt glorious, but she forced herself to hurry, straining her ears for any sound outside the cabin door. Still, she could not help thinking of Ransom, who had been sitting in her place a few minutes before, and the memory of his naked body made her shiver in the oddest fashion.

She shook off the mood as she stepped from the tub and hurried into her clothes, hoping, for her own sake, that Ransom was not a stickler for cleanliness, for this bathing business was too nerve-racking. When the *Reckless* reached warmer waters, she decided firmly, she would do her washing in the ocean!

Once dressed again as a boy, Cat immediately went up on deck to make sure the captain noted her clean state. It would not do for him to start checking on her bathing habits, and besides, she wanted him to trust her.

As the days passed, Cat's desire was granted, for she did earn her captain's trust. She was assigned additional responsibilities, including taking care of the ship's accounts, yet her hopes of kindling a friendship with Ransom dwindled. Although she spent more time with him, he reminded her little of the fellow who had rescued her from Edward, and she began to wonder just what kind of man the captain was.

She knew that he was held in high esteem by the crew. In the kind of life where death could suddenly loom imminent, a man with the ability to make quick decisions was invaluable, and Ransom had proved himself many times over to his men. He kept them healthy, too, using the newest techniques to clean his ship and fend off illness, even if it meant serving up plates of onions for supper. The choicest varieties of vegetables and fruits, now thought to aid in the sailor's constant battle against disease, were not always readily available, but the crew of the *Reckless* was never without some food that served the purpose.

Most important to his crew, Ransom paid good money. Although the sailors on most privateers received minimal wages and did not share in any booty from the prizes taken, Ransom paid each man in accordance with the wealth of the ship seized, ensuring a loyalty that was rare on any ocean.

Yet, despite the fierce devotion most of the crew felt for their enigmatic captain, few could claim his friendship, for Ransom kept his distance. He was not stiff-necked but somewhat cool, Cat thought, trying to pin down an explanation. He held himself apart from the crowd, except for Bosun, the only one aboard who seemed on easy terms with the man.

Why, he barely looks my way, Cat thought irritably, and though she could not explain why, she very much wanted him to notice her.

Chapter 4

Whenever Cat finally captured her captain's attention, she could have wished for a more propitious moment. The storm had struck around midnight, sending the *Reckless* pitching and rolling from side to side so that Cat was sure the huge ship would capsize at any moment. Her fear of storms, which she thought she'd conquered long ago, burgeoned with each deafening crack of thunder. As no lamp would stay lit, the darkness in the cabin was absolute until a bright streak of lightning rent the sky, illuminating the room with its eerie glow.

The captain had instructed her to stay in his cabin, and Cat did not argue, but as the night wore on, she longed for the presence of another soul, for reassurance from some old salt that the "little blow" would soon be over. Just as she loosened her grip on the bedpost, determined to seek company, the door burst open and a sudden pitch of the floor sent her across the room smack against the captain like a sack of potatoes.

With several well-chosen oaths, he finally got Cat to her feet, and she helped him from his greatcoat as water poured from the cloth and dripped from every inch of his body. He stripped off his sodden clothes, too, and Cat threw a blanket over his shoulders before she scurried about in the darkness to find him fresh clothing. "You can light the lamp, lad," he said as he sank into a chair, and Cat did, her heart warmed by the tiny flame that chased away the shadows.

"Is it over then?" she asked, realizing that the ship did seem steadier, the pitch less wild.

"The worst of it," Ransom answered.

Cat turned and was shocked by the look of him. His face was pale and drained, the wet curls matted to his face, and his body just hinted at the exhaustion that would have laid another man low. She knew that he had not slept at all, had spent the night fighting sheets of biting rain on a tossing deck so slippery that just staying aboard took all one's strength. Although seemingly invincible, the captain was human, something Cat had almost forgotten.

Without a word, she poured him a whiskey, which she pressed into his icy fingers. Grabbing a towel, she walked behind him and stood drying his hair as he drank. Her first movements with the towel were brisk and businesslike, but her hands gradually slowed their task as she became aware of the way his dark locks gleamed in the dim light. His hair was vibrant and alive beneath her fingers, and when Cat felt a shiver run through her, she laid the towel aside, suddenly acutely self-conscious.

Cat turned away, but as she did, she noticed that the blanket had slipped down Ransom's shoulders. Chiding herself for placing her own silly nervousness before her captain's comfort, she tentatively laid her hands on the wide shoulders and began kneading his tired muscles. Her efforts were soon rewarded as she felt him relax. "Can I get you some supper, captain?" she asked, trying to ignore the feel of his smooth, cool skin beneath her fingers.

"No, lad." He sighed, pulled the blanket close

around him, and stood up. "I'm for bed, but see if Bosun wants anything. Mr. Peabody is in charge."

"Well, we needn't worry then. If the storm starts blowing again, Old Stone Face will just stare it out of countenance," Cat said dryly. As soon as the words left her mouth, she caught herself and shot a glance at the captain. After all, she was making fun of the ship's master. Relief washed over her when she heard him laugh, soft and low, and the sound was so delightful, she decided then and there to make the captain laugh more often.

"So, Mr. Peabody is Old Stone Face, is he? And what am I?" he asked.

"Oh, you're too perfect for a nickname, sir," she answered ingenuously. "You don't have anything glaringly wrong with you, like Stinkard . . ."

"Let me guess. Hmmm, the red-haired fellow . . . Marlowe! He *is* worse than most."

"Or Blubber Belly . . ."

"Cook."

"Or Shark Bait . . ."

"Hmmm, I suspect that is someone you've developed an extreme dislike for, although none of the others you've named are particularly pleasant . . . It's Mule, isn't it! I would not let him hear you call him names, little Cat, or you might lose one of your nine lives," Ransom said as he slipped into bed.

"I think I just lost one in the storm," Cat said. When her captain made no response, she smiled because she realized he was already asleep. For a time she stood watching his face, the strong features softened by slumber, then quietly she tucked another blanket around him before leaving him to his dreams.

After those moments of comfort and laughter shared during the storm, the captain unbent a little, and before long an easy comradeship developed be-

tween Ransom and his cabin boy. Although Cat was
popular with many of the sailors, her latest conquest
came as a surprise to nearly everyone, and more
than one head turned at the sound of Ransom's
voice raised in laughter at his cabin boy's quips.

Cat enjoyed her new friendship and reveled in the
warm weather when the *Reckless* sailed into Caribbean waters. She thrilled with excitement when they
took their first ship, a bloodless event involving a
great deal of shouting and the discharging of a few
nine-pounders that Cat viewed as the height of her
career. The captured cargo was to be transferred to
a warehouse Ransom owned on Windlay, and Cat
begged a place beside the captain on the first boat
ashore.

When they reached the island, Cat marveled at
the palm trees, which she'd previously seen only in
books, and gawked at the blacks and mixed-blood
women wearing gaudy kerchiefs and gay flowers.
Her footsteps were light as she strode between Bosun and Ransom, pointing out each new wonder that
caught her eye until Bosun said, "Lord, captain,
you'd think the lad had never been out of the nursery."

Although Ransom let out a low laugh in response,
Cat saw the truth in Bosun's words and reminded
herself just who she was supposed to be: a boy with
a much less sheltered background than her own. She
put a firm clamp on her enthusiasm, vowing to enjoy her outing but a little less loudly.

Her gay mood was soon gone, however, for when
they reached the site of the warehouse they were
stunned to find nothing but charred rubble. The
building and its contents had apparently burned to
the ground very recently. Cat could only gasp in
dismay as Ransom stood silently looking over the
remains of his warehouse and Bosun poked about
in the ruins, mumbling obscenities. No one spoke,

making the grim scene seem deathly quiet, although the noises of the street could still be heard behind them, a dim echo to Bosun's grumbling.

"Devlin," Ransom finally said, and his first mate immediately jerked upright at the single word, as though his fingers had been burned by a smoking ember.

"What makes you say so?" Bosun asked.

"It bears his signature," Ransom said softly. "Look around you, Bosun. None of the other warehouses were touched."

"But you settled with him!"

"So I thought," Ransom said dryly.

Cat could see Bosun was still not convinced, for the older man looked down at the rubble, shaking his head. "I don't know, captain. I just can't see it. Not after what you done to him." The first mate looked up again at Ransom's hooded eyes. "And how would he know the warehouse was yours, anyway?"

"The man has spies everywhere," Ransom said, shrugging. He stood staring at the ruins, but to Cat it seemed as though he saw something else.

"Devlin? Who's Devlin?" she whispered to Bosun as Ransom stared off into space.

"Tremayne Devlin. He's an old enemy of the captain's," Bosun grumbled.

Although the look on his face warned Cat not to ask any more questions, she persisted. "Why would he burn the warehouse?"

Bosun simply glared at the lad, but the captain, his thoughts returning to the present, answered. "Devlin himself did not burn the warehouse," Ransom explained. "That's not his way. He only directed the burning of the building because he seeks to ruin me . . . an old grudge."

"Is he trying to kill you?" Cat asked, her familiarity with such behavior leading her to wonder if it was widespread.

Bosun choked back an oath, but Ransom held up his hand, smiling coldly. "Now, Bosun, give the boy some credit. The question is logical." Turning to Cat, he said, "So far, he has not tried to kill me, only to best me. I doubt if he would reap satisfaction from my death . . . unless he ruined me first," Ransom mused. "I suppose he will have to be dealt with again."

The quiet menace in his words made Cat shiver, and she said nothing more. The bleak warehouse site robbed the island trip of its promise of gay adventure, while the talk of vengeful, plotting enemies raised the hairs on her neck. She did not argue when Ransom ordered Bosun to take her back to the ship.

"And get Peabody down here," Ransom said. "I want the three of us to look over the area and nose about. Let's see if we can find any clues in the rubble."

Chapter 5

Sunlight streamed through the windows of the captain's cabin, warming Cat's bare feet as she sat cross-legged in a patch of light on the bed, humming a ditty and mending Ransom's shirt. She was a poor seamstress, but she had improved since Bosun had first set her to sew some sail and, upon viewing her work, declared it the worst job he had seen in more than thirty years of sailing the world's oceans. In disgust, he had sent her to Bull Marston for a lesson.

A large bear of a man with scars from head to foot from pirating, privateering, and brawling, Bull had meaty fingers that fairly flew with a needle. He had done his best to teach her, telling her the skill was not all in the fingers, but in the head, too. "You've got to want to sit still long enough to do the job right. That's the problem with you young whelps; you don't want to take the time," he said. But time was something Cat had in abundance, and so she practiced, surprising herself when she actually began to enjoy it. There was something infinitely peaceful about sitting on the deck mending the huge lengths of sail. With a shrug, Bull had tried to explain it. "Sometimes I just need to keep to myself, instead of getting in a ruckus."

Cat held up the captain's shirt and surveyed her

work critically. Not too bad, although Ransom would grouse about the cabin boy who couldn't sew a straight stitch. Cat smiled at the irony that the one talent at which, as a female, she should be proficient was the one at which she least excelled. But then she had never been skilled in maidenly accomplishments, as her stepfather had repeatedly lamented.

Although her manners were acceptable, Cat's needlework was atrocious, and she could not pretend to paint watercolors. She was an excellent horsewoman but could not sing a pleasing note, nor engender anything but dismay by her turns at the pianoforte. She spoke fluent French and knew a healthy amount of Latin and Greek, too, but she evinced no interest in running a household.

The life of a lady, which seemed to involve only the dullest of activities, had held little allure for Cat, whose tastes ran toward more active pursuits, such as climbing trees and frequenting the stables. During the past few years, Cat had ignored her destined role, staving off time itself by sheer force of will as she enjoyed her prolonged childhood . . . and now its extension aboard the *Reckless*.

Unaware of her own obstinacy, Cat lived for the moment, and at the moment her life suited her just fine. She delighted in the new sights and sounds of the Caribbean, and she found no fault in her shipboard activities—especially when they included Ransom.

Her worship of the captain had earned her the nickname Ransom's Bootlicker among some of the more obnoxious members of the crew, but Cat didn't care. She liked being with him. She had come to love the lazy smile that reached to his eyes and the sardonic lift of his brow. A soft grin played on Cat's lips as she thought of her captain, and with a sigh, she folded the shirt and placed it neatly away. It seemed that he was forever invading her thoughts, and she dislodged him with a quick shake of her head before going up on deck.

There she came upon Harry Fields and Joe Williams lazily throwing their knives at a knot in the wood. Harry, small, dark-haired, and wiry, had become a special friend of hers, and he was seldom without Joe, who loomed over his smaller counterpart. Although his slow wits often made him the butt of Harry's jokes, Joe was devoted to his companion, and few said a word against the prankster Harry in front of Joe Williams.

When the two invited Cat to join them, they were shocked to find she did not possess a blade. Nothing would have it but that they teach the lad how to throw, and they were laughing loudly at Cat's first efforts when the captain sauntered into their midst.

"Williams, you couldn't hit a barn," Ransom commented, sending Harry into guffaws. "Watch, Cat." With that, a blade sang through the air, landing squarely in the middle of the knot. Harry's voice stilled in mid-laugh, and Joe looked at the captain, dumbfounded, for Ransom had drawn the knife from his boot and hit his target before any of the three could "spit nails," as Harry said.

The captain chuckled at their astonishment and, to Cat's delight, he proceeded to instruct her in the fine art of knife throwing. They whiled away the afternoon, watching Cat's efforts and criticizing each throw until she could send the captain's handsome blade with its mother-of-pearl handle flying straight toward a target.

All agreed, however, that the boy just could not attain the stealth necessary to pull the knife undetected. Cat refused to accept that judgment, and in the weeks that followed hardly a day went by that she did not pester one or the other of her fellows to borrow a knife and practice, until all swore the first thing they would do upon making port was to buy Cat a knife.

Knives, however, were the last thing on the sailors' minds when the *Reckless* anchored off Tortola. They were thinking of the Cock and Bull, a local brothel, and precious little else, as they prepared to head for shore. Harry and Joe insisted that their new friend accompany them on what promised to be a delightful expedition, but Cat, ill at ease with the idea, declined politely, to the distress of her companions.

"Well, maybe the lad's a bit young yet," Joe mumbled.

"He's not! Gawd, you're never too young," Harry said. "Look at Danny." He pointed at the youngest member of the crew, a twelve-year-old even smaller than Cat who was joining a party bound for shore. "And he was there last year," Harry added, his voice rising as his irritation grew.

At that moment, Mule, a less than civilized member of the crew, walked past. "Maybe he's got his cravings satisfied better right here," he said, sniggering. Cat glared at him, then smiled at Mule's expression when he suddenly noticed the captain standing nearby, his eyebrow cocked questioningly at Mule's crude comment. Mule, although taller and heftier than Ransom, backed away without a word and joined his fellows.

Dismissing Mule without another glance, Ransom turned to Harry. "If the boy doesn't want to go, let him be," he said curtly, leaving the three staring after him.

"*That* man reminds me of a cat," Harry said with admiration. "Always turning up in the damnedest places and without batting an eye, too."

"You're right, Harry," Joe said. "Sometimes you just think about him and he's there. Gives me the willies, it does!"

Cat paid no attention but watched Ransom depart instead, admiring the lean lines of his body. "The captain's going, too?" she asked.

"Hell, yes," said Harry. "He's a real favorite of Sally Knotts. She runs the place."

Cat felt her insides churn at the thought of the captain and the brothel owner and, determined to have a look at this Sally, she decided to give in to her shipmates. "All right then, let's be off," she said, drawing whoops of approval from Harry and Joe.

When Cat entered the establishment, she had cause to regret her decision, for Sally was quite comely, with hair as black as midnight and eyes the color of the sky. Her grin was wide and friendly, despite a chipped tooth, and she looked round and smooth in all the right places, Cat decided glumly. Try as she might, she could find nothing lacking in the brothel owner's looks, with the possible exception of her waist-length hair, which could use a decent brushing, Cat reflected critically, unconsciously fingering her own shortened tresses.

"Ransom Du Prey, you gorgeous rascal!" Sally called in a melodious voice that Cat felt made her own husky tones resemble frog croakings. As if sleepwalking, Cat found herself pushed into a chair while all around her scantily clad females squealed and sailors caroused. She ignored them all, her attention only on Ransom, who was swinging the luscious Sally up in the air, her black curls brushing his shoulders. As Cat watched, Ransom took the brothel owner in his arms, lowered his head, and kissed her in a fluid motion that set Cat's heart to pounding.

"Oooh, you've brought us a young one," a ripe-smelling female cackled at Cat's elbow. "Lord and he's a pretty one, too! I'll teach him a few tricks!" With that, the hefty woman deposited herself heavily on Cat's lap, her prodigious bosom only inches from Cat's face. Caught unawares, Cat jumped from her seat, depositing her burden neatly on the floor, to the accompaniment of hearty laughter.

"He needs to learn some manners, don't he?" the wench spat from her position on the floor, and Cat read murder in her eyes before a sailor scooped up the woman and flung her, shrieking and giggling, over his shoulder. Grimacing with annoyance at the interruption of her observation, Cat glanced back to where Ransom and Sally had been locked in their embrace, but they were gone. She walked among the tables, ignoring Harry's calls and sidestepping zealous sailors, looking in vain for the captain.

Disgruntled, Cat dropped into a chair at a vacant table and tried not to imagine what the missing duo was doing, her heart pounding still from the sight of their embrace. There, seated by the wall, she spent the better part of the evening downing rum syllabubs and fending off the advances of one Blossom Demorney, a comely young thing who gave Cat an earful of everything from the ingredients of the syllabub to the skills that had earned her a reputation in her chosen profession.

After suffering the indignity of a kiss full on the mouth from her admirer, Cat beat a retreat back to the ship, where she spent the rest of the night and most of the morning in a curious series of dreams in which Sally, Blossom, and the captain moved in and out.

When Cat finally roused herself, the sun was filling the cabin with bright light, and she jumped up in alarm. What a dressing-down she would get for sleeping late! Glancing furtively at the captain's bed, however, she saw that she had no cause for worry because Ransom's bed had not been slept in. Why, then, was she not relieved?

Cat was up on deck when the captain, with a gleam in his eye, finally returned to the ship. Cat instantly regretted the education she had received from Blossom, for she pictured Ransom and Sally doing everything the girl had described, and what had sounded exotic and exciting after a night of rum syllabubs took on a decidedly different cast in the bright light of day. In fact, Cat was not sure what Blossom had described and what she herself had dreamed up, for it all seemed very strange and a bit embarrassing. Some of her preoccupation must have shown on her face for, to her annoyance, Ransom asked, "Have a nice evening, Cat?"

"Yes, very fine, thank you, captain," she answered lightly, feigning interest in the topmast as she craned her eyes upward.

The captain chuckled and threw her a small bundle. "Here's something to keep you busy for a while," he said. Looking up at him questioningly, she nearly missed catching the object he tossed so casually. At his nod, Cat slowly unwrapped the heavy cloth to reveal a small sheathed blade with an ornate silver handle. Slowly she raised her eyes, sparkling with delight, to his.

"For me, captain?" she whispered in awe.

"Yes, for you, scamp. Now you can quit pestering me to borrow mine." With a lazy grin, Ransom slapped her on the back, and Cat had to restrain herself from throwing her arms around him in exuberant thanks.

The two stood in companionable silence as Cat tried out her new blade, but nagging questions kept knocking at her concentration, forcing her to take a deep breath and plunge into conversation. "Captain," she began as she prepared to throw the knife, "why haven't you ever married?"

Ransom's short burst of laughter caused Cat to send her shiny new blade wide of its mark. "Marriage!" he scoffed. "Now there's a fool's deed! What on earth put that into your head, lad?"

"Well, I was just thinking on . . . women, sir, and I wondered," Cat mumbled.

"Hmmm. Well, I wouldn't give a shilling for any woman I know: a lot of spoiled, spiteful, and deceitful creatures," Ransom said while Cat squirmed in her breeches. "As for marriage . . ." There was a long pause before he laughed mirthlessly. "A man should put his faith in more solid things, lad!"

Then, as if to shake off the mood, Ransom's tone lightened. "Women on the whole are boring creatures," he explained. When Cat did not respond, he added, "When you're a little older I think you'll view women with a more jaundiced eye. Look at Tom Clapper. He's the fellow to talk to about marriage; I forget how many times he has wed," Ransom said with a low chuckle.

Cat could have answered him, for she had often laughed at Tom's stories. He had had three wives and complained about all of them on a regular basis. When asked why he kept marrying, Tom declared the vixens tricked him, one and all, but his shipmates maintained he collected wives the way some amassed seashells. Marriage was his hobby, and a right expensive one, too, they would add.

Before Cat could form another question, however, Ransom was called away by Mr. Peabody. She watched him walk off, admiring the way his body moved as she tried to absorb his words. So women are boring, are they? Cat thought resentfully. If you only knew.

Then, tossing his comments aside, she looked reverently down at her prize, running her finger over the intricate design on the knife's silver handle. Slipping it into her pocket, she swore to herself that his gift would never leave her side.

That night her dreams were sweeter, for she all but forgot Sally as the ship resumed sail.

Chapter 6

By cornering most of her crewmates at one time or another and pestering them to share their knowledge, Cat gradually acquired a host of new skills as the *Reckless* wended its way through the Leewards. Catching the captain in a good mood one lazy afternoon, she even learned some navigation. Expecting a rebuff, she had picked up the sextant and asked him to teach her, but he heaved a sigh and showed her a problem. His annoyance turned to astonishment when he discovered the extent of her mathematical knowledge.

"I assume your grandfather, the esteemed sailor, taught you this?" Ransom asked. Cat knew that few ordinary seamen possessed such skills.

"Who?" Intent on the problem he had given her, Cat did not see his raised eyebrow or catch the sarcasm in his voice.

"I thought as much," Ransom answered dryly, and Cat never realized her blunder. She only knew that Ransom was sharing his knowledge and precious time with her, and she glowed.

Cat loved being with him. Oh, she had many friends on the *Reckless*, and she especially cared for Bosun, but her companion of choice was Ransom. She adored his biting sense of humor, and sometimes choked on her dinner when he dryly related a story about some hapless sailor on a past voyage or the behavior of some greedy merchant. He was handsome, interesting, and amusing, and he treated her with a sort of reluctant affection that sent her heart skipping.

Her mind strayed from her navigational study to the events of just the other night, and Cat smiled at the memory. He had been in the best of moods and urged her to join him at supper.

"Come, lad, quit waiting on me and have a chair," Ransom had said, and Cat needed no further invitation. "How are you faring?" he asked when his cabin boy was seated across from him.

"Fine, captain!" she said with a grin.

"No troubles with—let's see, what were your pet names for them?—Blubber Belly or Shark Bait?"

"No, sir. Blubber Belly, or rather the cook, is more bark than bite, and well, you know Mule. It's best just to keep out of his way," she answered earnestly.

"Ah, yes," Ransom said. "I'm afraid that mariners in general are not known for their kind dispositions. Or their cooking skills," he added dryly as he gnawed a hard biscuit.

"Oh, I think there are more than a few good fellows aboard," Cat said with enthusiasm as she tackled her salt pork. "I wouldn't know about other ships, though, the navy vessels and the whalers and the stinking slavers . . ." Gauging the extent of his good mood, she paused, then blurted breathlessly, "Have you ever met any pirates?"

Ransom smiled, shaking his head at her excitement. "Yes and no. I've never fought a pirate ship, but I have met men who crewed on them. Believe me, lad, they're not the stuff of romantic legends. The pirates I've known are so filthy and mean they make Mule look like a model of decorum. They're the kind who would snatch your purse in broad daylight, then slit your throat as an afterthought. And some privateers are little better than foul criminals hiding behind a letter of marque," he said with disgust.

"No!" Cat gasped wide-eyed.

He laughed in response. "Yes! Even the *Reckless* was mistaken for a pirate ship once," he said, chuckling again when Cat eyed him skeptically. "We came upon a Spanish schooner, many-gunned but big and slow. She put up no resistance, and when we boarded her we found out why." Ransom paused, and Cat, though engrossed in the story, could not help noticing how nicely his lips curved when he spoke.

"The crew had mutinied, locked the officers below, and broken into some casks of rum in the hold," he said. "They were all as drunk as only sailors can get, and, certain we were pirates, they clamored to join our crew. We were nearly forced to fight them off and were lucky to get away without any extra crew members!"

Cat had laughed aloud, as much for the pleasure of Ransom's company as for the humor in his tale. Smiling at her recollection, she turned her attention back to her navigation lesson, and was interrupted by the slam of the door, signaling Ransom's abrupt exit from the room. Cat looked up, disappointed at his departure.

Putting her chin in her hand, she let herself picture him as he so often stood on the deck, his body taut and his hair windblown. He was always so strong, so sure of himself, so . . . Enough! The captain might be wonderful, but she need not dwell on him so, Cat chided herself. He already invaded her dreams at night; she did not need to spend every waking minute thinking of him! With an effort, she returned her mind to the task at hand and put her quill to the paper.

* * *

Despite Cat's increasing variety of skills, she was ordered to stay in the captain's cabin whenever a prize was taken, a command that did not sit well with her. After the frustration of peeking through the windows at a particularly thrilling battle, Cat tried to think of a way to circumvent the captain's decree without outright disobedience. Her chance came the day they suddenly scared up a French merchantman around a deserted reef.

Cat was up on the mizzenmast when the battle was launched, and she simply remained where she was, transfixed by the sights and sounds as the *Reckless* sent a warning shot booming over the other vessel's bow. She reasoned it was already too late to climb down from the rigging, and as if to prove her point, the warning shot was answered with a volley of twelve-pounders, beginning the battle in earnest.

Cat clung to her position until a shot nearly toppled the mast above her, the creaking timber and heavy sails pulling, in turn, on the mainmast. Without a moment's hesitation, she scrambled upward amid the perilously heavy canvas to cut the lines, freeing the mizzen royal and relieving the pressure on the mainmast.

Damage to the ship was minimal, for despite its efforts, the French vessel was no match for the many-gunned privateer, and soon Cat was racing down the rigging, flush with the thrill of her first real battle, while the *Reckless*'s crew began transferring cargo from the captured vessel.

"Good work, lad!" Bosun shouted, giving Cat a hearty slap on the back. She fairly beamed with pride, imagining nothing short of a promotion from her captain. Her Aunt Amelia in Barbados and, indeed, her very sex were momentarily forgotten as she envisioned a career on the seas, her sights on Mr. Peabody's position. Cat's plans were short-lived, however, for once the *Reckless* sailed boldly away in victory, the captain ordered her to his cabin. He looked extremely displeased.

"Well, I see that you are down to only seven lives, now," Ransom said as the two stood facing each other in his cabin.

"Aye, sir, I suppose so," she answered uncertainly, the cold fury on Ransom's face effectively draining all her satisfaction.

"I find it incredibly stupid of you to waste one of them on something as trifling as the mizzen royal sail." His words sent Cat reeling in dismay, for she had heard him use that arrogantly vicious tone before, but never on herself.

"The damage would have been slight, but you easily could have been killed. I had expected more of you than the action of a foolhardy braggart."

"But, captain—" Cat began.

"This is *not* a lark, boy," he said, cutting her off, his voice filled with quiet rage. "This is *not* a pleasure trip, and it is *not* a game. It's *real*, and it's deadly." Suddenly, he grabbed Cat by the arm as if to shake some sense into her. "Why do you think the gun deck is painted red?" he demanded, pausing only long enough for Cat to shake her head in ignorance. "So that you won't notice the blood," he answered softly. Releasing his hold on her, he turned on his heel and exited the cabin, leaving Cat to gape at the closed door, astonished by his behavior.

Ransom's words stung Cat, and she moped around like a wounded puppy before righteous indignation took hold. Everyone else approved of her action, and even if the captain didn't, he had no cause to speak to her in that manner! She worked herself into a foul mood, and retaliated against Ransom by treating him with a frosty disdain guaranteed to set his teeth on edge.

At supper, she waited on him silently, her face grim as she shoved his plate before him, and she returned his attempts at conversation with bleak monosyllables.

"Well, what hideous fare has cook prepared tonight?" Ransom asked without glancing up.

"Same," Cat mumbled. Giving him a sidelong glance, she noticed that she had captured his attention.

"The same as what, yesterday?" he asked, a hint of irritation in his voice.

"Aye."

"Hmmm," he grunted, returning his attention to his plate. "And have you kept out of further trouble today?"

"Aye."

Again he looked up, his brows drawing together. "Have you lost your tongue, lad?"

Cat simply shrugged, and Ransom gave up for a time, eating silently. But she could swear he stole a glance at her now and then, grimacing as he did so.

"What exactly ails you?" he finally asked. When Cat only shrugged again, he reared up from the table and stalked from the room. Serves him right! Cat thought as the door slammed behind him.

Unfortunately, Cat discovered after several days that her revenge was not so sweet, for Ransom could be far colder than she. Her anger evaporated in the ever-widening rift between them, and the reason for their falling-out no longer mattered; in fact, it seemed rather silly when she thought about it. Suddenly the world was bleak and empty, and she wanted the comfort that only his friendship could provide.

Cat's state of mind was not improved when Bosun approached her on deck, and with a nod at the captain's distant back, asked, "What ails you two?"

"Nothing," Cat mumbled into her chest.

"Well, you best take care of it, lad," the first mate said. "Don't let the captain fool you. For all that he seems cool as ice, the man has a temper, and I, for one, don't like to see it."

"I've already seen it," Cat said glumly.

"Have you? Now, what have you been doing, lad, to get the man's ire up?"

"He yelled at me for cutting those mizzen lines!" she burst out.

"He did, did he?" Bosun asked, rubbing his chin thoughtfully.

"I'm not supposed to be on deck during a battle, but I hardly could have climbed down in time, and, anyway, I don't see why I should have to stay cooped up in the cabin! He says I'm more use to him than most and he doesn't want me blown to bits, but it doesn't seem fair to miss the excitement all the time," Cat complained.

"I see," said Bosun, his grizzled features set and serious. "Now, you listen to me, lad. The captain's right, and you should be glad he's taken a liking to you. There's precious few that he has, God knows!" the first mate mumbled under his breath.

Louder, he said, "Now, the man doesn't want you to get hurt is all. The people he cares for have a habit of dying on him, so maybe he just wants to make sure you don't go the same way. Now, be a good lad, and don't let the captain down."

"What do you mean?" Cat asked, wondering if Ransom was an orphan like herself, but Bosun only shook his head.

"Back to work with you, boy," he said, and Cat swallowed back the questions that rose to her lips. Although she did not follow all of Bosun's words, she understood that Ransom's anger, although not justified, sprang from concern for her, and she felt guilty over her own childish behavior. She resolved to mend the breach between them and determinedly headed for the cabin, where she found him seated at the large table, glancing over the books.

Cat soon discovered that a reconciliation would not be easy.

"Good day to you, captain," she said. As her first try at conversation, it failed miserably.

"Hmmm," was Ransom's response, his eyes never rising from his work.

"Is there naught I can do for you?" she asked.

"No."

"Well, if there's anything you need, just speak up," she urged. Her words were met with total silence. Cat decided she was becoming heartily sick of the sound of her own voice. With a wrench, she realized that only a few days before she had given Ransom the same treatment. First she would not speak to him, and now he was not talking to her! What a pretty kettle of fish, she mused, not at all comforted by the realization that she had had a hand in its preparation.

Unwilling to give up, but uncertain as to her course, Cat perched on her sea chest and began mending a tear in her pants, periodically looking over at her still-silent captain. She stayed, quietly sewing in the corner, in the hope that he might speak to her or she might be struck with an inspiration on how to achieve that end.

As she sat, Cat brooded on how she missed his company. She loved to be with him, to listen to his strong, deep voice and watch his face surreptitiously while he looked over the books. She loved his dark eyes, his lazy grin, and the sound of his laughter. She loved the shape of his long, lean fingers grasping the pen and the way the sunlight brightened his shiny dark locks as he bent his head. She loved . . . him.

The gasp caught his attention, but he only flicked

a glance over her stricken face, and when she did not speak he returned his attention to his work.

She loved him. The realization hit Cat like a broadside, knocking the wind from her. She saw his quick glance, and she wanted to say something, but "I love you, captain" did not seem quite appropriate. She could only stare miserably at him, her mind turning over the implications of this wonderful and terrible discovery.

She loved him, but what good did it do her when the man would not even speak to her? By supper she was nearly at her wits' end, conceiving and rejecting several plans for reconciliation, and she hovered over Ransom like a fly on a hot day. Finally, he slammed his fist down on the table, sending the cook's hard-as-nails biscuits sailing through the air.

"God damn it, Cat! If you don't stop this moping immediately, I'll put you off on the first island I see, and I can only hope it will be populated by man-eating Caribs!"

He had spoken to her! Although the words were not promising, Cat grasped at her chance. "Whoa, captain! Watch those biscuits! Do you want to put a hole in the paneling?" she said lightly as she stooped to pick up the errant foodstuffs. "We could always put 'em in a nine-pounder." She held up one of the missiles. "Use them as cannon shot," she added, smiling up at him.

Their eyes met briefly across the room before she was rewarded with his lazy grin. "He thinks if he makes them hard enough, they will repel the weevils," Ransom commented, and Cat beamed.

So the rift between them was healed, and to Cat all was right with the world again. She certainly had no intention of acting on her discovery that she loved her captain. What could she possibly do about it? Simply to have his companionship again was enough for her . . . for now.

The reconciliation pleased Ransom, too, although he would hardly admit it to himself. Smiling as he watched Cat clear the table, Ransom decided he was glad to have the youngster with the lively sense of humor aboard, yet even as the thought came, a voice in the deeper recesses of his mind derided him. Ransom realized that he was looking at the youth with something akin to fondness, and he straightened, the smile leaving his face. *They'll be calling you "mother hen" soon*, the voice warned. *Perhaps you'd like to take in a few more strays and turn the* Reckless *into a floating nursery* . . .

Ransom shook his head, remembering how he had carried on over the boy's small act of courage during the recent battle. He'd been surprised and annoyed at his own loss of temper over the incident. He had vented his wrath on Cat for recklessness, and yet, he'd been irritated with himself for caring. Ransom told himself that, as captain, he must be concerned for the welfare of everyone aboard, but he knew damn well that if anyone else had cut the sail, he would have handed out praise instead of ridicule.

He had sailed for years in comparative peace, and now . . . Ever since Cat had erupted like a boil into Ransom's existence, the captain found his carefully structured life disturbed with alarming frequency. He was beginning to rue the day he first looked into those green eyes on the quay at Barton. What did he care if the little idiot was killed? He was becoming all too fond of his cabin boy. Sailors died. That was a fact of life, and it was best not to become too attached to any of them.

Chapter 7

Cat kicked a stone in the road, then glared, suddenly disgusted with her dirty bare feet. Her delight in going ashore with the captain had vanished when he'd excused himself to escort a couple of idiotic females to their destination.

The *Reckless* was again anchored at Windlay, which Cat was beginning to think lay under an ill wind, for it seemed every time she looked forward to an outing, some mishap occurred to spoil her fun. She'd been promised a trip to Ransom's offices, but now she stood forgotten, her heart in her throat, watching him walk away.

Cat had seen the women stare at Ransom, then smile and simper when he noticed them, and she had nearly retched at their coyness. Oh, she had seen others light after Ransom like bees for honey, and she had grown accustomed to those women like Sally, who dressed in brightly colored skirts, blouses slipping from their shoulders and bold invitations dripping from their painted lips.

These two were not of that ilk. They wore fine silks of beautiful design and elegant hats, and they carried tiny reticules. Their voices were soft, their accents sophisticated, and they came from the kind of life Cat had left behind. She watched Ransom look them over appraisingly before slipping off, and the boyish disguise that allowed her so much freedom suddenly seemed about as appealing as sackcloth.

As she walked back to the beach to swim Cat wondered with unexpected longing what it would be like to return to female form, acutely aware of the irony that she was desiring the very things she had once despised. Even as she longed for the feel of clean, soft fabric beneath her fingers, a pretty ribbon for her hair, or a warm apple tart swimming in fresh cream, Cat cursed herself. She was living the life of adventure that she had once only dreamed about; how could she want anything more?

With a sigh, Cat closed her eyes against the bright Caribbean sun as if to shut out the new feelings assailing her. She had rarely given a thought to her female state, but now . . . She was so much more aware of her body lately, as if it had a life of its own, especially when she was around the captain, and *especially* when he was naked. Then her heart would trip apace and her breath would catch in the strangest fashion.

It was as if her body was suddenly maturing, the growing pains appearing as odd prickles and tickles that had an unnerving tendency to strike when Ransom was near. Perhaps her weight was only shifting, but she had the notion that even her legs, though long and slim, were becoming awfully shapely for the average sailor.

Cat was thankful the *Reckless* was heading south toward Barbados, for she knew it would be best to end her masquerade soon, although so far her secret remained safe. Ransom allowed her some measure of privacy in his cabin, owing to her sad scar story, and she kept to herself when swimming and rarely removed her disguise. She even slept in her clothes, but then everyone did except the captain, she thought with annoyance.

Although the masquerade had begun to prey on

her mind, Cat was reluctant to abandon the ship she called home to face an uncertain future with a relative she could barely recall. The thought of actually leaving her newfound friends at Barbados weighed down her heart, making it difficult for her to choose the right course.

And, of course, there was Edward. She had been too busy and too happy of late to brood on her cousin's treachery, but she had not forgotten, and she had no intention of letting the man enjoy the spoils of his wickedness in peace. Justice would not be served, however, while she frolicked on a privateer. Her thoughts whirling in her head, Cat raced through the waves and dove into the turquoise waters as though the salty sea could wash away her confusion.

From the very first time she'd plunged into the ocean, Cat had decided the best thing about sailing was the swimming. Jumping into the clear blue-green Caribbean to enter a silent world of fantastic coral and schools of sparkling fish was a far cry from paddling among the lily pads of Wellshire Manor's duck pond.

Best of all, she loved to swing from a line off the ship, dropping gracefully into the water below, enjoying the way sky and water swirled about her and the lurching feeling in the pit of her stomach just before she released the rope. Surely, there was nothing better on earth, Cat thought, clinging tenaciously to her boyish existence. With a sigh she stepped from the water and threw herself on the hot sand, feeling oddly torn by the pull of two separate worlds.

Heaving another sigh, Cat sat up and rested her hands on her knees. She dug her heels into the wet sand, enjoying the feel of the water, as it gently washed her toes, and took in the scene about her, trying to imprint it on her memory forever. Not a cloud marred the azure sky, almost indistinguishable from the sea, and the only object in a world of sea and sky was the *Reckless*, her hull towering over the tiny figures swimming by her side and her masts soaring into the heavens.

As Cat marked the scene in her mind, she knew it would be hard to break the ties that bound her to the ship, for she could feel Ransom's inexorable pull. Despite her yearnings—or perhaps because of them—Cat wanted to remain right where she was, and for emphasis, she dug her toes into the sand as if to take hold of the island and all it represented.

Ransom returned to the ship not long after she did, and Cat, elated to see that he was not happy, briefly hoped that one of the fine ladies had either picked his pocket or snubbed him. Her petty thoughts turned to concern, however, when she registered the grim cast to his features, and hearing him call for Bosun, she tagged along, anxious to learn the source of his troubles.

Neither man seemed to take note of her small figure hovering behind them as they stood on deck in the gathering twilight. "It's worse than I thought," Ransom said so softly that Cat strained to hear him over the rush of the wind and the din of ship's activity.

"What's that, captain?" Bosun asked.

"It's not only the warehouse. I learned that two of the shipping vessels were taken by Ben Pike."

"Butcher Ben, the pirate?" Bosun asked, scratching his head in puzzlement. Cat pricked up her ears at the mention of the dreaded Ben, whose penchant for hacking his foes to pieces had earned him the nickname Butcher.

"Two ships, captain?" Bosun questioned, and at Ransom's cold nod, he shook his head. "I can see that jackass having the luck to come across one, but two . . ." The first mate shook his head again. "That sounds deliberate."

"So I thought," Ransom answered dryly.

"What were they hauling?" Bosun asked, his eyes under the heavy brows darting up to Ransom's.

"Sugar."

"Sugar! What the hell would Ben want with a load of sugar?" Bosun scoffed, his brow crinkling in disbelief.

"That's just what I intend to find out," Ransom answered, and the cold determination in his voice made Cat step back toward the rail. She watched Bosun walk away, still shaking his head, and moved to go herself, but a voice stopped her.

"Well, did you hear all you wished?"

Ransom had not even turned around to look at her, and Cat frowned at his back before guiltily slinking away from the rail. "How do you do that?" she asked.

"What?"

"See through the back of your head," Cat grumbled, not daring to look at him. But Ransom chuckled, and seeing that he was not really angry with her for eavesdropping, she was encouraged to satisfy her curiosity.

"Captain, why would Ben take your ships?"

Ransom sighed and looked out over the waves. "I'm not sure, but I suspect Devlin's hand in this."

"Devlin," Cat whispered as though the name itself were an ill omen. "Who *is* Devlin?"

Ransom was silent for so long that Cat thought he would not answer, but finally he spoke softly and slowly. "Devlin has made himself my particular enemy. It goes way back . . . to when I was young and cocky—or foolish, depending on your choice of words," he said grimly.

"One of Devlin's people approached me with an offer to invest in some island property, and I saw myself as a grand plantation owner," Ransom said, his lips curving into a self-deprecating smile. "The promise of riches was enticing, too, as I was rapidly depleting my inheritance. The phrase 'rich as a Creole' had become so widespread it was easy to imagine all those who invested in the islands returning with great fortunes." Ransom shook his head at his own foolishness.

"Unfortunately, I wasn't the only one who labored under this delusion, my lad. Devlin, along with others of his ilk, brought down many a man through unscrupulous investment schemes in the West Indies, and they continue to do so. They tender the credit to purchase land, but once the land is cleared they call in their loans, leaving the hapless planter without money to buy stock or slaves. These same moneylenders then offer to buy back the land, cleared through no effort of their own."

"How can they get away with this?" Cat asked, outraged.

"Oh, it's all perfectly legal." Ransom sighed. "There was nothing left to do but pay the man or lose the land. Although I could ill-afford the former, I was loath to give away the land so easily. Then Devlin was so kind as to give me a third alternative . . ." His words trailed off, and Cat watched his face grow grim. "He was willing to extend the loan in exchange for sexual favors."

At Cat's gasp, Rasom's face grew less rigid. "Oh, I wasn't shocked; I had seen too much in my misspent youth for that," he said with a crooked smile. "I never thought to be bought like a street whore, though." His laugh was humorless. "Maybe it was the insult of being offered money for such services, or it might have been Devlin's contemptuous sneer, but I lost my temper." He spoke as though such an occurrence was both rare and disgraceful. "He had to call in two of his assistants to tear me off him, and still I nearly broke his jaw.''

Ransom shrugged. ''You see, Devlin had mistook his man. I was a different bird from his previous pluckings and not quite the witless carouser I appeared to be. In the end I paid him off, although my holdings were badly damaged and I could no longer continue my free-spending revels.''

He was quiet, seemingly lost in thought as he looked out over the waves, but Cat's curiosity had not been satisfied.

''Why, then, does he continue to harass you?'' she asked.

Ransom grunted in response. ''That's a good question, lad. Would that I knew the answer myself, but I can only guess. Apparently, Devlin cannot forget that I scorned him, and my subsequent success rankles him so much that he loses his better judgment.'' Ransom shook his head.

''When the first sugar crop of my hard-won plantation was burned to the ground, I suspected, but had no proof, that Devlin was responsible. After that, there were minor incidents, and, of course, the spies, including a lovely young 'widow' intent on giving me the clap,'' he said with a smile. ''It was not until I began the shipping business and found several cargoes damaged or missing that I was able, by exerting some pressure on the appropriate parties, to connect Devlin to the deeds.''

Ransom's face grew grim again. ''I sought him out, but he was not easily found. Finally I came upon him in one of his warehouses overseeing the transfer of some cargo, which I simply diverted to one of my own vessels as payment due.''

''That cannot have made him happy!'' Cat said.

''Since I had a pistol aimed at his heart, he gave me no argument. I suggested that we call the game even and warned him that I had discovered some of his dealings, which would greatly interest the authorities. That was more than a year ago, and I've not been troubled by him since . . . until the warehouse."

"And now the ships," Cat said softly.

"Yes, the ships," Ransom said. "I would like to learn more about Ben Pike," he added, finally turning away from the rail. "And I know just the place to look for information."

Ransom spoke softly, as if forgetting Cat's presence, but then he looked down at her, his eyebrow raised as though daring her to speak. "And I think I have given you more than your fill of answers for one day, my lad," he said. Cat, recognizing the dismissal in his tone, smiled winningly before scurrying off, highly pleased to have shared his confidences.

Cat tossed and turned in her hammock, troubled by images of her captain. Finally, she flipped onto her back, opened her eyes, and listened for Ransom's steady breathing. By the silence, she knew he was not in his bed. She sighed in the darkness and crossed her hands behind her head. If this was love, why did the poets all aspire to it? Ever since her self-discovery, her emotions had tossed like waves between elation and gloom, and she was beginning to get seasick. How on earth had matters come to this pass?

Oh, it had begun subtly enough after the visit to Tortola. Ransom just slipped into her dreams while she slumbered. Cat dismissed them; after all, she had no control over her dreams. Then the visions sneaked into her daylight hours, and she found herself imagining what would happen if she threw her arms around him or how it would it feel to kiss him.

These were dangerous thoughts, Cat knew, and her healthy instinct for self-preservation beat back her lovesickness. But still, unbidden, the images came to mind. Surely he cares for me, Cat thought in the darkness. What if I confessed all? You might be thrown to the sharks, she answered herself, and with a grimace she rolled from the hammock.

On deck she spoke briefly to the watch before walking to the rail, where she propped her elbows and took in the glorious night. The moon was a shining sliver and the bright stars seemed endless, while all about the ship the black ocean pitched and tossed. The roar of the sea, the groan of the timbers, and the flap of the sails sounded eery in the darkness.

"Beautiful, isn't it?"

Warmth flooded her chest at the sound of the captain's familiar deep voice. She felt him beside her, and a shiver danced up her neck, but she only grunted, "Aye."

"This is one of the reasons I stay at sea," he said, leaning into the rail. The two stood in silence for some time before Cat finally spoke.

"What are the others?" she asked. "The other reasons?" She felt rather than saw him shrug beside her. Both figures, one tall and dark, the other small and light, faced the ocean.

"It's an honest fight," he finally said softly. "Can you understand that, little Cat?" he asked, turning to look at his cabin boy.

"I think so, captain." Cat paused, carefully choosing her words before she continued. "The ocean's not for you or against you; she's just there."

"Very good, lad," he said softly and smiled at Cat affectionately before returning his gaze to the sea. "I learned early on that most men are scheming bastards. It's all a fight, one way or the other, but out here, the fight is more real."

Cat stood quietly staring at the black waves as she digested his words and felt a sudden bolt of insight.

"So . . . most men are scheming bastards, and most women are boring creatures. You don't have a very high opinion of mankind, do you?" she asked.

For a moment she thought Ransom had taken offense at her comment, but then she heard his soft chuckle.

"Touché, lad. I'll admit, there are few people in this world who win my respect," he said wryly. "Take a lesson from me: you come into the world alone and you leave it the same way, and the only one you can count on in between is yourself."

Cat, ever optimistic, found his philosophy depressing, and she frowned down at the railing. "Have you no family, sir? No desire to have babes of your own?" she asked, her words trailing off lamely into the darkness. She felt him stiffen in response.

"No. I have no family, and as I said, it doesn't pay to care for people, Cat," Ransom answered. "Good night."

Cat looked over only to see his dark figure striding away. Hurt at his curt dismissal, she wanted to call him back, to argue with him, but instead she tore her gaze away and, disillusioned, blinked at the moon. Although she'd never thought it out coherently, in the back of her mind she had harbored the fantasy that somehow, someday, she would blossom into a beautiful woman, Ransom would suddenly fall madly in love with her, and they would sail off into the sunset.

Oh, she was well aware of his low opinion of women and his detached nature, but somehow she had thought to change him. Somehow, someday, things would be different. He cared for her a little, no matter what he said, and when he found out who she really was, why, he would sweep her off her feet!

Ha! What childish nonsense, she realized now.

She would never be anything more than a skinny girl who could pass for a boy, and he would never fall in love with any woman.

Her romantic illusions shattered, Cat put her chin in her hands and looked glumly out upon the dark ocean, now bereft of its mystery and allure.

Chapter 8

Cat moped about the ship for days after her depressing conversation with Ransom. Even the festive mood of the crew when they made port failed to cheer her. Harry tried to talk her into going ashore, but they were anchored off L'Etoile, a disreputable place if ever there was one, and Ransom had warned her to stay aboard the ship.

Chafing under her captain's restrictions, she sulked about the deck until Bull collared her with an invitation to join him and his fellows. She was about to refuse again but caught herself, and with a rebellious nod, she tagged along.

She was determined to enjoy the outing, but her group, louder and more boisterous than Harry's, seemed to draw unwanted attention, and the tavern that Bull chose looked filthy, even by Cat's relaxed standards. She dared not glance too closely at the glass from which she drank, hoping that the vile rum in it had washed away any insects making their home in the brackish bottom.

She viewed the other occupants of the place with a wary eye, for they were a foul-looking lot, the kind who would as soon slit your throat as look at you. L'Etoile, a refuge for those with no love for the laws of any country, was a favorite haunt for the numerous pirate crews and privateers that worked these waters, and Bull had unerringly chosen the place where the worst of them congregated.

A scuffle across the room made her think twice about staying, and she urged her neighbor, the odoriferous Marlowe, to gather his fellows together for an early exit. He would have none of it, though, assuring her that they were having a fine time, so Cat searched for Bull, hoping he would have more sense than the rest.

Her faith was misplaced, for when she found him Bull was loudly insulting Napoleon in front of several Frenchmen who adored the emperor. As soon as the words left Bull's mouth, all hell broke loose among his audience, and before long it seemed that everyone in the place dove into the fray, with fists flying and more than a few knives flashing.

Cat managed to leap atop a high cupboard, from which she dispensed bottles of liquor over the heads of the appropriate parties. But despite her continued support, the battle seemed to be going against the *Reckless* crew, and she eyed the door, hoping to escape. Suddenly, the breath was knocked from her lungs as someone pulled her leg out beneath her and dragged her outside by her shirt collar, despite her screaming, kicking and biting.

"Hold, you feline!" a familiar voice shouted as she was thrown to the ground at the back of the tavern.

"Captain!" Cat cried in surprise, rolling to her feet.

"By my count, you are losing your spare lives far too quickly, urchin! What possessed you to go anywhere with Bull Marston, a man known for his attention to trouble?" Ransom asked furiously. Cat promptly quelled the exhilaration that rushed through her at the sight of him and, instead, took umbrage at his tone. But before she could answer, he ordered her firmly to stay put and walked back into the tavern.

Annoyed at his curt command, Cat stepped to the door, opening it a crack to peek inside. She stared in reluctant admiration as he dispatched more than one burly fellow in an effort to reach Bull and the small band from the *Reckless* that remained standing, but her eyes were suddenly drawn to a swarthy man on the other side of the room.

The fellow's stealthy movements, so out of place among the other rampaging, drunken brawlers, riveted Cat's attention, and her blood began to race with apprehension as he drew a knife and began to move purposefully through the crowd. Too purposefully, Cat thought, for while the other sailors lashed out at anyone in their vicinity, the swarthy man with the knife seemed intent on someone in particular.

Ignoring her captain's orders to stay outside, Cat slipped back into the tavern, her eyes fixed on the knife-wielding man who edged ever closer to Ransom. Suddenly the fellow made his move, and Cat's heart leaped into her throat as she watched him raise the blade to Ransom's back. Without even thinking, Cat threw herself at the offender with a shout, knocking him to the floor, and the two rolled in the dust until Cat gasped for breath underneath his weight, her eyes fixed on the knife raised high above her heart.

She might be weak but she was wiry, and as the swarthy man's arm descended, she jerked sideways. The movement saved her life, but it did not prevent the blade from cutting through her flesh, and Cat's eyes widened in surprise at the pain that shot through her. Then the breath was knocked from her as the dead weight of her opponent landed full upon her.

Ransom felt the next few moments pass in dreamlike horror after he heard the lad shout and turned to find a knife poised over the boy's heart. His own blade somehow found a home in the cutthroat's back, but as he knelt to push the body aside, he felt a pressure in his chest he had not felt in many years.

It tightened, threatening to constrict his throat, as he sought frantically to discover if his cabin boy lived . . . or died. In that long second, Ransom realized he cared too much about the lad, but it was too late; the emotion was already invested, and he cursed his own foolishness. Then Cat's eyes fluttered open, and Ransom breathed freely again as his fingers searched for the wound, assuring himself it would not be fatal.

It was a draggle-tailed bunch that made its way back to the ship, Bull nursing a cut over his eye, two men carrying the unconscious body of John Fitzsimmons, and a white-faced Ransom carrying his cabin boy in his arms.

"It's just a scratch on my arm," Cat grunted through clenched teeth, but Ransom ordered her to be quiet, and the effort it took to argue with him seemed ill-expended. She felt dizzy with rum and pain, but she fought the urge to drift off and join poor Fitzsimmons in blissful oblivion.

But Fitzsimmons's loss of consciousness mattered not in the slightest, whereas Cat's disguise, her identity, and perhaps her very life depended on her staying awake. She simply could not faint away because she knew what Ransom would do when he got her back to his cabin.

He would strip off her bloody shirt.

Cat gritted her teeth but could not prevent the groans from escaping her lips at each jostling movement.

"Hold on, lad," Ransom whispered, and Cat found herself wondering if perhaps this reckoning was fated. Stories of women—harbingers of bad luck—found aboard ships returned to haunt her. Surely Ransom would not throw her overboard . . . or worse.

After what seemed like an eternity of rough usage, Cat heard the voices of her fellow crew members and opened her eyes to the familiar masts of the *Reckless*. If she could just hang on a little while longer, she remembered thinking, and then Ransom was laying her on his bed, putting whiskey to her lips. The warmth of the liquor revitalized her, and she gathered the remnants of her strength as her captain's hands moved to her shirt buttons.

"It's my arm!" she said forcefully, managing to put surprising annoyance into the words.

"Let me see it," Ransom urged softly.

"Here. Look, then," Cat said, pushing up the sleeve.

"God damn it, Cat. Let me get that bloody shirt off you!" Ransom said, his temper flaring.

"My scars . . ."

"Your scars be damned!" Ransom said, but Cat raised her other arm to her shirt, her hand feebly clinging to the fabric as tears welled in her eyes.

"Oh, for God's sake," Ransom cursed in vexation, and Cat felt the blood drain from her face as her destiny hung in the balance. Then, with another oath, he released her shirt and pushed up her sleeve, exposing the torn flesh on the inside of her arm.

"It's just a scratch," he confirmed, his relief so intense it unnerved him, a feeling both foreign and unpleasant to the captain of the *Reckless*. He struggled to regain the unruffled, chilly detachment he had cultivated for years, knowing he must distance himself from the lad of whom he had become entirely too fond.

His face grim, he cleaned and neatly dressed Cat's wound, then tossed a clean shirt onto the bed with the warning, "I hope you can manage to get that shirt changed, for I have no desire to bed down on bloody linen.''

His unexpected callousness cut Cat sharper than the knife. "Aye, captain," she muttered, smarting from both wounds.

"Now," he said, pouring them each a glass of whiskey, "suppose you tell me why you disobeyed my orders and went back inside that tavern."

"He was going to kill you," Cat mumbled, keenly aware of the coldness in Ransom's voice. "He went after you, captain. I saw it. Maybe that man Devlin has changed his tactics."

"A knife in the back?" Ransom scoffed. "I fear that's a bit too literal for Devlin. Perhaps your man simply chose me out of the crowd as a good target," he suggested, swallowing his whiskey.

"I don't think so," Cat said. The liquor and her exhaustion were coming together, and she fought back the urge to cry. She longed for comforting from her captain, not this cold interrogation, and she knew in her heart with a sudden, piercing certainty what she had guessed the other night. Her love for Ransom was hopeless because the man before her was incapable of caring.

"Whatever the man's motive, you had no business going back in there," he was saying, and Cat tried to concentrate on his words.

"But—"

"But you saved my life," Ransom said stiffly, looking down into his glass. "I am indebted to you."

"No," Cat mumbled, closing her eyes. "We're even."

"What?"

"Let's leave it at that," she whispered bitterly, blaming her hero for falling short of her expectations. "Just . . . just take me to Barbados."

"Barbados?"

"I'll need help until my arm heals," Cat lied

softly. Although dressing would be difficult, Cat knew she could probably manage, so it was not the wound that spurred her words, but Ransom. His coldness had finally pushed her to break the ties binding her to the ship . . . and binding her in girlish infatuation to its captain.

"Fine," Ransom said tightly. He saw his cabin boy's unexpected defection as a slight that threatened to hurt him if he let it. Ransom was in control of himself again, however, and he had no intention of allowing this ragtag youth to pain him further.

Let the ungrateful wretch leave, he cursed to himself, knowing it would be better for his own peace of mind. "I'll work up your final pay," he said, his eyes flicking over Cat with finality before he walked to the door.

Cat listened for the sound of the latch, then let the tears run down her cheeks, the pain of heartache blending with the ache of her wound until she drifted into a troubled sleep.

"Well, captain?" Bosun asked as he watched Ransom pour himself a shot of whiskey. The two were in the first mate's small cabin, where Ransom could let down a small measure of his guard. Bosun could see from the slump of his shoulders that the night had not been a good one.

"It's just a scratch," Ransom said, the coldness in his voice surprising his first mate.

"Shall I have a look at it?" Bosun asked, and he was again surprised when Ransom shrugged indifferently before taking a seat.

"Well, I guess not, then," the first mate said softly as he sat across from his captain, his keen dark eyes taking in the grim set of Ransom's jaw. He sat quietly while Ransom swirled the liquor in his glass. The movement was an absent one, but Bosun noted the tight grip of those lean fingers.

"It seems that some of Ben's friends did not care for the questions I was asking," Ransom said, jolting Bosun with the change of topic.

"Ah. You learned something, then?"

Ransom's snort of laughter was derisive. "Indeed. I discovered that Ben has been doing a little work lately for an old friend of ours."

"What?" Bosun asked suspiciously.

Ransom smiled coldly. "It seems he's found a new partner . . . Devlin."

"No!" Bosun started. "Devlin may be a bad one, but he's not one of Ben's kind."

"You think not?" Ransom asked, his brow raised sardonically. "You give him too much credit. Those two are cut from the same cloth; only the design is different."

Bosun grunted in disgust before looking sharply at his captain. "And now?"

"And now," Ransom answered, his dark eyes glittering strangely in the cabin's dim light, "we look for Devlin." He downed the rest of the whiskey in one swallow. "I have a score to settle with him— once and for all."

Chapter 9

When the *Reckless* anchored in Carlisle Bay two days later, dawn was spreading over the neat shops and houses and wide, clean streets of Bridgetown, Barbados, while Cat, her few possessions trussed up in a blanket, took leave of the shipmates who had become her friends.

"You'll miss these wooden walls when you land in prison," Harry said, slapping her on the back so hard that her wounded arm ached.

"You'll be back when you see how you fare on land," Bull warned, and the other sailors hurled a few coarse jests her way, their idea of a fond farewell, Cat thought with a smile.

"Whatever you do, don't marry any young lasses," Tom advised, and Cat assured him there was not even a remote chance of that. She was still smiling at the notion when Ransom appeared.

How he stands out among this rabble, Cat thought. He was half a head taller than most, yet it was not his height that set him apart, but rather an intangible air about him that made him so different from these men.

Ignoring the sudden melancholy that enveloped her at the sight of Ransom, Cat moved toward Bosun, awkwardly shaking the first mate's hand with her left. "Good-bye Bosun, and thank you," Cat said sincerely.

She grasped his hand longer than necessary, but the sailor did not seem to mind. "Good luck, lad," he said, a ferocious grin on his face.

"I'll take you ashore," Ransom offered, and Cat nodded silently, not even glancing at his tall figure.

He was quiet in the boat, and Cat did not say a word, memories of the past couple months at sea moving in front of her eyes like a multicolored canvas, dipping and swaying. Each scene that met her mind's eye in seemingly random recollection was a poignant reminder of whom she was leaving behind.

She remembered the night of the storm when she felt Ransom's shoulders beneath her fingertips, and the memory was so vivid she could sense his smooth skin. Her thoughts ran shamelessly to every innocent contact between them, then drifted to the more exotic and less innocent activities described by Blossom of the Cock and Bull. There she dallied, her recollections halted, for memories of Blossom gave her an idea that tripped her heartbeat with its boldness.

She looked at Ransom. The breeze tossed his dark locks and caught his open shirt as he manned the oars, his wide shoulders moving rhythmically, and her whole body tingled in response. She let her eyes travel over him one last time, from the tips of his long, lean fingers to his dusky hair, lingering on all those places that spurred her senses and finally coming to rest on the smooth, firm lips that had so fascinated her from the first. Her heart hammering in her chest, she knew she should not, could not, do the thing that had come to mind.

Ransom, who had been ignoring his cabin boy's gaze, finally looked up, and Cat nervously glanced away, but the image remained. She knew his every feature like the back of her own hand and continued to savor each one in her mind, even as she fought the longing that burgeoned in her chest.

When the boat came to rest, Cat agilely leaped out and turned to face her captain. ''Well, lad, this is it,'' Ransom said, a little too coolly for her taste. ''I wish you well,'' he added perfunctorily, and suddenly Cat knew she must follow through with her scheme.

Despite her nervousness, despite the risk, she reached for Ransom, knowing that soon he would be gone from her life forever and she would never have the chance again. Her lithe fingers grasped his shirt, pulling him toward her, and throwing an arm around his neck, she pressed her lips against his for one brief moment.

In the span of seconds it took the astonished Ransom to recover himself, Cat was already disappearing among the people on the streets of Bridgetown.

Hot, footsore, and irritable, Cat trudged along the road to her Aunt Amelia's house, longing for the *Reckless* and questioning the wisdom of her departure.

Her quest had begun promisingly when she received directions to her aunt's from a Bridgetown shopkeeper, but since then she had been dusted by a cart that nearly ran her off the road, and she had begun to feel the island heat in earnest. With a sigh, Cat took off her hat and rolled up her sleeves, but she dared not remove the vest that helped hide her female curves, although sweat trickled between her breasts and her skin began to itch under her bindings. What a sight I must be, she thought dejectedly. Aunt Amelia will probably shriek in horror!

As she rounded a bend in the road, Cat kicked desultorily at a stone and watched its path, wondering just how much farther she would have to walk when she looked up to see a picture-book cottage surrounded by orange and tamarind trees and nearly engulfed by gardens. It was made of stone, the differing shades creating a patchwork on the walls, and its arched windows were flanked by brightly painted shutters. A neat flagstone path wound its way among a profusion of shrubbery and flowers to the stone steps and tall doors.

Looking down at the well-worn cap in her hands and her dusty bare feet, Cat hesitated. More than a little aware of her ragged appearance and uncertain of her reception, she was reluctant to stand before the massive front doors. Then she spied another path leading around the side of the house and followed it to the rear, where a large terrace was surrounded by even more flower beds, overflowing with roses, orchids, and exotic tropical blooms of every description.

Straightening her shoulders, she walked under a spanking white trellis covered with trailing honeysuckle to the rear door, ducking along the way to avoid pots of plants perched here and there on railings and pillars. Her initial trepidation eased as she looked about her, for she sensed this was a friendly house.

She knocked once and waited, then knocked again. After a seemingly interminable delay during which she had time to wipe her face with her sleeve, leaving a streak of dirt along her cheek, a dusky young woman appeared at the door. Although the servant tried to shoo her away, Cat insisted upon seeing Amelia Molesworth, and finally, after looking Cat up and down, the girl shrugged her shoulders and opened the door. She led Cat down a narrow hallway, past several doors, and finally into a cool parlor where a little, birdlike woman sat writing at a secretary in the corner.

"This boy says he must see you, ma'am."

"What? What's this, Marie?" The little lady turned, and Cat could see pink cheeks and flyaway white curls. "Well, sir, what can I do for you?" she asked, still holding her quill pen. Cat looked pointedly at Marie and then back at her aunt. "Fine, Marie," Amelia said, rising from her desk and waving away the maid. She walked over to where Cat stood nervously clutching her hat in her hands and smiled. "Yes, boy, what is it? Speak up now."

Cat, who towered over the lady, suddenly felt big, awkward, and uncertain. "Aunt Amelia, it's me . . . Catherine Amberly," she said.

The lady took this pronouncement with equanimity, as if scruffy boys frequently announced themselves to be female relatives, and stepped forward to look closer. "Catherine?" she asked as she put a hand to Cat's face, wiping away a smudge of dirt. Cat looked into the warm blue eyes and suddenly found herself weeping in her aunt's arms.

"There, there, my child. Everything's all right now," Amelia murmured, gently patting her niece's back until the tears turned to sporadic hiccups. "Little Catherine! I don't believe it," she said softly, holding Cat back to take a good look at her. "Look at how you've grown! How old are you now?"

"Sixteen."

"No! I don't believe it. Belinda's little girl sixteen! My, how the years have flown. Oh, but my poor girl, you look so thin! Let's get you some food." She smiled gently and put her arm around her niece as she called for the maid.

Cat, struck with a sudden inspiration, gulped back her hiccups. "Oh, aunt, what I would like above anything in this world is a bath . . . a real bath!"

In a very short time Cat was luxuriating in a brass tub filled with piping hot water and trying to choose among a variety of scented soaps. She lathered her entire body with a bar that smelled deliciously of lavender and washed her hair until it squeaked. The water had long since cooled when she finally stepped from the bath to dry herself with some beautiful linen towels piled high on the bed.

Marie had laid out one of Amelia's dressing gowns, which Cat gamely donned, although the sleeves stopped short of her wrists and the hem showed a long stretch of calf. Cat, accustomed as she was to baggy, rough seaman's gear, thought the robe was heavenly, and she reveled in the feel of the soft, velvety material against her skin and the smell of the lemon fragrance clinging to the fabric.

Seated cross-legged on the bed, Cat was brushing her hair vigorously when Amelia herself brought a breakfast tray and placed it on a table flooded with sunshine from a large arched window. Taking a seat across from her aunt, Cat was dazzled by the array of fresh food: cheese, cold ham, slices of melon, and huge, soft rolls. She tried not to gobble the meal, but after the ship's biscuits, the warm rolls, topped with great globs of honeyed butter, were ambrosia. Perhaps living on land would not be so difficult!

"You poor dear, you must be starving," Amelia murmured, and Cat looked up with a start, stopping herself in the middle of a bite as she realized she had been oblivious to her aunt's presence. Where had her manners gone? Chagrined, she put down her fork and fidgeted with her napkin.

"Go ahead, dear, eat," Amelia said with a smile of encouragement. "Now, about your clothes . . . I've sent Isaac off to Bridgetown for my dressmaker, Madame Roussard. She does very nice work and her charges are reasonable." Amelia's hands moved restlessly as she spoke. "Though, perhaps later we should try Mistress Shaw, as she is quite popular with the young ladies, more stylish I suppose. That is, if you are not too tired . . ."

Amelia's voice trailed off as she observed that

Catherine's brows had furrowed. "Oh dear, perhaps I shouldn't have taken it upon myself, but we
must get you dressed, my dear . . ."

Cat looked closely at her aunt, but detected no
censure, only pleasure in the little lady's face. "No,
I'm not the least tired, and I don't mind your getting
the dressmaker," she said. "Of course, I must have
some new clothes, but I don't expect you to pay for
them. I have some money of my own, aunt."

"Oh, dear!" Amelia broke in. "I've said something wrong. Oh, I'm so used to living by myself,
you'll find I'm just a silly old fool," she said, looking flustered. "My Horace left me quite comfortable,
and if I can't take care of my own niece, why, heavens! I don't want to hear another word about money.
Don't you worry about a thing," she admonished
and reached over to squeeze Cat's hand. "I'm just
so glad you're here. You must tell me if I say something that's not quite the thing. Now," she said
briskly, "you finish eating and tell me everything."

Truly comfortable, well-fed, and clean for the first
time in a long while, Cat sat back to tell her tale to
an astonished Amelia, who was soon pale with
shock as Cat related her harrowing experiences at
the hands of Edward and her sudden flight from
Wellshire. "Oh, Catherine, you poor child. If only I
had known! When Belinda died, I should have sent
for you!" she fretted.

"No, aunt! Father and I were happy enough together until Edward came," Cat said, her eyes holding a faraway look that was not pleasant.

"He'll never find you here, a world away,"
Amelia assured her niece. "We are far from the fashionable circles, thank God! You're safe now, my
poor child, and you must forget about the whole
horrible experience!"

"I will never forget," Cat said softly. Returning
her attention to the present, she glanced up and saw

the concerned look on Amelia's face. "Oh, you needn't worry, aunt. I'm sure you're right; he'll never find me here. In fact, I doubt if Edward is even worried about me," Cat said, absently fingering a flounced pillow. Her tone was light, but when she raised her eyes, Amelia saw a glint of pain that took her aback. "But he should be," Cat added, "for he should hang."

Amelia started at the words, spoken so forcefully. "Catherine," she said, shaking her head. "It would be very difficult to prove his guilt. You would need a powerful ally, and I have no contacts at home."

"Yes, I know," Cat said, "and I have no plan to bring him to justice. But sometimes I think how he's still free to commit other crimes and how he'll never suffer for this one. No one should get away with murder."

Chapter 10

Amelia's efficient dressmaker soon had several lovely gowns ready, and for days boxes arrived from town loaded with slippers, underthings, stockings, hats, and all the necessities of a young lady of fashion. The quantity of accoutrements staggered Cat, who had never taken an interest in the world of fans and reticules and spangled shawls. While others her age were polishing their watercoloring skills, she had been climbing the ratlines, which made for quite a gap in her education.

Still, Cat made the transition from cabin boy to lady with surprising ease; her young boy's swagger became long, graceful strides and her body blossomed in the heady island heat. She abandoned her nickname along with her breeches and made an effort to eliminate telltale mannerisms from her speech. She looked to Amelia for guidance in the finer points of etiquette, and soon only rarely committed a faux pas, easily overlooked by others too smitten by her features to notice.

For Cat was beautiful. She had been an attractive young girl, but that promise of loveliness had now been fulfilled, and no one seeing the lithe, blonde young lady would ever recognize her as the scrawny youth of the *Reckless*.

Her sun-lightened hair, which curved in soft

waves about her face, was perfectly in vogue, for both the fashion and the climate called for short tresses. Still, she stood out in sharp contrast to those women of European descent born on the island, with their pale skin and languid movements, for Cat's face was always rosy or browned by the sun, much to Amelia's distress, and she moved with an unconscious confidence.

The restlessness Cat felt in her youth had calmed, perhaps because of her stint at sea or because of the warmth of her aunt's love, but she still glowed with the vitality of her spirit, and her striking features and intriguing manner combined to make her a unique beauty.

Pleased with her niece's transformation, Amelia was even more delighted by Cat's eagerness to help, for although she had sold the plantation and great house to Lord William Claremont, baron of Whately, Amelia retained the guest house where she now lived, along with several acres on which she indulged her interest in botany.

There was always something to be done in the orchards, fields, and gardens where Amelia attempted to grow "everything under the sun," as Lord Claremont put it, and the lady was not content simply to direct her servants. She enjoyed working with the soil herself and would have been sorely disappointed with a missish niece who feared to dirty her hands.

Cat certainly had no qualms about getting soiled, and soon she was helping her aunt each day, happy to be busy with something less frivolous than making afternoon calls.

"Of course, it's unheard of for a lady to do anything interesting, but they view me as a harmless eccentric," Amelia explained to Cat one day as they pruned roses. "Let the old fool putter around with the plants if she wants," she said, laughing gaily.

"Surely, Lord Claremont doesn't feel that way," Cat said above the *clip-clip* of the shears. "He seems quite interested in your work."

"Pooh! You'll find, my dear, that very few men appreciate a woman who thinks for herself. They like to call her a bluestocking and treat her as something less than human. Thank God my Horace was not one of those kind! He was very open-minded. Such an intelligent man. Ahead of his time, I used to say."

Cat wondered idly if Ransom would appreciate her intelligence. Probably not, since he had so little regard for women! The thought irked her vaguely. How could he lump all women together? Why, look at Amelia . . . How could anyone not care for this gentle lady? She shook her head in disbelief. "You were very lucky to find him," she said to her aunt.

"Oh, yes, indeed," Amelia said, stopping her work for a moment. "A wonderful man! Fortunately, he had inherited a tidy sum from his grandmama, or Father would never have consented to a love match for me. Of course, he had practically given me up for a spinster by that time, so he might have let me have my way, but I doubt it. He was not in favor of your mother's love match, and when your father's death left her penniless, he felt justified."

Amelia stopped her trimming to stare off into space and sighed. "Oh, my, but they were happy— Belinda and your father—if only for a little while!" Returning briskly to her task, she continued, "Of course, Father wasn't about to let her do the same again, and married her off in a thrice to Lord Pembroke, who had no idea what to do with her!"

Cat smiled softly. "I think I baffled him, too."

"Oh, most certainly. Make no mistake, Catherine; Pembroke was a good man. He just wasn't right for Belinda. I'm a firm believer in love matches," she said, standing back to view the results of her work with approval. Turning to Cat, she said, "Now, we must find someone for you! He must be an islander, so you may stay close to me! Who catches your fancy?"

Cat ran her mind's eye over the eligible men she had met, and try as she might she could not picture one as a future spouse. They all seemed to fall far short of her imaginings, and the vision of a tall, dark figure laughing into the wind kept intruding, pushing aside all others. She looked over to find Amelia eyeing her closely and laughed uncertainly. "I'm happy with you; don't cast me out yet!"

"Oh, I won't, my dear!" Amelia assured her. "But I can't help looking," she said with a wink. "Mark my words, I'll find you a husband."

After a sharp knock, Bosun entered the captain's cabin. "Brought your dinner, sir," he said.

Ransom didn't look up. "Put it on the table," he instructed as he continued making notations in his log.

Bosun set down the tray, but remained where he was, hands clasped behind his back. "Captain?"

"Hmmm?"

"We've sailed together a fair number of years now," the first mate began. He had succeeded in gaining Ransom's attention, for the captain finally stopped writing, his eyebrow lifting in question as he turned in his chair to look at his first mate. "I've sailed with you because you're a good man and know how to run a right ship." Again Bosun hesitated.

"This sounds like the prelude to a real dressing-down," Ransom said dryly.

"Aye, that it is," Bosun answered. "You've been hard on the men for weeks now—ever since Cat left." The first mate paused again before continuing. "Captain, we miss the boy, too."

"Ha! That pesky whelp." Ransom snorted in derision.

"You miss the lad, and what's wrong with saying so? There's piddling few aboard that don't, and I don't mind telling you some of these fellows never cared for anyone in their misbegotten lives." Ransom's eyebrow rose again. The look he shot Bosun would have sent anyone else from the room, yet the first mate plodded on. "But they're not mad at the boy for following his own path. Each man has his own destiny, as well you should know."

A full minute passed before Ransom responded. "You're getting pompous in your old age, Bosun," he said. "I never thought the day would come when I'd hear you preaching about one's destiny."

Bosun appeared uncomfortable but withstood the captain's withering glance, looking him straight in the eye when he spoke again. "He's not dead," the first mate said softly, and Ransom's head jerked involuntarily in response, as though Bosun had struck him. Again, neither man spoke for a moment as Bosun wondered if he had gone too far and Ransom struggled with his own private demons.

"You're right," Ransom finally said, forcing his voice to be light. "But he might as well be, for he's gone just the same, which goes to show the folly of such alliances. Fortunately, I would be relieved at *your* demise, for I would have no more interference from an impudent fool!" he said, his grin mocking his words.

"You're right, of course," Ransom repeated abruptly, the smile leaving his face as quickly as it had appeared. "Possessive, aren't I? But what can you expect from such a misbegotten—I believe it was—sort such as I? All right, we'll be making port soon to sell the cargo. We'll stay a few extra days to let the poor devils have some sport." Ransom turned back to the desk and picked up his pen, indicating the conversation was closed. Bosun released the breath he had been holding.

Her eyes sparkling with mischief, Cat raised her glass to Amelia's and popped up with a toast from her days as a cabin boy.

"One for me, and one for the crow, and one for them that lie below!" she said, sending her aunt into gales of giggles. They were sitting in the parlor toasting Cat's seventeenth birthday with a syllabub Cat had prepared for the occasion. The rum, much stronger than the light spirits the two were accustomed to drinking, was making its presence known to both ladies, and Amelia was just a little bit giddy.

"Wherever did you learn such a thing?" she asked, knowing full well that most of her niece's odd behavior and the bits of whimsy she sometimes spouted could be traced to her time aboard ship.

"From one of my shipmates," Cat said, a secret smile playing on her lips, as it usually did when she spoke of the *Reckless*. Although she rarely discussed her sailing days with her aunt, Cat often thought of them as a treasured interlude, a childhood adventure that was seemingly unreal in comparison with her life on Barbados.

Amelia recognized her niece's wistful expression and sought to draw her out. "From what I hear, the London ladies are all dressing up as their pages," she said. "So it appears you were quite in fashion, my dear!" She pushed back a wisp of white hair and smiled fondly at her niece.

Catherine was seated on her favorite chair, back straight, her gown of creamy ivory satin falling into delicate folds and her hair curling softly about her face. It was hard to imagine anyone taking her for a cabin boy. "How on earth did you get away with it?" Amelia asked.

With an easy grace, Cat set down her glass and

smiled at her aunt. Her hands folded neatly in her lap, she leaned over and whispered solemnly, as though imparting the wisdom of the ages. ''It was simple!'' she said, and the two dissolved into giggles. ''Since I slept with the captain, there was no—'' Amelia, in the midst of swallowing when Cat spoke, broke into a fit of coughing. Cat jumped from her seat and rushed to her aunt's aid, but that lady brushed her assistance aside as she regained her composure.

''What?'' Amelia finally managed weakly.

''I slept in the captain's cabin, so there wasn't much chance of discovery,'' Cat finished. She concentrated on settling herself comfortably on the floor at Amelia's feet, thereby missing the relief that flooded the older woman's face at her words.

''Catherine, my dearest child,'' Amelia said, patting her shoulder, ''as much as I admire your resourcefulness, you must promise me you will never tell anyone else of this!''

''I don't have to promise you that,'' Cat said with a smile. ''I doubt that anyone else would understand, dear aunt.'' Cat knew that her past somehow isolated her from others, but despite her apparent changes, she remained proud of her seagoing days, and the opportunity to share her adventures, if only with Amelia, was inviting.

Her mood mellowed by the syllabub, she wove delightful tales for her aunt, her expressive voice taking Amelia through storms and leading her along sunlit beaches. She passed over the battles lightly, judging that her aunt might not appreciate those stories, and focused instead on the excitement of lighting a cannon, the thrill of diving off the side, and the friendships she had developed with the many characters aboard the *Reckless*.

When Cat paused, Amelia refilled their glasses and looked down at her niece's golden head. ''Well, now, this captain of yours certainly sounds interesting. Tell me more about him.''

''Ransom Du Prey? Oh, he is simply the handsomest man alive.'' Cat giggled, her tongue now thoroughly loosened.

Amelia chuckled. ''Is that all?'' she asked, drawing a laugh from Cat.

''Well, he is tall, above six feet, with dark brown hair,'' Cat said, unconsciously moving her hand to her own golden locks. ''And the deepest brown eyes.'' She stared off into the window of memory, and for a moment the room seemed utterly still. ''And a smile like . . . no other.'' She shook her head and grinned at her aunt. ''I guess he sounds like any other man, but he isn't. He could be kind and gentle and yet strong and . . . so exciting,'' she finished lamely.

''He sounds most intriguing,'' Amelia said. ''Quite popular with the ladies, I assume.''

''Oh, yes! The first mate said he could charm the petticoats off any woman he took a notion to,'' Cat said. ''But he doesn't think too much of women, so he rarely makes the effort. He says they are silly, boring creatures,'' Cat added, frowning into her glass.

''I see. Well, something tells me the young captain will have cause someday to change his opinion.'' Smiling slyly at Cat, she took another sip from her glass. ''I assume you learned to prepare this delightful concoction while on your ship.''

''Oh no,'' answered Cat. ''Actually, I got this recipe in a brothel,'' she said matter-of-factly, then leaped to her feet to slap her aunt on the back, as the poor woman was stricken with another fit of coughing.

Chapter 11

Cat stood cooling herself with a fan of mother-of-pearl and kid, a birthday gift from her aunt, as she scanned the small crowd in the largest receiving room of the Grayson plantation house. The heat seemed to rise in waves from the polished fruitwood floors, and she was grateful that the current fashion called for thin gowns, although even the tiny puffed sleeves on her white spotted lawn dress seemed heavy tonight. She had long since abandoned her matching lace-edged shawl on one of the chairs lining the walls of the room.

Cat always looked forward to the parties held on the island. Most of the planters lived like country squires—drinking hard, keeping a good table, and nursing their gout. Social gatherings were rare, and in the six months that she had lived on Barbados, she had attended only two such entertainments. Life in the islands was a far cry from London's endless balls, parties, and routs lasting till dawn, but to Cat, who had never been to London or attended a party until coming to Barbados, the festivities were entrancing. How she loved the lemonade sparkling in crystal decanters, the elegant suppers laid out in the dining hall, and the dancing! She had received some quick lessons before her first party and had easily

mastered the steps, a simple task for someone who
had run the rigging with grace and agility.

Tonight, however, even the dancing could not ex-
cite her. The glow of the candlelight and the scent
of the gardenias grouped in profusion on the satin-
wood tables had lost their power to enchant, for her
mood had been spoiled by a mincing fop from London who had been hanging on her skirts the entire
evening. In exasperation, she had finally sent him
for some punch.

At the thought of Mr. Pettibone, she snapped her
fan more vigorously. Because these entertainments
were few, she liked to savor every moment, but how
could she with that simpering fellow dogging her
footsteps? Unfortunately, the heat had kept many
guests away, making it difficult to find an escape
from her admirer.

Her eyes swept the room again for an ally, flicking
over the entrance for the hundredth time, but on
this pass her gaze was drawn irresistibly back to the
curving staircase leading up to the huge, carved mahogany doors flanked by footmen in colorful livery,
and her breath caught in her throat. At the top of
the stairway, one foot negligently resting on the first
step, stood her captain.

He seemed untouched by the heat, elegant in his
black evening clothes. His mahogany hair was
brushed back from his face in a fashionable tousle,
and his cool gaze assessed the crowd with a self-
assurance that set him apart from the other guests.
Had only six months passed since she had seen him?
He must have grown more attractive in that small
span of time, for surely he had never looked more
handsome than he did tonight, the white of his cravat and waistcoat contrasting starkly with the black
tailcoat and pantaloons.

Captain! My captain! rushed alarmingly through
her head, while a flock of gulls seemed to have

lodged in her chest, rapidly beating their wings against her ribs and tickling her throat with their feathers. She tried to swallow, succeeded, realized she was staring and quickly dropped her gaze. Willing her breathing back to normal, she forced her body to move—*slowly now!*—and turned, walking toward the doors that led to the gardens.

Once outside, Cat took several deep breaths and was relieved to notice a slight breeze. Did her distress show? The hands that flew to her cheeks felt warmth. Was it simply the heat, or was she blushing? She'd lost that quaint feminine trait long ago aboard the *Reckless*, hadn't she? The *Reckless!* At the thought of the ship, Cat was suddenly struck with a stab of panic that Ransom would recognize her and she would be ruined.

With a grimace, Cat put a firm clamp on her whirling emotions and glanced about to make sure she was alone. Assured that no one would see her, she walked to the enormous Grecian fountain that graced the gardens, dipped her hands in the cool waters, and pressed them to her heated face. The splash of coolness seemed to soothe her, and, she hoped, would eliminate any lingering telltale flush.

With a sigh, she dabbed at the droplets with her handkerchief, deciding to find Amelia and leave the party immediately. Ransom spelled danger for any female, she thought grimly, but especially this one, and she had no desire for a chance encounter with her captain.

Turning away from the fountain to return to the house, she nearly collided with Phineas Pettibone, whom she'd forgotten about when Ransom arrived. "Oh, you startled me!" she accused the portly man.

"I was but admiring your beauty, Miss Amberly," he simpered. "How I long to escort you on a stroll through the gardens." Compared to Ransom's understated elegance, Cat found Pettibone's attire even more ridiculous than before. His coat, breeches, and waistcoat encompassed every color in the rainbow and dangled with several fobs and watch chains.

"That would be quite improper, sir," Cat answered irritably, pushing past him toward the doors.

"Oh, how droll you islanders are! Come, walk with me," Pettibone said, holding out his hand. "These surroundings suit you, you know. You have the look of a Greek goddess." Although Cat ignored his outstretched hand, the man was undeterred. "Don't deny me, my lovely, for I fear I cannot control myself any longer. I am overcome by your beauty," he gushed and made a move as if to embrace her. Without a pause, Cat stepped forward and indelicately trod on his foot, causing him to stumble backward, an oath on his lips.

"Oh, I beg your pardon! How clumsy of me," Cat said, her voice filled with disdain, and walked impassively back into the house.

From his vantage point in the shadows, Ransom stood chuckling to himself. "Well done, my dear," he said softly.

He had come to the Grayson plantation in search of a merchant interested in the *Reckless*'s cargo, a dull enough business, and yet the evening was turning out to be far from boring. First he had nearly caught one of Devlin's men shadowing him when he left the ship. He had recognized the redheaded fellow immediately as one of those present during his last confrontation with Devlin, but when he turned to give chase, the man had disappeared into the dark streets of Bridgetown.

But that was not to be the only unusual episode of the evening, Ransom discovered, for even while searching the crowd for his associate, his mind back on business, he had noticed the extraordinarily beautiful blonde staring at him with the oddest expression.

In his twenty-eight years, Ransom had received more than his share of admiring glances from the female population, but there was something different in this one's gaze. He could not quite pinpoint it, but he felt almost certain he knew her. Her subsequent flight to the gardens had piqued his curiosity, and he had followed, catching a fairly good look at her while she washed her face in the fountain. Now *that* was unusual! Although he could not recall ever laying eyes on her before, there was something about her that seemed familiar.

Mr. Pettibone again forgotten, Cat made her way through the arched galleries to the ballroom, where she spied her aunt deep in conversation with an elderly matron on the other side of the room. She was but a few steps away when Lord Claremont halted her with an invitation to dance. Cat was trying politely to fob him off when she heard a deep voice from behind her. "I'm sorry, but Miss Amberly promised this dance to me."

Her heart in her throat, Cat spun around, coming face to face with a casually tied cravat that she had probably pressed at one time or another. Before she knew it, she felt his arm around her waist and his hand over hers, and she was whirled among the dancers in one elegant movement.

Cat felt lighter than a feather as Ransom led her through the waltz. Ah, but he was a far cry from the provincials she had danced with before! He could give her dancing instructor lessons, she thought, and she wondered distractedly how his hand could feel so cool and smooth while hers was uncomfortably hot and—horrors!—damp in his grip.

As they glided smoothly across the floor, Cat let herself relax, surrendering to the pure joy of the dance and being in his arms. How she had once longed for this very moment! Smiling—idiotically, she was sure—up at him, she let her eyes caress the familiar face.

He is more handsome than ever, she thought as she let her gaze wander from his dark locks over those mobile brows to the warm brown eyes. There she stopped short, for the eyes were no longer warm, but cool and distant, and disappointment pricked her as she realized this was the face he presented to the world. You fool! He doesn't recognize you, and if he did, do you think you would receive a warm welcome? The smile left her face to be replaced by a thoughtful purse of her lips when he spoke.

"We've met before?" It was half question, half statement.

"Oh?" Cat asked lightly. "And what did you say your name was?" She saw the corners of his mouth lift in the ghost of a smile.

"Touché, my lovely. I am Ransom Du Prey, duke of Morcester," he said, inclining his head gently and raising that infernal eyebrow.

Cat's eyes flew to his in astonishment. My God! The man has the gall to masquerade as a nobleman, Cat thought wildly. No paltry peer either, but a duke, the highest rank!

"You look surprised."

"Why, your *grace*"—the title dripped with sarcasm—"from the way you swept me away from my intended partner, I never would have thought you a gentleman."

He chuckled softly. "Your intended looked as though such an effort would severely aggravate his gout."

Against her will, the corners of her mouth started to twitch.

"And, if you find my invitation to dance rather impulsive, I can only plead that I was overcome by your beauty."

"You *are* no gentleman!" Cat gasped, realizing that Ransom had overheard her encounter with Pettibone in the gardens.

"Hmmm. You're repeating yourself, my love, and I was just beginning to think you were endowed with . . . more than average wit," he said while his gaze traveled slowly over her in a way it never had when she was his cabin boy.

Why, he was looking at her as though she were one of his idiot female admirers who threw themselves at his head! Cat's shock was quickly followed by outrage. "Do you make a habit of eavesdropping in bushes, or was this a special occasion?" she threw at him.

"Oh, I engage in such practices about as frequently as young ladies wash their faces in lawn ornaments."

Seething, Cat glared up at him to no effect. He returned her black look with a lazy grin that threatened to pull an answering smile from her lips. Silently, she reminded herself not to succumb to his allure, for as Bosun had been wont to declare, Ransom could "charm the very pants off a body" when so inclined.

Although she was no longer wearing pants, Cat felt the phrase was even more applicable to her female persona. The look on his face—definitely not brotherly affection—did nothing to reassure her. On the contrary, it set her whole body astir with a strange trembling, which she quelled sharply, irked at his effect on her. "For heaven's sake, stop looking at me as if I'm a stuffed mackerel you're preparing to devour!" she snapped.

Ransom threw back his head in a deep-throated laugh. Cat had forgotten how delightful he could sound. She could not help the warm rush of affection that his laughter engendered, and suddenly she felt at home, as though she had returned after a lengthy and unwilling absence.

Watch yourself, a voice warned her, but she ignored it to enjoy the tingling sensation that emanated from her heart and coursed through her entire body. She felt a surge of disappointment when the dance ended, and although she thanked him curtly, her eyes sparkled, destroying her attempt to give him a good set-down.

Ransom watched her leave with a smile lingering on his lips. Yes, Miss Amberly was definitely unusual; quite refreshing, in fact. He was calculating whether he could take the time from his busy enterprises to pursue a relationship with the beautiful blonde, while his instincts advised him that something was not right with the lovely lady. She denied meeting him before, yet she appeared to know him or know of him, and there was something so familiar about her . . .

Tim Calhoun sat in the half darkness just outside the circle of lamplight that marked the Grayson house, chewing on a straw and cursing the luck that had him watching Du Prey.

Tim had been doing well enough until somebody had learned that His Nibs, as Tim called Du Prey, would be going to Barbados. Lord, the time and money the boss spent watching *his* every movement could have been well spent on something more profitable, if you asked Tim, but nobody was asking him, nor were they likely to, so he kicked his heels, watching the bay and waiting for Du Prey.

It wouldn't have been so bad if he could have tucked away some spare coin on the side by picking a few pockets along the bustling waterfront, but Tim had strict orders to keep out of trouble and out of sight, and he had no wish to earn the wrath of his employer. Devlin was not a man to cross, he thought

with a shiver as he watched the coaches drawing up
to the plantation house. Still, this latest job was not
to his taste, by any means. Trotting around to fancy
parties; bloody hell! If his dear mum could see him
now!

Tim's thoughts broke off as he watched a lovely
blonde step through the doorway. Now there was
one worth watching, he thought as she walked
gracefully down the stairs. Why, that golden hair
shone in the lamplight just like an angel's, but the
way her dress fell around that body . . . The rest of
Tim's thoughts had nothing to do with heaven. Im-
pulsively he stepped from the shadows to hand her
into the coach, eager for the lady's touch and hoping
for a smile to brighten his evening.

It was granted. Although Cat had other things on
her mind, she did not ignore the courtesy of servants—having been one aboard the *Reckless*. When
the small man stepped forward to hand her up into
the coach, she smiled distractedly and nodded.
"Thank you," she murmured, and that was all the
invitation Tim needed to loosen his own tongue.

"You are quite welcome, my lady. And let me
wish you a fine evening!" Tim said, grinning from
ear to ear. For his trouble he received another smile,
this one more genuine, that left him gaping after the
lovely lady.

Once he handed Miss Amberly and her older companion into the coach, Tim slipped back into the
shadows, warned by the sixth sense professional
thieves cultivate that eyes were upon him. He
groaned to see Du Prey standing at the entrance
looking down at him. Now there would be hell to
pay! Not only had Tim been seen, but it looked as
if Du Prey was coming after him! Sure enough, His
Nibs was stepping down those stairs, and that was
all Tim waited to see, taking flight into the darkness
as if the very hounds of hell were on his tail.

Ransom had seen the wiry fellow dart forward, recognizing the bright red hair from earlier in the evening, and had watched the man's exchange with Miss Amberly with interest. Although he intended to seek a word with the fellow, Ransom halted when the redhead disappeared into the darkness. No sense racing off after someone long gone and, no doubt, familiar with the countryside. He turned back to the house as he mulled over the scene he had just witnessed.

Hmmm. Perhaps the lovely Miss Amberly was connected to the red-haired ruffian only by coincidence, Ransom mused, or was she, too, one of Devlin's cohorts? It would not be the first time his nemesis had sent a woman to spy on him, but this one was certainly not the same sort as the "widow" who carried the clap. No, this one was definitely different.

Resolutely ignoring a twinge of disappointment at his suspicions, Ransom decided that Miss Amberly was worth pursuing. After all, he had been searching unsuccessfully for Devlin, since the man's increasingly criminal activities had forced him underground, making him difficult to find. These two, one of them obviously in Devlin's employ, might provide a clue as to his whereabouts.

Although the red-haired coachman had made his escape this time, Ransom thought as he gazed into the night, the lady herself might give him the information he sought—and she would undoubtedly be more interesting company.

Chapter 12

Cat tried to concentrate on cutting gladioli, but her hands kept falling idle as she replayed the scene with Ransom in her mind and gave herself decidedly better lines. The bonnet Amelia had insisted she wear fell unheeded down her back, and tendrils of hair escaped from their proper place to curl about her face as Cat snipped away. The air was hot and still, the silence broken only by the occasional raucous sounds of the frigate birds and a few stray gulls.

Amelia was bustling about the roses, her gloves lying forgotten on the stone walk. "Catherine, please put on your bonnet! Your face is already brown as a berry," she said.

"Oh, aunt, don't scold." Cat laughed. "The sun feels so nice." She raised her face to catch its warmth as she spoke. "I love the out-of-doors. Why dress to suit some silly fashion in your own garden?" Before her aunt could answer, she added, "Besides, you've left off your gloves again."

"Why, so I have and you, too, my dear. What a pair we are! I've lived too far from society for too long to chaperon you properly." Amelia shook her head at her own shortcomings as she retrieved the gloves.

"I think we are delightfully suited. And I don't give a fig for society!" Cat said with feeling.

"Oh, dear, you can say that, but you don't know how *they* are, the *ton*. They can snub you so dreadfully, if you have just a hair out of place."

Cat unconsciously patted her own curls, but bit back a retort when she saw Marie approaching. The maid spoke softly to Amelia, who was bending next to a particularly untidy rosebush. At a word from Marie, she dusted off her hands and rose to her feet. "Finish cutting your gladioli, dear. I think they'll make a lovely arrangement for the hallway," she told Cat while distractedly rearranging her white hair as she walked to the house.

Cat sat back on her heels and looked unseeing at the cloudless sky, her thoughts straying to Ransom once more. She had never thought to see him again, and suddenly she had been dancing with the man! She resolutely stifled the tendency of her heart to soar at the memory. She would *not* see him again. There were few enough balls on the island; she would simply avoid them until the *Reckless* left the harbor.

She was well rid of him! She simply could not risk recognition. The captain had the devil's own temper when roused, and she could not imagine him being pleased to find she had shared his cabin and confidences under false pretenses. She had fooled him, and that would not sit well with Ransom, not well at all.

And why on earth was he posing as a duke? The audacity! She did not remember him being so arrogant. Why, he'd treated her as though she were one of his tarts! And the way he'd looked at her . . . She shivered despite the heat as just the thought of that look set her skin to tingling in the strangest fashion. She shook her head in annoyance and gave an especially vigorous clip to the stem between her fingers.

The object of her thoughts was but a stone's throw away examining a lovely piece of porcelain in Amelia's hall. Officially, he had been shown into the morning room, but he had wandered back out into the hall to escape the stifling heat there. He returned the vase to the side table and paused to study a portrait hanging over the table.

A middling work, the painting depicted two golden-haired beauties, obviously related, although one appeared dainty and frail, while her taller counterpart held herself with more confidence. Leaning closer, Ransom noted more than a passing resemblance between that beauty and the intriguing Catherine Amberly. He turned from the painting to see the other of its subjects, come to life as a wispy woman with hair now white as snow, walk toward him.

"Oh, dear, I hope you weren't expecting the girl in the portrait, your grace," she said, waving a tiny hand at the painting. "Goodness, but that was done long ago!" She smiled tremulously at the picture and for a moment appeared to be lost in her own thoughts, then she looked up at him as if seeing him for the first time and smiled.

"Good day, Mrs. Molesworth!" Ransom said, bowing graciously over her hand. "I hope I have not called at an inconvenient time. I met your niece last night at the Graysons' ball," he explained.

"You have my leave to call whenever you wish, your grace," Amelia answered amiably. "But why are you wandering about? Didn't Isaac show you into the drawing room? Oh, dear, the servants just can't be depended upon." Before she could continue Ransom held up his hand and smiled at her.

"Actually, Mrs. Molesworth, your man is not at fault. He very politely conducted me to the morning room; my own appalling manners are to blame for my wanderings." He bowed slightly. "Please forgive me."

Amelia chuckled, delighted at the handsome charmer towering over her. "A bit close, was it? I don't doubt it. The room is always shut up. It receives all the morning sun and is insufferably hot," she explained. "Aptly named, I suppose, but most uncomfortable. We'll go to the parlor, where it's cool."

Ransom's eye was caught by a movement behind her, and he looked over his shoulder to see Catherine approaching. He turned slowly to face her, and suddenly the very air seemed charged with the magnetism between them, causing Amelia to step back out of the way.

"Ah, here is Catherine. I'll leave you in her capable hands," she said, her eyes twinkling, "while I see to some lemonade for us." Her words were lost on Ransom, who had eyes only for the beautiful blonde woman now standing stock-still in the hallway.

The sun from the rear of the house lit her golden hair, lending an ethereal cast to her beauty. His eyes took in the charming disarray of her tresses and traveled down the slim column of her golden neck to where the heat had dampened her bodice, leaving a triangle of material clinging provocatively to her breasts. The puffed sleeves of her white gauze gown were pushed up past her elbows, and in her arms she carried a huge basket of cut gladioli and sprays of greenery. She could have stepped out of a painting except for . . .

"You've neglected to wash your face this time, Miss Amberly," he said, surprising himself by the softness of his voice. He stepped toward her until he stood so near that he could feel her breath, then lightly wiped a smudge of dirt from her nose with his thumb.

Cat could only stare at him, dumbfounded. The sunlight was shining on his handsome face, lighting the familiar brown eyes and the curve of his lips in a way that the candlelight had not, and she realized that he was still far and above the handsomest man she had ever seen.

He was so close she nearly reached up a hand to touch the visage that had so often haunted her dreams, but caught herself. His own light touch so unnerved her that she turned to the side table and, to hide her confusion, plucked a flower from her basket to place in the empty vase.

"Here, let me help you." His voice was like silk as he took the basket from her. Her hands now free, Cat began plucking the gladioli and greenery from the basket that he solicitously presented to her and arranged them in the vase. She felt like a drowning man being lulled by the hum of the deep as the warmth of his charm pulled her under.

With an effort, she struggled to the surface and to cold, clear reason, which told her he had caught her unawares and woefully unprepared. Amelia had somehow disappeared, drat her hide, leaving Cat to entertain her former captain, whose overly friendly manner bespoke his intentions. When Cat found her voice, she asked, "What are you doing here?" with more than a touch of irritation.

"I'm sorry to disappoint you; you were expecting Mr. Waistcoat perhaps?" He leaned too close to her ear.

"Certainly not! And his name was Pettibone," Cat answered without looking at him.

"No! How appropriate!" he said lightly, causing Cat to smile unwillingly. "Then you were expecting another suitor perhaps?" he queried.

Another suitor? What was he getting at? "I have

no suitors," she said with a trace of scorn. At his silence, she turned to find his eyebrow raised in disbelief. He was certainly acting strangely, she thought, putting the finishing touches to the flowers and stepping back to appraise her efforts.

"Very lovely," he said of the arrangement. "But, then, so is the artist. So much so that I find it difficult to believe she is lacking in admirers." She caught a curious undertone in his voice, as though he were accusing her of something, and she looked at him sharply, but his face revealed nothing of his thoughts.

"Believe what you will. I've been meaning to find a husband, but the task seems so tedious." She shot him a withering glance. "Men being a lot of boring rogues."

Ransom grinned broadly. "I see. Well, if Pettibone is any indication of the company you've been keeping, your opinion is understandable."

What a conceited oaf! As if you are better than any other man, Cat fumed inwardly, forgetting that she had often held that very belief herself.

"Perhaps I can endeavor to redeem the reputation of my gender," Ransom began.

"I doubt that, your grace, as I see no difference between you and any other fellow. Now, if you will excuse me, I need to freshen up, as you pointed out so graphically. Please don't feel you must stay on my account." With that parting shot, she climbed the stairs without another glance.

Ransom was left standing in the hallway holding an empty basket and his smoldering temper. He disliked the bowing and scraping his title engendered when he used it, yet he was not accustomed to having it totally disregarded, either. What a rude little chit! He felt like storming up the stairs after her and giving her a good thrashing, but then, maybe that was what he was supposed to feel. His anger dissolved as he thought again of Devlin. Was her performance being staged by his old nemesis?

"Have you been abandoned, your grace?" He heard the older lady's voice behind him. "Come, join me in some lemonade," she said, gesturing toward an open doorway, where the manservant stood holding a tray. "Or, perhaps something a little stronger for yourself?" Ransom, who found himself in the unusual and uncomfortable position of being at a loss, assented and was soon seated on a small divan in the cozy parlor.

"I am so glad to meet you," Amelia said with a smile as Isaac presented him with a sherry. Ransom waited for the lady to continue, but no further conversation appeared forthcoming. She simply sat looking at him, smiling and shaking her head as if she were daft. He was about to comment on the weather when she finally spoke again.

"Oh, you'll do. You'll do," she said, looking quite pleased with herself.

"I beg your pardon?"

"Oh, it's nothing, just an old lady's rambling. I am so pleased that you are calling on Catherine. May I speak frankly?" At Ransom's nod she continued. "I must admit that I have not provided all I should in the way of social opportunities, and Catherine needs a husband." She paused briefly, turning her mild blue eyes to Ransom. "You see, Catherine is not what she appears."

I believe that, thought Ransom. This is getting better by the minute.

The little woman leaned over conspiratorially. "If I may confide in you, your grace," she said, lowering her voice. "Catherine has taken refuge here from a wicked guardian, who would do her ill," she announced with all the gravity of the romantic novels which Ransom could only assume she had read too frequently.

"She simply must marry before he discovers she is here," Amelia said, nodding sagely while Ransom's eyebrow shot up. "Oh, yes. I probably should not be telling even you, your grace, but I trust you will not reveal her whereabouts." She sat back upright in her chair and sighed as if a great weight had been lifted from her.

"Yes, the child needs a husband. Someone who has no fear of reprisals from the new baron of Wellshire. Someone bold and reckless, such as yourself, if I may say so." She smiled sweetly at Ransom, then blithely sipped her lemonade as though she had said nothing out of the ordinary.

"Now, the child has good blood. Her father—her real father, mind you—was one of the Hampshire Amberlys, part of the old earl's brood, and, of course, my father—her grandfather—was a baronet, although I suppose that means little enough to you." She paused, frowning, as if struck by a sudden misgiving. "I imagine that Catherine would prove to be a handful, though. She is a headstrong girl."

Lord, thought Ransom, was the old lady in on it too? "I fear I must disappoint you, Mrs. Molesworth, but I have no plans to wed as yet," he said, his face revealing nothing of his thoughts.

"Oh, dear, I've said too much! Oh, do excuse me, your grace," the little lady said, fluttering her hands. "Do forgive a silly old woman and say you'll sup with us."

Ransom agreed on Wednesday evening for supper and rose from his seat. "By the way, I wondered if I might have a chat with that red-haired coachman of yours," he said casually while eyeing Amelia carefully. "He appears to be quite a hand with the horses."

It was the little lady's turn to look puzzled. "Coachman? Why, I have no red-haired coachman," she said innocently. "Isaac handles all our needs. You may certainly speak with him, though you won't win him away from me, I hope!" She smiled as she stood and, patting Ransom familiarly, she lowered her voice to a whisper. "As to our other conversation, I'm sure I can depend on you to keep it confidential. Catherine would be so distressed if she discovered I was talking out of turn."

Only a lifetime of schooling his features kept Ransom's astonishment from showing on his face, and he left the Molesworth cottage feeling more than a little baffled, another alien emotion for which he had little use. The little old lady appeared too giddy to be involved in any scheming, yet there was definitely more to her than met the eye.

Someone bold and reckless, she had said. Was this a subtle reference to his ship, or was he simply chasing shadows? Either the lady was daft, utterly daft, or a superb actress . . . but in what play?

Chapter 13

Cat was mortified when she learned of the supper invitation. "Do you realize who that was?" she asked, her voice rising in direct proportion to her horror.

"Why, yes," Amelia answered mildly. "The duke of Morcester. I remember his family well." She looked past her niece as though fondly recalling some episode long ago.

"That was my captain!" Cat squeaked. "The captain of the ship where I served as a cabin boy!"

"Well, my goodness! There's no need to get so excited," Amelia said. "Since you already know him, we will most certainly have a pleasant evening together."

Cat could only stare aghast at her aunt.

"But, my dear, what could be objectionable?" Amelia asked. "He's not as young as you are, but not in his dotage, either, and a young girl needs an older, experienced man." She was pouring tea, but stopped to tick off on her fingers Ransom's finer points. "He's handsome. He has manners . . . so very important in a husband! You don't want him picking his teeth at table as Squire Peterson was wont to do."

"A husband?" Cat squeaked. "Are you mad? He was my captain! What if he recognizes me?"

"Pooh! No one could imagine you as a boy, my dear."

"Ransom is no fool. He thinks we've met before," Cat argued.

"The man will hardly leap to the conclusion that you were his cabin boy," Amelia said. "I like him. He's personable, and he comes from good stock. The Du Preys were always head and shoulders above the rest of the Midlands crowd."

Good God! Cat looked up, startled, as Amelia's words sank in. Ransom was impersonating a *real* duke! Lord help us, she thought. Calmly she took the forgotten teapot from the table and began to pour. "How do we know he is who he claims to be?"

"You're the one who recognized him."

"All I know is that he was the captain of the *Reckless* and ran some shipping concerns on Windlay," Cat said without looking up. "I never heard he had a title until last night."

"What? Do you think he's not the duke?" Amelia asked, taken aback. "It wouldn't be the first time we've been fooled by a masquerader on this island, you know. Living so far from England, it's difficult to verify these things, but I'll have Lord Claremont look into it at once."

"No, no," Cat said. She realized that no matter what Ransom was up to, she did not wish him ill. "I just wondered." She shrugged casually. "Don't bother Lord Claremont about it. Really." She turned her attention to a tray of tarts and so missed the satisfied smile that Amelia sent into her teacup.

The night of the supper seemed to arrive with untoward speed, and the minutes raced by while Cat fidgeted in front of the mirror, even though she had dressed carefully in one of her favorite gowns. Made of the palest green lawn, it had deep green leaves embroidered about the hem and neckline. She threw a transparent shawl with gold fringe about her shoulders and, although she disdained jewelry, at the last moment she donned the diamond earrings Amelia had said she could borrow. With one last look in the mirror, she admonished herself to keep her wits about her at all times.

Cat had alternately dreaded and looked forward to Ransom's visit. If only he would act like his old self, she thought wistfully. His behavior when he called at the cottage had been, well, a trifle odd. What if he acts strangely during supper in front of Amelia? She would run to Lord Claremont with the tale. Cat did not care to have Ransom's role as imposter unmasked, no matter how he might irritate her. Let him simply go about his business, whatever that may be, she thought, and then be gone.

She need not have worried. From the moment he stepped into the house, looking dashing in forest green, Ransom put the entire household at ease. He had Amelia so charmed she would probably let his horse tread over her, Cat thought with a trace of disgust as she heard him questioning her aunt about the gardens.

She narrowed her eyes suspiciously as he spoke knowledgeably on the region's produce and discussed the finer points of crop cultivation. Although she knew he owned a plantation, she'd never dreamed he was so involved in the management. When he began describing his sugar-producing property on Windlay, Cat remembered just how he had come by the land and could not refrain from planting a barb or two in his side.

"I suppose this property has been in your grace's family for years," Cat said dryly while serving up some ragoût beef.

"No. Actually I purchased the land myself a few years ago. I had some *difficulties* at first"—he looked

pointedly at Cat, to her bewilderment—"but I'm
happy to say the last few years have been quite successful." He smiled serenely at Amelia, who, not
knowing what to make of the exchange, offered the
duke some particularly fine, plump grapes.

"I congratulate you, your grace, on your success," Amelia said. "I know only too well how difficult it can be to build a life in the islands," she said
with a sigh. "There were many lean years when
Horace and I were starting out and, of course, here
we have a four and one-half percent duty on exports
to pay off Carlisle and his friends, who supposedly
sold the island back to the Crown after the restora-
tion," she explained. "On any of the islands there
are so many variables: the weather, pests, prices,
wars, taxes."

"That's true. However, I have eliminated one of
those variables by dispensing with the need for a
shipper." Again he looked meaningfully at Cat, his
brow raised sardonically. "I ship my own goods and
can count on a fair price for my product as long as
the market is stable. I'm sure you're aware of the
number of unscrupulous men doing business in the
islands."

Cat was becoming annoyed at the strange looks
Ransom was sending her way and was beginning to
wonder if he had lost his reason. Here he was, masquerading as a duke and acting as though *she* were
guilty of something. He didn't recognize her, of that
she was certain. What then ailed him?

"My, you have *so* many interests, your grace. How
do you keep track of them all?" she asked acidly.

"I keep track of *everything* that concerns me, Miss
Amberly. Have no doubt of that." Though smooth
and silky, his voice held a hint of menace, which
made Cat bristle.

"What gossip do you hear from London?" Amelia

interrupted, blithely ignoring the tense undercurrents.

"Not much, I'm afraid," Ransom answered, his charming smile back in place. "I haven't been to England recently." His lack was immediately remedied by Amelia, who chattered gaily about the latest news she had received from her friends in London until the mood at the table lightened. By the time dinner was over, Ransom and Cat were enjoying a playful argument about Greek literature while Amelia sat back and sipped her wine, a pleased smile on her face.

Although Cat had rejected the idea of piling the table with Ransom's favorite dishes, she did make sure he liked all the choices on the menu and smiled to herself when he remarked on the excellent meal. When he saw the stuffed mackerel, that lazy grin Cat knew so well spread across his face, and his eyes met hers across the table with a message that sent shivers down her back.

Emboldened by sherry and Ransom's good mood, Cat suggested a game of backgammon when they retired to the parlor. Ransom raised his brow in mild surprise, and he inclined his head slightly in acquiescence. Privately, he noted that the girl had done her work well; his fondness for the game was not common knowledge.

When Cat saw the surprise on his face, she immediately realized her invitation was too risky, considering how often they had played as captain and cabin boy. Would she give herself away? She quickly discounted the idea. After all, the man had played countless games with many players in his lifetime; he'd never recognize her strategy as Cat's. Besides, her manners had certainly changed since then! She smiled to herself remembering when he had taught her the game on a lazy afternoon in his cabin, sun spilling through the diamond-paned windows onto the heavy mahogany table.

She had been bored. Ransom had been going over the accounts, and she'd been walking about the room, trailing her fingers along the woodwork as she waited for him to approve her work. Finally, she fished a set of dice from her pocket and cast them against the wall. "Want to play hazard?" she asked, expecting a prompt rebuff.

"Games of chance are for the feebleminded," he commented without looking up. Cat pocketed the die again and glanced about for another object of interest when she stopped, surprised to hear the sharp *thwack* of the books closing so soon. "Since I believe you are not one of that vast group which, by the way, includes no small portion of the British aristocracy, I have a challenge for you. Would you care to learn a game comprising both chance and skill?"

Cat jumped at the chance to bask in the warmth of his company, and she was soon seated across from Ransom, the backgammon board between them, learning the rules of play as they spent the first of many enjoyable afternoons engaged in the game.

She was still smiling slightly at the memory while placing the board on a small table in the parlor, little realizing how seductive that smile was to Ransom. He thought again how very lovely she was, bathed in the glow of the candlelight that gave life to the spangled shawl she had draped casually around her arms. As Ransom watched her place the stones, he felt a growing desire to bare those gleaming shoulders and bury his lips along the slim line of her neck.

"Your grace?" Cat looked innocently puzzled by his stare as she offered him the dice box. With an effort, he shook off the desire that had descended so quickly and smiled at her. Either she was a gifted seductress or she was as inexperienced as she appeared. He was not quite sure for which choice to hope.

The luck appeared to lie with Cat at first, who smiled benignly after each favorable roll of the die. She abandoned the angelic air, however, when the game turned to Ransom. "How rude!" she accused when he sent one of her stones to the bar. "I don't believe you have a shred of decency."

The next game was even more animated as she laughed with delight over each successful move and vilified her opponent when he gained the advantage. Enchanted, Ransom chuckled at her antics and ignored a nagging tug on his memory. He'd never been under this lady's spell before; of that he was sure.

Ransom took the first two games, but Cat won the third. "I was warming up," she explained saucily. When she also took the fourth, Ransom suggested they retire the board for the evening. "Afraid I will best you again?" she asked wickedly.

"I live in dire fear of that result," he said, laughing. "I am up to another game, if you wish, but it is late." The moment the words left his mouth, he wanted to call them back, for his companion looked at the mantel clock in alarm.

Cat was suddenly aware that the evening had fled and Amelia along with it, leaving the two of them alone in the stillness of the salon. The light that had illuminated their play suddenly seemed woefully inadequate.

"It *is* late," Cat said, rising. Drat that addlepated Amelia! She led Ransom into the dimly lit hallway, where the quiet of the house bespoke the absence of any servants. "I'll call Isaac for your horse," she said with a touch of annoyance.

"No need." Ransom said softly, putting out a hand to stop her.

Cat's heart hammered in her chest as she realized

how near he was standing. "I'll light the lamp," she said, moving to the door, but again he halted her steps, and she shivered at his light touch upon her arm.

"Don't bother." His voice, smooth and deep, poured over her like cream. He's going to kiss me, she thought wildly, her heart racing. His hands lightly grasped her arms, urging her to him, and she raised her eyes to his, but she saw only his lashes as his head bent and his lips, soft and warm, captured her own. Her hands pressed against his chest, the satin of his waistcoat smooth underneath her fingertips. How often had she imagined this?

Reality took on a dreamlike quality as she surrendered to her senses. Her very being seemed to melt, her shawl slipping unheeded to the floor as his tongue moved lightly across her lips and into her mouth. Her hands slipped around his neck of their own accord while his moved slowly down her back, pressing her full against him. To Cat his body seemed warm and safe, delightful and exciting, all at once.

She felt his lean fingers under her chin, drawing her lips closer as his kiss deepened. "Kiss me, love," he urged against her mouth, and the self-satisfaction in his tone acted on Cat like a dash of cold water. Oh, he was all too sure of himself, speaking softly and moving oh-so-smoothly, and here she was falling into his arms like any of his other giddy females! The conceited bastard! She broke the kiss and pushed her hands against his chest, stepping back.

"Out!" she whispered hotly. "Out of my house!" Ransom chuckled at her sudden change, which riled her further. "You are no better than Pettibone!" she accused, pushing him out the door. She hesitated only a moment before slamming it soundly. Let Amelia wake up, Cat thought angrily. She's the one who invited him!

Ransom was still chuckling as he mounted his steed and proceeded at a brisk trot down the roadway, surprised that he had enjoyed an evening spent in the company of two ladies, one old enough to be his mother and the other, by all appearances, a virgin. What's more, he had the feeling he could grow to like both women, an absurd notion that made him faintly uneasy and more than a bit suspicious.

Certainly the two appeared to be nothing more than they seemed, an aged eccentric and her charming young niece, yet there were too many things that didn't quite fit, beginning with Devlin's red-haired minion who had conveniently disappeared. Although enjoyable, the evening had not brought him any answers. Perhaps his old friend René could help, Ransom thought as he urged his horse on to Bridgetown and the *Reckless*. Yes, René would do nicely, and he had an idea where to find him. Tomorrow he would set sail for L'Etoile.

Chapter 14

The following morning Amelia was treated to a ranting litany such as she had never heard from her niece. "That conceited ass! He thinks every woman waits only to fall into his arms!" Cat was pacing back and forth in the dining salon while Amelia calmly ate her breakfast.

"But, my dear, I don't understand why you're so angry. Most men try to steal a kiss from the young ladies. At least that's the way it was in my day," Amelia said sensibly. "And although every gently reared female would deny it, many of them allow a gentleman to do so. Of course, it wouldn't do to have such a thing get about. It could damage your reputation."

She rambled on while Cat paced, and for the first time since she arrived at her aunt's, Cat lost patience with the lady. Amelia was an intelligent woman; why did she rattle on so stupidly? Cat stopped in mid-stride and watched her aunt blissfully sipping chocolate.

"If you were so concerned about my reputation, why did you retire without a word? Even I cannot believe *that* is proper behavior for a chaperon," Cat said. Amelia put down her cup, a hurt expression on her pale features, and Cat immediately wanted to call back her hasty words.

"When I left, you two were having a delightful time," Amelia said, tilting her dainty chin defensively. "And I was under the impression, apparently mistaken, that you were able to take care of yourself. It seems to me that a girl who can manage a ship full of pirates should be able to handle one simple duke."

He is neither simple nor a duke, and *he's* the one who managed the ship, Cat thought as she went to Amelia's side. Aloud she said, "You're right, dear aunt. I'm sorry." She put her arm around Amelia's shoulders and gave her a quick squeeze. "Forgive me?"

"Of course, dear," Amelia said, patting her absently. "Now, I must attend to the gardens."

Cat watched her leave the cottage and plopped dejectedly into a chair. Curse my wretched tongue! And curse that snake Ransom, she fumed. "Isaac!" she suddenly called, leaping from the chair and sweeping into the kitchen.

"Ma'am?"

"If the duke of Morcester should call for me, I am out," she instructed. He nodded, but Cat thought she caught the hint of a smile and looked again. Although slavery still existed on the island, Amelia had freed Isaac, along with Marie, on the heels of the abolition movement. Dignified and quiet, Isaac looked wiser than the lot of them, Cat thought ruefully. Like Ransom, he was distant yet he seemed to know a lot more than he was telling, reminding Cat of shipboard stories of Hispaniola slaves and their witch doctors.

"Ma'am?"

"Isaac, what do you think of the duke?" she asked.

Again there was that hint of a smile before he answered in soft Caribbean cadences, "I'm sure I wouldn't know, ma'am."

* * *

As he suspected, Ransom found his quarry in the Devil's Spawn, a fancy gambling establishment on L'Etoile. There was no mistaking the black locks and small mustache of René Troussaint, his bright blue eyes shaded by the long, thick lashes that were the envy of all his women.

He was seated at a faro table, holding the bank and slouching negligently in his chair, but Ransom knew he was anything but inattentive. He watched as the Frenchman won a large sum of money from a tall, thin fellow who was totally unaware that he was out of his depth, and looked very displeased with the outcome. As Ransom watched, the thin fellow rose from his seat, sputtering, as if to challenge René's good fortune.

Ransom stepped to the table, knocking aside another chair, and growled at the Frenchman, "Get up, bastard, or die where you are."

"Du Prey," René hissed evilly, while his erstwhile opponent, who stayed only long enough to watch the Frenchman's response, fled the scene of what looked to be a bloodbath. The man was barely out of earshot when the other two burst into laughter.

"René," Ransom said with a smile as he extended his hand.

"Ransom, you son of a whore!" René rose and grasped Ransom's hand, then threw his other arm around his friend in a rough embrace. "Did you fear for my life?" he asked, nodding toward the door where the thin man had vanished moments earlier.

"No," Ransom answered. "I sought to spare the poor fellow. He obviously had no idea with whom he was dealing!"

"That is so," René said, laughing. The Frenchman gestured toward an empty table and called for some brandy. "Sit, my friend," he said before dropping gracefully into a chair.

"I see you've made yourself at home," Ransom said wryly.

"Ah, yes, but I am at home in all places," he said, spreading his arms smoothly through the air as though to encompass the entire globe. "Even though I like these Americans so well that I now call myself one of them." Leaning back in his chair, he clasped his hands in front of him and eyed Ransom. "It is good to see you, my friend. What brings you here, business or pleasure?"

"A bit of both," Ransom answered, smiling. "I hear you are heading to England," he said, raising his brow in question.

"*Oui*, I have some business there. I plan to sail within the week. You were lucky to catch me," he said as generous glasses of rum were placed before them. Ransom took a drink, the corners of his mouth curling as the liquor hit his throat. "Can I interest you in a little job for me?"

"Perhaps," René answered with a grin. "Go on."

"It's easy enough. Just some background work. I want you to find out all you can about a Catherine Amberly, daughter of the previous baron of Well-shire. History, money, relatives, friends . . . that sort of thing," Ransom said with a shrug.

"Aha!" cried René, his blue eyes twinkling. "A woman! How very interesting, Ransom Du Prey. May I ask why this interest in the lady?"

"You may take that gleeful smirk off your face. I think she may be in Devlin's employ."

"Ah," was the Frenchman's only response as he eyed his friend closely under his thick lashes.

Ransom toyed with his drink, watching the liquid swirl in the glass. "She's living outside Bridgetown now, with an aunt. A most intriguing lady. Although Miss Amberly denies knowing me, she seems familiar. I want to know just who she is and what her connection, if any, is with Devlin."

"And describe this one to me," René urged with a smirk.

"I don't know if I should," Ransom said, looking up quickly at his friend. "Your voyage might be delayed by a stop on Barbados."

The Frenchman threw back his head and laughed with glee. "This gets better and better, my friend! But, come, you must at least tell me something. How will I know if I have the right lady?" he asked.

"You wily bastard," Ransom said softly, drawing another gale of laughter from his friend. "She is small. Blonde hair, green eyes."

It took the laughing René some time and a few more drinks to try to get more out of Ransom, and when it became apparent that his friend had said all he was going to, René shouted in disbelief. "But, *mon ami*, if the blonde one is under your skin, why not take her to bed?" he asked.

"She is not under my skin," Ransom denied. "No one gets under my skin. She is simply of interest to me. Let's find out if she is who she claims to be. If she is one of Devlin's minions, I want to know exactly what she is up to. If not . . ." He shrugged. "Unlike a certain rutting Frenchman, I don't make a habit of sullying virginal young ladies of quality."

"Bah! You use the excuse, my friend, because you are afraid of her. You, who fear no man. It is all the same with you English—you are all so afraid of love! You think you will not be men if you fall in love!" René scoffed. "I have been in love many times and I am not ashamed to say so!" He raised his glass in salute. "To *amour*, my friend. *Amour*."

Cat moved restlessly through the house, her hopes of snubbing the alleged duke having faded, since several days had passed without a word from her unwelcome caller.

Good, Cat tried to tell herself. Perhaps the thick-headed captain had finally realized he was not wanted, or maybe her rebuff of his attentions had discouraged his plans for seduction, sending him back to the *Reckless* with his tail between his legs. She should be glad, not disappointed, that he had given up so easily and more than likely moved on to a more cooperative female. At that thought she threw down the tasseled pillow she had been fingering and strode from the parlor, nearly colliding with her aunt, who was standing in the hallway adjusting her hat.

"Would you care to stop pacing long enough to go to town with me?" Amelia asked, her dainty mouth curved into a sweet smile. Cat leaped at the prospect of an excursion. She firmly pushed aside the unwelcome idea that formed in her mind that in Bridgetown she could see if the *Reckless* still lay in the bay. If the ship had sailed, so much the better, she thought. If it had not, well, just because she did not want Ransom calling on her did not mean she wanted him calling on anyone else!

Standing outside the milliner's shop, near the bay, Cat shaded her eyes with her hand as she had done so often from a perch in the ship's rigging while Amelia chatted about a particularly appealing confection displayed in the milliner's window. Cat was trying to pick out the *Reckless*'s masts from the other ships that lay in the bay, but realized she would have to get closer.

"Looking for me, ladies?" Cat nearly jumped from her skin as Ransom spoke close to her ear. How did he do that? And how could she have forgotten his habit of appearing out of nowhere when least expected?

"Your grace, how delightful to see you again," Amelia said, taking his hands while Cat stood by sullenly.

"I fear I have neglected you while business sent me on an errand," he said smoothly.

"Well, I'm certainly glad you've returned. Catherine's been—oh!" Amelia grunted as Cat laid an elbow firmly in her side.

"I'm sure you'll excuse us, your grace, as we have some shopping to do," Cat said, taking her aunt's arm to pull her away.

"Do have dinner with me," he urged, smiling.

"We would love to!" Amelia said, shaking off Cat's grip and innocently turning those mild blue eyes on her. "Wouldn't we, dear?"

"Oh, *yes*. It would be lovely," Cat said sarcastically, provoking a grin from Ransom.

Dinner at the Golden Bell consisted of a rich turtle soup and a hearty black-crab pepper pot, along with capons, mutton, fruits, and sweets. But Cat barely noticed the food. Her attention was taken by Ransom, who, it soon became apparent, had set out to charm her.

He was relentless, poking fun at her sober expression, whispering asides designed to send her into peals of laughter, and telling wonderful stories. Holding out as long as she could, Cat finally succumbed when the sisters Montrief descended upon him in full force. Daphne and Elizabeth were good-tempered but unattractive, and they were notorious for pouncing with untoward zeal upon any unmarried male who crossed their path. Ransom was no exception.

Elizabeth was as tall and thin as Daphne was short and squat. Indeed, they little resembled each other except in their talkative and overly friendly manner, especially around eligible men. Their excitement at meeting a duke was such that they were both breathless in a short span of time.

"Your grace, your grace," said Daphne. "You simply must come and dine with us. Our cook is

French, and he has such a way with the native foods. Why, they are transformed!"

"Yes, do say you will come to visit," Elizabeth said with a little more restraint. "We were both born here on the island," she noted, shooting a glance at Amelia and Cat, as if to point out that they were not. "And you will find no better guides to the sights."

"Why, yes, yes, we do know Bridgetown!" put in Daphne.

"We are familiar with the entire island," Elizabeth said proudly.

"Well, I'm really not sure how long I will be staying," Ransom hedged.

"Oh, but you *must* see the city," said Elizabeth.

"And the theater, the theater. You simply must attend! We have *two* theaters, I'll have you know," added Daphne.

Cat could barely keep from giggling as she watched Ransom politely fend them off, his wits his only weapon against their zeal, and she decided to join in the fray. "Why, Daphne, his grace was just telling me how much he enjoyed the theater," Cat said sweetly, receiving a look from Ransom that sent her diving behind her napkin.

When the ladies finally exited the inn in a flutter of parasols, packages, and invitations, leaving behind the unstated desire that Ransom marry one of them, Ransom turned to Cat, his eyes twinkling. "You, my love, are in need of a sound thrashing!" His endearment caught Cat in the chest, and when he commented that it was too bad about Miss Elizabeth's peg leg, she nearly sent her soup spewing across the table.

"What on earth?" she gasped.

"Oh, I thought from her gait that she was missing a limb," Ransom said with a straight face.

"You are incorrigible," Cat claimed, and from that moment on, she was his, dissolving into giggles at his tales and warming to the delicious sound of his voice. She was enjoying herself so thoroughly she had to catch herself before she said, ''Tell Amelia about the ship whose guns were painted on,'' or ''Tell Amelia about the Portuguese merchant.''

For the most part, Cat's aunt sat in quiet satisfaction, watching the sprightly interchange. Ransom's dark head would bend near Catherine's golden one, causing her to break into a dazzling smile or a sparkling laugh, and when Catherine spoke to her aunt, Ransom's dark eyes followed the curve of her mouth, the line of her cheek, the movement of her lashes. Amelia sighed softly to herself, declaring the dinner a complete and utter success.

When the last raspberry tart and cake confection had been consumed, and the trio finally rose to leave, Cat felt a twinge of disappointment. She was loath to part with her captain and realized, too late, how dangerous it was to spend time with him. Her fear of discovery was fading as she remained undetected with each new encounter, yet her former life held a warning for her. She had once fancied herself in love with this man, and she had no desire to relive that misery.

All thoughts of suffering fled, however, when he took her hand, his touch sending shivers up her arm and on to various parts of her body totally unrelated to that appendage. His lips against her hand seemed far more intimate than a simple farewell gesture and even more unnerving than his kiss of the other night. Perhaps it was the fact that his mouth was touching a part of her body that she never expected to be so sensitive, or maybe it was the look in his eyes as his lips lingered too long against her skin. Cat only knew that her composure had slipped, and that the slow grin he gave her upon parting showed that he was well aware of his effect on her.

Chapter 15

"Such a nice young man," Amelia gushed as the carriage rolled homeward. "Don't you agree?" she asked, looking slyly at her niece, who was watching the countryside, her finger at her lips.

Receiving only a noncommittal response, Amelia pressed on. "You two seemed to be enjoying yourselves again, if I do say so." She sighed. "Catherine, don't chew on your finger," she admonished before launching into a one-sided discussion of their recent dinner, followed by another recitation of Ransom Du Prey's merits.

Although not attending her aunt, Cat was also thinking about the estimable duke. She was wondering just how long he planned to stay in Barbados and thinking the sooner he left, the better it would be, especially for her peace of mind.

She would not have been encouraged to know that Ransom had returned to the island strictly on her account. Unwittingly, she had captured her former captain's interest. The sale of his ship's cargo had been completed and the crewmen were enjoying themselves, so, since he had no other pressing plans to take him from Barbados, Ransom decided to spend a few extra days furthering his acquaintance with her. He had to admit she was a delightful companion, beautiful and witty, and it had been a long time since he had established more than a passing familiarity with any female besides Sally Knotts.

There was a good reason for that, the duke reminded himself. He was too busy to listen to the simpering demands of a mistress, and his wealth was too hard-won to throw away on greedy wenches masquerading as ladies, who liked to be ''kept.'' A man away at sea was apt to find his gold supporting not only a luscious lady but her amours as well.

Perhaps Devlin hoped that the intriguing Miss Amberly would charm him into establishing her as his mistress, then bleed him dry. If so, he was to be disappointed, for no woman held Ransom's interest for long. But since Miss Amberly *had* succeeded in capturing his attention, he might take a few days to pursue her . . . and see where it led him, he thought with a smile.

Cat was curled up in the parlor, concentrating on translating some difficult Greek, when Ransom was announced. Despite a stern self-admonishment, a thrill surged through her, and she hastily rose to her feet, the volume falling, forgotten, to the floor. Ransom bent smoothly to retrieve her book, his brow rising at the title.

''When you spoke so lovingly of the tragedies, I had no notion that you read them in their original text,'' he said in a tone that hinted at disbelief. Cat felt her ire rise. Gone was the warm charmer of the Golden Bell, replaced by the distant stranger who viewed her as a stuffed mackerel, a side of beef, or worse! She did not know what annoyed her more, his ability to turn his charm on and off like a garden pump or his condescending attitude.

''No matter what *you* may believe, women are not all mindless ninnies,'' Cat snapped as she snatched the volume from his hand.

She caught the flicker of surprise in his eyes,

which only irritated her further. "Have you never met one who could *read* before?" she asked in a voice heavy with sarcasm. Her taunts seemed to make no impression on him, however, for he only shook his head with amusement. Cat, infuriated, wanted to slap the slow grin she saw forming on his face.

"I'm afraid I have never made the acquaintance of one who could both read Greek and pass for a goddess from its pages," he said as he took the errant volume from her hands and set it on a nearby table.

Cat looked up at him, realized that he was standing far too close, and fought the trembling that seemed to accompany his nearness. Her anger stood her in good stead as he raised a hand to her face, for she brushed it aside in exasperation.

"And not all women are panting for your caresses, either, your grace," she snapped, stepping away from him to put the table between them. "Gad, what arrogance you must have to think that every simpering miss is waiting to fall at your feet!"

"So you are not one of those, all of whom are manufactured by my . . . enormous arrogance?" Ransom asked, his brow rising again, his lips curled into amused skepticism.

"No! Yes, I mean, I have no desire for your continued attentions, if you wish me to make myself plain," Cat said firmly, the words sticking in her throat for some idiotic reason.

"I see," he said softly. "Well, I certainly have no desire to force my presence where it is unwelcome." He turned to go, and Cat stepped from behind the safety of the table, struck by a pang as she realized that he was truly leaving and she would never see him again. With conflicting emotions, she followed him silently to within a few steps of the parlor doors, then nearly collided with him when he turned suddenly.

"But first I have a desire to make a liar out of you, Miss Amberly," he whispered, and before she knew what he was about, he cupped her chin in his hand and lowered his lips to hers.

The pressure was gentle yet firm as it sent messages of delight throughout her body. Softly, insistently, his lips moved against her own until he coaxed them apart, and she felt the warm smoothness of his tongue. Its movements, although limited to the inside of her mouth, seemed to touch every part of her. She felt a strange but wonderful tingling from her hair to her toes, then his hand slipped behind her head, his fingers threading through her golden hair until she felt limp.

Cat raised her hands to his chest, leaning against him as she tilted her head up to his, and it was then that he released her. She slumped like a rag doll, staring dully at the tall, lean body that was leaving her, and could only hope her mouth was not hanging stupidly open when he turned to smile at her.

"Until next time, Miss Amberly," he said softly as he bowed, the self-satisfaction in his voice like a knife against her skin. It wasn't until he was gone that she realized he had never even put his arms around her.

"I don't believe it," Tremayne Devlin choked, his bloated stomach shaking with the force of his incredulity.

"It be true, sir," Tim Calhoun said from across his employer's huge mahogany desk. Tim had forgotten how disconcerting it was to deal with Devlin and, in nervous reaction, he glanced around the office. It was stark and plain, devoid of the opulence with which Devlin usually surrounded himself. Tucked as it was in a warehouse in the Rue de la Paix, it had no need for finery, Tim decided. The office served its purpose, and since its location was in one of L'Etoile's seedier neighborhoods, it was better left undecorated.

"I simply cannot believe that the cold and self-contained Du Prey has fallen for a *woman*. How disappointing! I thought he was above such drivel," Devlin said with a scowl. From behind the imposing desk, Devlin exuded a commanding presence that belied his short stature and round figure. Dark featured and menacing, he sported a tiny, pointed beard that made him appear more so. His small, thick hands moved gracefully as he spoke, sending off sparks of light from the many jeweled rings he wore, but whether the motions were unconscious or a purposeful distraction to others, Tim could not guess.

"You say he's actually returning to Bridgetown for no other reason than to pursue a vapid young virgin?"

"Yes, sir," Tim asserted. "I have it on authority of several of the crew. I took to drinking with them, to get them to tell me what they knew. The night before they left, they had no idea where they were bound, but they were told they would be back soon for some sport, and more than one claimed it was because the captain had his eye on a filly."

Devlin still looked skeptical, his small, dark eyes seeming to bore into Tim's soul, and Tim tried not to finger his hat nervously. There was no need for him to tell Devlin that Du Prey had recognized him. Bloody hell! He had done his job well enough, hadn't he? Why did the fat man have to stare at him so? It was enough to make a body sweat.

"And you say he saw a lot of this . . . female while he was there?" Devlin finally asked.

"Yes. He saw her at a party, and then went to her house twice."

"That hardly constitutes an obsession," Devlin

said caustically, while Tim shifted from one foot to the other.

"Well, I thought you would want to know, sir, but I can go right back. Perhaps I shouldn't have come . . ."

"No. You were wise to come to me, and I appreciate your initiative," Devlin said curtly, causing Tim to breathe a little easier.

"Now, what is this female's name?"

"Amberly, sir. Catherine Amberly. She's supposed to be a baron's daughter, though she lives sparse enough in a cottage with old Mrs. Molesworth, who used to own a big plantation there."

"Amberly . . . Why does that sound familiar?" Devlin said softly as his eyes drifted away and his hand moved thoughtfully to his chin. "I never forget a name or a face," he noted. "I cannot put features to that name, but I have heard it . . . in connection with Edward . . ." His voice trailed off and then was raised again in a shout. "Richard!"

Tim nearly jumped out of his skin when the fat man bellowed aloud. "You'll be well paid if your story is confirmed," Devlin said as his eyes darted back to Tim. "Now get out."

Tim backed away from the desk toward the door, so eager to escape the oppressive atmosphere that he nearly collided with the blond-haired man who entered in response to Devlin's shout. Richard Blakely's blue eyes moved distastefully over Tim as he stepped aside and casually walked to Devlin's desk, nodding in acknowledgment.

Devlin waited for the door to close behind Tim's departing figure before he spoke, his fingers knotting together as he eyed his favorite secretary. Richard was an efficient and capable assistant, with no equal in Devlin's organization, but his performance in other, more personal, areas was lacking, and Devlin decided quickly that he would not miss him. "It seems Du Prey might have fallen under the spell of a female," he said, his lips curling into a smirk. "Get over to Bridgetown and find out if it is true."

"Certainly," Richard said, his gaze expressionless.

"Amberly," Devlin continued. "The creature's name is Catherine Amberly. I want you to find out everything there is to know about her. *Everything*. This is important, Richard. I have my suspicions about this girl . . ." he mused as his hand curled around his mouth, one finger absently stroking his beard.

"Above all, keep an eye on the creature," Devlin said. "Don't lose sight of her, Richard," he warned, the smooth coyness of his voice masking his inherent threat. He became silent, his thoughts elsewhere for a moment, then said briskly, "I'm closing up the office here. I'll be going to England for a while. I have some business that's been waiting, and now a new question demands my attention." He moved his hands impatiently over the desk as if in dismissal, then eyed his secretary for a response.

Richard stoically accepted the backhanded announcement that he would not be going with his employer this time. He was used to sudden trips and to being kept in the dark about the details. Devlin, as he well knew, did not trust anyone, but that was only sensible. Richard shared his employer's suspicions, and his closemouthed efficiency had made him Devlin's right hand man. Whether he retained that position remained to be seen, but Richard did not pause to consider it now. Instead, he concentrated on the mission ahead. "And if Du Prey is smitten with this female?" he asked.

Devlin's thin lips curled into an evil smile as he answered without hesitation. "Why, break up his little romance, of course."

"Ahem." Richard cleared his throat. "Would not this lady be an asset to us if she could be bought?"

The thin smile tightened before Devlin answered, as though he were contemplating with delight such an occurrence. "Most assuredly," he answered, the smirk leaving his lips as quickly as it appeared. "But if I know Du Prey, and I do, the wench must be pure as the driven snow to have held his attention for this long," he said with disgust. "If you discover otherwise, spend whatever is necessary to enlist her in our cause.

"Of course, if we discover her identity, we may have the means to . . . persuade her, for if my suspicions are correct, this female is related to Edward Moore, an old associate of mine, and is quite possibly a runaway. In that case, she may have value to us other than her ability to charm Du Prey," Devlin mused, speaking softly. "An interview with Edward will prove enlightening, I'm sure."

The fat man paused to look Richard in the eye as he smiled again. "But that is for me to discover. Your job lies on Barbados. You can stay at a plantation owned by William Montgomery; he owes me a favor," Devlin said with a smirk. "Make a good job of it, Richard," he added. "Just make certain that Du Prey is sorely used, with or without the lady's help."

Chapter 16

Cat was still bristling over Ransom's kisses as she dressed for supper. The conceit of the man! And she had practically swooned at his feet like any other besotted admirer! Cat berated her treacherous body again and again while she tried to explain away her response by remembering how often she had dreamed of his touch while serving on the *Reckless*. Unfortunately, even Cat could not accept that excuse or any of the others she'd manufactured, including curiosity, to explain her rapid surrender.

She seethed as she donned an elegant creamy satin gown with matching spencer and clasped a modest necklace of pearls around her throat. Cat, who never took stock in her own beauty, was even less attentive than usual to her toilet while her thoughts concentrated solely on how to bring her former captain down a peg or so. Thus occupied, she did not spare a thought for the upcoming evening at Lord Claremont's. She and Amelia were invited to the plantation house for supper at least once a week, so it was not until she stood before the waiting landau that Cat felt a twinge of foreboding.

"Now, aunt, there's no need to tell Lord Claremont about the duke," she suggested tactfully as she stepped into the open carriage and settled beside her aunt.

"My heavens, why not?" Amelia demanded, fluttering her fan. "I think he'll be impressed that a duke is calling on you. After all, my dear, Lord Du Prey would make a fine match, and you certainly haven't had any interest in the local fellows. I think you should seriously consider his suit. Imagine, my little Catherine a duchess." She sighed.

Cat laughed out loud. "Somehow I find that hard to picture," she said, looking out over the passing palm trees. "And suit? What suit? If you think the man has marriage in mind, my dear aunt, you are daydreaming. Rogues like Ransom don't believe in marriage."

"I swear I can not keep track of which way the wind blows. One day the man is wonderful, the next he is a demon. I certainly wish you would make up your mind," Amelia began, but Cat interrupted, unable to bear another recitation of Ransom's finer points.

"Please, aunt. Promise me you won't bring it up."

"Catherine Amberly, what has gotten into you? You have been acting most strangely of late. Perhaps some island malaise is affecting you. Have you a fever?" Amelia asked, dropping her fan in her lap and pressing her fingers to Cat's forehead.

"I don't have a fever," Cat said, pushing her aunt's hand away and staring moodily over the landscape again.

"It must be love, then," Amelia teased.

"I am *not* in love with Ransom Du Prey, so get this duchess business out of your mind. Honestly, aunt, I think you're the one acting strangely!" Amelia only sighed knowingly, making Cat sink back into the cushions, her hand to her head and a whispered "Oh, Lord" on her lips.

Cat began to wish fervently that she had stayed home. When she was ushered into Lord Claremont's drawing room, she had cause, once again, to regret her presence. Lord Claremont, tall and thin but robust, walked forward to greet them. "Ladies, it is a pleasure as always," he said, leading them into the room. "Let me introduce another guest to you," he added, and Cat knew, even before she saw him, who that guest would be.

"Your grace! How lovely," Amelia gushed, fluttering her fan as Ransom stepped forward.

The smile died on Cat's lips as he bowed over her hand. "Your grace," she acknowledged through clenched teeth, much to Ransom's delight.

Without releasing her fingers, he turned to Lord Claremont and smiled. "The lovely lady is well known to me."

"Good, good," Lord Claremont said heartily, while Cat tried desperately to retrieve her hand, a smile pasted on her face.

Lord Claremont prided himself on setting a good table, and the supper laid before them was no exception. Cat chose from an array of turtle, mutton, creamed onions, potatoes in herb sauce, sweet baby peas, sugared pears, and delicate pastries.

"It appears we are to have the pleasure of your company for some time," she said sweetly, smiling at Ransom, who knew very well the lie behind the words. "I would think the duties of your ship would have called you back by now."

"I have been conducting some business, but, alas, I will have to return to the sea soon, Catherine," he said with exaggerated regret. "As much as I enjoy the company here on Barbados"—he grinned wickedly at her—"I must not neglect my business."

"Oh, how disappointing," Cat said, longing to toast a speedy voyage.

"Well, you're welcome to stay here with me if you like," Lord Claremont told Ransom, to Cat's dismay. "The house is always open to visitors, and I don't think you will find better accommodations.

They can say what they like about the islands, but
the people are hospitable. I did a lot of traveling
hereabouts in my day and always found a good bed,
if not a good table.'' He laughed.

Cat refused to look at Ransom, whom she pictured grinning luridly at the prospect of encamping
nearly on her doorstep. She clamped her mouth shut
and let the other three carry the conversation, refusing to take another look in her captain's direction.
The supper seemed interminable as course after
course was trotted out, and Cat wondered if she
could get away with pleading a headache afterward.
As they all rose from the table, she was about to put
forth her excuses, but Lord Claremont had other
plans.

''Since we're a nice, cozy foursome,'' he said,
rubbing his hands with relish, ''let's have a game of
whist.'' Cat groaned inwardly, knowing somehow
that she would draw Ransom as her partner. When
she did, she again thought of running home, but
Ransom's next words changed her mind.

''You do know how to play?'' he asked her dryly.
Cat, who considered herself a better than average
player, rose to the challenge like a fish to a line.

She held back a biting retort when Lord Claremont answered for her. ''I say, Du Prey, you are
lucky to have drawn Catherine. She's an excellent
player.''

''How fortunate for me then,'' Ransom said, a lazy
grin spreading across his face while Cat fumed. The
group moved to take their seats, and as Ransom solicitously pulled out Cat's chair, he leaned over and
whispered in her ear, ''I'm sorry about yesterday. A
truce?''

Cat, who'd nearly jumped at the feel of his breath
against her hair, shot him a glance of incredulity that
made him laugh aloud, drawing the attention of the
elder partners. Ransom ignored their questioning

gazes and took his seat, his brow raised as he looked at Cat. She felt the corners of her mouth twitching and sighed, nodding slightly to her partner in acceptance of a truce against which her better judgment warned her.

Although Lord Claremont and Amelia had played whist together for years, earning a reputation as a more than able team, it soon became apparent that Ransom and Cat were the better players as they handily won a succession of games.

"Are you sure you two haven't played together before?" Lord Claremont asked irritably as he watched the seemingly effortless collaboration. Cat smiled to herself. They had never played together; she had learned whist from her reluctant stepfather when the vicar and his wife had visited and pressed for a game, and her skills had been honed right here at Lord Claremont's house. She had never played aboard the *Reckless,* for even had Ransom asked her, who would have completed the set? Her lips curved gently as she tried to picture a few of her burly friends from the ship seated nicely playing whist.

The secret smile that played upon Cat's lips as she recalled her days as cabin boy departed quickly at Ransom's next words. "I was hoping to persuade Catherine to go riding with me tomorrow," he declared with a devilish grin.

"By all means, feel free to use the stables," Lord Claremont suggested, and Cat glared at her host. Lord Claremont had never offered *her* the use of the plantation stables, but let a supposed duke waltz in, and he had the run of the place. Men!

"Let me show you around the property, give you an idea of how things are run," Lord Claremont continued. "They look a little different from horseback," he added, nodding in Catherine's direction.

Cat fairly steamed at his comment. As if she had never been on a horse! She opened her mouth for a blistering retort when she felt the soft squeeze of Amelia's hand on her own. Cat glanced at her aunt to see that lady's face shining with silent amusement, and she swallowed her scathing comment. Ransom could get her so worked up that she was ready to snap at everyone! She sighed inwardly as she watched him, now engaged in a deep discussion of horses with his host, and thought what a crime it was that he was so handsome, so charming . . . and such a rogue!

When the evening finally wound to a close, Ransom left the plantation with the now-familiar feeling that he enjoyed Catherine's company but was no closer to solving the mystery of her. Lord Claremont had talked volubly about the two ladies before their arrival, without the slightest idea that he was being quizzed, yet he made them out to be two helpless females in need of male protection.

Ransom discounted Claremont's judgment as wishful thinking, for he could not imagine two more independent females. Ransom inferred that Claremont would offer for the old dame at the slightest urging, but since the two had known each other for many years, Ransom doubted any encouragement would be forthcoming.

The old fellow saw nothing unusual in Catherine's precipitous arrival six months ago and apparently knew nothing of any other relatives. No doubt Amelia had spun the little tale of Catherine's wicked guardian in hopes of snaring the title of duchess for her niece, but somehow that did not seem right. Ransom's instincts told him something else was afoot here besides a lovely young lady's marriage prospects.

His brow rose in puzzlement, for Miss Amberly was proving to be an enigma. She was appealing— beautiful, intelligent, high-spirited, and, above all, interesting—far different from those women he had dealt with before. She was certainly not the typical drawing room bore, nor did she seem to be the deceiving seductress he had suspected. But Ransom was not ready to accept her innocence as yet, and common sense advised him not to dismiss the notion that Devlin had sent her.

Chapter 17

As she dressed in her pristine riding habit, Cat could not help feeling a thrill of excitement. How good it would be to ride again, to watch the countryside fly by at a good gallop and feel the rush of the wind! And Ransom would be with her. What should have been a drawback to the excursion only heightened her anticipation, and she scolded herself. But, then, he would be leaving soon, and what could possibly happen while Lord Claremont was with them?

Cat rushed down the steps to the sound of hoof-beats outside the cottage, and before Isaac could reach the front of the house, she had already flung wide the door. Her graceful strides quickly took the brick path to the lane, and there she stopped. In front of the cottage was her captain, riding a hand-some stallion, alongside a spirited filly with no rider.

"Where is Lord Claremont?" Cat asked in the long-suffering tones used by nursemaids, tutors, and other handlers of small, unrepentant children.

"His gout was troubling him," Ransom said, his lips twitching.

With a sigh of resignation, Cat shook her head, her own mouth threatening to curve into a smile, and stepped to her mount. "I can only hope you did not harm the poor man," she threw at Ransom while she stroked the filly's neck.

"Her name is Beauty—not original, but applicable," Ransom said while the filly stamped, impatient to be off. "I thought you would be able to handle her."

Ignoring the jibe, Cat introduced herself to the animal, talking softly to her and calming her before mounting. As the horse pranced about, she pulled sharply at the reins, bringing her under control. "I'm glad you had faith in my ability," Cat said dryly, causing Ransom to chuckle. "Now, let me show you around the plantation."

"Are you certain you can find your way, keeping in mind that things do look different from horseback?"

Cat looked over to see him grinning wickedly, and she had to laugh. So Ransom had caught that comment, too! She had to admit she was heartened to know he thought it as silly as she did; at least he gave her credit for having some sense. In fact, though he disdained women as mindless bores, he did not treat her as such, she thought suddenly. He might act strangely at times, sending odd glances or remarks her way, and, of course, his conceit was boundless, but he always acted as though she were an equal, an intelligent being capable of joining in his most subtle humor.

She quickly quashed the spark of hope that appeared in her chest, hope that somehow he had found her different. Most likely he treated all women in this manner, then complained to his fellows of how dreadfully tedious they were. The thought that Ransom was telling some new cabin boy about how insipid she was sent her temper soaring, and she gave Beauty her head. She was not going to let him ruin her outing.

Cat let Beauty race along the edge of the cane

fields, and oblivious to all but the wind and the horse, she felt an exhilaration she had not known since she had last swung from the rigging, high above the world. At the orchard, she sent Beauty galloping between the rows of orange trees, a green and orange blur on either side. Immersed as she was in her own world, Cat had not noticed the stallion, but as Ransom's shouts penetrated she slowed the filly to a stop.

"What the hell did you think you were doing?" Ransom lashed out at her with such fury that Cat could only blink in astonishment. "Are you trying to get yourself killed?" When Cat, calmly watching him with wide-eyed wonder, made no response, he inched his horse closer. "Well?"

"If you can't keep up, then wait for me back at the great house," Cat said matter-of-factly, and made as though to turn her horse about.

"Oh, no you don't," Ransom said, his hands on her reins. "I'm responsible for you, you little idiot, and I have no intention of dragging a broken body back to your aunt."

So much for being treated as an equal, Cat thought with disgust. "Are you saying I can't handle this horse?" she asked seriously, looking straight into those angry brown eyes. For a long moment, the two remained as they were, dark eyes blazing into green, then Cat saw something she had never thought to witness: a crack in her captain's facade. For the blink of an eye, Cat caught a glimpse of another Ransom underneath the controlled exterior, a Ransom she longed to know better. His eyes faltered for only an instant, though, before he loosed her reins and shrugged indifferently.

"I can see you are a skilled horsewoman, but I would prefer no more foolhardy displays."

Cat wanted to shriek in anger and call back the man who lay beneath the nonchalant pose, for she sensed something behind his rage other than a misjudgment of her abilities. "Oh!" she snapped in frustration as she sent Beauty into a brisk trot.

They rode through a section of Lord Claremont's property, Cat pointing out as best she could the main parts of the plantation while Ransom explained the finer points of sugar production. Then Cat veered off to her own favorite spot, a grove of ancient locusts and wild roses falling in short, natural terraces to a small stretch of beach. There they dismounted and walked to the edge of the rise, where Cat seated herself, her feet tucked neatly under her. Ransom relaxed beside her, leaning back on an elbow and looking out over the ocean.

For a long while they simply enjoyed the quiet together as they often had aboard the *Reckless*, and Cat's mood gradually improved. When Ransom finally spoke, it was to ask her more about the island, and Cat eagerly responded. With a natural enthusiasm, she described the climate, economy, and politics of her new world while Ransom watched her. As she spoke, sometimes an inflection in her voice or a movement of her hands would strike him as familiar, and his mind groped in vain to find the reason.

Even as he sought the answer, Ransom admired her. She was describing with amazing skill and precision a certain fishing technique she had observed, and Ransom wondered idly just how many females, outside of a fishmonger's wife, paid attention to such things. When she finished, she looked at him as though she knew he would share her interest, which surprised him. He *did*, but damn it, how did she know that?

It was as if she knew him well already, he thought as he reached over to lift an errant golden lock from her cheek. The gesture led his thoughts back to less ethereal matters, and he laid his palm softly against her face. Her skin felt as smooth as silk beneath his fingers, and he experienced a surge of desire, along with some strange, unfamiliar emotion as he looked into her bright green eyes. Without a word he slid his hand into her hair and pulled her toward him. She came without demur, and her lips pressing tentatively against his own jolted him with unexpected force.

It was different this time, Cat thought as she leaned over Ransom's hard chest. There was no gleam of self-satisfaction in those brown eyes, only a warmth that she had not seen since her days as his cabin boy. Sensing a vulnerability in her captain, she kissed him again.

His mood might be different, but his effect on her was the same, for her heart began racing and her body sang with excitement. Breaking away, she raised herself up to take a breath, which caught in her throat as she looked down at the face that had haunted her dreams. His lips were still parted as if urging the return of her own, and his eyes were dark with something she did not recognize but which seemed to strike an answering need in her.

Cat raised a trembling hand to his hair and ran her fingers with wonder over his smooth locks. Who would have thought that hair could be so beautiful and feel so alive? she thought, before what little breath she had was knocked from her as he pulled her close and took her mouth with his.

Ransom's kisses became deeper and longer until Cat's heart was nearly bursting from her chest. She moved her tongue against his in imitation of his own movements and felt him pull her tightly to him and roll her onto her back. The pressure of his body against hers sent new sensations flowing through her flesh, and she knew with a primitive instinct that this sort of behavior could lead to things best avoided. But she was helpless to stop the warmth that surged through her. She reached up to curl her hands into his hair as his lips moved along her jaw and up her neck to her ear, and she gasped as his tongue roamed its ridges. She gasped even louder as the presence of a large, wet, snorting nose startled her from her languor.

With an oath, Ransom pushed aside the wandering filly's head, then rose to make sure the horse would interrupt them no further, but Cat did not lie passively awaiting her lover's return. With a mixture of dismay and embarrassment, she sat upright, running her hands nervously over her hair and eyeing the strong, virile body that had but recently left her own.

The mood was gone; she knew it from the cold line of Ransom's mouth. Perhaps he was only irritated at Beauty, but Cat was relieved that the moment had passed, and she blessed the animal's interference. If I could convince Amelia to buy you, I would repay you for the rest of your life, my little Beauty! she swore silently.

"I must be going," she said aloud, without really looking at Ransom when he sat down beside her.

"No, stay," he said, putting his hand on her own, but Cat removed hers from his touch with a wry shake of her head.

"You broke the truce," she accused softly. At Ransom's questioning gaze, she smiled. "You said you were sorry about the other day," she reminded him gently.

"Hmmm?" Those brown eyes looked briefly puzzled. "Oh, and so I was," Ransom said with a chuckle as he recalled his words. "I was sorry you became angry, not that I kissed you," he explained.

"I see. I must heed your words more carefully," she said, and she appeared so lost that Ransom could have kicked himself—and the stupid horse.

"Tell me more of your island," he urged, leaning

back once more. When he made no move toward her, Cat obliged, her voice at first stilted with self-consciousness but soon rambling on as if there had been no intimate interlude between them.

Ransom leaned casually back against the grass to watch her, idly listening until he could recapture her in his arms, his attention focused more on the curve of her cheek and the swell of her breast than her conversation. In fact, he was so inattentive, he almost missed her slip of the tongue. But then Ransom did not miss much, as Cat, in her more lucid moments, could well attest.

She was describing Bridgetown when she noted that the business district "looks like where you have your offices on Windlay." The moment the words left her mouth, Ransom's head tilted imperceptibly toward her, his brow raised curiously, and Cat cursed herself.

"So you've been to Windlay then?" he asked without missing a beat, and Cat felt her throat constrict as though she were a rat caught in a trap.

"You've been to Windlay?" Ransom repeated after a pause of deathly silence.

"Why, yes," Cat managed as she pulled at a tiny flower dotting the grass. "I have friends there."

"Do you? What are their names? I know more than a few people on the island."

"Gallsworthy," she answered, plucking the names of her neighbors in England from her memory.

"Hmmm. I haven't heard of them."

"I'm not surprised; they moved several years ago," Cat said, wondering why she was so infernally nervous now when she used to lie to this same man on a daily basis. Before, it had seemed such a lark, and she realized with a start just how perilous her adventure on the *Reckless* had been. Perhaps she had been too young and naive to know it at the time, but she knew now that the man before her could be dangerous. She recognized that, despite his careless pose, he was oozing menace from every pore.

"I see," he said softly as he gazed out over the ocean. "And what did you think of my offices?"

"What?"

"You said you had been to my offices."

"I've never been to your offices," Cat said. "You simply mentioned that they were located on Windlay."

"Did I?"

"Yes," Cat lied. "And you said you had a plantation there, too," she added with just enough irritation to show she was bored with the topic.

"Hmmm. Perhaps I did," Ransom said. Although he sounded unconvinced, Cat dared to hope that the incident was closed.

She longed to slap herself silly for such carelessness. Thank God she had said nothing even more revealing . . . or mentioned the ship! Oh, how simple it was to fall back into the habit of friendship with this man, especially when he began treating her with his former warmth. Then it was easy to talk freely . . . but more than the warmth of his manner was at fault today, Cat thought wryly. She blamed the heat of his caresses for scattering her thoughts. After all, she was used to keeping her head in touchy situations. It was the lovemaking, alien and mindnumbing, that had tripped her tongue, she decided as she scowled at the grass.

Her companion also frowned in distaste at the inane answers he had just received. Ransom knew damn well that he had never mentioned the location of his offices to the lady. She had obviously seen them, yet she denied it. Why? He could only think of one explanation: her connection to Devlin.

Ransom hated intrigues, and he was getting a bellyful of this one. If it weren't for a lingering doubt, which, he admitted, had more basis in feeling than fact, he would grab her by the throat right now and throttle some answers out of her. Instead, he decided on another tack. If Miss Amberly was one of Devlin's harpies, he could get her to show her true colors easily enough with the right offer. With a studied nonchalance, Ransom looked over at his companion. "So you like living here?" he asked.

"Oh, yes," Cat answered without hesitation. "It is a beautiful place, don't you think?"

"Yes," Ransom nodded. "And what of your aunt? Are you happy with her?"

His tone was innocent, but Cat glanced sharply at him, only to find him eyeing her shrewdly. "Why, yes, of course I'm happy with Amelia," she answered, irritated with herself for hesitating. She still felt like a baited rodent, for from the look of him, Ransom was up to something. Despite her slip of the tongue, Cat doubted that he now recognized her, so she turned the tables back on him. "Why would you ask such a thing?"

Ransom shrugged. "A young lady as clever and beautiful as yourself might become . . . bored buried in the pleasant cottage life. Back in London, you could be moving in the smartest circles, around the court . . ."

Surprised by this new topic, Cat could only look puzzled.

"Wouldn't you rather be attending the theaters and assembly rooms, dancing till dawn every night, dining on cut-glass plates, and gossiping over the latest court intrigues?"

"Pooh! It doesn't sound very alluring to me, except maybe the dancing, though I can't imagine dancing till dawn every day because I would miss my sleep," Cat said seriously.

Ransom smiled oddly. "Ah, but you could sleep until noon," he said.

"Why, half the day's gone by then! It sounds like a lot of farrago to me," Cat declared, her expression guileless. "Besides, only the very rich live that way." And I'm penniless, she did not add.

"You're a resourceful young lady. I'm sure you could arrange something," Ransom said, cocking a brow at her.

Cat's eyes narrowed. "Just what are you insinuating?"

"I'm not insinuating anything," Ransom disclaimed. "I merely wondered if you sought to improve your . . . means."

"You conceited bastard!" Cat huffed as she turned to stare at him. "And I suppose I am to better my circumstances at your hands . . . by playing the mistress! Is that it?" Cat saw Ransom's smile as a confirmation of her charges and leaped to her feet, fighting the urge to slap that grin from his face.

"I'll see that the horse is returned to Lord Claremont," she said through clenched teeth. Ransom, sprawled casually on the grass as though completely at ease, smiled more broadly. "I trust you can find your way home," she added, preparing to mount her horse.

"No, my lovely," Ransom said, finally getting to his feet. "We will ride back to the cottage together. Letting a little innocent like you out alone among the perils of the world would plague my conscience," he said with a chuckle.

Cat let him fall in step beside her, but spoke not another word, irritated at how easily she had lapsed into the old pattern of enjoying her time with him—until he emotionlessly offered to lead her into a life of disgrace. How difficult it was to accept the change in her status from a favored cabin boy to a faceless female who could be used and tossed aside. Her pride stinging, she held her chin high and studiously ignored him all the way back to the cottage.

She dismounted without speaking, but he would not let her go without a word.

"Cheer up, my love," he said, tilting her chin up with his fingers. "I'll be leaving soon."

Cat jerked her head away. "That's what you keep saying," she called as he urged his horse forward, "but I have yet to see you go!"

Cat slammed the door with relish, although she knew Ransom could not hear, and wandered sullenly into the parlor where Amelia was opening her correspondence. "Ah, Catherine," she said, glancing up at her niece before returning her attention to the page before her. "How was your ride?" Before Cat could answer, she added, "It is unseemly both to slam doors and to shout at one's companions, no matter how provoking they may be.

"My, my, look at this bill. Madame Roussard is certainly becoming expensive! If she thinks she can raise her prices just because Lady Lawton patronized her when she breezed through, well! We simply must have Mistress Shaw do our gowns from now on. I've said all along that her work is much more fashionable. What do you think, dear?"

"Whatever you wish, aunt," Cat said, throwing herself onto the divan and swinging her crop through the air.

"Please don't hit anything with that, dear," Amelia said from her position at the secretary. "Oh, an invitation from Lord Claremont. He's having a party! How lovely. I suppose it is in honor of his grace."

Cat groaned. "Then I'm not going."

"Don't be silly. I know how much you enjoy dancing, dear. And I know you will want to have a new gown made, although I'm sure you will outshine all the other girls, whatever you wear," Amelia said, smiling with the look of a cat in cream. "Oh, but I do love a party," she murmured, fanning herself with the invitation.

Cat, her mind's eye running over the other young ladies, both unmarried and wed, who would probably attend Lord Claremont's function, decided she might just have to make an appearance after all. But not to see Ransom. Certainly not to see him!

Chapter 18

Cat was not surprised to learn that Ransom had availed himself of Lord Claremont's offer and was now staying at the great house, but the news did little to improve her mood. When Amelia told her, she jabbed her spade viciously into the dirt as though to prick the blackguard's heart, a futile gesture, she was certain, for the man obviously possessed no such organ.

"Catherine, please control yourself," her aunt admonished mildly. "If you intend to destroy these seedlings, there's no point in repotting them. Perhaps I should get one of the gardeners to help me."

"No," Cat grumbled, realizing that she sounded like a sullen child. "It simply irks me to have that scoundrel so close. And why is he still here, anyway? If he has legitimate business, he's certainly taking his own sweet time about it! I've never known him to dally this long anywhere."

"Did you never consider that he may be staying here simply to see you?" Amelia said with a sly smile.

"Ha! Don't be absurd! The man has never been *that* interested in any female, and what he wants can be had on any dock," Cat added before catching herself.

Although her aunt's devotion to Ransom's shal-

low charms galled her, she had no desire to shock
or hurt the lady, so she had not breathed a word of
his recent untoward actions or his appalling proposition. If the truth be known, Cat was none too eager to reveal her own embarrassing . . . compliance
in his lovemaking, either, and so protected her own
peace of mind, and Amelia's, with her silence.

As she pressed a little too firmly on the dirt around
her tiny plant, Cat wondered if her willing response
to Ransom's caresses had given him the idea that
she would gladly be his mistress. Still, he had no
right to insult her so, and he certainly wouldn't wish
her such a life if he cared for her at all, Cat thought,
shaking her head. The life of a pampered, well-kept
woman was no more secure than that of a dock
whore, and a fall from grace could plunge any
woman dependent on male whims into a life not of
her own choosing.

"So you are at odds with him again?" Amelia
asked, breaking into Cat's reverie. "What has he
done now?" She was scooping up more soil, her
attention focused on her task as though Cat's answer mattered little. Her niece had to bite her
tongue.

With studied nonchalance, Cat shrugged. "I told
you I simply have no desire for the man's company.
He is an arrogant and conceited rogue."

"But you used to think he was wonderful."

"I was just a child, then. Any captain would have
been my hero," Cat answered scornfully.

"So he is not the man you thought he was?"
Amelia asked. Her brow furrowed in question, she
put down her spade to gaze at her niece.

"No, he is not! Oh, I don't know," Cat said,
shaking her head, unable to sort coherently through
her own jumbled feelings for Ransom.

"Or is it that you are not the boy you once were?"
Amelia mused softly.

"I tell you, he is just an irritating boor now, and if I hear one more word about him, I will surely scream!" Cat said vehemently.

Her aunt only chuckled. "Well, I think we should wait until you are not so angry with him before we do any more potting," she said gently as she took off her gloves and looked disapprovingly at Cat's efforts. "Perhaps an afternoon call will drive away your blue devils. Come, let us abandon our gardening today and go for a visit!" she urged.

Although Amelia finally coaxed her niece into paying a call at the Grayson plantation, the visit, far from cheering Cat, put her into an even blacker mood.

The outing seemed doomed from the moment the landau entered the curving driveway of the Grayson home and they spied the unmistakable pink and green equipage of the Montrief sisters ahead of them. Cat groaned aloud, but they could hardly turn back at that point, so they were soon taking tea with Daphne, Elizabeth, their cousin Charlotte and Aunt Immaline, along with Mrs. Grayson and her three unmarried daughters. The ladies' conversation immediately turned to Ransom, and like hungry dogs with a bone, they clung to that subject tenaciously.

"I hear he's as rich as a Creole," gushed Immaline as she stuffed her mouth with powdered cakes.

Cat nearly hooted in disbelief. She had kept her lips clamped tightly shut under Amelia's nervous gaze as the assembled ladies admired Ransom's looks, charm, and title, but this was too much. With a determined sigh, Cat sought to change the topic. "Has anyone yet seen the new play Hobson's presenting?" she ventured. A few murmured no's testified to the general lack of interest, before Daphne steered the way back to the main subject.

"I hear his grace simply *loves* the theater. We really must get a party together."

"Oh, yes," chimed in Charlotte, and the voices became enthusiastic again.

Cat grimaced in disgust. If only Courtney were here, she thought, wishing wholeheartedly for her friend to appear. Courtney Westland, a red-haired beauty of seventeen years, shared Cat's sense of humor and disdain for ceremony and, if present, she would probably have voiced her exasperation with the conversation in no uncertain terms. Cat smiled to herself at the notion, but thoughts of Courtney brought on a twinge of guilt.

Courtney was her best friend, and yet, anxious to avoid any questions or teasing concerning Ransom, Cat had not visited her since his arrival. Granted, they did not see each other frequently because they lived a fair distance apart, but if everyone was talking about the duke, Courtney would soon hear of him and wonder why Cat had not sought to share her confidences.

Cat frowned but shook away her guilt with the hope that Courtney was too busy with her own family to take notice. For now, Cat would have to make do without her friend, and since the discussion continued in the same revolting vein, she attempted to engage Sir Grayson's elderly mother in private speech. As the lady was deaf, Cat did not meet with great success, so she simply concentrated on sipping her tea, trying her best to ignore the comments of those around her. She was not allowed even that small measure of peace, however, for the Montrief sisters had not forgotten who had introduced them to the duke.

"But Catherine, you and Amelia were dining with him at the Golden Bell. Surely you can tell us more about him," said Elizabeth.

"Yes, and didn't he take supper at your home? How could you keep such a visitor all to yourself?" Immaline asked maliciously.

Cat squirmed in her seat as all eyes swiveled in her direction. She groped for words, uncertain exactly what to say. Her rage at Ransom demanded that she tell them he was a cold, unprincipled deceiver, yet she hesitated, unwilling to expose him and unable to fabricate glowing tales of his virtue.

Just as her long pause was becoming embarrassing, Amelia came to the rescue, reciting her usual litany of praise for the duke while doing nothing to discourage the wildest speculation of her audience. When Immaline again mentioned Ransom's supposed wealth, Amelia waved a hand as though it were boundless. "Oh, he has a plantation on Windlay, a shipping business, and goodness knows what else," she said.

"The Du Prey holdings were vast," Grandmama Grayson shouted, having caught the name often enough to finally glean a measure of the conversation.

Cat gritted her teeth as she listened to their nonsense. Although she disdained the discussion, she had to bite her tongue many times to avoid jumping in, especially after she heard a particularly absurd comment. When Immaline said, "The man is an inveterate gambler who loses enormous sums on the turn of a card," Cat nearly leaped from her chair to argue that it just wasn't so.

For, while few of the ladies present had ever even spoken with Ransom, Cat sometimes knew what he would say *before* he spoke. She had rubbed his tired shoulders, brought him coffee in the cold and rain, seen him bathe. Surely not even his lovers could claim a closer relationship in most regards, she thought irritably, for despite her anger with him, Cat remained very proprietary about her captain.

However, she was certainly unaware of her feelings. She only knew she was heartily sick of the conversation and the company, and before Immaline could quiz her again, she reminded Amelia that they really must be going, with a determination that bordered on the grim.

Even Amelia dared not bring up the afternoon's fiasco, although Cat thought she caught her aunt smiling several times later in the day. By evening, Cat retired to her bedroom in disgust, but she could find no peace there, either. That night her dreams were haunted by snatches of the afternoon's conversation and visions of Ransom, who appeared in various incarnations as a dear friend who laughed at the descriptions of himself she passed along to him, a cold seducer who left his mistress after a few nights of pleasure, and the embodiment of all the virtues with which he had been credited by the hopeful ladies at tea.

Cat tossed and turned restlessly, raging at the thought that the rogue could intrude so thoroughly into her activities, her conversations, and even, it seemed, her dreams.

No dreams troubled Ransom's slumber, but he woke early. After a tiresome evening spent listening to stories of Lord Claremont's youth, he had retired sooner than usual only to rise before dawn, unused to such a great amount of sleep. Even the servants were not about when he dressed quietly, enjoying the cool of the lingering darkness.

Ransom slipped from the silent house with the idea of taking a stroll around the grounds, but his feet strode unerringly toward the Molesworth cottage, where Catherine, presumably still wrathful over his questions of the other day, would be abed. He found the picture that thought formed in his head—of her in slumber—enticing to contemplate.

The walk was pleasant, and Ransom soon left the main road to strike through the gardens that marked the rear of Amelia's property. Moving silently through the trees, he decided that he should have a tour during the daylight hours, preferably with Catherine and not her aunt, he noted as he imagined the expedition culminating in a soft, grassy nook where he could enjoy her charms more fully.

Although he still had not pieced together the puzzle behind his lady, he had been heartened by her response to his proposition. If she were truly one of Devlin's spies, surely a position as his mistress would be her goal. Instead, he could swear she was the outraged innocent she appeared. Still, she was hiding something . . .

Ransom had no plans but to wander by the cottage in his walk, enjoying the break of day. He certainly did not expect any of the occupants of the house to be up and about, and had no wish to startle any of the servants, so he skirted the edge of the terrace, intending to return to the main road. He took a moment, though, to enjoy the perfume of the gardenias and roses that surrounded the rear of the house, for they reminded him of Catherine, who always carried the hint of those fragrant blooms about her.

Shaking his head at his own whimsy, Ransom suddenly stopped in his tracks, for a sound that was not made by bird or animal broke the stillness. He moved instinctively back into the darkness, peering at the rear of the cottage. For a long moment all was silent, as though the noise had been a trick of his imagination, but Ransom knew better. Something stirred in the shadows close to the house.

He watched from the tamarinds as a shadowy figure slipped across the terrace. He moved with it, trying to catch a glimpse, then looked again, closer, to be certain there was no mistaking his subject before he followed.

Chapter 19

Cat climbed gingerly from the natural terrace and glanced up and down the short stretch of deserted beach. Dawn was just a pale ghost on the horizon, but she wanted to make sure no one was about in her tiny hidden cove where she liked to swim.

Amelia certainly did not know, for even that open-minded lady would not approve of her niece, stripped down to her chemise, striking out to sea in long, swift movements. With that in mind, Cat had limited this one carryover from her former life, but there were times when she simply had to feel the cold, clean salt water washing over her, had to cut through it with strong strokes until her heart pounded and she finally floated on the surface, spent.

Cat eyed the dark water longingly as she removed her slippers. Next, gleaming in the dim light, came her knife, the lovely silver blade Ransom had given her. She now carried the gift she had once cherished, out of habit—for protection, Cat told herself as she placed it atop her stockings. With unconscious grace, she stretched upright again, slipping off her gown and carefully spreading it over everything.

Enjoying the feel of the air against her skin and

the smooth and pliant sand beneath her feet, Cat slowly walked toward the ocean and sighed with pure pleasure as the water lapped about her legs. She waded ever deeper into the waves in the hopes that the swim would soothe her—and wash that devil Ransom from her thoughts.

As her sure strokes cut through the blue-green waters, Ransom, his tall form barely visible, climbed down the terraced earth and seated himself casually next to her clothing. Blending in with the shadows, he leaned back on his elbows, his eyes never leaving the dim shape in the waves, and tried to identify the strange feelings coursing through him.

When he had seen Catherine slipping warily from the cottage at this hour, he had followed her to the grove, not quite sure what the lady was about. All his suspicions had returned with remarkable speed, and he had wondered if she had an assignation set with a lover or, worse, one of Devlin's people. It would be easy for a ship to anchor off this cove, he thought grimly.

No one else appeared on the small deserted beach, however, and it gradually dawned on Ransom that Catherine had gone alone to swim.

Amazement hit him first, for despite his growing familiarity with the lady, she still surprised him at every turn. Then, briefly, he was relieved that she was not meeting anyone. But that emotion, too, was soon overshadowed by another: anger. He knew the sea and how quickly it could turn against one. The pull of the tide or the crash of a wave could send a lone swimmer down to his death, not to mention the sharks and poisonous stingarees that roamed these waters.

Fast on the heels of his anger, though, was appreciation for her bravery and skill. The woman was so damn unusual; every part of her seemed designed to pique his interest. And while on the subject of

parts . . . the desire that she always engendered was
shooting through him even as he sought to quell it.

It had rushed over him when she first began to
remove her clothes on the beach, nearly sending him
after her like a horned youth, for her graceful dis-
robing affected him more profoundly than any
brothel temptress or coy mistress ever could. His
breath in his throat, Ransom had watched her walk
to the water, admiring the long, slim legs and yearning to remove the chemise that hugged her breasts
and brushed her thighs. Even now he felt a need for
her as she rose from the waves, not unlike Venus,
the thin undergarment molded to her breasts.

He watched her casually push the hair from her
eyes as she stood in waist-deep water surrounded
by the pale light of sunrise. Then he saw something
else beside her in the water. At first Ransom thought
it was a slow-moving sea cow, but soon he recognized the shape of a playful porpoise. As the animal
ventured closer, he watched Catherine reach out to
touch the wet skin. Laughing aloud as it nudged
her, she lost her footing, went down for a dunking,
and stood again, throwing her arm along the porpoise's flank.

Ransom, never a superstitious sort, for one brief
instant nearly believed in sirens as he watched Catherine Amberly charm the fish from the sea. Although he had observed many porpoises, considered
by some sailors to be bearers of good luck, he had
never seen one frolicking with a human being as
though the two were kindred spirits.

He watched in wonder as Catherine and the animal splashed about together in the magical glow of
dawn, the great beast nudging against her and playfully knocking her back into the water like some giant pup. As he gazed at the fantastic scene, he was
conscious that the sound of the splashing and Catherine's throaty laughter wafting along the breeze

were affecting him in some way he could not name.
He had identified all the emotions that she sent
rushing through him, but this last one eluded him,
and with sudden irritation, he decided that too much
introspection made for ill luck.

Taking a deep breath, he tried to ignore whatever
feeling it was that seeped into his bones at the sound
of her merriment and instead concentrated on getting a good glimpse of the porpoise. Perhaps aware
of his study, or mayhap in response to a call from
another of its kind, the animal suddenly swam away
with a shake of its tail in farewell, leaving Ransom
to wonder if he had dreamed the whole enchanting
episode.

A smile lingering on her face, Cat turned back to
the shore, hugging her experience with the porpoise
to her tightly as something she would never forget
and regretting that she couldn't share it with anyone. Still thinking of her delightful encounter and
watching her step through the waves, she was nearly
out of the water, the sea swirling round her shapely
calves, before she realized that her captain was
seated casually on a rocky outcropping in front of
her. Her heart leaped in her chest and her smile
sparkled as his name pounded in her blood like
primitive drumbeats.

Did you see it? she wanted to ask, to share the
thrill of the porpoise with him, but all that had
passed between them stood in her way, slowing her
steps and wiping the greeting from her lips. Ransom
answered her first, unguarded smile with a lazy grin
while his gaze leisurely caressed every inch of her
body. Cat felt her knees grow weak before she realized just how little she was wearing.

The thin, wet chemise clung to her skin and rode
high on her thighs, threatening to expose more than
her long legs as she walked out of the water. Her
heart began tripping along at an alarming pace, and

she felt a slow, deadly heat coursing through her limbs, while her mind, which threatened to abandon coherent thought at any moment, noted in passing that she was melting fast and he had not even touched her.

Reason returned when she noticed that he was seated next to her clothing, and the heat of her anger replaced the more dangerous warmth that had surged through her. The devil had sneaked up on her to lounge about on the beach and watch her bathe, as though she actually were his mistress! It was bad enough that he spied on her, but if he thought to make her stand here, wet and nearly naked, under his perusal, he was sadly mistaken! She stiffened with determination as she stalked toward him. "If you are finished gawking, I would like my clothes," she hissed though clenched teeth.

"Hello, my love," he said softly, surprised at the catch in his voice.

"I want my clothes."

"Certainly." Ransom swept his hand toward the pile beside him, and Cat lunged for her dress, sending a slipper flying into the sand. With a mumbled oath, she flung the dress over her head, thrusting her arms through the sleeves with enough force to burst the seams. "May I?" Ransom asked, and Cat stopped fighting with the back of her dress long enough to look at him, down on one knee in the sand, holding her slipper. The infamous eyebrow was poised in question, while the lazy grin was spreading across his face.

"No, you may not!" Cat declared, stamping her bare foot for emphasis. With a nonchalant shrug, Ransom rose gracefully to his feet, slipper in hand.

Cat had prepared several scathing speeches concerning his proposal, his character, and his lineage, but all flew from her mind now that he stood before her. "You have molested and insulted me!" she sputtered. "And now you have sunk to spying upon my bath!"

"Perhaps you should bathe somewhere . . . less public," Ransom suggested with a grin.

"You blackguard! You have not one shred of decency!" Cat shouted as she hopped on one foot, angrily jamming on a slipper.

"I've neither molested nor insulted you, my love, though I do admit to spying on your bath, quite unintentionally, I assure you."

Cat was caught off guard by his words, spoken softly and with a hint of humor. She nearly lost her balance as she gaped at him, and Ransom chuckled softly at the look on her face. "Now you are saying that your odious offer was not an insult?" she gasped. "Why, you—"

"I never offered you a position as my mistress," Ransom said innocently. "You are the one who made the suggestion, not I."

"Ha!" Cat grabbed her other slipper and put it on her sandy foot. "You did not deny your words yesterday!"

"You seemed to be enjoying yourself thoroughly. Why should I spoil it?"

"Oh!" Cat groaned in disgust. Ignoring him, she reached for her remaining garments, and for a moment there was a glint of silver in the early light as her fingers closed around the blade he had given her. Startled, she looked up at him, fearing that he had noticed the knife, but Ransom's eyes had apparently remained on her face. She thrust her hands behind her back and glared at his warm brown eyes, the corners of which were creasing into tiny wrinkles.

"I regret that I said anything to offend you," he said with mock solemnity. The ring of truth underneath the humor made Cat eye him dubiously. Of all the conversations she had imagined having with him—in which she destroyed him with a few well-chosen words—she never expected to hear him apologize.

"Yes, I can see that," Cat finally said sarcastically. "You look *so* contrite." Ransom threw back his head and laughed, and the warm, familiar sound was almost her undoing, for despite her words, Cat's anger was nearly spent. No longer raging against Ransom, she unconsciously raised a hand to her hair, realizing how utterly dreadful she must appear in her wet, sandy, and disheveled state.

Ransom caught the meaning behind her gesture and grinned, for she looked beautiful. Tiny wisps of hair were drying golden in the morning's glow, framing a face flushed delicate pink with her anger. The way her dress clung wetly to certain prominent parts of her body was so unerringly provocative that he could only marvel that, even at her worst, Catherine Amberly was more seductive than any woman he had ever known.

"What would you have me do . . . to make amends?" Ransom asked, his voice becoming a low purr as he took a step toward her.

"Not that!" Cat snapped, correctly interpreting his inclinations. The resulting look of innocence on his face nearly wrested a laugh from her. You had better quit now, before he somehow gains the advantage again, Cat told herself, one eye on the glowing horizon. As it was, he had already delayed her. She would have to sneak into the cottage in her sorry condition and hope that the ever-alert Isaac was not about; she had no time to stand here fencing with Ransom.

"Dare I hope that you will change your mind?" he asked wickedly, stepping closer.

As she gazed at those inviting brown eyes and warm smile, Cat knew that her limbs would soon turn to liquid if she let herself trust him. Her reckless heart wanted to take him at his word, to believe that he never thought to degrade her with an indecent proposal, but her head, thankfully if only temporarily in control, would not.

"No, there is no hope," Cat said saucily as she seized her remaining possessions from the sand. "I have no intention of changing my mind about your insults or your . . . amends! Why, I would sooner have a viper in my bed!" With a toss of her head, Cat stalked off, proud of her cool control. It was time she took a lesson from Ransom and reined in her volatile emotions; let him be the one left standing to stew in his own juices! Even as she congratulated herself, she missed a stride at his parting words.

"Viper in your bed," he repeated. "And what sent your thoughts straying to the bedroom, my love?"

Chapter 20

All the way back to the cottage, Cat mulled over Ransom's words, especially his denial that he had offered her a position as his mistress. Once back inside her room she sighed aloud as she considered the possibility that he was telling the truth. Perhaps she really had misconstrued his words, and he, amused by her antics as usual, had let her play out the hand, enjoying the entertainment she provided.

Cat shrugged as she sat before her mirror, absently brushing out the tangled locks, still slightly damp from her swim. She was chagrined at the thought that she might be taking Ransom—and herself—all too seriously—a result of becoming a lady, no doubt. With a shake, she reminded herself that only a few months ago she had been a ragged lad, telling ribald jokes with a group of coarse sailors more dear to her than the most polished gentlemen. Surely, the fun-loving boy she had once been had not entirely disappeared.

Maybe she was just too tetchy around Ransom—far more thin-skinned than she had ever been before, Cat thought as she recalled how he used to tease her when she was a lad. He was partially to blame, however, for the man seemed to excel in getting her goat. Had she been more tolerant before, Cat wondered with a frown, or was she losing her sense of humor?

That would never do, she decided, rising from her dressing table and walking to the bed, where last night her maid had laid out a lovely morning dress. As she picked up the fresh gown, Cat resolved not to take Ransom so seriously. She was not ready yet, but she did not rule out the possibility of accepting his apology.

After all, she reasoned, Ransom did seem sincere. She could not help the quickening of her pulse at the memory of his words, his grin, and those warm brown eyes. He said he didn't mean to offend her, and so it must be true, for she didn't think Ransom was a liar. Still—she paused as the gown fell about her slim body—he was masquerading as a duke, certainly not the act of an honest man.

Cat raised a finger to her lips, pondering the apparent contradictions in his character, and her brow furrowed slightly as she once again wondered just how well she knew her captain. She had seen him so clearly before, when they'd shared their days and nights aboard the *Reckless*. Oh, she had always sensed his complexities, but she felt she knew Ransom better than any other person did, with the possible exception of Bosun. Now she was not so positive. He was doing and saying things that struck her as odd, and she was not sure if he had changed or if the difference lay with her . . . or if she had never really known him.

Clinging to her memory of Ransom at his best, Cat refused to consider the last possibility. If he began acting strangely again, then she must laugh at his absurdities and ignore him, instead of letting her temper rule. And it would be best to avoid being alone with him, she thought with a shiver, just in case his mind turned again to seduction.

With these plans firmly decided, Cat found her mood improved, and she soon made her cheerfulness known to the entire household. Marie, unfortunately, was caught unawares by Cat's display of happiness, and, startled by an unusual piercing sound from the upper apartments, dropped a tray of china. As she gathered up the broken bits, the maid was heard mumbling to herself certain uncomplimentary comments concerning any lady who whistled while Amelia raised her eyes from the book she was reading and smiled slyly to hear the notes of a jaunty jig coming from her niece's room.

Pleased by Cat's change of mood, Amelia coaxed her into going to town, and the ladies spent the afternoon visiting the local shops. Cat enjoyed herself thoroughly, her spirits buoyed by her new attitude toward her captain, while Amelia chatted gaily as though her heart, too, was lifted by some secret pleasure.

The sun shone brightly as they strolled along the tidy streets of Bridgetown, and it seemed as though nothing could alter Cat's new mood, not even a brief encounter with the Montrief sisters. Her pleasure waned, however, when Amelia stopped to see an old friend and business associate of her husband.

Orin Tawpenny, a friendly enough sort whom Cat had met before, was not the source of her dismay, nor was his secretary, a nondescript gentleman whose name she had forgotten, the cause of her displeasure. It was the party exiting Mr. Tawpenny's office whom she eyed askance.

Ransom, grinning ear to ear when he saw them, was cordiality itself. "Why, Miss Amberly," he said, bending over her hand, "if I didn't know better, I would swear you were following me!"

His smooth appropriation of her own accusation, made that very dawn, had Cat gritting her teeth in frustration even as she suspected him of somehow engineering this coincidental meeting. "Your grace," she said through clenched teeth, "it does seem that you're always underfoot!"

Uncomfortable with such banter—directed toward a duke no less—Mr. Tawpenny laughed nervously and hoped that his grace would not blame him in any way for the young lady's disrespect.

"Why, it seems only hours since we last met," Cat added dryly, her smile less than congenial.

"Does it?" Ransom asked with a genuine smile. "To me, the hours not graced by your sweetness pass like days."

Cat bit back a retort while Mr. Tawpenny tried his best to herd them from his offices before any further words were exchanged. "But, Orin dear, I've come to see you," Amelia protested, refusing to be budged, even though dear Orin looked less than thrilled at her announcement.

"If Mr. Tawpenny is busy," Ransom said, "perhaps I can persuade you ladies to accompany me on a visit to my ship."

"Oh, how very kind of you," Amelia exclaimed while Cat nearly gasped in horror. "I would love to see your ship, your grace, and I'm sure it would be most educational, but I'm afraid I did want to speak with Orin. Catherine dear, do go; I know you will enjoy it."

"No, really, I can't," Cat said, pulling Amelia's sleeve in an attempt to catch her eye.

"Oh, I insist," her aunt replied, taking the hand that was desperately trying to get her attention and gently patting it. "I simply won't have you miss such a lovely excursion on my account."

Cat's repeated attempts to avoid the engagement met with more of the same: Amelia, smiling sweetly, would have none of it, while Ransom's grin returned in full force. Finally, Cat gave in, but as she left Mr. Tawpenny's offices, her arm entwined in her captain's, she did not know with whom she was angrier, Ransom, who was his usual suave and insufferable self, or Amelia, who appeared to be throwing her niece at his head at every opportunity.

When they arrived at the *Reckless*, Cat could not subdue a surge of excitement at seeing her old ship, but the thrill was combined with trepidation that some member of the crew would recognize her.

Her fears proved groundless, however, vanishing the moment she set foot on the deck, for by wearing a dress she guaranteed that not one sailor observed anything but the curves that it graced. The men either ignored her totally or ogled her with a shameless admiration that saw no further than the outline of her gown.

Cat's lingering doubts were put to rest by Bosun, who did not look beyond the fact that she was female, a situation which obviously made him uncomfortable and disinclined to introduce himself. Ransom collared him, however, and Bosun ambled over, putting on his most ferocious grimace, intended, Cat assumed, to scare the daylights out of any sensible female. His gruffly mumbled greeting sounded more like a growl, but Cat smiled sunnily in affectionate pleasure and held out her hand to him, a response that so surprised him that he momentarily lost his composure. Cat's lips twitched as she watched those heavy eyebrows rise while he fumbled over her hand, then scooted off as if not sure what to do with a woman of quality who was not the slightest bit thrown by him.

Breathing easier, Cat let herself enjoy the visit to her former home. With a nostalgic smile, she ran her hand over a thick ratline, realizing how very rough it now seemed to her tender flesh. How long had it taken to transform her work-hardened hands into a soft-skinned tribute to idleness? she wondered curiously as she looked down at them, remembering full well how Amelia had not let her remove her gloves until they had reached their current silky-smooth texture.

Cat only half listened as Ransom explained the

workings of the ship, enjoying the sound of his voice and his tall presence beside her. When they walked over to the rail, Cat decided that the small beribboned chip hat adorning her tresses would have to go, and giving a few tugs to the pins, she slipped it from her head, shaking her golden hair out so she could feel the wind.

Her unconscious gestures told Ransom that she was a woman who enjoyed the feel of different textures beneath her fingers and the stirring of the wind in her hair. Although her movements did not give away her identity, they spoke loudly of her sensual nature, sending a surge of desire through her companion, who imagined her response to more . . . concentrated stimulation.

So it was that her tour of the ship—an expurgated version for ladies that avoided the less attractive sections of the vessel—ended in the captain's cabin, and Cat found herself staring at Ransom's wide bed, her thoughts uncontrollably drawn to memories of him in it.

Cat heard the door shut quietly behind them, and her nerves, already tingling, sounded a warning that rang through her blood and positively exploded in her ears. Still, it took her some moments to tear her eyes away from the familiar bed and the image of Ransom sleeping naked there, a blanket slipped carelessly over him. What had unnerved her then made her knees weak now, for the thought of that bare chest tossed her insides with a mixture of fear, embarrassment, and desperate longing.

With an effort, she tore her eyes away and turned, only to run into the object of her thoughts, who had been standing behind her, and was now, thanks to her misstep, poised just inches away.

"I really must be going," Cat choked out. "Amelia . . ."

"So soon?" A hand reached up to caress her

cheek, and she knew she could not be trusted to look into his eyes. She dropped her gaze. It rested on the trim waistcoat in front of her, a seemingly safe sight until her traitorous senses remembered what the skin beneath that coat and the thin material of his shirt would feel like. Her heart pounding, Cat shook her head as if to clear away such ideas, thereby dislodging his hand.

Her movement made no matter, for he simply ran his lean fingers along her neck, sending chills of pleasure through her flesh, while her thoughts, far from abandoning their embarrassing bent, focused more firmly on their subject, and she battled a desire to press *her* lips to his neck. What would it taste like? Warmth and cologne and that indefinable smell that was Ransom?

Like a shield, she clutched her hat before her, creating a space between them, for she knew if she touched his body again, she would be lost. By now, her breath was coming shakily with the effort of fighting her desires, and the cabin seemed stuffy and small. Ransom's deft fingers were still roaming her neck, traveling to her hairline as he bent over to barely touch his lips to her forehead.

With a will born of panic, Cat broke free, stepping back and gasping for breath. ''Please take me to Amelia now,'' she whispered, and the simple request took on the color of a plaintive plea. For a long minute he stood gazing at her, his face impassive and inscrutable, then his voice, deeper than usual, grounded out a ''Certainly'' that, although it sounded none too pleased, was the response she desired. With a slight hint of resignation, he held out his arm, and they exited the cabin.

''Well, did she seem familiar to you?'' Ransom asked his first mate, his voice grating with irritation. ''Not a bit,'' Bosun said, shaking his head. ''A pretty enough little thing, though, and spirited, too, I'll bet.''

''Yes . . . spirited,'' Ransom repeated with mild distaste as he stood at the rail.

''She doesn't seem like Devlin's sort,'' Bosun offered. When he received no response, he shook his head again. It was not like the captain to moon over a female, no matter how pretty, but it looked as if he was doing just that. With a grunt of wonder, the first mate walked away, leaving his captain to gaze moodily out over the waves.

Lost in thought, Ransom barely noticed Bosun's departure. A slight wind ruffled his dark locks, and he was suddenly struck by the image of Catherine's golden hair swept by the breeze.

The memory both delighted and frustrated him. It would have been so easy to take what he wanted today in his cabin, for Ransom knew that Miss Amberly's reluctance, whether real or feigned, could have been overcome with little effort. The lady was blessed with a sensual, perhaps even passionate, nature that could not be disguised, and her earlier responses to his caresses had only whetted his appetite. Unfortunately, his plans for today had been thwarted by her expression when she begged to go. She had resembled a frightened rabbit caught in a snare, and he, exhibiting some kind of strange weakness, had done her bidding instead of taking her to his bed.

So he still lusted after her. Damn! He was not used to his body making such imperious demands. It was inconvenient and idiotic, and he only hoped it did not cloud his judgment, for although he had not admitted as much to his first mate, he was fast reaching the point where he did not give a damn who Miss Amberly was, as long as he had her . . . and soon.

Chapter 21

As a precaution, Cat reminded Isaac that she was not at home to Lord Du Prey before she set out for the farthest orchard to pick oranges. Despite her often enjoyable interludes with Ransom, she had no desire to spend any more time cultivating a relationship that could go nowhere and that had the potential to make her uncomfortable in any number of ways. These coincidental meetings, coupled with Ransom's visits, were becoming all too frequent. Although her heart might yearn for him, her brain resounded with warnings, and her brain, thankfully, was in control . . . for now.

Cat hitched the donkey to a small cart, which she loaded with baskets and a ladder, and headed toward the fields, looking forward to a peaceful day without the temptation of her captain's company.

In the stillness of the grove, the rustling of the donkey's movements was the loudest sound, the soft drone of the bees a peaceful hum. Cat looked for fruit that was perfectly ripe, as Amelia had taught her, and after filling the first basket, she plopped down in the tall grass.

Flushed pink by the heat and her exertions, she unfastened the top buttons on her muslin gown and lay down on her back, watching the sun play through the leaves overhead. Turning on her stom-

171

ach, she glanced at the small rise along the tree line, wondering what was beyond and debating whether to go exploring. It was probably just Lord Claremont's sugar fields, she thought idly, then smiled as she realized her view would be vastly improved if she were up higher . . . in the tree, for instance.

With a mischievous grin, Cat sat up and looked around her before getting to her feet. Not a soul stirred the grasses of the orchard or watched her swing gracefully onto the lowest-hanging tree branch. From there, she stepped lightly onto the next branch and finally took a seat with a view of the orchard and beyond. Who needs ladders when they have climbed among the rigging to touch the clouds? she thought with a smile.

As she suspected, the rise barely hid the long stalks of sugarcane, and, her curiosity satisfied, she knew she should get down, but her perch was comfortable, and the oranges smelled tangy and sweet among the greenery. She plucked a ripe one nudging her shoulder and, taking a deep breath, looked lazily over the orchard. She had to stifle the shriek of dismay that rose in her chest at the sight that met her eyes. Ransom, dressed handsomely in brown breeches and a matching coat thrown casually over his arm, was strolling through the tall grass as if he owned the place.

As Cat saw it, she had two choices, both ignominious. She could stay where she was and hope against hope that her persistent captain would fail to see her, or she could leap to the ground, undoubtedly providing him with an interesting view of her skirts that no decent woman would think of allowing. But then, she did not claim to be decent, she thought wryly. As Cat wavered between the two choices, she watched Ransom unerringly approach the tree in which she was seated and look up at her.

"Do you want to come down or shall I come up?"

The grin on his face was so engaging that Cat could only smile back at him in exasperation. "Well, come up, then, if you must," she said. He did, in a smooth motion of long limbs and lean muscle, and her heart beat just a little faster to have him seated next to her up above the earth.

"My God, I don't think I've been up in a tree since the day I hid from my tutor and pelted him with plums, a deed for which I received more than adequate punishment," he said, and Cat laughed at the thought of a small Ransom misbehaving. She realized, with a shock, that she knew next to nothing about Ransom Du Prey. Oh, she knew his ways, his humor, his temperament, but what of his past, his family, his childhood escapades? Where had he grown up? When did he take to the sea, and why? Such questions were never asked aboard a sailing ship, where an unwritten code prohibited interrogation of your shipmate, yet she could certainly ask them now.

She sneaked a peek at him from under lowered lashes and caught him contemplating the countryside. He was leaning against the trunk of the tree, one arm resting casually on a knee, one firmly muscled leg swinging free. The finely tuned body was relaxed, his strong chest rising and falling with each deep breath of the scented air, and as Cat watched him, her heart began beating so loudly she was sure he must hear it. She looked quickly out over the cane fields and concentrated on keeping her breathing even. Good God, what was happening to her? She had reached a sorry state if one look at her captain left her weak. Weak-witted! she amended, giving herself a mental shake, and when she spoke her voice was calm and collected. "Where is your home?" she ventured.

"Wherever my ship is."

"I meant, where did you grow up?" Cat persisted.

"In the Midlands," he answered indifferently, and she remembered that the man before her was masquerading as a duke. It would be unlikely that the captain of the *Reckless*, whoever he was, would tell the truth about his past when he was living a lie. With a disappointment that surprised her, she dropped her inquiry and gazed out over the orchard.

"And you, my intriguing Miss Amberly, from where do you hail?"

Cat caught a caustic note in his voice and eyed him skeptically before answering just as vaguely, "Hampshire." He smiled slightly without even glancing her way, his eyes on the orchard. "You have a good orange crop here," he said, nodding at the surrounding trees.

"Oh, yes," Cat enthused. "Aunt Amelia's oranges have the most wonderful flavor. Once in a while you might find one that looks perfect yet is sour inside, but for the most part, they are all sweet."

"Hmmm. And what about you, my love? You are all fire and mystery on the outside. What are you really like . . . underneath?" His voice was deep and low and spread over her like warm molasses, while his eyes held hers, the look in them setting her pulse to hammering again. She decided there was something in the way he said "my love" that triggered all her bodily fluids, and she really should not let him call her that, for the sake of decorum and her own well-being.

He reached over to run his finger down her cheek, and Cat nearly fell off the branch.

"Your grace," she began.

"Please, call me Ransom."

"Ransom." His name, which she'd savored so

many times in her thoughts, sounded strange when spoken aloud. "Ransom, I really must return to the cottage." Without waiting for his response, Cat stepped to a lower branch and jumped to the ground, landing neatly on her feet and looking up at him.

Ransom could not repress a quick shout of laughter at her agile escape, for being with her made him feel like a boy again, without a care in the world. The pins in her hair had loosened, allowing her golden tresses to fall in waves about her face, while the smile she sent him sparkled mischievously.

Cat never knew what made her run; perhaps the look of devilish exuberance on his face—an expression she had never seen before, but which recalled their old friendship—or maybe her own soaring spirits were to blame. Whatever the provocation, she began running through the tall grass, along the wide expanse between the rows of orange trees, and Ransom gave chase.

Cat was hindered by her skirts and he easily caught her, but she broke free to run again, laughing and shouting, until Ransom grasped her waist and pulled her toward him with a shout of triumph. Still laughing and trying to catch her breath, Cat lifted her hand to push an errant lock of hair from her face, and suddenly she was in his arms.

It happened so fast. In an instant her feet were lifted off the ground and his mouth moved over hers with a passion that bore no resemblance to the gentle and deliberate kisses he had pressed upon her lips before. His arms, tight around her, loosened only long enough to let her drop sinuously down his body, but Cat did not feel the earth beneath her feet or the grass waving about her knees. She moved without thought or reason, instinctively throwing her arms around his neck and pressing against him.

His hands stroked her back, then traveled up to

cup her face almost roughly as his tongue plunged into her mouth, his lips moving over hers. Cat's breath came in gasps, and her fingers curled into his hair, threading through the dark silkiness, yet still she could not get enough of him and she frantically pressed her lips harder against his mouth, then his eyes and his cheek, as though to touch every part of those handsome features.

Ransom responded in kind. With a reckless passion that threatened to whirl out of control, his open lips moved along her neck, then again he kissed her, while he buried his hands in her hair and they dropped to their knees on the grass. His fingers moved to unbutton her dress as their mouths locked, broke apart and met again in a driving rhythm that seemed to propel them to the ground.

Cat did not notice the soft, tall blades giving way beneath her; she was conscious only of the lean, muscular body pressing against her and the feeling that it was not near enough. She ran her hands across his back, pulling him closer, and when his mouth moved along her cheek, she buried her face in his neck, pressing wet kisses along his throat. She was rewarded with a heart-stopping kiss before his fingers slid along her shoulder, slipping the gown to her waist, and she felt his hand, smooth and dry, against her naked breast. The sensation, so new and intimate, made her gasp aloud.

Ransom stilled her with his lips, delving deep into her inner recesses as his hands moved over her. She was shocked to feel his fingers against her nipple, but pressed against him, wild with longing. Her heart hammering in her chest, Cat was unable to think as her senses, alive as they had never been, held sway. Her hands coiled in Ransom's hair while his lips trailed along her shoulder, and she felt an exquisite jolt that stopped her breath when his hand moved down to cup her buttocks, pulling her against his hardness.

It was all too overwhelming for someone whose experience was limited to a few kisses, and when his lips moved down to her breast, Cat felt a jolt of another kind. The alien, warm wetness of his mouth over her nipple, and the resulting pull as he sucked gently at her breast, shocked her so that she struggled upright again, fighting for possession of her faculties.

Enmeshed deep in a passion the likes of which he had never known, Ransom was slow to respond to the arms that were no longer grasping and pulling him close, but pushing him away. Finally releasing her, he sat back and watched her fasten the top button of her dress with trembling hands, tears pooling at the corners of her eyes. "Catherine," he whispered, reaching up to caress her cheek.

Cat was so appalled at her own behavior she did not know whether to laugh or to scream. She was still breathing so hard that she would have been unable to speak had she thought of something to say. Helplessly, she struck blindly at Ransom's hand, then rose jerkily to her feet and fled, heedless of all but her escape.

Chapter 22

Cat closed her eyes and splashed cool water on her hot cheeks, letting it drip through her fingers and back into the washbasin. Straightening, she pressed a towel against her face and looked in the mirror. Was this Catherine Amberly? Her skin was flushed, but otherwise she looked the same. How then to explain her recent behavior, which bore more resemblance to that of an untamed animal than that of a woman?

With a sigh of defeat, Cat sank into a chair, the towel still clutched in her hands. What *had* happened? What *had* made her . . . Cat could not even finish the thought as the memory of herself, wild with passion, pulling at Ransom and gasping for breath, made her groan in embarrassment. She had wanted him so desperately, ached for him to do those things to her, longed to touch every inch of him—without a thought for the consequences.

She had lost all reason. Did this happen to everyone? Did fallen women fall because they yielded to some handsome blade's caresses, unable to help themselves? Something must be wrong with her, Cat decided.

Maybe her masquerade aboard the *Reckless* was to blame. Surely, she would not have succumbed so easily to Ransom if she had just met him, if she did not know him so well . . . if she did not love him so.

The words entered her consciousness against her will, for she had not allowed herself to examine her feelings for Ransom too closely since his precipitous return to her life. Now, however, she could no longer ignore the source of all her distress. If only she were not so hopelessly, helplessly in love with him.

Sighing, Cat admitted that she had probably fallen in love with him the first moment she saw him, and the situation had fluctuated from bad to worse ever since. Leaving the *Reckless* had done no good, for her love had skulked in the back of her heart, coloring her perceptions of every man she met while waiting to burst, full-blown, when her captain reappeared. What a traitorous organ the heart was, that it would not take direction from the head, she thought miserably, wondering with a kind of horror if she would love Ransom all her life.

Cat shuddered at the thought of that grim burden. Oh, when she was with Ransom, when he smiled at her, her heart soared, and sometimes when she thought of him, hugging the image of him close to her secret self, she was filled with wondrous joy. More often, however, her love brought her nothing but frustration and gloom, for it promised only heartache.

Cat remembered all too well how easily Ransom's coldness could cut her to the quick and how miserable she had felt when she'd finally broken away from him—for good, she thought. Yet here he was again, tormenting her with his presence . . . his caresses. If only he would leave her alone, she thought, indignant at his relentless pursuit.

Why, not too long ago she had been berating herself for taking him too seriously when, apparently, she had not taken him seriously enough! She was certain now that Ransom had designs on her virtue, and it appeared that he would not leave the island until he could claim it.

Cat felt righteous anger break through her depression and disgrace. He was toying with her, like a cat with a mouse, for she knew full well that he did not return her feelings. With a frown of distress, Cat made herself examine the facts: Ransom was a cold, heartless creature who would never love any woman. He thought them all boring and deceitful, and lest she let herself think that he felt differently about her, Cat reminded herself that if he cared for her at all he would not want to ruin her, something which it seemed he had every intention of doing.

Well, she would put a stop to his little plan, Cat decided. Avoiding him seemed impossible, but what if she told him outright that she no longer wished to see him? The idea tugged momentarily at her heart, but with fierce determination, Cat decided it was the only solution. With a gulp, she admitted that she could not trust herself with him, therefore, she must eliminate *him* from the picture entirely. Since she held out little hope of his imminent departure, and fate—or other, more corporeal parties, she suspected—seemed to conspire to throw them together, she must take matters into her own hands.

Cat was surprised at the relief she felt once her decision was made, but then, she was a woman of action, and to make a move, rather than blindly moaning in distress, suited her nature. Better to get the thing over with in one clean break than to spend her life mooning over the man, she decided firmly, before straightening her shoulders and folding the towel that had been clenched in her hands.

Walking to the window to take several deep breaths, Cat realized with surprise that the day was fast disappearing and she must hurry or be late for supper. Without even ringing for her maid, she quickly changed into a fresh gown and made her way to the dining room where Amelia was waiting.

"Ah, there you are, dear," said her aunt, her white brow wrinkled in worry. "I was just coming to check on you. Isaac said you rushed into the house earlier as though you were in some distress."

Isaac saw and said more than anyone should, Cat thought. "No, I'm fine," she answered with a reassuring smile before taking her seat.

"And famished, I hope, for the cook has outdone herself tonight," Amelia said. Cat smiled less enthusiastically this time as she wondered if she could even force down a bite. The afternoon's escapade and the ruminations that followed had left her with little appetite, but for appearance's sake she made an attempt to taste what the cook had worked so hard to prepare.

She tried the baby carrots, fresh from the garden and delicately seasoned with herbs, and ignored the mutton that seemed to lie heavily on her plate, and she was toying with some shrimp baked in a pastry when Amelia delivered a broadside attack.

"So, did your captain find you this afternoon?" she asked innocently.

Cat almost started from her seat. "What? Oh, yes, I . . . spoke to him briefly before coming home," she answered as nonchalantly as possible before taking a sudden interest in the asparagus.

"Good. I was thinking he must have missed you since he did not come back with you," Amelia said.

"Well, he decided to walk through Lord Claremont's fields," Cat responded between mouthfuls. "He is interested in that sort of thing, you know."

"Yes. He did say he had a plantation of his own." Amelia nodded. "I was just going out to the gardens when he arrived, so I directed him to the orchard. I thought to see him upon his return, so I did not stay to talk with him. I always like to see that handsome charmer,'' she confided.

Cat nearly gagged on the large bite of asparagus she had just taken, but picked up her fork for another.

''But, then, I did invite him to tea tomorrow, so I imagine we will have a nice little chat then.''

Cat's fork clattered to her plate.

The asparagus, never her favorite to begin with, seemed to lodge in her throat as she struggled to speak. ''You invited him to tea?'' Cat finally squeaked.

''Really, dear, I wish you would not talk with your mouth full,'' Amelia chided, her tiny brows drawing together in disapproval. ''I thought you had better table manners. Perhaps we need to brush up on the rules, for I certainly would not want you to embarrass yourself at a supper gathering.''

Cat simply stared at her aunt until the little lady became flustered. ''Well, good heavens, dear, I did not mean to insult you,'' she said.

''Aunt,'' Cat began, trying to gather her thoughts, ''you must stop trying to throw me together with Ransom.''

''Why, my dear,'' Amelia said, putting down her knife and fork, ''whatever makes you say such a thing? As if I would 'throw' you at anyone.''

''You know what I mean,'' said Cat softly, holding up a hand to stop the denial on Amelia's lips. Although she was not eager to argue with her aunt over Ransom's faults, some measure of the truth was called for before Amelia did further harm.

Taking a deep breath, Cat marshalled her thoughts and chose her words carefully. ''You think that Ransom—the duke—would be a matrimonial coup, and I really cannot blame you,'' she said seriously. ''He is handsome, he can be charming, and it would appear that he is wealthy—an attractive combination.

But believe me, I know this man. His opinion of women is . . . contemptible, and he is an accomplished rogue and seducer. He has no intention of ever marrying," Cat said.

"Nonsense," Amelia replied with surprising force as she turned her attention back to the meal. "Opinions can be changed, habits abandoned, and intentions altered, my dear child. I have not spent so much time in this world without learning a thing or two about people, and your captain is not as certain of things as you imagine him to be."

Cat sighed in frustration at her aunt's obstinacy while she watched her daintily consume a pear in mint sauce, their conversation apparently no longer of interest to her. How could she convince Amelia that Ransom was after naught but her maidenhead? With a shrug, Cat thought to let the matter drop, unwilling to reveal any more intimate proof of Ransom's intentions, but she made one more effort to curb Amelia's actions. "Aunt?"

"Yes, dear," Amelia answered without looking up from her pear.

"At least promise me that you will no longer invite him to the cottage," Cat pleaded.

"Why, Catherine, I'm surprised at your wanting to restrict my callers," Amelia answered blithely. "No one is forcing you to be here when he visits."

Cat frowned sourly. No one *was* forcing her to be present at tea tomorrow; that certainly was true. She could easily claim another engagement, but Cat bristled at the thought. She was not about to run and hide from Ransom like a scared rabbit! She would attend tomorrow's tea all right, she thought grimly, for she had something to get off her chest . . . and it would not be what that rogue wanted to hear!

Richard Blakely coolly admired his surroundings as he followed the manservant through William

Montgomery's plantation house. The residence might not be as grand as some others on the island, but it was still a far cry better than many of the places where Richard had served his master.

Dismissing the servant, Richard settled into his rooms, noting the absence of his host during his arrival. Well, let the man avoid him, for Richard certainly had no interest in befriending William Montgomery. He knew that despite an apparent distaste for his houseguest, Montgomery would cooperate, which was all that mattered. Indeed, Montgomery's only function would be to provide Richard entrée into the appropriate circles when the time came.

For now, Richard had no plans for socializing. His first matter of business was to gather information on Miss Amberly and assess the situation, work that he would do quietly, as he had no wish to be seen and recognized by Ransom—yet. Oh, Richard had formulated a plan already, in his usual efficient manner, and that scheme demanded that he be eventually noticed by Ransom, but it would be quite ineffective if he tipped his hand too early.

Chapter 23

When she rose the next morning, Cat found that the shock of her wanton behavior had begun to fade, leaving in its place a trace of nostalgia for the feelings of excitement and abandonment and an unexpected emptiness, as if she had woken from a particularly pleasant dream she could never recapture in her waking hours.

She shook aside the fancy, for although her distress had abated, her anger with Ransom remained. The insufferable snake had tried to seduce her, right there in the grass like a common field hand! Damn it, why did he always get the upper hand? He had the arrogance to lump all women together, yet was she any different from the others who melted in his embrace? Cat thought not, and the notion galled her.

Well, he would get some of his own back today, she resolved as she dressed in a silky pale pink dress dotted with roses. With perverse pleasure, she was determined to look her best, and she avoided helping her aunt, spending the afternoon instead with her book in the parlor.

She was so engrossed in reading that she started when the duke was announced. Although nothing in his demeanor or smile hinted at the intimacies they had shared, Cat frowned at his handsome face when he leaned over her hand. For the moment her wrath fled as memories of her behavior in the orchard flooded back, and she cringed in embarrassment. What must he think of her?

Cat could barely look at Ransom while he glanced at the book she had put aside and took a seat next to her. He nodded toward the volume of Greek, his smile soft and sincere. "Although you may not believe it, I'm impressed by your choice of reading material. You did not give me the chance to tell you when we'd discussed the matter previously," he added wryly.

"I don't believe it," Cat said, scowling. Ransom only shrugged casually in amusement.

"You are a woman of many skills," he said.

"And just what is that supposed to mean?" Cat asked.

"Nothing, my love. No innuendos or secret meanings were hidden in the words. I was simply complimenting you," Ransom said.

Cat's disgusted retort was halted by the arrival of Amelia, bustling into the parlor wreathed in smiles.

"Oh, how delightful! I see you two are carrying the conversation without me! Isaac," she called over her shoulder, and the manservant silently appeared with the heavily laden tea tray. "Catherine, please pour. Your grace, do sit down," she urged, her cheeks pink with delight at the cozy gathering.

Cat found the tea a stilted affair, and she sat straight in her chair, sipping the liquid with barely a glance at the two other parties. Amelia appeared to take no notice of Cat's silence, while Ransom did his best to charm her, to no avail. Soon the conversation drifted between Amelia and the duke while Cat sat mired in her own thoughts. She realized when she heard that deep voice, rich with appeal, that her plan was going to be difficult to execute, and she tried her best to harden her heart against the pull she could feel even now from across the room.

"Catherine . . . Catherine," Amelia repeated until Cat looked up in surprise, "his grace has expressed an interest in our gardens. Would you be so kind as to give him a tour?"

"Oh, yes, of course," Cat said softly, knowing that a stroll alone with Ransom would provide her with the perfect opportunity to give him the set-down she had planned. Unfortunately, the words she had rehearsed well into the wee hours of the morning had scattered from her memory like leaves tossed in the wind.

As Isaac cleared away the remains of tea, Cat rose to take Ransom's arm with a distracted air, not even noticing the slight frown of concern on his face as he watched her. With Amelia waving them off gaily, she walked with him into the sunshine, where she dropped his arm almost immediately, ostensibly to pick a bloom from along the terrace.

Stiff and businesslike, Cat led her captain along the paths beside her aunt's flowers and vegetables, giving a recitation worthy of a botanist, while her mind ran riot on another topic entirely: how to rid herself permanently of this man. "You might recognize the breadfruit," she said as she pointed to a tree with brownish-green round produce. "It was brought to—"

"Ah, yes, a most noteworthy specimen, but I find that my interest in the gardens is lagging," he said. "Perhaps if we stopped for a rest? Those cream pastries your aunt forced on me at tea lie heavy on my stomach," he said, his lips curving.

The corners of Cat's own lips turned down in response as she looked about. They were in a remote section of the garden, enclosed by trees, and Ransom's alert eyes obviously had noted an ancient and worn bench, used by the gardeners, a few feet away.

"Certainly," she said, motioning to the bench. "Please be seated. I prefer to stand." Ransom did not sit, however, apparently having lost interest in the bench when Cat refused to join him. Instead, he leaned his tall frame against one of the trees, his brow raised curiously at her obvious discomfiture.

"Your grace," Cat began as she unconsciously paced back and forth along the path.

"Ransom," he supplied.

"Your grace," Cat said, pacing a length again before stopping abruptly. "I no longer wish to see you," she blurted out, her prepared speech forgotten.

"Why?" Ransom asked, his features registering only mild interest.

"Because you do not treat me as a gentleman ought to treat a lady," she answered, immediately disliking the pious tone of the words.

"Is that what this is about?"

Ignoring the question, Cat rushed on, irritated by his apparent calm while she felt extremely uncomfortable. "I'm asking you to no longer call at my home and to no longer make any attempts to see me. You may stop arranging 'coincidental' meetings in town and cease following me everywhere I go!" She finished on a firm note, proud of her recitation, but only briefly, for instead of looking pained or outraged by her outburst, Ransom burst into laughter.

"What is so funny?" Cat demanded as he shook his head in amusement and stepped away from the tree.

"You are, my love, for accusing *me* of arranging our meetings, when I have done no such thing. Although I admit to a few occasions where I sought you out, your skill in tracking me down far exceeds my own abilities," Ransom said with a chuckle.

Cat felt her palm itch to wipe the smile off his face. "Are you accusing me of chasing after you?"

she demanded. When Ransom made no answer, she whirled away from him, but he caught her arm.

"Don't rush off, my love, for I'm willing to meet you halfway. Let us say our meetings have been co-incidental and leave it at that," he said.

"Oh, I don't care what you think," Cat snapped as she pulled her arm away. "I just want you to leave me alone. Do you understand? I do not wish to see you again," she said more softly, for she discovered, to her horror, that her eyes, focused firmly on the ground, were filling with tears.

"And what have I done to deserve such punishment?" Ransom asked, his voice silky and cajoling. "How can you be so inhospitable as to consign me to such a cruel fate?"

"What are you talking about?" Cat asked, looking up in puzzlement.

"How could you hate me so that you would condemn me, on my last few days on your island, to the company of Lord Claremont!"

Cat felt her lips twitch, but pulled a face instead. "There are many other inhabitants of this island whom you may keep company with, and I know that you have met some of them."

"Ah, yes, the ogre sisters," Ransom said. "The tall one would eat me alive in one bite!"

"The Montrief sisters," Cat corrected, smiling in spite of herself. "And Elizabeth is not so bad. In fact, they are both quite kind; it is their Aunt Immaline who is ill-tempered."

"Good God! More of them exist? There you have it." Ransom moaned. "You would leave me in the clutches of an ill-tempered ogre and an elderly gentleman prone to endless reminiscences!"

Cat laughed and felt herself wavering, her resolve to put Ransom from her entirely slipping away under his appeal. *You must remain firm,* she told herself, yet hadn't he said he would be staying on the island for only a few more days?''

"Just when do you plan to leave?" she asked suspiciously.

"I'm committed to my dear host's ball, I'm afraid. Then I am free to go."

The ball was set for the day after next, and Cat felt her determination to ignore Ransom slip another notch.

"You are coming to the ball?" he asked, his hand moving to caress her cheek.

"I'll be there," Cat said, the last vestiges of her fortifications crumbling under the warmth of his gaze. It seemed that he always knew just how to deflect her anger, she thought ruefully as she looked up into those dark eyes.

He was standing close, his thumb rubbing as soft as a butterfly's wing along her cheek, and she felt the familiar tingling his touch evoked, as well as the anticipation that he might kiss her. Just one little kiss, she thought.

"Oh, there you are!"

Cat broke away guiltily at the sound of Amelia's voice, and she turned just in time to see her aunt hurrying around a curve in the path. "I sent the gardeners off to pick oranges and thought I might conclude the tour with you," she said brightly, her large, floppy work hat bouncing over her white curls.

"That would be lovely," Cat said, smiling with relief. Certainly she did not feel regret . . .

"I'm sure Catherine has been doing a superb job," Amelia said, "but, of course, I am a bit possessive about my work." While Amelia chattered, Cat watched Ransom's tall, lean body tower over the elderly lady, his head cocked toward her with what appeared to be rapt interest.

With a sigh, Cat berated herself for the failure of

her mission. It seemed that she would always be the loser in a battle of wills with Ransom, who simply laughed or charmed her anger away. Her hopes of never seeing him again were dashed, but was she really disappointed? Traitor! she moaned at her misbehaving heart.

Oh, well, she thought with resignation as she fell into step beside her aunt, she would soon be rid of him for good. And until then . . . well, what could happen in a day's time?

Richard Blakely accepted the tray that a maid had delivered as just one of the benefits of his stay in William Montgomery's plantation house. He had not touched the food; indeed he was little interested in the overindulgences of the wealthy, but he appreciated the well-ordered environment of Montgomery's residence and the tasteful objects gracing it.

Devlin's lifestyle, with its emphasis on rich food, extravagant decor, and emotionalism, had always held little appeal for Richard, but there were advantages to serving such a master, and Richard was well aware of them. His lodgings today were one such boon, for it seemed that Devlin knew innumerable people who owed him favors—or money—or simply feared him in one way or another.

Obviously, William Montgomery was one of them, Richard thought dispassionately as he bent his hand to his notes. He did not waste a moment wondering about Montgomery, who continued to politely avoid him, for he had what he needed from the man: an invitation to Lord Claremont's ball.

Richard's information on Catherine Amberly was scrupulously accurate and as complete as he could make it. All that remained was the final chore Devlin had given him: to break up the romance between Catherine and Ransom. It seemed one of the easiest tasks he had ever been assigned, and the upcoming party would provide the perfect opportunity to implement his plan. It was simple, really, Richard thought coldly, for all that was required was his presence. Oh, he would make an effort to enlist the girl to Devlin's cause, but if she accepted, it would merely be a bonus. The main thing was to make sure he was seen talking with her by the only person who would care: Ransom Du Prey.

Chapter 24

~~~~~~~~~~~

Cat held a melon in each hand, gingerly testing their weights, while all around her the voices of the marketplace filled the air with smooth Caribbean accents. A gentle breeze, tinged with salt and a blend of spices, wafted over her as she concentrated.

"They look deliciously ripe," a familiar voice spoke in her ear.

"Too ripe," Cat said, replacing a melon, one of the few varieties Amelia did not yet cultivate. "I'll take this one," she said briskly, haggling briefly with the vendor before putting it in the sturdy straw basket she carried to market. Without glancing beside her, she turned and headed for the carriage, calling for Isaac.

"I sent him home," said the voice at her side.

"You what?" Cat asked, turning to confront the bearer of these tidings. She faced six feet two inches of a smoothly muscled body that looked so masculine dressed in a buff jacket and breeches which matched the cuffs on his boots, that she suppressed a shiver.

"I told him I would escort you safely home." Showing his most rakish grin, Ransom leaned toward her and took the heavy basket from her arms.

"How amusing!" she jeered. "And who is to protect me from you?"

"You seem quite capable of performing that task yourself."

In exasperation, she let him lead her to the waiting landau, where he stored her market basket and waited to hand her into the open carriage. Cat stood looking at him, undecided, while he waited with that infernal grin on his face. "I'm not going to let you drive me about as though you are my slave," she finally said, drawing a chuckle from him.

"Then come up with me," Ransom answered, easily lifting her to the driver's perch. She frowned as he slid in beside her, his long limbs too close for her peace of mind.

"I suppose you have nothing better to do than accost innocent young ladies in the marketplace."

"My love, innocent young ladies do not swim nearly nude in the ocean alone," he said, snapping the reins smartly.

"They do if they wish to remain innocent," Cat countered, deliberately misconstruing his words. Ransom laughed, and Cat let the delightful sound wash over her. Leaning back against the seat, she took a long, deep breath and looked around her at the beautiful day. Snow-white clouds adorned the bluest of skies, but did not obscure a golden sun, and she tilted her head to feel its warmth on her face beneath her wide-brimmed bonnet.

Lowering her lashes, Cat surreptitiously glanced at Ransom, whose brown locks were tossed back from his forehead by the breeze as he watched the road ahead. He was leaning forward slightly, one glossy boot higher than the other, while his long, slim fingers held the reins lazily. Eyeing his firmly muscled thigh, she was thinking just how well his clothes fit him when, his eyes still on the road, he said, "Do I meet with your approval, my love?"

How *did* he do that? The man must have eyes

where his ears should be, she thought not for the first time.

Ignoring the question, she returned her gaze to the sky, and the warmth of the sun combined with the *clip-clop* of the horses' hooves to lull her into relaxing her guard. Falling back into an old habit, she began finding shapes in the clouds, and before long she was pointing them out to her companion. "There's a unicorn," she said suddenly, gesturing gracefully to a puff of white.

Ransom cocked his head to the side. "Yes, but she's about to be consumed by the lion."

"Oh! Yes, I see him," Cat said with a smile, then sat bolt upright in her seat. What was she thinking of? This was a game Cat had played many times with her captain, and it was best not to jog his memory too much. She had begun to take for granted his failure to recognize her, yet this sort of negligence could very well result in her discovery. She shot him a glance, but he appeared not to have noticed anything unusual.

"Have I grown a snout?" he asked, and she breathed a sigh of relief and settled back in her seat, determined to remain vigilant. Her relief was short-lived, however, as she soon watched him direct the landau down a fork in the road that led away from her aunt's home.

"Stop this carriage immediately and turn around, you . . . you . . ." Cat thought of several fitting epithets, all of them unusable.

"It's a beautiful day for a picnic, don't you agree?" Ransom's mouth twitched irrepressibly, but Cat would have none of it.

"What?" she fairly shrieked.

"Oh, I'm so sorry that your hearing is failing . . . and at such a young age, too."

"Take me home right now!"

He ignored her glare and only noticed that her

face was flushed quite becomingly. "Calm down, my love. What say you to a truce? I'll behave with the utmost propriety," he teased. She tried to remain adamant in the face of his slow smile, and as if sensing that she was weakening, he played his trump card. "And your aunt's gone to such trouble to pack us a delightful picnic basket."

"Rubbish! I hardly think even Aunt Amelia at her most vague would approve an unchaperoned picnic," Cat said.

"Well . . ." The lazy grin struck again. "Not possessing your naturally suspicious nature, she probably failed to anticipate my relieving Isaac of his duties."

"You're incorrigible," Cat declared.

"Ah, here we are, my love," he said as the carriage rolled into her locust grove. Ransom jumped smoothly from the carriage and reached up to help her down, his eyebrow raised in challenge.

Cat hesitated as she looked down at his handsome face. "As I recall, you broke the last truce I agreed to by kissing me," she accused.

"As I recall, we agreed that kisses were not covered under the truce," he claimed, his eyes holding a glint that both beckoned and warned her away.

Cat glanced at his outstretched arms, her will wavering. She knew she should not give in, but suddenly it seemed that all she really wanted was to be in his arms, and she felt the barricades she had been building and rebuilding since his arrival on the island come tumbling down. Still, some remnant of good sense remained. "Promise you will take me home *whenever* I ask—with no argument," she demanded. "On what little honor you possess."

"Done," he said with a laugh, and Cat let him swing her down from the seat. His hands seemed to linger a moment on her trim waist, but then were gone.

Together they explored the grove and the beach below, discovering tiny sand crabs, gathering flowers and shells, and standing breathlessly still as they watched a hummingbird only inches from them. This was the Ransom Cat knew and loved, a man who appreciated the beauty of nature and maintained a lively curiosity about the world around him. He was gentle and witty, and Cat was thoroughly at ease as they wound their way from the beach back up into the grove, where they stood admiring the view below.

"This is a lovely spot," Ransom said. "Have you ever painted it?"

"Oh, no! I never learned to do watercolors. I'm afraid painting could not hold my attention," Cat said, shaking her head. "I much prefer being part of the scenery to painting it." She smiled mischievously up at him, and he was dazzled.

"You have a beautiful smile, Catherine. I love to see it," Ransom said. Unnerved by the tug in his chest, he pressed on, "So you were not interested in watercolors; what did capture your attention?"

"Oh, none of the things that were supposed to. I guess I took delight in being different, making myself even less acceptable to a stepfather who was already unsatisfied with me." The truth of the words startled her, and she pricked herself on the rose bloom she was fingering. "Oh!" she gasped, pulling back her hand to put the injured finger to her lips.

"Here, let me see." Ransom stepped toward her and gently took her hand in his own.

"It's nothing," Cat said and tried to pull away. He was standing so close she could see the tips of his boots by her toes, and her bent head was only inches from his chest. His touch made her catch her breath as she dazedly watched his finger lightly trace the curves of her palm. The scent of wildflowers washed over her, and her skin tingled everywhere. Raising her eyes shakily to his, she found in them something she had never seen before, something warm and lazy and wonderful. His gaze never wavered as he lifted her hand to his lips and placed a lingering kiss inside her wrist, where the pounding blood was certain to give her feelings away.

A parrot shrieking at her shoulder broke the spell, and Cat snatched her hand from his as though it were ablaze. A series of alarms sounded in her head, urging her to go, but she had so enjoyed the afternoon that she hesitated, and before she could speak, Ransom took her hand and tucked it against his arm.

"Well, Catherine, let's see what delicacies your delightful aunt prepared for us," he said lightly, as if nothing had happened, and Cat could not bring herself to leave him.

Along with the large basket of food, Amelia had provided a faded quilt, which they spread on the sun-dappled grass. Ransom removed his boots, and when Cat glared at him reprovingly, he only raised a sardonic brow as though daring her to do the same. "Go ahead," he urged. "Surely you are not hampered by convention."

Cat gave him a black look, and with a toss of her head, she turned around to strip off her shoes and stockings. Damn! The man can read me far too well, she thought. She sat down quickly and tucked her bare feet under her skirts, to the sound of Ransom's soft chuckles.

Amelia had stocked the basket with ham, leg of mutton, boiled eggs, cheese, and cook's delicious rolls and pastries. Ignoring the lemonade Amelia had supplied, Ransom produced a bottle of champagne with a flourish. As Amelia served spirits infrequently, Cat soon felt the effects of the sparkling wine, and, sated and drowsy, she leaned back on her elbows to glory in the sunlight.

As she felt the warm glow of the wine, Cat found it hard to believe that while aboard the *Reckless* she could down several glasses of rum with nary a blink of her eye! The memory made her smile softly to herself. Now here she was dressed in a lovely white gauze gown, her bare toes peeping out from beneath her skirts, stretched out on a blanket with only a basket between her and the very same captain she had once served.

Lying on his side, his glass held casually between two long fingers, Ransom watched the slow smile play on her lips and felt as if the air had been knocked out of his lungs. He noticed how the sun sparkled on her hair and longed to run his hands through it, but she looked so innocent tilting that pert nose up to the sun, the champagne obviously making her giddy, that he only drew a deep breath. " 'What is your substance, whereof are you made, That millions of strange shadows on you tend?' " He quoted Shakespeare's sonnet softly.

" 'Since every one hath, every one, one shade, And you, but one, can every shadow lend,' " Cat recited the next lines for him. Too happy to consider the connotations of his words, she laughed and said, "My, aren't we waxing romantic!"

"I beg your pardon!" he said with mock effrontery. "I suppose this is more to your taste: 'There once was an old man from Brennart, who met up with a pretty young tart,' " Ransom began.

" 'She sat on his lap and gave him the clap and then ran away with his heart!' " Cat capped off the bawdy limerick by raising her glass in salute and finishing her champagne to the delightful sound of Ransom's deep-throated laughter.

"Where did you pick up that doggerel?" he asked, but Cat just smiled slyly. Peeking at him under her lowered lashes, she could not help admiring his handsome features and the fine figure he made lying on the quilt. Her heart pounded in response as her eyes moved over him, and she knew she had tarried long enough on the grass alone with her captain. With a small sigh of regret, Cat rose to her knees to gather the remains of their meal, but Ransom's hand on her wrist halted her.

"Wait, my love. Your aunt put something else in the basket, a favorite of yours, she says," Ransom said, with no intention of letting her go as yet. He rummaged in the hamper, found what he sought and grinned wickedly. "Close your eyes and open your mouth." To his surprise she did as requested, and for a moment he admired the pretty picture she made seated back on her heels, her golden hair tossed teasingly about her face. Long, dusky lashes caressed her cheeks, and the pink bud of her mouth curved into a small O.

A wave of desire hit him with a physical force that surprised him in its intensity. But even more surprising was the tenderness that welled up in his throat. Gently he placed a ripe, red strawberry in her mouth and was rewarded with a glad cry as her bright eyes flew open. "Good?" he asked huskily. His hand caressed her cheek, while his thumb delicately outlined her lower lip.

His touch sent Cat's thoughts scattering. She was vaguely aware of a voice telling her to knock his hand away, but the warmth that shot through her drowned it out, and she struggled instead to concentrate on the question. "I adore them," she said, savoring the tiny fruit. "And you?" She did not wait for his answer, but dipping a delicate hand into the basket, she held a strawberry just out of his reach, laughing when he tried to take it. He finally caught the fruit between his lips, and her laughter ceased when she found her fingers captive in his mouth, his tongue running over each one in turn.

When he released her hand it fell limply into her lap, and she could only gaze at him wide-eyed. He offered her another strawberry, and as though in a dream, she moved her mouth toward his fingers. As she bit into the fruit, a drop of sweet juice trickled down her chin, and suddenly Ransom's lips were there, his tongue capturing the errant fluid, then he was meeting her lips with his own, and the flavor of the fruit mingled with the taste of him as his tongue explored her mouth.

The sensation sent her reeling, and her head fell back, but his strong hand was there to support it. Her own hands slipped over his shoulders to his hair, her fingers threading through its thickness. She heard Ransom make a sound deep in his throat, and then she was lowered down, onto the quilt.

"Catherine. Catherine, my love," he whispered against her lips before burying his face in the golden waves of her hair. Her breath quickened as she felt his lips along her neck and in the soft flesh behind her ear, and she gasped aloud as his tongue found the tender curves of her ear and his teeth lightly nipped her lobe. Her breasts against his chest felt tight, her clothing too constricting as she pressed herself to him.

"Kiss me, love," he urged in her ear. Her eyes flew open to gaze into his, soft and warm and deep with passion, and slowly she raised her lips to his, closing her eyes as her tongue slipped into his mouth to explore the redolent depths. She heard his breath catch in his throat and the sound sent her pulse racing even faster. She tightened her arms around his neck.

"Oh, yes, my love. Yes, that's it," he breathed. "You are delicious." The kiss that followed left her breathless, and her heart was pounding alarmingly as his palm covered her breast. Surely, he can feel it, she thought dizzily as his hand traveled upward to remove her gown from her shoulder. She heard a soft moan and was unsure whether it was his voice or her own, when he began to explore the curves beneath her gown, his long, lean fingers gently caressing her naked breast.

"Your skin is like silk," he whispered as he cupped her breast in his palm, which then slid along her shoulder, up her neck, and into her hair. As his fingers moved along her nape, his lips teased the slender column, drawing the very soul from her. Cat could no longer claim control of her own hands, which slid along his shoulders to his neck, where they began pulling at his shirt, eager to feel the smooth skin beneath.

Cat never meant to touch him so intimately. She never meant to allow him such liberties, but the warmth of the wine and the sun and her captain's presence were too powerful to resist. The smell of wildflowers, strawberries, and Ransom filled her senses, and she sighed with pure pleasure, all her firm resolve and modesty disappearing with his shirt.

His skin felt alive beneath her fingers, and she raised her head to kiss the smooth muscles, her lips trailing among the dark hairs of his chest until her delicate exploration made Ransom capture her lips again. She was not aware of the tiny sounds escaping her throat, but Ransom was, and he pressed against her urgently, his mouth moving downward along her neck to the curve of her breast.

Cat arched against him, grasping his dark head as he took her nipple into his mouth, her chaotic breaths stirring his hair, and Ransom felt the situation moving beyond his control. He had intended to taste her charms, that was certain, but did he really mean to take her? He had never fully resolved that question in his mind, leaving it in limbo with the answer dependent somehow on her identity. But he still had no solid proof that she was not what she seemed: an innocent young virgin. Was he prepared to take that from her?

Ransom's conscience vied with overwhelming desire until he raised his head, certain that he should stop himself now—before it was too late. His ingrained aversion to losing control stood him in good stead as he sought to still his rapid breathing. His passion for the woman in his arms was like nothing he had ever known, bringing with it a frightening tendency to wipe out all else. With cool determination, he fought the urge to finish what he had begun and, taking a deep breath, leaned back to take a good look at the lady who had such power over him.

Her eyes were closed, her delicate, pink mouth was tilted open slightly for an intake of breath, and her golden hair lay tousled and glistening in the sun. She certainly did not appear innocent at this moment, but neither did she have the look of an experienced lover. Ransom felt his resolution sorely tested as his eyes moved lower, to the smooth, pale breasts displayed in front of him.

Her hands had been slack against his shoulders, but now that he was still, they tightened, and he felt the firm pressure of her fingers urging him downward. "Catherine," he began softly, intending to explain to her why their tryst must end. At his words she opened her eyes, the green pools awash with desire, and smiled.

"Ransom." The word was like a caress, imbued with so much feeling that he nearly caught his breath. "My beautiful, beautiful captain." She sighed, running her fingers along his cheek as though in awed wonder. "Kiss me, love," she said, her voice deep with desire. The request, the very same that he had made not so long ago, shattered his resolve into a thousand pieces. With a groan, he lowered his head to hers, capturing her soft lips with his own.

Cat met his mouth eagerly, her heart soaring with love too long denied and passion which demanded his touch. Those few moments when she'd felt him draw back had seemed cold and empty, and although her mind told her that she was getting into water far too deep, she could no longer help herself. She sighed as Ransom's hands slid over her skin, and his lips trailed downward again to her breasts, closing over each nipple in turn.

Just as Cat thought she could bear the exquisite torture no longer, Ransom slipped the gown and chemise from her body and removed his own garments. He stood for a moment gazing down at her, the sunlight behind him, looking just as he had the very first time she saw him naked in his cabin . . . only better.

She saw him hesitate, and in one swift moment she realized the enormity of what she was doing, but it was too late. All the love and desire she had ever felt for him, every laugh they had shared, each kiss and caress, and even the cross words between them seemed to have been leading up to this moment, and nothing could make her turn away. Cat threw caution to the winds and reached out her hand to him.

In a moment he was pressed to her, the feel of his naked body against hers more luscious than she could ever have imagined. Their mouths locked and broke apart, their breaths mingling, while their hands moved over each other, roaming in delightful abandon. Cat gasped aloud as his fingers caressed the most intimate part of her, reveling in the feeling even as she longed for something more.

"Ransom." She spoke his name as if it were a plea.

"Yes, my love?" He raised his head to look into her eyes.

"You . . . It's you that I want," she whispered. He groaned in response, taking her lips as he moved his body over hers, and Cat arched against him. She sighed with abandon as he entered her, but the pain which soon followed made her open her eyes in surprise, to gaze into his, dark with passion—and clouded with guilt.

"I'm sorry, my love," Ransom whispered hoarsely. "I never meant to hurt you." He pulled her close again, breathing endearments into her ear, and soon the pain was forgotten as she moved with him, her feet pressed into the quilt, her fingers clutching the smooth muscles of his back until she was drowning in sensations that made her cry out his name.

"Ransom, I love you," Cat gasped as he shuddered in her arms.

Chapter 25

Ransom's conscience returned with a vengeance as he folded his arms around the slender beauty beside him, his words to René coming back to haunt him. *I don't make a habit of sullying virginal young ladies of quality,* he had claimed, yet apparently he had done just that. Catherine's tender declaration of love rang in his ears, and he wondered just how the hell he was going to extricate himself from this mess.

Her passionate response had led him to believe that she was a veteran of such encounters—until he'd met the proof of her innocence. Yet he could hardly blame her when he, too, had been unable to halt their lovemaking despite his firm resolve. And now what? Perhaps the lovely young woman who had given herself to him in a moment of abandon did not realize the consequences of their union, but Ransom did, and the ramifications stung him to the core.

What if she should reveal the details of this afternoon to her aunt? The idea made him grimace, for he had little faith in that sweet but whimsical lady's good sense. The way she prattled on, the story might get out and Catherine would be ruined—a social outcast, a pariah to all but the bravest of her peers.

Gone would be her way of life, along with Amelia's hopes for an advantageous marriage. Oh, per-

haps some dull shopkeeper might be persuaded to
wed her; although beneath her, he would provide
an alternative to a life of spinsterhood. Such an arrangement would not be unusual, but the picture of
the nubile beauty in his arms spending her days as
the wife of some nondescript bourgeois wrenched at
his gut.

Ransom frowned at such fancies. No one need
know of the afternoon's indiscretion, and Catherine
would undoubtedly continue her life without further complications. She would probably go on to
snag some old, rich fellow like Claremont in marriage, take dozens of lovers, and never worry her
pretty head about a thing. This scenario, unfortunately, held nearly as little appeal as the previous
one, and Ransom, rarely given to such flights of
imagination, tried to get a firm grip on himself.

His attempt faltered as another vision appeared to
torment him: she could be carrying his child even
now. Ransom sharply quelled an odd thrill of excitement at the notion while he calmly tried to calculate
the odds of such an occurrence. He had already
made up his mind that it would be best not to touch
Miss Amberly again, and the possibility of procrea-
tion simply reinforced his decision. But, as if in argument, a jolt of desire surged through him as her
slender form stirred in his arms.

Ransom scowled at his own weakness. Of course,
he thought as he absently stroked the golden head
resting on his chest, he had not considered the obvious solution to his dilemma: that he wed the girl
himself. His hand stilled suddenly as he furiously
rejected that option. Catherine was definitely beautiful and intriguing and a virgin to be sure, but innocent? How could he be certain that her passion
did not spring from an urgent desire to be a duchess? That nagging doubt joined with his natural dis-
trust of women to rule out the idea of marriage.

God, what a coil! This was not the sort of situation he let himself get involved in. He had little use for females, especially virginal ones, but his normally good sense and cool, calculating brain had apparently exited the scene when Miss Amberly appeared, leaving his groin to rule in their stead.

Yet even as he regretted his actions, Ransom had to admit that he had never experienced such love-making, nor that strange but pleasant warmth that lingered in his chest as he held her in his arms . . . He raised his hand to her cheek, smoothing back the golden hair, and he was struck by the realization that he wanted her again, now.

Tenderly cupping her innocent face in his hands, Ransom was seared by a sudden, fierce pleasure that he was the first. It was irrational, he knew, but intense just the same, and he struggled with the desire that demanded he claim her again. With a groan of exasperation, he rolled away, unintentionally waking the beauty beside him.

It was not the movement but the sudden absence of warm arms cradling her that woke Cat. She shivered slightly in the fading sunlight and realized with a desperate emptiness that the spell was broken. The wine was gone, the strawberries overturned in the grass, and the magic of the afternoon had slipped away, leaving only a love-struck young girl who was suddenly embarrassed by her nudity.

Cat looked to Ransom for comfort as she nervously reached for her clothes but saw only his smooth, muscled back as he jerked on his breeches. She raised a hand to touch him but let it fall back into her lap as she saw the firm set of his jaw. So that was the way of it, she thought, swallowing a painful lump in her throat.

Well, it was not the first time she had felt that cold withdrawal, Cat mused as she dressed silently. She remembered all too clearly Ransom's rejection of his cabin boy. With Ransom one could never get too close . . . Shaking her head forlornly, Cat knew that she had no one but herself to blame for her current predicament. She was the one so adrift in desire that she could not let him go, and she was the one so overcome with love that she had to blurt it out. Well, she had enjoyed the moment; now she must deal with the aftermath.

With a determined set to her shoulders, Cat rose, resolving not to let her weakness show. If Ransom expected a mewling, clinging female begging for further attentions, he would be surprised. "We should be going," she said softly.

Ransom, still struggling with his own guilty conscience, nearly jumped at the sound of her voice. Turning to face her, he saw only a composed young lady and agreed gratefully with her words. "Yes, it's late. I wouldn't want your aunt to be worried," he said, then frowned at his own turn of phrase, grimly aware that her aunt had good cause to worry.

As the duo rode home among the lengthening shadows, Ransom was too caught up in his own uncharacteristic emotional turmoil to feel anything but appreciation for his companion's silence. Never one to delve too deeply into a woman's thoughts, he missed the small signs that would have told him her heart was aching.

Once inside her room, Cat wept furious tears at Ransom's cold withdrawal. How could he change so quickly? She wondered frantically what would have happened had she not fallen asleep. He had been so tender, so passionate as he made love to her—she shivered at the memory—and then when she awoke, her warm lover was gone, replaced by his icy counterpart.

With a sigh, Cat wiped away her tears, resolving to savor every remembered moment, each touch of his lips, each tender caress and every whispered word. Despite Ransom's cool farewell, Cat could not regret the afternoon and would not have forgone one single moment, for now she had the most wonderful day of days, the most beautiful experience of her life, to hold close when he was gone.

Gone. The thought of his departure rent her heart again.

When the maid called her for supper, Cat pleaded illness, and when Amelia herself came up, Cat pretended sleep, for she was not ready to face her aunt's probing questions. Underneath her flighty exterior, Amelia was a little too astute, and although Cat had managed many a deception, she knew that right now her ability to dissemble was at rock bottom.

She spent a restless night dreaming of her captain and skipped breakfast, delaying the inevitable conversation with Amelia until dinner, when she finally appeared downstairs, looking refreshed and natural.

"Oh, Catherine, I'm so glad to see you!" Amelia said. "I was so worried; I wanted to go up, but the maid said you were sleeping still, and I didn't want to disturb you. How are you feeling?"

"Fine, now, dear aunt," Cat said, bending over and kissing Amelia on the cheek. If she hugged her aunt a little too closely, the lady appeared not to notice, demanding instead that she sit and eat a good meal to chase away the lingering effects of her illness. "It was just a headache," Cat reassured her with a laugh.

"Well, I'm glad," Amelia said as she restlessly moved her hands. "I mean, I'm glad it was nothing more, and that . . . well, I thought you might be angry with me."

"Oh, aunt, how could I be?" Cat asked.

"Well, you told me to stop interfering between you and the duke, but when he came looking for you, I couldn't very well lie to him, and then when he asked if he could picnic with you, well, I naturally. . . . I mean, cook was right here and I saw no sense in his grace going to any trouble, for you know Lord Claremont's cook is an evil fellow, so I just knew he would have a difficult time of it up there, and I really couldn't imagine him going to an inn for the food—''

''Aunt, aunt!'' Cat laughed, holding up her hand to halt Amelia's nervous chatter. ''It's all right, really. The picnic was just fine . . . Perhaps it was the ham that did not sit right with me or the pickled eggs, but I am fine now.''

''Well, ham can have that effect on one, and I have often wondered if those pigs we've been getting from the plantation are quite as they should be. Perhaps we are receiving the runts and the thin, old, tough porkers! I will have to speak to Lord Claremont about it,'' she said with determination, and Cat was only too glad to have the subject turned away from Ransom.

Cat was spared any further questions about the picnic, for Amelia's agile mind flitted to another topic, bubbling with cheer over that night's party. Cat, whose mind had been elsewhere since yesterday afternoon, was jolted by her aunt's reminder that Lord Claremont was to hold his ball that evening.

Cat viewed the event with a mixture of anticipation and sadness, for despite Ransom's recent coldness, she was eager to see him again and to dance in his arms one last time. Therein lay her disenchantment, too. She knew the gathering signaled his departure, but how, after all that had happened, could she let him go?

As she listened to Amelia relate the exhaustive preparations for the event, however, Cat could not help becoming infected with her aunt's high spirits. From the sound of it, Lord Claremont was planning the social event of the year . . . and Ransom would be the guest of honor. With an excited smile, Cat decided she would focus all her energies on enjoying the night.

She began by preparing for the ball with unheard-of care, surprising and pleasing her personal maid, Tess, who felt she was wasted on a mistress who would just as soon dress herself. Cat was well aware that some of the wealthier ladies present would be arrayed in the latest London fashions and draped in sparkling jewels. What Cat lacked in funds, however, she more than compensated for with taste and ingenuity, and the gown she had ordered for the ball was both beautiful and unusual. Although the sea-green tulle was a little darker than was strictly fashionable, the color matched her eyes, and the effect made Tess clap her hands in admiration.

The square neckline was cut so low as to make the bodice only a few inches deep before it met the high waistline. But Cat refused the necklaces and bracelets that the maid pressed upon her, leaving her neck and arms bare. For jewelry she wore only pearl earrings, and on a whim she had Tess wind through her hair a chain of tiny shells that she had collected in her travels. She wrapped a shimmering blue-green shawl about her and spared but a glance in the mirror to admire the effect before hurrying down the stairs to the waiting landau.

While Cat's carriage rambled up the lane to the great house, Ransom was beginning to regret his easy acceptance of Lord Claremont's hospitality. He had been bored stiff for the past few days by his genial host, and tonight promised to be more of the same as he was introduced to guest after guest, including an alarming number of unmarried ladies and their mamas. The reason he had quit this existence came back to him in a rush as he stood next to his host, uttering inanities: he detested such functions.

With an impatience he had not felt in years, he longed for Catherine's arrival. An evening of serious introspection had revealed to him just how his behavior after their lovemaking must have appeared to her, and he felt an urgency to—if not explain himself—at least apologize for his coldness. He still had no immediate solution to his dilemma, but he was hoping to discover her thoughts on the subject. The sudden notion that his lady might not appear or might not wish to see him—a definite possibility considering their stiff parting—set his teeth on edge.

"Your grace, do say you will be dancing this evening," gushed an enormous woman in a white turban, whose name he could not recall. "All the young ladies are so looking forward to a dance with you," she trilled, fluttering a handkerchief so powerfully scented as to offend his nostrils.

"Yes, your grace, do take a turn around the floor," Lord Claremont urged.

"Your drink, your grace," a servant intoned at his elbow, and Ransom nodded in gratitude. Excusing himself, he ducked into one of the receiving rooms, then strolled through the house, casually sipping his drink while the tension dropped away.

Wandering into the dining hall, where a late supper would be served, Ransom hailed a servant for another drink and drained the glass before turning his attention to the ballroom. His gaze swept the crowd and the entrance for Catherine, the odd sensation of anticipation catching him unawares. He could only liken it to his feeling upon sighting another ship, when the expectation of battle and the challenge of capturing a vessel were in the air. His lips curved in a smile as he imagined capturing this prize: the lovely Catherine, once again wild with passion and moving beneath his body. But since the object of his desire was not in view, Ransom had to be content with his imaginings. Where was she?

At that very moment, Cat was wondering the same thing. Attempting to keep the dust of the roadway from her gown as she stood with Amelia alongside the carriage, Cat was trying to determine just how far they were from the great house. Placing some familiar landmarks, she mentally gauged the distance, then glanced dismally down at her thin slippers and sighed heavily. Restlessly, she moved closer to the carriage, straining to see what Isaac was about as he labored with the wheel.

"Catherine, please don't step into the roadway. You will simply ruin that gown," Amelia warned, fluttering her fan.

"Well, I just want to take a look."

"Now, Catherine, do you want to insult Isaac? I'm sure he is taking care of whatever the problem may be as quickly as possible."

Cat sighed again. "Perhaps we should start walking," she suggested.

"And arrive at Lord Claremont's ball looking like two chimney sweeps? No thank you, my dear. There is nothing wrong with being fashionably late and making a grand entrance," Amelia asserted, her pink cheeks wrinkling into a knowing smile. "A little anticipation never hurt anyone."

Amelia ignored her niece's scowl and serenely continued her fanning. "Please don't pace, dear," she added as soon as Cat took a step.

Cat fidgeted for what seemed like an eternity, stepping forward only to catch herself mid-stride. Grimly remaining rooted to the spot, she fought the urge to take off along the edge of the roadway. "Oh, why doesn't a carriage come by? We should have taken the main road!" Cat finally burst out.

"Goodness, dear, I had no idea you were in such a hurry," Amelia said, her blue eyes twinkling. "I recall you originally were not going to attend Lord Claremont's party at all."

Cat gritted her teeth in the face of her aunt's teasing and told herself to relax even as her eyes searched the bend in the road for other travelers. Just when she was about to look at the wheel herself, Isaac finally came around the carriage, his face as always revealing nothing as he helped them back to their seats.

"What was the problem, Isaac?" Cat asked, leaning forward.

"I'm not quite sure, ma'am, but all looks well now," he answered before climbing onto the driver's seat.

Cat looked askance at her aunt. " 'I'm not quite sure, ma'am'?" she mouthed silently to Amelia. Totally puzzled by the servant's response, she had the uneasy feeling that absolutely nothing had been wrong with the wheel. Amelia only smiled sweetly, however, as the carriage began moving again with a jolt, and Cat's thoughts returned to the ball.

While Cat was suffering through her delay, Ransom again scanned the crowd for her. Irritated at his own impatience, he sought out a partner for the waltz, choosing a young girl of not more than sixteen whose porcelain hair framed a pale, heart-shaped face that neared perfection. Her conversational ability, however, was limited to monosyllables.

His next partner was a sophisticated lady with rouged cheeks and a twinkle in her eye, but he disliked the bold way she licked her lips, and her innuendos were so lacking in wit that they left him cold. As he left her side, interrupting a blatant invitation to her bedroom, he decided that if Catherine did not arrive soon, he would grab a bottle and duck into the gardens, never to be seen again.

"Who are you looking for?" his third partner asked him as they sailed across the floor. When he raised his eyebrow slightly, she continued, "I've been watching you dance, and you seem more intent on the doorway than on your steps, though you dance very well.''

"Thank you," Ransom said dryly, his brow soaring.

"It's no good denying it, you know. You are looking for someone, though you needn't name her, your grace. Gossip has it you have been seeing a lot of Catherine Amberly."

"I never respond to gossip," Ransom said, giving the young lady a quelling look.

Unfortunately, Cat was standing in the doorway and was not close enough to see Ransom's expression. Yet as she watched him dance with Courtney Westland, her heart sank. Unaware of her own beauty, Cat thought her friend Courtney, with her auburn hair and blue-gray eyes, was the loveliest resident of the island. They made a striking couple, and Cat knew Courtney was intelligent and witty, a favorite with any man who valued more than a pretty face. Viewing Ransom's arm tightly around her friend, Cat felt jealousy well up, for surely Ransom could not think of the bright and beautiful Courtney as boring! Perhaps her friend would succeed where Cat had failed, and Courtney Westland would win her captain's heart. The idea brought her up short, and she wrenched her gaze from the waltzing couple.

"There she is!" Courtney announced with a smile, nodding toward the door, and Ransom's eyes flicked, emotionless, over Catherine just as the dance ended. Although his every impulse insisted that he rush to her side and question her tardiness, his mind rebelled at such immature behavior, and as the strains of the waltz faded away, he returned his partner to her companions, a look of icy disdain his only response to her knowing smile.

"You will excuse me?" He nodded curtly to the stunning redhead and strode into the receiving room, where he ordered another drink and cursed himself for ever coming to Barbados. He moved to a vantage point where he could see Catherine without drawing too much attention to himself, and as he looked at her a warmth that could not be wholly attributed to the liquor coursed through him.

She resembled a sea siren, dressed as she was, her iridescent cloak the color of the ocean, with shells woven through her hair. Not a piece of jewelry adorned her throat or arms, and the effect was one of extreme sensuality, as though she were naked but for the frothing waves of blue-green that covered her. How could he have thought the white-haired china doll beautiful? Catherine glowed with life from the top of her shining golden hair to her slim fingertips, making her far more lovely than any other woman there.

"Ah, there you are, your grace!"

Ransom's scrutiny was interrupted by a voice behind him. "I have someone I want you to meet," the man announced loudly, and Ransom turned to Sir Alec Grayson, who had been introduced to him earlier. Ransom forced himself to smile as he was presented to a dowager who claimed they were in some way related. She appeared to be slightly deaf, for she ignored his demurs and listed an interminable number of kinsmen, searching for the connection. Finally, exasperated beyond endurance, Ransom agreed that his mother's brother—who had died in infancy—was married to the lady's cousin. By the time he escaped, however, the object of his interest was nowhere to be seen.

A glass of champagne in hand, Cat slipped off to the portrait gallery before taking a healthy swallow, followed by a deep breath, in an effort to calm the jealously that had consumed her at the sight of Ransom and Courtney dancing. With a gulp she tried to erase

the memory that haunted her—a vision of Ransom
leaning over her, his chest bare, his eyes warm with
desire, his mouth tasting of strawberries and wine.

What a fool she was for succumbing to his seduc-
tions when he cared nothing for her! Ransom Du
Prey, go to hell, she seethed, tightening her grip on
the slender stem of her glass.

Caught up in her own misery, Cat spared not a
thought for the other revelers. Yet one of the guests,
watching her movements with the keenest of interest, had followed her into the gallery. Unaware that
she was no longer alone, Cat struggled with her
temper, telling herself that Ransom meant nothing
to her. Let him dance with whomever he pleased!

Finishing the champagne, she abruptly put down
her empty glass next to a tray temptingly full of
freshly filled glasses, and hesitating only briefly she
took up another, annoyed that, despite her disclaim-
ers, the thought of Courtney and her captain still
bothered her.

"Miss Amberly! Hello!" Her reverie was broken by
a thin, blond-haired stranger hurrying along the gallery toward her. "I have been looking for you. How
nice to find you!" he said, and Cat nodded slightly,
her eyes holding a look of mild inquiry at the intrusion. "Oh, beg pardon! My name is Richard Blakely.
I believe we have a mutual acquaintance."

"Do we, sir?"

"Yes, I think you know the duke quite well,"
Blakely said, pausing just long enough to add an
extra layer of meaning to the words. "I've known
him a long time. I usually find that his friends . . .
interest me greatly."

"Do you?" Cat asked. "Well, I certainly can't
claim to be a friend of his."

"No? Then I have been misinformed. Forgive
me," he said, bowing slightly. "Please, sit down,"
he urged, motioning to a small gilt and brocade sofa.

Cat, curious, complied. Another lady might have hesitated to join a stranger in the deserted hallway, but Cat, confident in her ability to protect herself, felt no such qualms. She gave no thought to how it would look, and she certainly had no idea that Ransom was searching for her.

He was stalking the rooms, his jaw clenched in anger. Where the deuce had she gone? Passing by the refreshment table, he sought another drink and found himself drawn by his host into a debate on the merits of irrigation systems. Inwardly raging, he wondered why he of all people, the calm, cool, and controlled Ransom Du Prey, should be losing his temper over a simple female. Things that would normally not cause him to bat an eye were infuriating him: that she was late, that she had disappeared immediately upon her arrival, and that he was stuck listening to this dull conversation on her account. With an effort, he extricated himself from the cozy group to continue his search.

He nearly collided with an officious servant who presented him with a drink and smirked. "If you are looking for Miss Amberly, your grace," the fellow said slyly, "I saw her heading for the portrait gallery . . . with a gentleman." Ransom raised a brow at the fellow's insinuating tone, effectively dismissing him, and scowled as the man disappeared into the crowd. What was that all about?

With a puzzled grimace, Ransom turned his steps toward the portrait gallery, instinctively watching his back as he entered the dimly lit corridor. At first, he saw no one. A few steps gave him a better vantage point, however, and then he spied her. Out of sight of the other guests in the quiet of the shadowed gallery, the seemingly innocent Miss Amberly was seated cozily beside Richard Blakely, Devlin's favorite sycophant.

Chapter 26

Ransom ignored the sudden pain in his chest and coldly, calmly, watched Catherine Amberly sip champagne as she reported to Devlin's right hand man. In his mind Ransom congratulated Devlin on his choice, for the . . . lady . . . was highly skilled, at least in piquing his interest, and certainly in arousing his appetites.

He downed his drink in one swallow as he stood staring at them, burning the picture into his head in an effort to dull his desire for her. He could nearly kick himself for becoming so enamored. His usually reliable instincts had played him false this time.

Christ! He had become enthralled like some damp-palmed schoolboy, panting to steal up a maiden's skirts in the grass. His pride rebelled at the thought that he should look so foolish—especially to that bastard Devlin. Devlin. The man's laughter was probably shaking the entire West Indies, Ransom thought as his lips twisted into a grimace.

It was time to attend to that scoundrel. Revenge had never attracted Ransom, but Devlin's games were becoming too bothersome. There came a point when a man lost his patience, Ransom thought coldly, his mind already traveling from the scene before him to a confrontation with his enemy.

What had been the plan this time? To make Catherine his mistress? She had refused that suggestion, but would she acquiesce now that they had made love? Or perhaps that was not the goal, and Devlin thought . . . No, even Devlin could not hope to snare him into marriage! With a short laugh that would have chilled Cat to the bone, Ransom looked down at his glass and loosened his violent grip on the fine crystal.

The sharp pain in his chest eased to a dull throb while he calculated just how to locate his nemesis. Devlin now traveled from one hiding hole to the next, covering his tracks with expert care. But Ransom had an idea how to discover where he was skulking. With a grim smile, he turned on his heel and slipped into the shadows to wait.

Cat was well into her third glass of champagne before she realized that something was not quite right. She was already a little light-headed from the sparkling wine, but she was alert enough to become suspicious of her smooth-spoken companion as he inched closer to her.

At first, Cat gave the man no thought. She made the appropriate replies to his small talk while her mind, haunted by visions of Courtney and the captain, roamed far from the conversation. As he droned on about the party and the island, she stared fixedly ahead, sipping champagne and unwilling to make the effort to rid herself of his company.

Even when he turned the conversation to Ransom, Cat paid no heed, for the duke seemed to be the topic of everyone's discussion, as she well knew. She answered politely, if rather distractedly, as he posed innocuous questions, until something in his tone of voice suddenly made her attend to him.

She turned and looked at Mr. Blakely, really *looked* at him for the first time, and she did not like what she saw. His head was tilted slightly to the side, his lips curved into an odd smile, and there was something about his eyes . . . He reminded her of nothing so much as a weasel, and her own gaze narrowed as she wondered if the resemblance extended to his behavior, for this was no chance occurrence, she surmised. Mr. Blakely had sought her out for a purpose.

He continued talking, softly and smoothly, as though oblivious to her sudden scrutiny, but somehow Cat did not think him unaware. She imagined, with an eerie certainty, that not much escaped him as she began to concentrate on his words. ". . . Of course, those of us who know the duke are well aware that you have captured his tendermost feelings," he said. "Can nuptials be too far in the future?"

"I'm afraid you are mistaken, Mr. Blakely," Cat answered softly. "His grace holds me in no more regard than any other acquaintance. Or perhaps you do not know the duke as well as you profess?"

Her companion's lips thinned in response, but he bowed his head in a nod of sham cordiality. "You are too modest," he murmured. "Ah, well." He sighed and looked down at the floor, then he tilted his head again as his blue eyes, alight with intent, shot to her face. "But if one were to have influence with the duke, such influence could be very valuable, don't you think?"

Cat, her wits dulled by champagne, struggled to grasp his meaning, but she was in no shape to decipher obscure underlying messages. "What on earth do you mean?" she finally asked.

Richard gave her his most ingratiating smile while wondering if he had been sadly misinformed about Miss Amberly's intelligence. So far she seemed exceedingly dim-witted and lifeless, hardly a consort for Du Prey, unless the man had fallen victim to her physical beauty alone. "There are always people

willing to pay for influence with the nobility, Miss
Amberly," he explained patiently. "Such practices
are commonplace in London."

"You are willing to pay me to influence Ransom?" she burst out, her tone incredulous.

"No, no." Richard laughed, demurring. "I was
only pointing out that such business arrangements
are prevalent with the rich and powerful. Lud, Miss
Amberly, I would never include myself among such
as they!" He smiled thinly. Obviously, the feeble-
brained chit could not be bought. Richard was mildly
disappointed, for Devlin would have been thoroughly pleased by her defection, but his attention
now focused on maintaining the conversation. He
still had to break up the romance, and Miss Amberly
was assisting him, whether she knew it or not.

Calculating the time that had elapsed since the
start of their tête-à-tête, Richard decided that Du
Prey, directed hither by Devlin's hireling, was undoubtedly watching them by this time. But the
longer Miss Amberly remained by his side, the more
incriminating their discussion would appear, so he
spoke again.

"Tell me, my dear Miss Amberly, about your
aunt's gardens. I have heard so much of them,"
Richard urged, forcing a look of interest onto his
normally impassive features. Although he had failed
to win the lady's loyalty, Ransom would not know
it, and that was the core of his plan.

The change of topic, however, jarred Cat into action. "Perhaps another time, Mr. Blakely," she said.
With a sigh of confusion, she set down her empty
glass of champagne—the last one she would touch
tonight, she swore to herself—and glanced again at
her companion, his gaze now mild and unaffected.
Having no desire to play the pawn and feeling too
fogged by drink to discover the mysterious Mr.

Blakely's motives, Cat rose and excused herself politely, then retreated.

He let her go without a murmur, and Cat wondered with annoyance if the wine was affecting her judgment and the man was only a harmless, foolish creature. She smiled as she exited the gallery, shaking her head at her own imaginings and confident that Mr. Blakely had gained nothing from her. Had she turned back in time to see his smug smile, Cat would have known differently, for Devlin's man had accomplished just what he had set out to do.

After she left, Richard remained standing in the dim gallery, apparently pausing to study a portrait, then turned at a sound behind him.

"Richard Blakely," Ransom said coolly as he stepped through an archway. Although the blond man remained still, exhibiting no signs of nervousness at his appearance, Ransom was not surprised, for nothing much ever showed on Blakely's face.

"Your grace," Richard answered just as coldly, bowing slightly. "How delightful to see you again."

"Do you think so? I would be sorry to have to change your mind," Ransom said. Without a moment's hesitation, his fingers curled around Richard's neck, slamming him against the wall with a dull thud, and there the man dangled, his feet inches off the floor, while he struggled for breath.

"Where can I find your master?" Ransom demanded. Receiving only a choked gurgle for his trouble, he increased the pressure of his fingers on Richard's thin neck. "Where is he?" Ransom asked again, the cold calm of his voice belying his actions.

"L'Etoile . . . the Rue de la Paix," Richard choked.

"Very good," Ransom said, as he loosened the grip on Richard's neck, and let his feet slide to the floor. The blond man gasped for several deep breaths, eyeing Ransom warily, for his neck was still enclosed in a fearful grip.

"And that one?" Ransom asked, nodding slightly toward the entrance to the gallery.

"What?"

"Who is the girl?" Ransom asked, his fingers tightening again.

"I never saw her before," Richard answered, his blue eyes mildly returning Ransom's gaze. This time, the force of Ransom's movement slammed Richard's head against the wall.

"Is she in Devlin's employ?"

"Yes, yes," Richard breathed as he struggled to stand. "She was to ensnare you . . . to make you look foolish."

"Thank you, Blakely, you have been most cooperative," Ransom said, abruptly releasing his quarry. He moved smoothly away, looking as elegant as when he had arrived, his eyes flicking emotionlessly over Richard, now hunched against the wall. Then, without another word, he turned, his long strides taking him from the gallery without a backward glance.

Richard slid down the wall to slump near the floor, rubbing his neck and orienting himself as the wave of dizziness passed. He did not even bother to congratulate himself on the success of his plan. Instead, he was silently berating himself for his miscalculation.

Miscalculations were dangerous and messy, and, in this case, painful. Yet who would have expected the cold-blooded Du Prey to become violent? Richard would accept no excuses, however; it was his job to foresee all possible problems, and he had not seen just how touchy Du Prey would be about the girl. Yes, he had definitely miscalculated, for Du Prey was not just taken with the girl. He must be in love with her.

Shaking off the odd encounter with Mr. Blakely, Cat ducked into the blue salon to freshen up, her thoughts turning once again to Courtney and Ransom. She pinched her cheeks and checked the mirror, noting dismally that there was little change in the face that returned her gaze. It was certainly too late to hope that she would sprout a cloud of red hair accompanied by a pale complexion of milk and honey. Looking glumly back into the glass, she watched the features she had hoped to attain appear before her and turned in surprise.

"Courtney!"

"Catherine Amberly, why didn't you tell me?" Courtney asked breathlessly, taking both of Cat's hands in her own.

"Tell you what?"

"Only that a duke is so taken with you that he can't keep his eyes off you!"

"What?"

"It's true!" Courtney said excitedly, and they sank into two elegant gilt chairs. "Of course, when I asked him, he denied it and gave me quite a setdown, but it was obvious to anyone watching him. Oh, Catherine, he is simply mad for you!"

Relief flooded through Cat with the knowledge that her friend had no interest in Ransom, but she remained skeptical of his supposed tendre for herself. Courtney tried to convince her, detailing in excited whispers Ransom's every movement since he stepped into the ballroom, until Cat felt giddy with confusion.

"He was watching the door like a hawk until you arrived, and then I think he would have rushed to your side if I had not teased him about it." Courtney laughed. "Of course, he disliked me instantly." Seeing the faintest glimmer of a smile on her friend's face, she continued, "I think he is the handsomest man I have ever seen. Intelligent, dashing, *very* sure of himself, and so . . . aristocratic!" she enthused. "Well, tell me, what is he really like?"

What is he like? There's the rub, Cat thought, for she did not know what to tell Courtney. Although they were the best of friends, Cat had never divulged the secrets of her past to the red-haired beauty. "I really don't know him that well," Cat mumbled.

"Don't be coy with me, Catherine! Rumor has it that you two have been seeing quite a lot of each other!"

"Rumor probably spread by Amelia, whose eyes have been glazed ever since she saw his title," Cat said scornfully.

"Well, who can blame her? After seeing him, I admit to being a bit dazzled myself. Of course I am terribly cross with you, you goose, for not rushing to me immediately with the details!" Courtney said, smacking her friend playfully with her fan. "How often is there a tall, gorgeous, *unmarried* duke chasing after you, my girl? And I can't understand how you can be so nonchalant about the whole thing. Why, I would be perfectly bursting at the seams!"

Cat laughed along with her friend. Courtney's enthusiasm was catching, forcing Cat to rein in her soaring spirits. After all, her friend knew nothing about Ransom, neither his views on women nor the bold way he had seduced her. If Ransom was "mad" for her, it was strictly lust that drove him.

"Tell me," Courtney coaxed. "Did he kiss you?" The words were so close to Cat's own thoughts that she looked up in startled surprise, effectively answering the question without uttering a word. "He did! Oh, how glorious! Tell!" Courtney urged, making a face when Cat shook her head. "Oh, unfair! I've told you about my kisses, although they were not from anyone as exciting as the duke. I am quite jealous, you know! Why, just think, you might be a duchess!"

"Believe me," Cat assured her grimly, "the rogue does not have marriage in mind!"

"No!" Courtney gasped. "He would seduce you? Oh, how exciting! Don't you wish that you could let him? I can't wait until we're married, and then we can accept such offers! Personally, I plan to have lots of handsome lovers." She laughed gaily, but her laughter died when she saw the weak smile on the face of her friend, who stood up and turned again to the mirror.

"Oh, but Catherine, aren't you flattered? The only men who try to seduce me are old, balding merchants or gawky young boys . . ." Her words trailed off, and the room, so filled with gaiety a moment ago as two young women giggled over whispered confidences, suddenly seemed quiet and empty.

Courtney tilted her head and looked closely at Cat, who was adjusting the shells in her hair. With a start of revelation, Courtney leaned forward. "You love him," she accused, her voice soft with surprise and awe.

"Don't be silly," Cat said, concentrating as her slim fingers deftly straightened a shell.

"Oh, Catherine, how do you know he won't consider marriage? I know he's been smitten by you. Any fool can see that."

"You have been known to exaggerate," Cat said lightly, turning from the mirror and smiling at her friend.

"Catherine," Courtney began, but she was interrupted by a group of shrill matronly women entering the room.

"Come, Courtney, we're missing the party," Cat said, taking her friend's arm as though nothing unusual had occurred. Courtney silently followed her to the ballroom.

The two had barely stepped into the room when they saw the duke, looking solemn and determined—and gazing intently in their direction.

"What did I tell you?" Courtney whispered behind her fan. "Why, he resembles a vulture ready to swoop upon us, and you, dear Catherine, appear to be the main course."

Cat, her spirits buoyed, could not help stifling a laugh, for Ransom was wearing his most serious face, and he was coming straight toward them.

"He is sinfully handsome," Courtney said, "but much too ferocious for me." She shook her head, sending her auburn curls floating around her in charming disarray. "My goodness, if I were married to that one I would not dare take any lovers; he looks far too possessive. But with him, mayhap you would need no others," she added with a giggle.

"Shh!" Cat whispered, having visibly started at the word "lover" while Ransom approached.

"Miss Amberly, Miss Westland," he acknowledged with a nod. Then, taking Cat's arm none too gently, he turned to Courtney. "You will excuse us?" He asked the question in a tone that brooked no argument, leaving the red-haired beauty speechless as he whisked Cat peremptorily onto the dance floor.

Cat was bereft of words herself, her heart leaping into her throat at Ransom's boldness and his powerful effect on her. As she placed a trembling hand on his arm, she realized that it was the first time she had touched him since they had made love. Had that been only yesterday? It seemed as if centuries had passed since she had felt his warmth beneath her fingers. The attraction between them was almost tangible tonight, like the heat from a pot ready to boil over, and she was afraid to lift the lid and look at him. She was concentrating instead on his cravat when the smell of alcohol assailed her nostrils.

Hardly believing her own nose, she looked up at him quizzically, but his face, cold and drawn, told her nothing. Her own head a bit fuzzy, Cat blurted out, "You've been drinking!"

"So have you, my love!"

"Not as much as you, I'll warrant! My God, you fairly reek of it!" Cat declared, staring at him in wonder tinged with amusement. Her merriment was short-lived, however, for to her amazement his features went rigid with cold fury.

"Hush, my love. Your employer would not like that tone," he snapped.

"My employer?" Cat's brow furrowed in puzzlement. "Why is everyone talking in riddles tonight? Either the champagne has addled my brain beyond anything, or everyone else has been affected. Let me tell you of the odd conversation I had earlier," Cat began as she recalled Mr. Blakely's claim of friendship with Ransom.

Her partner cut her off, however, his lips curving into a frown. "The subject is *you*, my dear, and let's return to it." Cat, taken aback by his angry tone, could only stare up at him, her bright eyes searching his cold ones for his meaning.

"You are a fine little actress, but the play grows thin. Let me assure you that I am no longer an interested audience," Ransom said. When she still stared blankly at him, he asked irritably, "Have you ears, or am I speaking over your head? I tell you there is no need to continue playing the innocent, for I know who you are."

Cat gulped back her surprise. So that explained his foul mood! Ransom had finally recognized her, and he was furious that she had masqueraded as his cabin boy, privy to his thoughts and deeds. To be taken in by a woman, one of those "boring creatures" he held in so little respect, must be humiliating for him! And what's more, he had been close to that woman, for Cat had not only served beside him on *The Reckless*, she had earned his regard—or so she had thought.

Whatever warm feelings, if any, he had once harbored for his young friend had long been spent, Cat realized as she watched him smile cruelly at the surprise and guilt on her features. Cat cursed herself again for picking tonight of all nights to indulge in too much wine as she struggled for the words to deflect his anger. Finally, she simply sighed, raising luminous green eyes to his. "I did what I had to do," she said softly, "to save my own life."

"Spare me the heart-wrenching excuses, please," Ransom said coldly. "I haven't the time or the stomach for them." Despite his words, Ransom hoped that there was a reason for Catherine's deceit and that she *was* acting under duress, for he knew that Devlin had many ways of getting others to do his bidding, and not all those who worked for him did so willingly. The hope he nurtured, unacknowledged, was shattered, however, when the woman in his arms spoke again.

"Have I committed a crime, then, *your grace?*" Cat asked, snidely stressing what she deemed to be his spurious title. "The islands are a refuge for those with irregular histories, and masquerading seems to be quite the rage!"

Ransom fought a second sickening wrench in his gut at her words, a brazen admission of her guilt. Now he knew that she was one of Devlin's own, bought and paid for. Nothing showed on his face, however, but disdain.

"Good," Ransom said, looking anything but pleased. "It is so nice that we understand each other. I'm sure we can work out something to our mutual satisfaction." Although he intended to learn the details of Devlin's scheme, such conversation did not belong on a dance floor. He wanted to speak to the treacherous Miss Amberly privately, and, now that he had taken her true measure, he might even sample her skills again.

"The game might be up, but that does not mean

we cannot find new amusements to entertain us. Don't you agree, Miss Amberly?'' he asked, raising his brow sardonically.

Cat, still smarting from his angry words, could only look puzzled again at these new remarks. Was it the champagne that made his actions so bewildering, or was Ransom himself so drunk he was unable to make sense? As she sought an answer, he leaned so close to her as to be indecent and brushed his lips against her ear. ''I'm leaving here tomorrow, so let us make our last night together a memorable one, Catherine.''

Although his whisper sent chills along her neck, Cat was too wary of his meaning to respond. Her heart plummeted at the news that he really was leaving, and she looked up into his eyes, searching for some sign that he would miss her. But those brown orbs were so cold and hard, she slid her eyes away. His mouth, too, had hardened into a tight smile as he spoke again. ''Claremont has put me in the Carlisle bedroom in the west wing. Do you know it?''

Perplexed at this new change of topic, Cat only nodded mutely. Was he dissatisfied with his apartments?

''Meet me there when our dance has ended,'' Ransom instructed coldly.

This time his meaning was clear, and Cat's head snapped back as though he had slapped her. ''You conceited oaf!'' she hissed. ''You think just because of what happened yesterday . . . that I . . . God!'' she sputtered, so angry she was unable to speak. She fought the urge to strike out blindly at him, halted only by the desire not to make a spectacle of herself on the dance floor.

''Come now, let's not drag out this charade any longer, love. I won't be back, so if you want something from me, you had better move quickly,'' Ransom said curtly.

"I want nothing from you but your total absence from my life!" Cat said. "Let me go this instant, Ransom Du Prey, or I will do more than trod on your foot, as I did with Mr. Pettibone," she breathed hotly. "Instead, I will gladly give you my knee right here in front of everyone. Then maybe you will be less cocksure!"

"As you wish." Ransom shrugged and let her go with a graciousness that did not extend to his eyes. Too angry herself to take note, Cat did not see the threat implicit in his gaze, or she would have realized that Ransom was too furious to give in with such ease. They were in public, so he was forced to respond accordingly, but his stare held a promise that all was not done between them.

Cat, unable even to look at him, resisted the urge to rush from his side, an action that would only draw attention to herself. With slow, measured steps, she walked across the floor, putting a hand to her throbbing temple in an effort to still the headache brought on, she was certain, by Ransom and not by drinking three glasses of champagne in too short a time.

"But we just arrived," Amelia protested when Cat announced she was leaving. "And you were so impatient to get here, I had to restrain you from walking the whole way!" The look on Cat's face, however, stopped her chatter for once, and Amelia scooped up her reticule and shawl without another word.

She followed Cat's swaying skirts to the doorway, and as her niece made excuses to their host, Amelia turned to pick Ransom out of the crowd with her eyes. She found his tall, handsome figure easily enough. He was lounging negligently, his shoulder against one wall, glowering at them with a fierceness that made her start. Even Amelia began to doubt the wisdom of interfering in that one's life.

Chapter 27

Cat tossed and turned in her bed, knocking her fist into her pillow in an effort to make it more comfortable, but to no avail. She could not drive the night's horrible experience with Ransom from her thoughts. Amelia had wisely kept her mouth closed on the way home, and Cat, with no intention of volunteering any information, had gone straight to bed. Still, her fury with the man was so intense she was unable to sleep. Finally, she swung out of bed with an oath and threw a wrapper over her thin nightgown.

Without even thinking she slipped her knife into the pocket, for she carried it with her constantly. Begun as a sentimental gesture with a vow that her only gift from her captain never leave her side, the practice had long since given way to custom, and she no longer thought of Ransom when fingering the blade.

The terrace was cool and quiet. A slight breeze stirred in the trees, while the moon was bright above in a sky brimming with stars. Up at the great house, they would have finished supper and returned to the receiving rooms and the ballroom to continue dancing and socializing. Cat shook herself at the thought of the ball that continued without her and took a deep, calming breath. The air, a mingled perfume of roses and orchids, acted as a balm to her senses as she walked among the shadows.

Tearing an orchid from its stem, Cat lifted it to her face and breathed deeply of the heady scent. She looked down at her bare toes, peeping from underneath her wrapper, and scolded herself for coming out without her slippers. Too many months of running barefoot over the decks of the *Reckless*, she thought. Had she really changed so much since then? One thing remained the same: whenever Ransom entered her life, her emotions ran awry and confusion reigned.

She felt as though she had been through a battle, pounded and battered by cannon shot, but who was the victor? Ransom! she answered, for he had won the prize of her maidenhead. Cat cringed to remember how she had gasped in his arms, returning his kisses and even tearing at his clothes in passion, and she felt hot with shame. She realized painfully that she could not claim the victory in this contest of wills. In fact, she felt too much the casualty to be satisfied, and she longed to give her captain a little of his own back. It stung her to know that he walked away from this engagement with not one scar.

Right now, she hated Ransom Du Prey, hated him with all the force of her bitter, stinging pride and all the disillusionment and betrayal that wrung her heart. He had meant to seduce her all along, offering her the role of his mistress then claiming he had not, she thought angrily. And this time there had been no talk of her becoming his mistress—which at least would have been a commitment of sorts! No, she had been offered only a night in his bed, no more and no less, and a bitter, cold offer it was, too.

Cat still could not believe Ransom's rage at discovering her deception. She had expected him to be angry, but deep down she had hoped he would remember the closeness they had shared and look

upon her escapades on board the *Reckless* as fondly
as she did. In a pig's eye! The man had been furious, accepting no explanation, and assuming that
anyone who would masquerade as a boy was of low
moral character. He was the one lacking in character
and principles, she thought, her ire rising.

Despite whatever stupid yearnings she might feel
for him, Cat saw Ransom now with crystal clarity as
a coldhearted privateer posturing as a nobleman, the
kind of man who thought all women could be
bought by a shiny coin and a handsome face.

She had begun to pace slowly along the terrace,
unknowingly becoming a pale beacon drawing the
attention of a figure hidden behind the trees. That
figure, when he saw her moving like a specter
among the orchids, drew in his breath.

Cat's hair, shining softly in the moonlight, fell in
waves about her face, rippling as she gracefully walked
along the flagstones, while each step made her thin
garment cling to her body, delineating its curves and
accentuating her long legs. She looked entirely serene,
almost otherworldly, as she lifted an orchid to her
nose, and Ransom longed to break the spell. He
yearned for the passionate girl whom he knew lay underneath the graceful exterior, not this cool vision,
and he was struck by a sudden desire to have her,
all of her, here and now among the orchids.

Ransom was chagrined to find he still wanted her,
despite her ties to Devlin and her utter lack of scru-
ples. But desire raged through his blood like a physical thing, an outside force that he had to control
with an effort. It was like nothing he had experienced before, and it infuriated him, for since the first
lesson he had learned from Devlin, he had been in
control of himself, his business, his future. Until
now. Until he had met this devious beauty with the
power to throw his entire existence off balance.

Angrily he fought down the demands of his body

and forced cool control to flow through him before
he stepped quietly onto the terrace. "Out for a
moonlight stroll, my love?"

Cat nearly jumped out of her skin, then whirled
to face him furiously. "How dare you skulk around
my own terrace in the middle of the night like a
common housebreaker!"

"We have some unfinished business, my love,"
Ransom said ominously as he stepped closer.
"Surely, you did not think me such a compliant buf-
foon that I would leave without finding out a few
details of your little enterprise."

"Get the hell out of here!"

"Not until I obtain what I came for," he said, ad-
vancing until he stood but a hair's breadth from her.

"You're drunk!" Cat accused. She turned from
him in disgust, but he grasped her arm and pulled
her back.

"Hardly, my pet," he answered, annoyed at her
perception. "Now suppose you tell me exactly what
this charade was to accomplish?"

"Let go of me!" Cat ordered, more angry than
afraid when his hands closed around her arms. She
tried to break away from the fingers that gripped her
tightly and kicked at his shin. But without her shoes,
she only succeeded in hurting her own toes. "Have
you taken leave of your senses?" she snapped.

"Not entirely." Struggling in earnest now, Cat
raised her knee to his groin, but he anticipated her
action and stepped out of the way, whirling her
around in the same movement. "You are making me
lose all patience, you conniving baggage," he whispered menacingly. Before she had time to catch her
breath, he wound her hair around his hand and
snapped her head back. "Now, what was the
scheme? I want to hear it from your sweet, innocent
lips, my love."

"What the hell are you talking about?" Cat

choked, now alarmed by his behavior. Ransom was making even less sense than he had in Lord Claremont's ballroom, and his face, a cold mask in the moonlight, told her nothing. She had never known alcohol to affect him so, and she was at a loss as to just what to do to bring him back to his senses.

"If you are delaying in the hope of receiving compensation, let me assure you that you will not be getting any money from me," he said smoothly. "I'm sure Devlin is paying you enough already."

"Devlin!" Cat's shocked gasp rent the night. "Devlin paying me? You *are* insane!"

"I thought we had settled this already," Ransom said wearily. "I know who you are. I saw you with Blakely, who, after a bit of persuasion, confirmed your employment."

It took Cat several long, dark moments to connect Ransom's accusations with the man she had met in the portrait gallery. When she did, wild emotions soared through her, not the least of which was relief to find a reason for the behavior she was beginning to think signaled an unbalanced mind.

Her thankfulness quickly changed to outrage that he could think such a thing of her. She knew what kind of man Devlin was. That Ransom could believe her involved in some way with that horrible man was beyond anything, and that he would take some stranger's word over her own was worse.

"Pardon me for being so confused," Cat snapped. "Am I to understand that you believe I have been paid by this Devlin to do something to you? And when you claimed to know who I was, you were talking about the entertaining fiction that I am one of his employees?" Cat asked, not really expecting an answer. She laughed humorlessly at the thought that Ransom had not the slightest notion who she really was, nor did he seem too interested in discovering the truth, having already judged her guilty.

Cat's questions were met with stony silence, and, in truth, she expected little else, although deep in her heart she had hoped for more. Finally, since he seemed to be expecting some sort of confession, she complied. "I met the man for the first time tonight. You can believe me or not. I don't give a damn," she said with indifference. Their eyes locked in the darkness, his cold and suspicious, hers blazing with indignation.

Although it seemed an eternity, only a moment passed before he let her go so abruptly that she stumbled back, gasping for breath. He turned away from her with a grunt of disgust, and that was his mistake, for in the space of seconds the tables were turned and she was holding a knife to his throat.

"Very good!" Ransom said dryly. "Devlin certainly has taught you well."

"Understand this," Cat whispered, breathing hard. "I am not going to stand here defending myself to you, you bastard! You have done little else but insult me since you came here! I don't know from what lunatic asylum you escaped, but don't you *ever* lay your hands on me again." Her voice cracked with anger and hurt as she circled around to face her accuser, still holding her blade to his throat.

Although Ransom could feel the cold steel against his neck, he was more interested in Catherine's eyes, large and luminous in the moonlight, and throwing off more sparks than a bonfire. Her struggles had tossed her hair into a wild mane and had thrown open her wrap, exposing the creamy skin above her breasts that rose and fell rapidly with each breath.

Cat was watching him closely, her ire just barely in check, and when she saw where his gaze wandered, her temper exploded. Forgetting she held the knife in one hand, she slapped him hard with the other, then his arms shot out to pull her roughly to him, and the knife fell unheeded to the terrace stone, a thunderous crack of noise in the stillness of the night.

His mouth moved roughly on hers, and she responded with abandon, her arms wrapping around his neck to pull him closer. His hands against her back pressed her body to his while his tongue roamed her mouth passionately, for Ransom lost control the minute he took her in his arms, abandoning logical thought to his overwhelming desire. Catherine filled his senses: her smooth skin, her silky hair, her sweet taste and scent.

His hands slipped underneath her wrapper to the thin nightgown beneath, causing his breathing to double its pace. The thought that he was behaving like an unseasoned boy passed briefly through his consciousness before something else intruded: a sound. With some difficulty, Ransom pulled himself out of the depths of his passion to listen. It was definitely a door opening. And footsteps. With an effort he pulled his lips from hers, heard her soft protest, but it was too late. There stood Isaac with a lantern spreading its light on them.

Cat blinked stupidly and looked up at Ransom. His eyes were bright, his features sharply etched. "Good-bye, my love," he said, and quickly cupping her face in his hands, he kissed her fiercely. Although her heart was racing, her body, languid and lethargic, was slow to respond, and it seemed a full minute passed before she realized she was staring at the empty air where he had been.

"Are you all right, Miss Catherine?" Isaac's voice, betraying nothing, broke the stillness.

"Yes, Isaac. Thank you," Cat said, dazedly glancing at the barefoot butler. There being nothing else to say, she walked past him with as much dignity as she could muster and returned to her room.

Chapter 28

Ransom's return to the ship was greeted with relief, for "Too much time ashore left a sailor skint and sore," as the adage went. When Ransom's mood became known, however, more than a few of his crew wished the captain would head right back to land. Hounded by a lingering dissatisfaction with his handling of Miss Amberly, Ransom restlessly snapped orders and complained of the laxity that had developed in his absence.

"And where the hell did Blakely come from?" he barked at Bosun as soon as he set foot on deck.

"God only knows, captain! The only other ship that's been here was one of the Simpson cargo vessels, and she's been and gone!"

"When?"

"Left yesterday morning, captain."

"I want to know how he slipped beneath our very noses without my knowledge and where the hell he is now!" Ransom said. "Send Peabody and as many as it takes to find out. The rest I want back on this ship, sober and ready to sail."

Mr. Peabody, efficient as usual, soon returned with the information Ransom sought, for he knew that a well-placed coin or two, a word in the right ear, and most people, gossips by nature, would tell all they knew. He dutifully reported that Blakely had arrived on the *Rampart*, recently anchored off the other side of the island, and stayed at a plantation there, owned by one William Montgomery. The ship, and Blakely, had sailed away that very morning.

At Mr. Peabody's words, Ransom snorted in disgust. "See that you're awake next time we're at anchor," he ordered his officers, "just in case Blakely should care to burn you in your beds!"

Beyond that, Ransom did not pursue the matter, for he had no intention of wasting another minute on Blakely or his cohort Catherine. Ransom's interest lay in the master of a chess game for which they only served as pawns. He was after Devlin. Blakely said he was on L'Etoile, so the ship would sail to the island to find him. It was time, Ransom decided, that this game ended . . . for good.

"Isaac can be trusted," Amelia assured her niece, satisfied that although the servant had already relayed the story to her, it would travel no further. Reclining amid a profusion of pillows on her bed, the elderly lady had rung for breakfast to be served in the privacy of her rooms while Cat had poured out the tale. "Honestly, Catherine," Amelia said, fluffing a pillow, "I'm sure I don't know what's gotten into you, sneaking out to meet a man in your nightclothes!"

"I did not sneak out to meet him! I left the party to avoid the blackguard! How was I to know he would creep into the garden in the middle of the night?"

"Well, I must say I can't approve of you wandering about outside at all hours," Amelia said. "My dear, it simply isn't done!" Cat groaned and jumped to her feet from her perch alongside Amelia's bed to prowl about the room like a caged animal.

"Of course, the best thing would be for him to

marry you, but it appears that course was not to his liking," Amelia said with a sigh.

Cat stopped her pacing. "Marriage to that . . . that . . ." Cat broke off as none of the names that sprang to mind were ones she felt comfortable repeating to her aunt. "No, thank you! The coward ran off rather than face that possibility! He has no intention of marrying anyone, ever!" Cat said.

The bitterness in her tone made her aunt glance up sharply. "Well, one would think he would have to, eventually, if only to have an heir to the title," Amelia said lightly, her eyes never leaving her niece.

"Ha! The man cares not a fig for family or home. I wonder if he really cares for anything," Cat said. She stopped her pacing while Marie arranged breakfast on a table for her and presented a tray to Amelia, still comfortable in her bed.

"It's not that I care a whit for what people think," Cat resumed forcefully, once Marie had gone. "I just don't want to be claimed as another in Ransom Du Prey's long line of conquests." She wondered idly if that was even his real name. Perhaps the true duke will show up, madder than a hive of hornets, she thought briefly. I wish he would go after Ransom's hide, but with my luck he's probably approaching seventy and bedridden!

"Oh, has there been a long line?" Amelia asked with interest. "I didn't know. Well, you know they say that reformed rakes make the best husbands." She ignored Cat's spluttering and buttered a flaky pastry.

"I would not call him a rake!"

"You just said he had a long line of conquests, though I suppose there are other things one must take into consideration before bestowing such a title. Of course, you know more about him than I do, having lived with him," Amelia said, nonchalantly popping the pastry into her mouth.

"And I thought he was angry that I had . . . lived with him, I mean!" Cat said. "At the ball he claimed to know who I was so I thought he recognized me as his cabin boy, when all the time he was accusing me of being one of Devlin's . . ." Cat could not finish the thought, her complaints about Ransom having finally wound themselves down to the crux of the matter. "How *could* he think I was involved with that . . . that creature?" she said, more furious and hurt by his accusations than by anything else.

"Oh, dear, you can't blame him for that," Amelia said softly. "You said the duke claimed this Blakely fellow told him you worked for Devlin. How was he to know the man was lying?"

Cat frowned at her aunt, unable to answer. *He should have trusted me* was her unspoken thought. If he cared for me at all, he would have given me the benefit of a doubt, she thought. Cat knew in her heart that something had happened last night between them, changing forever the way she looked at him, for now she knew that he had never cared for her and never would. How could he, when he did not even trust her? When he could make love to her and leave her?

Amelia's heart sank at the firm set of her niece's chin. "Well, the scoundrel is gone now, so we no longer have to worry about him," she said with a sigh as she dusted off her hands. "I have sent Isaac to town to see if his ship has left the bay. Believe me, my dear, he is the soul of discretion. He will say nothing about what he saw, and things can all return to normal around here!"

Ha! thought Cat, as if one could trust *any* man! For the next few days she went about her daily routines restlessly, alternately depressed and angry at Ransom's behavior, and apprehensive that word of their moonlight encounter would leak out.

But it seemed that Isaac was, indeed, to be trusted.

Cat heard nothing amiss—no sly innuendoes from shopkeepers' fat wives or impertinent offers from planters' eager young sons—and she breathed a sigh of relief. She had made a home on the island, and although she and Amelia were not social whirl-winds, she did not wish to be ostracized or to see her aunt's reputation suffer because of her own fool-ishness.

And what foolishness! To give her heart to a man as cold as ice and who would not even trust her! He was an idiot besides, Cat told herself, for who but the senseless would believe her to be in league with Devlin? As the days went by, Cat reminded herself of that and of each transgression against her that her captain had committed. She was determined to maintain her rage against him, for although her rep-utation was intact, her heart was not, and the force of her anger seemed to be the only thing that could keep her from sinking into despair.

Ransom stared coldly at the darkened warehouse on L'Etoile, empty but for a few useless crates and the trash that littered the floor, of interest to no one but the rats. The offices were just as deserted. Even the furniture had been removed, though in the larger of the two rooms, the floor still carried the imprint of where a huge desk had stood, and Ransom knew instinctively that it had been Devlin's.

Ransom's men had found other traces of Devlin's occupancy among the litter, but the markings on the floor were the only evidence Ransom needed. He knew with certainty that Devlin had been here, holding court in the spacious office tucked in the corner of a warehouse in the oddly named Rue de la Paix, but he was clearly gone now.

For how long? Ransom knew the *Rampart*, the ship on which Blakely had been traveling, and he doubted that the vessel could have arrived at L'Etoile before the *Reckless*. Even if it could have appeared soon enough for Blakely to warn his master, Devlin would not have had time for a move of this magnitude. No. Devlin had been long gone, and this building must have been standing vacant when Blakely gave away its location, Ransom realized with icy fury.

Ransom vividly remembered closing his fingers about Blakely's skinny throat in Lord Claremont's portrait gallery and demanding to know Devlin's whereabouts. Well, so much for the information he had received for his trouble. With uncharacteristic ruthlessness, Ransom wished he had killed the man then and there, for the little weasel had lied, saving his own skin by tossing Ransom a bone, an old and useless bone with no meat on it. How Devlin must be laughing up his sleeve right now.

With the realization of Blakely's deception, Ransom felt an odd hope burgeoning in his chest. If Blakely had lied about Devlin's location, could he not have lied about . . . other things? Had he lied about Catherine?

Ransom rapidly squelched the doubt that Catherine was one of Devlin's hirelings. There had been one too many coincidences where that lady was concerned . . . too many signs that pointed to her guilt. And hadn't he made enough of a fool of himself about her already? With a sharp intake of breath, Ransom dismissed the notion that Miss Amberly was anything but the conniving, deceitful wretch he knew her to be.

As for Devlin . . . Ransom would keep his ear to the ground. The man had to be somewhere in these waters, and Ransom had no doubt that he would find him sooner or later. In the meantime . . . He resisted an urge to blow the *Rampart* out of the water, should he come across her, for there might well be innocents aboard.

The same could not be said for the ship of Devlin's more infamous cohort, Ben Pike, however. The *Prize* carried no innocents, and Ransom had held no such reservations about its destruction. The pirate ship was not easily found, though, and rumor had it that Ben was now practicing his own brand of bloody harassment along the American coast, so Ransom doubted that the two would meet soon. He debated going in search of the *Prize*, yet so far he had no quarrel with the Americans. And the *Reckless* was not his personal instrument of revenge, but a business venture. One that he had sorely neglected of late, Ransom reminded himself.

There were prizes to be won and businesses to be run, he mused as he stared out over the sea that seemed to sing in his blood. The majestic blue was a fickle mistress but an honest one, and thus an improvement over any living woman, especially the one whose image would not leave him.

Chapter 29

$\sim\!\!\sim\!\!\infty\!\!\circ\!\!\sim\!\!\sim$

Edward Moore slumped in his chair, his cravat askew, his finely tailored jacket rumpled, and his heavy-lidded eyes dulled by his latest vice: opium. Right now, however, he was indulging in liquor, the London tavern where he sat having been a favorite haunt of his when he was young.

Then he had been willing to do nearly anything for money, and this had been a place of business, where he sought handouts from the wealthy nobles who came to the filthy place on a dare . . . or for more personal reasons. Yes, he had made some fat purses here, but somehow the money had never been enough, slipping through his fingers the way gin flowed like water in the public house.

When he had first come into his fortune, Edward had returned to the tavern, flaunting his title and his coin, but the thrill of turning the tables on his old cohorts was soon forgotten in the new and numbing haze of opium, and now he found it hard to remember just why he was there.

As if the devil himself divined his thoughts, a ghost from that past sidled up to his table, and Edward found himself looking at the thin, pinched face of . . . who was it? Corky. Yes, that was it. Not a very fitting name for a former pugilist well known for his ability to beat sense into those who, for one reason or other, were not sufficiently cooperative for his boss.

"Devlin wants to see you," the wiry man said, his leering grin showing the lack of several prominent teeth.

In spite of his benumbed state, Edward shivered, and the little man laughed. "Now," he said, stepping forward as though he would enjoy pulling Edward along with him like a bag of meal. Edward stood up and followed him through a bewildering trail of alleys and lanes to meet his former mentor, the man who, though Edward little realized it, was responsible for so much of what he was today.

After all the years, thing seemed little changed in Devlin's inner circle. A few of the faces were new but Edward would have recognized most of them had he taken the trouble; however, his attention was limited to the shadowy Corky, and then . . . to Devlin himself.

Edward stood, as one always did, before the massive desk and the man behind it, for Devlin always liked to keep others at a disadvantage. Edward, who knew that his new title meant nothing here, began sweating as he stood under the scrutiny of those small, dark eyes.

"You look dreadful. I'm disappointed in you," Devlin finally said, although he sounded pleased enough. "Sunk in gambling and drink and opium, too, they tell me. You've ruined yourself, Edward. Even your looks are going now. You are nothing but one of the dissipated dilettantes you once despised," he sneered. "But, then, blood will tell in the end, will it not? You are one of them, no matter how far removed."

Edward waited silently while Devlin paused, apparently finished with his ritual bloodletting. "I've called you here to do you a favor, my fine lord," Devlin said as he put his hands together. "I believe you have misplaced something. That cousin of yours. What was her name?''

Edward stared blankly before finally calling it to mind. ''Catherine. Catherine Amberly.''

''Ah, yes. I am in a position to collect this missing piece of baggage and return it to you, for a price.'' Devlin's lips curved into a smile at the look of bewildered surprise on Edward's face. ''Hoping she was dead, were you?'' he asked with a laugh. ''Well, she will be soon enough. And you, Edward, weren't you a little too eager for your inheritance?''

When Edward nodded, Devlin laughed scornfully. ''So I suspected when I heard of Pembroke's . . . untimely death,'' he said. ''You were always in a hurry, and it made you careless, didn't it?'' Devlin continued despite Edward's silence. ''No doubt you made a shoddy mess of the old man's murder, and then you let the girl escape. I assume she knows something?''

Edward nodded again, still saying nothing. ''Well, there will be no mistakes this time,'' Devlin said with assurance. ''I don't make them. But you know that, don't you? I know exactly where little Miss Amberly is, and I'll have her returned quietly and efficiently. I'll even eliminate her for you.'' Devlin paused, his fingers drumming together as he smiled. ''In return, I want a piece of that inheritance before you squander it all. How much is left?''

Devlin's lips pursed at Edward's gaze. ''So you don't even know? It's worse than I thought. I'll have one of my clerks look into the matter. I hope, for your sake, Edward, that it's not too late, for I'm sure you want this Amberly matter taken care of neatly, don't you?''

Edward asserted mutely, unwilling and unable to speak unless ordered to do so, while Devlin shook his head in disgust. ''Messy, Edward, messy. But then the whole business was, wasn't it? Showing up one day and murdering the old bastard immediately . . ." The fat man clucked. "I thought I had taught you better . . . Ah well, every teacher must have his failing student."

Edward did not even flinch, and Devlin, his sport ruined by Edward's lack of response, dismissed him curtly with a wave of his hand. Then he called for paper and began to write to a much more promising protégé, Richard Blakely.

I have a little job for our friend Ben Pike, he penned, smiling.

Richard accepted the packet of letters without expression, for unlike some of Devlin's less savory employees, he knew how to wait, and he had been waiting patiently for his next orders since he'd completed his mission with Miss Amberly.

He was not pleased with the delay, however, for the garret where he was staying was a far cry from his recent accommodations on Barbados, hearkening back instead to many of his first assignments. His extended stay in the Caribbean had prompted him to question his status in Devlin's organization and even consider striking out on his own. But no one left Devlin's employ unless he decreed it, and even then some did not make it out alive.

Once alone, Richard perused the correspondence, which would contain Devlin's instructions on various aspects of his businesses, and pulled out a letter sealed in red, denoting its foremost importance. The mission called for him to oversee the kidnap and transfer of Miss Amberly to Devlin's new base in England—a task that would return Richard to his boss's side, which was infinitely preferable to being stranded halfway around the world.

The letter was reassuring, noting only that Richard could be relied upon to complete the task with appropriate delicacy and efficiency. Flattery, no doubt, but it was a welcome hint of rewards to come, for the job of seeing Miss Amberly to England would not be an easy one. Ben Pike was notorious for his volatility, but finding another ship captain willing to carry a kidnap victim would be difficult.

The job itself could be handled simply, Richard thought, methodically going over the scheme in his mind. He noted, however, his last miscalculation in dealing with Miss Amberly that had resulted in his own injury when he had dismissed Ransom Du Prey too lightly. Word had it that Du Prey had left Barbados in a hurry, swallowing Richard's bait better than the hungriest of sharks, but it would not hurt to make certain just what the duke was up to now.

Ransom was on L'Etoile, throwing himself into gambling, wenching and drinking in an atypical fashion that fascinated the crew, especially since he seemed to excel in all three areas. Only Mr. Peabody, who was beyond such nonsense, and Bosun, who was worried, refused to join the men in recounting stories of the captain's exploits. Heartily sick of the endless carousing, the first mate finally took matters into his own hands, marching down to the captain's cabin with fire in his eyes.

At Bosun's noisy entrance, Ransom turned over in his bed, raising a hand to run his fingers through his hair. "What is it?"

"Well, well, here it is nigh on noon and you still abed like the lovesick swain you are," the first mate replied caustically, slamming down the breakfast tray with a bang that nearly jolted Ransom's eyes from his sockets.

"Good God, man! Are you trying to wake the dead?" Ransom asked, sitting up and putting a hand to his throbbing head. "What the hell are you babbling about?"

"You, lad! What are you doing to yourself? Let's put an end to this nonsense and be off!"

"You are the one who demanded that we make land," Ransom said coldly, his body stiffening in response to his first mate's words.

"Only because you were driving yourself and the men into the ground, tearing about after every piddling ship that you came across! Sick and tired they were getting, too, of the work and you driving them, but when I asked you to give the men a rest, I didn't have L'Etoile in mind!" Bosun huffed. "You know this isn't a good place for them, captain; they get into trouble here. There's a bad bunch anchored around us, and I don't mind saying that some of 'em make me nervous."

"Are you turning into a old woman?" asked Ransom irritably. "Where would you have me take them? To the King's park on a kite-flying excursion?"

"I'd tell you where, in a thrice, too, if I weren't suspecting that you'd take after me," Bosun grumbled.

"Ha! If you were afraid of me you wouldn't be in here now, airing your dissatisfaction so loudly," Ransom said dryly.

"Well then, lad, I'll tell you where you should go, and it's to Barbados!" At his words, Ransom's brow lifted slowly while his eyes bored into those of his first mate, who did not flinch from the iron gaze. "Take the whip to me if you will, but I'll say my piece. Maybe seeing this female again will get you back to your old ways, get her out of your blood."

"Who says she's in my blood?"

"You haven't been yourself since we sailed into that cursed Carlisle Bay. If it's something else that had you working yourself and the crew to death, and now has you working just as hard at roistering, then tell me. If it's the woman, there isn't any help for it but her, or maybe another one like her."

"There isn't anyone like her." The words were out before Ransom could catch them. Grimacing, he held up his hand in a warning to his first mate not to say a word as he stared down at the bedding in thought. Finally, he raised his head with a sigh. "We'll go to my plantation on Windlay," he said. "I'll check on the shipping, and the crew can frolic in safer taverns. How's that?"

Bosun, who knew when to quit, grunted in agreement.

Chapter 30

Bosun, anxious to see the last of L'Etoile, made haste to prepare the ship for sail, but before they could be off, the familiar canvas of the *Windmere* was sighted. Although there would be no leaving L'Etoile now, at least not right away, Bosun did not care. He actually broke into a grin to see the blood-red shirt of the *Windmere*'s captain, René Troussaint, for here was a man to shake the captain out of his gloom.

''Bosun, you old dog! Keeping the ladies satisfied, are you?'' René asked upon boarding, his blue eyes twinkling as he slapped the back of the burly older man.

''Trying my best! Trying my best!'' Bosun answered good-naturedly. ''I never thought I'd be saying this, but I'm glad to see you,'' he added with a fearsome grin.

''Since you are so happy to see me, you have not forgotten the ten pounds you owe me?''

''What? I don't know what you're speaking of,'' Bosun answered loudly, as if daring the man to refresh his memory. At the first mate's innocent pose, René laughed, showing his even white teeth, then turned to shout greetings at a few of the familiar faces among the crew, including a barely civil Mr. Peabody. After a mumbled answer, the ship's master turned and stalked away, the only man aboard who apparently was displeased at the sight of Troussaint.

"He'll never forgive me for the time I cried fire in the whorehouse, sending him into the street naked as a bird," René said, shaking his head at the departing back of the ship's master.

"Aye," Bosun agreed. "It wouldn't have been so bad if you hadn't lined up the crew outside and had that hornpipe a'playing."

"*Oui,* but the hornpipe added finesse," René said, grinning wickedly as he moved his hand in a gesture of appreciation. "He did dance a little jig as he tried to leap into his breeches! But now, where is your excellent captain?"

"In his cabin," Bosun grunted, "and in a fine mood. That's no lie."

"Then I am wanted. I will cheer the rutting stag," the Frenchman promised, the diamond in his ear sparkling in the sun, before he made his way below.

For once, however, Ransom was not heartened by the sight of his old friend. Once so eager to hear René's report on the mysterious Miss Amberly, Ransom no longer had the stomach for what would only be a confirmation of his own discoveries. And coming on the heels of Bosun's accusations that he was smitten with the wench, René's special brand of banter along those same lines would be difficult to take.

It was a less than enthusiastic Ransom, then, who greeted his old friend. Although he leaned casually against the paneling, René knew him well enough to see the tension in the lean body, and the Frenchman drew back, casting his friend a disparaging look. "I left a beautiful *fille de joie* to rush news to you and find you have lost your manners entirely."

"Sorry," Ransom said curtly and gestured to a chair, which René made a great show of taking.

Once his friend was seated, Ransom threw open the door and yelled for Bosun to bring the best bottle of brandy.

A few minutes later, René was leaning back in his chair, his booted feet crossed neatly on the captain's table. He looked entirely at ease, holding a glass of brandy in one hand and a cigar in the other.

"Well, do I have to pry it out of you?"

René smiled slyly. "*Mon ami*, this task nearly cost me an ear—my left one, which I am quite fond of, by the way—and I had to cut short my visit with the lovely Mademoiselle Armand. These developments were quite unanticipated."

"How much?" Ransom asked with a raised brow.

"I am insulted you think of me as mercenary!" René answered, starting from his comfortable position. "However, there was a small matter of a gambling debt," he said, relaxing once again. "The dens are not what they used to be! And Mademoiselle Armand had expensive tastes." He smiled. "Fifty for my trouble."

"It's yours."

"Good," said the Frenchman, taking a drink. He set his glass on the table and studied Ransom before relating his information. "Catherine Elizabeth Amberly was born September 14, 1788, to Charles Amberly and the former Belinda Naughton. An artist of little stature, Amberly died of pneumonia, leaving his wife and infant daughter penniless. The young widow married Lord James Pembroke, baron of Wellshire, and died herself not long after," René recited, his flamboyant gestures and accent all but disappearing in his concentration on his narrative.

"Pembroke held lands in the south, near the village of Coxley. A shrewd investor, he increased his inheritance to triple his income, but he was definitely a minor character. No court contacts. The fellow was killed by a poacher's bullet, in the summer of 1804.'' René took a long puff on the cigar and glanced at Ransom, who was watching the slow swirl of the liquid in his glass.

"His daughter was a handful by all accounts,'' René continued. "Grew up like a wildflower, careening all over the countryside on horseback and traipsing about the woods with the servants.'' He paused, looking for a reaction from Ransom, but his friend's face was impassive.

"The title passed to a cousin, Edward Moore, a hard one who is fast squandering all the money. The tenants are not happy with the change. Edward spends most of his time in London, gambling and cultivating new vices.'' René drained his glass and looked up expectantly until a scowling Ransom refilled the glasses while René looked on with a grin.

"The family always kept to themselves, this new lot especially, so everyone I talked to thought the girl was still living at the manor,'' René went on, holding his glass up to the light as if inspecting the liquid. "I was ready to leave it at that and return to my lonely *cherie* when an old tar caught me unawares and threatened to separate me from my ear.'' Ransom raised a brow questioningly, and René shrugged. "Even I am not invincible, my friend. I was enjoying the local hospitality when he caught me from behind.

"It was a most fortunate encounter. The old salt, Budd Simms by name, demanded to know why I was nosing about. He used to work at the estate and was quite protective of your little Catherine, so it took some fast talking and the blade I carry in my boot to save my lobe. According to him she fled, very suddenly, soon after the new lord's arrival.'' René glanced at Ransom through his thick black lashes and smiled when he realized he had caught the captain's interest.

"And?'' Ransom asked, but René did not answer

at once, taking time to casually blow three smoke rings and dust the ashes on the floor. "Damn it, René, you should take to the stage!" Ransom snapped, but the Frenchman, clearly enjoying himself, would not be rushed.

"*And*," René finally said, "she is now living with her aunt, a lady of unimpeachable character. So the girl is *exactly* who she claims to be, while you, my friend, have been sailing too long in these waters. You are seeing sharks behind every wave."

"She knows nothing of Devlin, then?" Ransom asked. He could hear the tension in his voice and cursed himself, but visions of Catherine under the tutelage of that fat, decadent slug had been dogging Ransom since he had left Barbados.

"I am saying that the little wildflower has had nothing whatsoever to do with Devlin."

Ransom's relief was almost physical, as though he had been struggling under a great weight that was suddenly lifted, and he turned his back, walking over to the windows to avoid his friend's penetrating gaze. Here was news he never expected to hear, and he tried to halt his exhilaration at the thought of her innocence while he methodically reviewed the evidence. Blakely had lied about Catherine, but why? There were still too many unanswered questions clinging to Miss Amberly . . .

Ransom turned suddenly, his brow poised high. "You're keeping something back. What?" he asked, his eyes narrowing as René studiously examined the end of the cigar.

"*Moi?* I am telling you what you wanted to know." The Frenchman shrugged. "Why would I keep something from you?" The blue eyes sparkled in challenge as they met Ransom's, and for a moment the two men stared at each other until René broke off his gaze with a mocking laugh. "Ask me

anything you like about your lady, my friend, and I
will answer you truthfully.''

Ransom eyed the Frenchman with a trace of sus-
picion, but he could not imagine what René saw fit
not to divulge. ''Why does she seem so familiar to
me?'' Ransom finally asked. The question, half serious, half rhetorical, hung in the air for a moment
before René grinned wickedly.

''Perhaps because you have met the lady before.''

''When?''

''Well,'' René said slyly, ''whether you remember
or no, I suspect you were once in the not-so-thriving
hamlet of Coxley, for the last time she was seen in
the village, the little wildflower rode in seated before
a stranger meeting your general description. This at
a time when you were crossing just that same bit of
country.'' René chuckled.

''The girl claimed to have had trouble with her
horse, from which, one can only assume, this
stranger rescued her. But all the village knew her to
be an excellent horsewoman, so some thought that
she disgraced herself with this fellow, and that is
why she was not seen again. I can only say for
shame, Ransom, ruining an innocent young thing!
And then not to recognize her.'' René laughed as he
shook his head.

''I did not touch her,'' Ransom growled as he dug
deep into his memory to recall rescuing a sweet-
faced child from a runaway horse. Such a minor incident, he'd tucked it away in the recesses of his
mind, but, yes, he could see now that the lovely
young innocent was indeed Catherine, and that
must be why he so often felt he knew her from before. And yet . . .

''Whatever you say, my friend,'' René said with
a grin, interrupting his thoughts, and Ransom had
to shake off a lingering suspicion that the Frenchman was not telling all he knew. Ransom could have

sworn there was a ghost of a laugh behind those clear blue eyes, but it was gone as René suddenly became serious.

"There is something else," the Frenchman said, putting down his feet and reaching for the bottle of brandy. He refilled the glasses and leaned his elbows on the table, speaking softly and seriously. "When I convinced the old man that I was not after his protégé's maidenhead or aught else of her, he confided in me. He thinks the father's death was no accident and names Edward as the man behind it, especially since no one admits to the girl's absence. He has no proof, of course, and who would listen if he did? He was not for stirring up the waters, thinking the girl was safe in the balmy isles." René took a gulp from the glass.

"I take it that situation has altered?" Ransom asked testily.

"*Oui*," René answered. "Someone brought the tale home that she is living happily ever after in the islands, and now there is a price on her head. Apparently Edward wants her back or dead . . . but he will not do the job himself. He has given it to someone much more accomplished in such areas, though how he made this one's acquaintance I am not sure."

Something in René's voice made Ransom look probingly at him, and the Frenchman nodded slowly. "*Oui*, my friend, you should be concerned. It is not the drunken Edward or some cheaply bought gaolbird who is after your lady. It is Devlin himself."

"Devlin? What would Devlin want with her?" Ransom asked, his voice icy.

René shrugged. "He may simply have been hired by the cousin . . . or he may hope to hurt you."

Ransom glanced sharply at his friend. "I'll kill him," he whispered.

"I thought as much."

"I've been meaning to attend to him for a long time, but the elusive bastard has always been just out of reach," Ransom said, his fingers closing hard around his glass.

"Well, he's set up his shop in London now, though how long he will remain there is anyone's guess. And exactly where in the city he has his den . . . that would take some hunting."

"Hmmm," Ransom grunted. "No wonder I had lost all trace of him here. But if he is in London, just how does he propose to stretch his tentacles this far?"

"Do not forget that he has friends and those who do his business for him," René said. "If you had some dirty work to be done in these seas, who would you take it to?"

"Ben Pike," Ransom answered, and his voice held a deadly menace.

"That is my guess, also," agreed René.

"I thought he was practicing his own brand of bloody harassment along the American coast," Ransom said.

"So he was, but I happened to hear that the *Prize* was headed south."

Ransom's brow inched up as his eyes met René's. "He's moving fast."

"He enjoys this kind of work."

"This is one job he will not complete."

"I would hope not," the Frenchman said, eyeing Ransom. "See that you take care of him—and Devlin, too, my friend," he said, raising his glass in a silent toast, "for I've a longing to meet this lady of yours."

Chapter 31

Cat twirled an orchid bloom between her fingers, her thoughts far from the garden where she sat on a bench among the day's lengthening shadows.

"I saw you cut the oldest Grayson boy quite rudely last night," Amelia said as she knelt a few feet away, clipping some of the choicest blossoms. "Really, Catherine, I'm surprised at you. And after he showed such partiality," Amelia added, eyeing her niece shrewdly from under her bonnet.

Cat shrugged. "He is far too stodgy for my taste."

"Oh, I see," Amelia said, as if those few words explained all. "A man has to accost you in your nightclothes to gain your attention."

Cat's chin jerked up, her lips turning down into a frown. "No, that is not the way of it at all," she said tersely, disgusted by her aunt's constant reminders of Ransom. She looked at the bloom between her fingers as if hesitating to speak, then said offhandedly, "If you must know, Charles Grayson has never appealed to me, and, besides, he disapproves of your gardening."

"Is that all?" Amelia laughed, sinking back on her heels to get a good look at her niece. "So does half the island!"

"That's exactly what *he* said," Cat answered, still frowning at the bloom between her fingers. "Why, he even claimed that Lord Claremont does not approve!''

''He doesn't,'' Amelia confirmed, pulling off her gloves and rising to her feet. ''Of course, the old goat would rather die than admit I'm smarter than he is. He'd be happy if I gave up the gardens entirely!''

''But I thought you two were such good friends,'' Cat said, looking at her aunt in surprise.

Seeing the bewilderment on her niece's face, Amelia sat down beside her and looked out over the gardens that meant so much to her. ''No, I would say we are friendly adversaries.'' She chuckled, then paused as if choosing her words. ''We are two old people drawn together by a common background and common interests. We enjoy each other's company, but that does not mean we agree on everything or even that we agree on the important things.

''Ah, but Horace.'' Amelia smiled wistfully. ''Now, with my husband, it was something else entirely, and that is as it should be.'' Taking both of Cat's hands in her own, she said seriously, ''You are too young to settle for less than that! Good heavens!'' She shuddered. ''Just imagine spending a lifetime with a man who disapproves of you! On second thought, I believe you were quite right in cutting that Grayson boy dead in his tracks,'' she said briskly, nodding for emphasis while Cat smiled.

For a moment, both women were silent, then Amelia spoke softly. ''Catherine, I think if you follow your heart, all will be well.''

That was the last thing Cat wanted to do, for her heart, that ignominious organ, persisted in yearning for the captain of the *Reckless*. Having no desire to admit to such traitorous thoughts, she merely shook her head and rose from the bench.

''Well, enough of such talk,'' Amelia said, a sad smile lingering on her face as she, too, stood up.

"Let us go in, dear. The sun is nearly down," she added as if suddenly noticing the day's passing.

"In a moment," Cat replied. "I think I'll watch the sunset." Frowning slightly, Amelia hesitated, but her niece's words held no invitation for company, so she finally turned to go, leaving Cat alone among the shadows.

After watching her aunt go into the cottage, Cat wandered to the edge of the gardens, then climbed down to an outcrop below, where she rested her elbows on her knees, cupped her chin in her hands, and scowled at the glorious display of colors on the horizon. A panoply of reds and yellows melted into the ocean in a breathtaking sunset, the golden colors reflected in her hair as she stared unseeing into its glory and mulled over her aunt's words.

Were two people ever happy together? she wondered as she tossed the now well-mangled orchid down the hill. Her mother and stepfather had obviously not been suited, and most of the couples on Barbados seemed to maintain a kind of distant tolerance. Was the type of relationship that Amelia recalled so lovingly with her husband possible, or were her aunt's memories simply sweetened by time?

Cat's own wretched experience with love seemed to bear out her theory that it did not lead to happiness, and as if to emphasize the point, she was struck by a sudden piercing longing for Ransom. Cat shook her head as if to clear him from her mind, but she could not stop herself from envisioning him. Where was he now? Was he standing on the deck, the wind tossing his dark hair, or bent over his ledgers, the windows sending the evening light glowing onto his features?

With a frown, she thought of every black thing he had ever done, each heartless seduction and cold word, culminating in his accusations about her and Devlin. It was no use, though, for she knew deep within her heart that, despite all, there was much in the man to love, and with a bitter certainty she acknowledged that she still did just that.

If only he had trusted her enough . . .

Cat shook herself; there was no point in pursuing that line of thought. She had tried her best . . . and she had failed. Her only choice now was to try to forget Ransom and get on with her life. Despite such good intentions, he was still on her mind when she heard a nearly imperceptible rustle in the bushes behind her, and she promptly reproved herself for thinking that she might have conjured up the object of her desires. She could not go through life hearing Ransom's footstep in every noise, expecting him to appear around every bend, she reasoned, standing up and dusting off her skirts resolutely.

"I'm never going to wish him near again," she declared aloud. But even her own mind defied her, and she was thinking of Ransom when a vicious blow from behind sent her crumpling to the ground.

Cat lay where she fell in the tall grass on the side of the hill, out of sight of all but a few birds and the two perpetrators who stood over her.

"Why must you crack her pretty skull, you jackass?" asked the first, a tall, skinny fellow brandishing a length of rope.

" 'Cause I didn't want a lot of caterwauling," growled the other, a burly man, dressed in seaman's clothes and armed to the teeth, looming over Cat's prone figure. He grabbed the rope with an oath, tied her hands and feet, stuffed a rag in her mouth, and threw her none too gently over his shoulders. "C'mon with you," he snarled, and with his fellow, he disappeared into the hedgerow.

A bright moon dipped low over the ocean, signaling that the sun would soon be rising over Barbados as the *Reckless* approached Carlisle Bay. After deliv-

ering his message, René had left the ship to return
to his own, and Ransom had stunned his first mate
with the sudden order to sail to Barbados. He had
been silently urging on the winds ever since.

The imminent sunrise reminded Ransom of the
morning he had caught Catherine swimming, nearly
naked, and he let himself savor the memory for a
moment before brushing it aside. He had been in-
undated with thoughts of her since René's visit.
Memories, visions, and images, each one more dear
than the last, had poured over him as though a dam
he had held forcibly shut had now been opened,
and it was all he could do to man the floodgates.

The absurd longing for her that he had been fighting since he'd left her doubled in its intensity now
that René had cleared her name, and all the half-
formed feelings he'd thought were neatly disposed
of had worked their way back into his blood at the
thought of his much-maligned beauty lying prey to
Ben Pike. He had made for Barbados with speed,
fighting off incipient anxiety and maintaining a cool
head, for should he be too late . . . well, he might
need his wits about him.

More than likely he would find Catherine blissfully asleep in her bed and outraged at any distur-
bance, he thought, his lips curving into a smile as
the ship entered the bay. He shrugged off the notion
that she might not be too happy to see him, considering their last encounter on her terrace. Although
she had no ties to Devlin, anyone who could wield
a blade with the skill Miss Amberly exhibited could
not be wholly innocent, he thought, remembering
how she'd held the knife to his throat.

Ransom smiled in admiration at the memory, no
longer sparing a thought for her mysterious past. He
realized without really admitting it that he no longer
cared what the enigmatic beauty had been up to before he had met her; he only knew he wanted to see

her again, to make sure she would be safe . . . and to hold her in his arms.

Ransom reached the Molesworth cottage as dawn was breaking, having nearly convinced himself that his headlong rush to Catherine's side was premature. But the sight of Lord Claremont's carriage in the drive at this hour made him set such notions aside and caused his throat to constrict oddly. He cleared it before stepping to the door and was immediately admitted to the parlor, where a disheveled-looking Amelia was in hot debate with his lordship.

"His grace, the duke of Morcester," Isaac announced with what Ransom could have sworn was a tinge of relief.

"Say, what do you know about this business?" Claremont barked at him while Amelia nearly swooned with relief.

"Thank God," she uttered, a dainty hand raised to her mouth.

"Now, see here—" Lord Claremont began, but Ransom ignored him, turning instead to Amelia.

"Catherine. Where is Catherine?"

"She's gone, your grace," Amelia whimpered, fear dulling her bright blue eyes and making her tiny shoulders slump in defeat.

"When?"

"Last night. She didn't come in for supper," Amelia whispered, then raised a hand to his sleeve. "You knew?" she asked, a measure of her strength returning at the sight of the duke's cool confidence.

"I had an idea," Ransom said, grimacing.

"Here, now. What is this about?" Lord Claremont demanded.

"Is there a plantation on the other side of the island?" Ransom asked evenly, his thoughts flying to the last time a ship had secretly berthed off the island. "Owned by a Montgomery?"

"Yes."

"What the deuce has Montgomery to do with anything?" Lord Claremont scoffed. "Why, the man's three times her age! I'm telling you, the girl's probably eloped with that Grayson boy, what's his name? Charles! I say head over to the Grayson plantation, and you'll probably pick up their trail," he argued loudly.

Ransom had been ignoring Lord Claremont as too ignorant of the facts to be helpful, but this last speech brought him up short. "What?" he asked coldly, his eyes on Amelia. "Is it possible that she has eloped?"

"No," Amelia answered scornfully, straightening her thin shoulders and giving Lord Claremont a look that made him mumble something unintelligible and sit down with a huff on the settee.

Ransom eyed her closely but, apparently satisfied with what he saw, he nodded briefly. "Where can I find this Montgomery's place?"

Cat drifted in the nether world between dream and reality, sometimes hearing the babbling of voices, sometimes sunk in her own silence, as she felt the jolting ride of a conveyance and, finally, the familiar roll of the ocean. The stench of belowdecks, acting as a poor man's hartshorn, finally roused her, and a man's image swam before her eyes. I must be dreaming, she thought as she let her consciousness drift.

"Miss Amberly, how nice to see you again," the image said, and Cat realized that it was not a dream, for her lashes fluttered open to pale blue eyes peering out of a thin face. He was familiar, but Cat, still drifting, could not place him.

As if reading her thoughts, he spoke again. "It is Richard Blakely, Miss Amberly," he said smoothly.

"We met at the ball your friend Lord Claremont held for the duke of Morcester."

Cat's eyes flicked in surprise, for she was rapidly coming awake, and the memory of that night at Lord Claremont's returned in a rush. The man before her now was one of Devlin's people, and he had lied to Ransom about her, although she had no idea why. Her brows knit together in puzzlement and anger, and she struggled to speak, but her mouth was full of cloth and her movements were halted by rope that bound her wrists and ankles. At these discoveries, alarm raced through her blood, yet she quelled it sharply, taking several deep breaths through her nostrils as she forced herself to be calm.

"Very good! I was hoping you would not faint dead away," Richard said. "Of course, I gathered you must be quite unusual, since you are the only woman ever to catch Du Prey's interest. I must admit I was not very impressed at our last meeting, but now I see that you do have a certain spirit, don't you?"

Not waiting for the answer it was impossible for her to voice, Richard continued in the same mild tone. "Pardon the accommodations," he said, looking about the cabin in distaste, "but Ben Pike is not known for keeping a clean ship." At his words, Cat guessed that she must be aboard Butcher Ben's ship, the *Prize*, and she looked around cautiously.

She was lying on a large unkempt bed with expensive but grimy hangings, and through the meager light she could discern crates, chests, and furniture in disarray and so filthy she cringed. Bottles and plates with the moldy remains of food still visible on a nearby table gave testament to a recent feast. No wonder the cabin smelled sour, she thought, and there would be rats . . .

Cat closed her eyes and forced the thought from her mind, focusing instead on her captor. "I have never had a desire to travel with Mr. Pike for obvious reasons,'' Richard was saying, ''but one must often face adverse conditions in the completion of one's duty.

''You really should have taken me up on my offer at Lord Claremont's house,'' he said, his blue eyes focused coldly on a spot above her head. ''If you had agreed to work with my superior against Du Prey, we might have avoided some of this . . . unpleasantness. I, for one, could easily forgo the drama of an abduction. However,'' he added with a shrug, ''I gather there is some problem with your cousin which will ensure your death in any case.''

At the mention of Edward, Cat's gaze leaped to Richard in dismay. Unable to believe that she had heard him correctly, she stared at him wide-eyed.

''Ah. I see you are aware of the problem,'' he said, and Cat's heart sank. She did not understand what Devlin's role in all this was, but she knew full well that Edward wanted her dead. Cat's hard-won calm rapidly disappeared at the realization, and fear, cold and acute, took its place.

Throughout the one-sided conversation, she had tried to speak, but the cloth in her mouth effectively blocked her efforts. Now she tried again, and although she succeeded in gaining Richard's notice, his next words put an end to her slim hopes that he would remove the gag.

''I have no intention of letting you speak, Miss Amberly, so you may as well cease your exertions,'' he said lightly, but with fiendish indifference. ''I have no doubt that your screams would incite the greedy rabble aboard this ship to break down the door, to claim their piece of you. I'm certain that scenario does not appeal to you, and I have no desire to return home with a dead body in my charge. So, you see, it really is best for you to maintain a discreet silence," he explained impassively, raising a hand to push a lock of hair from his brow.

"Of course, I'm afraid your silence may not deter our illustrious captain, although he has strict instructions not to damage the merchandise. My orders were to deliver you alive and in a reasonable condition, so let us hope, for both our sakes, that Ben can be counted on to, if not restrain himself, at least to limit his violence."

Cat's stomach lurched at the words, spoken so casually. Nothing, not even Edward, had prepared her for this cold-blooded creature reciting heinous crimes without the blink of an eye. Edward, she realized suddenly, was a rank amateur, while the man before her was something else . . . She felt the blood rushing past her ears and struggled with the dizziness that threatened to rob her of consciousness.

"Should Ben make a visit, I will need to take charge of your clothing . . . or the remnants. I gather my superior wants to make a little present of them to Du Prey," Richard said. "In that case, the bloodier the better, although I can always spice them up a bit . . . Despite your falling out, I imagine they will distress him. Don't you agree?"

Cat shook her head dismally as she fought down the bile that rose in her throat.

"Don't be so modest, Miss Amberly. The cold captain was quite infatuated with you; I have the lumps to prove it. And believe me, he has never been prey to emotional traps or we would have set them before."

He looked at her more closely, as though for the first time. "Yes, I have a notion that Du Prey was in love with you—until I told him you were in league with his enemy. Did he vent his anger on you, too, or just turn cold as ice?" Richard asked. "Ah well, I imagine you have no idea why your attentive suitor suddenly changed his mind.

"I suspect he'll be upset to learn that you were only an innocent victim. And although I care little for the theatrics my superior sometimes employs, I must admit that this little trick will probably do some damage to your noble duke." Richard was no longer looking at her but stared unseeing at the woodwork as he framed his next words.

"In fact, this time he may very well break," he said, and for the first time, Cat saw a thin smile crack his features.

Chapter 32

Cat nearly jumped out of her skin at a loud noise from above, certain that the dreaded Ben was rending the door from its frame. Even though she was bound tightly, she had to fight the urge to reach for her knife. She could only hope her precious weapon hadn't been discovered and was still strapped to her leg.

"Now, what is that?" Richard asked when the loud bang was followed by a commotion breaking out above them. Cat recognized the running and shouting as the sounds of battle preparations and prayed that the ship would be blown to bits. Better to go that way, she thought dimly, but she knew the chances of Ben losing the battle were slim. Ben preyed on smaller, weaker vessels, and no one purposely went after the *Prize*.

"Please excuse me," Richard said soothingly, rising from her side. She soon heard the door close, and holding her breath, she waited for the turn of the key. But there was no other sound, and she released her breath raggedly, realizing that on a ship run as sloppily as this, keys would have been lost long ago. And why would Richard lock her in, for where could she possibly go? Cat decided not to dwell on that question. Instead, she raised her knees to her chest and slid her hand underneath her skirts, breathing a sigh of relief when her fingers closed about the familiar silver blade.

She skillfully slipped the knife between her hands and began cutting the rope that bound her, straining so hard to hear every sound that her ears began to ring. The unnatural position made her wrists ache, forcing her to stop to rest several times, but she finally felt the rope slip from her hands. Sitting up, she slit the cord binding her ankles with one deft motion.

Cat rolled from the bed, glad to get away from the smelly bedding, and stole to the window, where she wiped a small patch of pane to peek out. She had been right about the battle preparations, for she could see another ship through the grime, and her knees went weak when she recognized it. For a moment, she stood staring out the window, dazed by her good fortune, before she sent up her thanks to the heavens, for whether by design or coincidence, the *Reckless* was bearing down on them, bringing with her the promise of Ransom, sanity, and safety.

Already plotting her escape, Cat hurried from the window to inspect the various crates and chests for anything useful. The first contained heavy materials, brocades and horsehair, the next finely crafted glassware no doubt valued at a fortune, but worth naught to her. Her third choice, a narrow wooden crate, held, of all things, cutlasses and swords, all too heavy for . . . A rapier! Praise God!

She returned her knife to its hiding place, and gripping the rapier, congratulated herself that, despite all his cleverness, Richard had underestimated her. He had left her, albeit trussed up, in an unlocked room with a box full of weapons! Why, he must have thought I would cry for some hartshorn rather than try to escape, she thought scornfully as her confidence returned in a flood.

She decided she needed clothes—escape would be

easier for Cat than Catherine—and rummaged
through a chest of pirated finery. Too gaudy! Too
big! There must be something . . . Desperately, she
rooted through a pile of silks and satins. Aha! In
another box she found more serviceable clothing and
pulled out some breeches, a shirt, and a coat. She
stripped off her gown and hurriedly dressed in her
newfound garments. Damn! Her hair was a little
long . . . Well, all she could do was tie it back. She
discarded her stockings and slippers as being too
feminine and, more than likely, a hindrance when
she needed to move with speed and silence. After a
quick glance at her disguise, she slipped the rapier
under her overlarge coat and crept to the door.

Cat took several deep breaths before stepping
stealthily into the narrow passage, thankfully deserted, but glowing with the dim light of a lantern
which hung crookedly on the wall. She took a step
toward the hatchway, but her attention was again
drawn to the lantern, and she stood for a moment,
undecided. Then, taking another deep breath, she
tore the lantern from its place with a strength born
of desperation and tossed it back into the cabin onto
the moldy bed. Fire, the sailor's most feared enemy,
sent its hot tendrils creeping through the blankets
while she ran to the hatchway.

On deck, Cat slipped unnoticed into the melee as
groups of seamen barked orders at each other, although no one seemed to listen. The *Reckless* had
slipped alongside the vessel, but no shots had been
fired yet. Her heart pounded at the sight of a figure
that could only be Ransom shouting at a garishly
dressed man who waved a cutlass dramatically.
Having no desire to view the infamous Ben at close
range, she inched away, keeping a lookout for Richard, who was nowhere to be seen.

Amid the mayhem, Cat made her way aft and
leaped into the rigging. Her recent life of ease had

rendered her ill-prepared for a fast climb up the rat-lines, but she threw herself into a task that her very life depended upon, hoping that no one on this poorly run vessel would notice her.

On board the *Reckless*, there was no confusion as each man crouched in his position, well-disciplined and ready at any minute to do battle. Most aboard knew that although Ben Pike manned the *Prize*, Devlin was the real force behind Pike's raids, and anyone who worked for Ransom Du Prey had been touched in some way by his enemy.

In fact, they were only too eager to get back some of their own, and Ransom overheard so many oaths and calls for blood that he reminded the crew to await his signal.

"Keep low and stay quiet," Ransom warned. "I don't want anyone to make a move until I've talked to Pike. He holds a prisoner, a lady, who must be returned unharmed. We are here to rescue her," he stressed. "When she's safe, then we'll deal with Ben Pike."

The crew had little faith that Pike would make an honest bargain, however, and all aboard were watching for any tricks he might suddenly think up. With that in mind, Tom Clapper, his eyes sharper than most, took quick note of Cat, scrambling up the rigging at top speed. "What's that fellow doing, Bosun?" he yelled to the first mate.

The crew of the *Prize* had also noticed Cat, one of the few figures aboard moving with purpose. "Who the hell's that?" asked one of Pike's burly minions to no one in particular before shouting up at her, "Hey, you! What are you doing?" His yelling caught the attention of Ben himself, who whirled around with a flourish.

"A spy! Kill him!" he ordered, and several men started eagerly up the rigging. But by this time Cat was nearly to the topgallant. As she reached for a free line, certain of her success, a ball whistled through the air, and she realized in a panic that they were shooting at her. The thought had barely registered when a sharp pain in her leg threw her off balance, and she almost lost her footing while reaching again for the rope.

Although her head was swimming, Cat pushed from the mast with every ounce of strength she possessed, and for one dizzying moment she was swinging across the ocean. It was like the old days when she would drop off to swim, but this time she knew that she must hold on until she reached the *Reckless* and safety. Her perception was hazy, however, and the ship that seemed so far away suddenly loomed large before her. Suddenly nerveless, her hands slipped, and she was floating free, her legs flailing vainly for a foothold as she felt the rope swinging back across the deck.

She landed hard, the breath knocked from her, on a piece of sail stretched taut to catch her. "God Almighty, it's Cat," she heard someone say as she opened her eyes to familiar faces that wavered before her. "That's a game lad!"

"Have you broken anything?" Cat recognized Bosun's voice, but she could not answer or even shake her head, lacking both the wind and the will.

Conscious only of a longing for her captain's strong, steady arms about her to still the careening world, Cat picked out his tall figure, facing away from her, from a group at the rail. Shakily, she raised a hand to point in his direction, her fingers vainly reaching toward him for one brief moment before her hand fell free and all went black.

"He's been shot, captain," Bosun said, looking up from where he crouched next to Cat's prone figure.

"Take him to my cabin," Ransom ordered over his shoulder without giving his former cabin boy a glance. Unable to spare a thought for anyone but

Catherine—and securing her safe return to the *Reckless*—his attention was focused on the *Prize* and its captain. "Give her up, Pike," he shouted across the waves.

"Go to hell!" the pirate screamed back, his laughter floating above the sea.

"I'm not leaving without her," Ransom countered, but a new commotion broke out on the pirate ship, diverting Ben's attention, its cause soon horribly apparent to all as smoke began to pour from several of the *Prize*'s windows.

"Close the distance, Peabody!" Ransom shouted when he saw the gray tendrils trailing into the air. But his direction to maneuver the *Reckless* nearer to the *Prize* was futile. Mr. Peabody, disobeying his first orders in a lifetime of punctilious service, steered clear and away from the flames which could easily leap to the *Reckless*.

Ransom, rooted to his spot, simply stared in horror at the smoke, now thick and black, that was engulfing the other ship. In all his preparations, in all his deliberations upon how to rescue Catherine from Ben Pike, fire had never been a part of the scheme. Bargaining, trickery, and finally pure force, he had considered them all, but this . . . His body urged him to action, but what course could he take to save her now?

Ransom refused to believe that Catherine could be lost after he had finally learned of her innocence and the feelings for her that he had buried were burgeoning forth once again. She was the only woman who had ever meant anything to him—surely she could not be trapped in the inferno that raged in front of his eyes. An anguished groan tore from his throat as he rejected the possibility that she might . . . die.

Fire was spouting from the side of the pirate vessel as Ransom headed to the wheel himself, unable to stand still and watch the ship burn. His normally cool reasoning was washed away in a flood of emotion and, heedless of the consequences, he could only think of getting aboard the other ship. Then suddenly the air was rent with explosions as the powder magazine went up, hailing debris down upon the *Reckless*, and it was too late. No one could board the fiery remains of the *Prize*.

With the unnaturally slow movements of a man long ill, Ransom stood with his jaw clenched and his hands locked in a deathlike grip on the rail until the pirate ship sank under the waves. Then, unnaturally quiet and still, he directed the rescue of survivors, searching for Catherine among a sorry lot of cutthroats that the crew of the *Reckless* would just as soon have watched drown.

Every man was questioned, and all denied knowledge of a woman aboard, but no one could be sure if they were telling the truth. Most of the crew had perished in the blasts and the flames, and Ben was not found among the survivors. Neither was Catherine.

Bosun neatly dressed the nick on Cat's leg, gave the former cabin boy a sleeping draught, and left her resting comfortably on the captain's bed. But he was painfully aware that Ransom's wounds would not be so easily remedied. When he returned to the deck, he found the captain still watching the waves intently, looking for a blonde head in every piece of flotsam. He was unable to stop the search, although it was apparent to the rest of the crew that they had found all the survivors of the *Prize*. There simply was no one else.

Bosun tried to tell his captain that Ben had never had her, that Catherine was still on Barbados, her disappearance a simple misunderstanding, but Ransom was not listening, and Bosun could not blame him.

"Well, there's no use staying here, circling the wreckage and staring down at the waters below," Bosun said softly. "Come away from the rail, lad.

The crew is beginning to wonder what ails you."
Finally conscious of the futility of his efforts, Ransom, cool and composed once more, went below to his cabin and the comfort a bottle would offer.

Bosun, conferring briefly with Mr. Peabody, ordered a course set for Windlay, where the captain might occupy himself with his businesses, before heading below himself. In the captain's cabin, Bosun again tried to talk, but Ransom, sitting at the table, staring unseeing at the walls, and downing liquor as though it were water, would not answer, and finally the first mate left him to his miseries.

Emotions Ransom would not name had been churning in his gut since he'd learned that Devlin had snatched Catherine, and now he suffered the pain he dreaded most, pain such as he had not felt since he was fourteen.

Death had again taken someone he loved, despite all his efforts to avoid that emotion. His denials had been useless. Ransom finally admitted it to himself. He loved Catherine Amberly, and now he had lost her.

Ransom raised his glass silently as regret, grief's fellow, joined him. If only he had told her. If only he had listened to her. If only he had not left her. If only he could have killed Ben with his bare hands . . . Soon Devlin would be laughing at the irony, for he finally had accomplished what he had so longed for: Ransom's undoing.

Bosun, checking on Ransom hours later, found him in the same position, as though he had not stirred except to lift the glass to his mouth. "Are you trying to pass out, lad?" the first mate asked. "Come on now. To bed with you," he urged. With a troubled sigh and a shake of his head, Bosun helped his captain into the bed, next to the sleeping figure of his former cabin boy.

Chapter 33

Certain she was dreaming the most compelling and delightful of dreams, Cat awoke to darkness and warmth and the scent of Ransom. In an attempt to prolong the illusion, she tried to burrow her head further into the pillow and discovered that the pillow was not her familiar soft feather bolster. In fact, it did not move at all and felt strangely smooth against her cheek, or rather it did move, up and down, with a rhythm of its own.

Her mind foggy, Cat struggled to separate dreams from reality, and her body tensed as the memory of Richard and Butcher Ben came flooding back. For long moments she could not place where she was, then with a shock, she realized she was in the captain's bed on the *Reckless*, lying with Ransom, one leg flung over his and an arm resting across his chest. Her cheek was pressed not against a pillow but to Ransom's naked chest, where she could hear the slow, steady beat of his heart and inhale his special scent, mixed with what smelled like an awful lot of liquor.

His chest felt so warm and inviting, the hairs tingling against her cheek, that for one dizzying moment Cat longed to press her lips to his taut skin. Her heart, which had quickened immeasurably since she awoke, now threatened to pop out of her chest, and she felt as though she were suffocating in the darkness. From the sound of his even breathing, Ransom appeared to be asleep, but the devil could just as easily be wide awake, staring at her, so she hesitated to move or look at him.

Cat decided to wait and listen to make sure her pounding heart had not awakened him, then roll from his body as gently as she could. It was a good plan, except that the minutes ticked by like centuries, and her heart, that fickle organ, was not cooperating in her efforts to slow its rapid pulsing. Just as she felt she could not keep still one moment longer, Ransom groaned and turned, flinging his arm about her in the process.

Cat had moved with him, but now she was truly caught, her legs in their boy's breeches intertwined with Ransom's and one bare foot touching his toes. His arm hung heavy on her chest, and Cat realized that he must truly be asleep, or passed out from the smell of him, she thought with amazement. As she lay on her back, contemplating her next action, Ransom stirred again, burrowing his face into her neck.

Her thoughts whirled around in her head, still groggy with what must be a sleeping potion, for she vaguely remembered Bosun forcing some obnoxious gruel down her throat. Damn! And just when she needed her wits about her! Calm yourself, Cat, she told herself. After all, the worst was over, for she was no longer in the clutches of Devlin's cold-blooded emissary. She drew comfort from that thought, and slowly, bit by bit, she gained control over her senses, her breath, and the erotic pull of the sleeping man beside her.

For Ransom was asleep. Now that she was more awake, Cat could almost swear it, and the fact that she was still dressed as a lad was reassuring. He obviously had not guessed her secret; she was simply Cat, an injured cabin boy, put in the captain's bed. But why was Ransom so . . . drunk? And what of the *Prize*? Was its meeting with the *Reckless* purely coincidental?

Cat fought the urge to shake her captain awake and ply him with questions, her feelings for him too confused to risk exposure of her identity. Although she longed to shower him with kisses for helping her escape from certain death, the accusations that he had hurled at her during their last encounter still rang in her ears.

Cat knew that Ben was no favorite of Ransom's and that he had, indeed, preyed on a couple of Ransom's shipping vessels. If Ransom had sought out the *Prize* solely to get revenge for past raids on his ships, then he would not believe Cat's tale of a kidnapping. On the contrary, he would assume that she was traveling happily with her cohorts, since he believed her to be in Devlin's employ. The thought brought a lump to Cat's throat, and she realized that she could not face his accusations and cold fury again. Better to remain hidden as Cat and turn tail for home, she thought.

With a groan, she lifted Ransom's heavy arm and crawled to the corner of the bed, stuffing her pillow between them for good measure, for she had no desire to awaken again in his arms.

When Cat opened her eyes once more, the bright light of day was dancing into the cabin. She yawned and stretched, drowsily aware of a sense of well-being that lingered from a lovely dream. With a sigh, she hugged the pillow to her and recalled waking in Ransom's arms, vaguely disappointed that it had all been a dream. Or had it? As she awoke more fully her pleasure dissipated, and Cat fought an increasing sense of dread. Finally, unable to put off the moment any longer, she opened her eyes to look directly into the face of her captain.

His handsome features, relaxed in slumber, confirmed her suspicions: her memories were no dream, and with a gasp, she slipped from the bed. She sank into a chair by the window, glad to be cloaked in her boy's disguise, and some measure of calm returned.

Cat looked curiously about the room, her eyes focusing on the empty bottles before her, and she picked up the glass and sniffed. Rum, and stronger than pitch, too. She shuddered, wrinkling her nose as she put down the glass. She shook her head in dismay, for she had never known Ransom to drink to excess. *But how well do you know him anymore?* she wondered.

With a sigh, she stood up. She could ill afford to remain here. Another night in Ransom's bed would be too risky—and too much of a temptation, she realized ruefully.

Her rumbling stomach reminded Cat that she had not eaten since she sat down with Amelia for a light dinner far too long ago, and she headed for the galley, knowing that even the cook's infamous biscuits would be welcome fare. She frowned in distress at the thought of her aunt, undoubtedly worried sick over her absence.

Would Amelia guess that Edward was to blame? If so, she would be fearing the worst, and Cat cursed her cousin again for his evil doings. With a grimace, Cat vowed to return to her aunt as quickly as possible to set her mind at ease, but then . . . She would have to attend to Edward somehow.

Cat found Bosun in the galley and smiled in genuine affection to see her old friend, who slapped her roughly on the back in a warm greeting. The two ate dinner companionably, Cat trying her best to recapture her old way of speech and her previous lack of table manners, for it would not do for the former cabin boy to act too refined! She thanked Bosun for tending to her leg while she struggled to avoid any direct questions concerning her presence on board the *Prize*.

"They impressed me, sir. Horrible it was! Laid me low with a crack to my skull," she explained, rubbing the back of her head for emphasis. Cat knew that her words were no lie, for she could still feel a small lump underneath her hair where someone had struck her.

"The bastards!" Bosun growled, shaking his head. "Seems a man can't take a drink anymore without someone waiting to drag him off on a ship."

"Why, they took me right out from behind my cousin Jack's tinsmith shop," Cat said, warming to her tale.

"I thought he was a carpenter."

"Well, he does a little bit of everything," Cat explained vaguely. "What made you go after the *Prize*?" she asked, veering the conversation away from the baldest of her lies.

"Ah, it's a bad business, lad, and that's a fact," Bosun said, frowning into his cup, then suddenly his head came up. "Say, you didn't happen to see a woman with those pirates, did you?"

"A woman?"

"A woman. Seems that bastard Ben took one, a female that the captain fancied, and now he's turning himself inside out thinking she's dead," Bosun grunted.

Cat nearly choked on her biscuit, prompting Bosun to slap her on the back with an "Easy, lad!"

"I find that hard to believe," Cat finally managed as she realized that the "fancied" female was herself. But if Ransom was feeling any remorse, it would only lie in being unable to question her again, she thought with disgust, never believing for an instant Richard's blabbering about Ransom being in love with her.

"Oh, it's true enough, and a sad sight to see," Bosun said, shaking his head.

"Well," Cat began, her brow furrowed in thought. "How do you know this woman was on the *Prize*?"

"We can't be sure. She was snatched from Barbados, and Ransom swears Ben took her onto his ship. But now that the *Prize* is blown to bits, who knows if she was there or not?"

His words brought Cat bolt upright in her seat. "Blown to bits?"

"That's right, lad," Bosun said. "Of course, you were a bit woozy by then, but the whole damn thing went up!" Seeing the shocked look on Cat's face, he shook his head in disagreement. "Don't waste any sentiment on them," he advised. "Good riddance, I say, for a bunch of more vicious dogs parading around as men I hope never to see again."

Still, Cat felt a surge of guilt over starting the blaze that had ended the lives of her captors, and the thought that she had caused so many deaths effectively silenced her. The crimes of the *Prize*'s crew were well-documented, and no one would miss them, or Richard, yet she found it difficult to justify the deed.

The memory of Richard made her shiver, and she wondered if it always would. Even in the light of day, safe inside the familiar wooden walls of the *Reckless*, the thought of his evil face sent a chill through her.

Thank God Ransom had come for her, Cat thought again. Whatever his motives, he had saved her, and for that she was wholly grateful. She wanted desperately to believe he was abjectly mourning her death and, for one moment, she thought of rushing to his side. But she no longer trusted her captain, or her own feelings toward him, so she simply shook her head.

"Well, I saw no such female on board," Cat announced with authority. "And I would guess that the lady will appear back home, sooner or later."

"You could be right, lad, and I hope you are!" Bosun said.

"Speaking of home," Cat began, "I expect my cousin . . . Jack thinks I was murdered. I really must get back to Barbados as soon as I can, him being worried and all, I'm sure. Where are we bound?"

"Should be at Windlay about sunset," Bosun said. "I don't know how long we'll be there, but we'd be glad to have you aboard until we can get you home, lad. I'm sure the captain will be wanting to go to Barbados, anyway. I just set the course for Windlay for want of any other direction."

"No," Cat said firmly, hoping to avoid any more of Ransom's company. "I really need to get home. I think I'll just look for passage from Windlay."

"I wish you would stay, lad," Bosun said, his bristled brows pensive. "I know you would do the captain a world of good."

Cat's cup clattered loudly onto the table as she nearly lost her grip on it. "I think not," she answered with a wry grimace.

When Bosun returned to his duties, Cat wandered to the gun deck, where she was greeted loudly and heartily by her former crewmates Harry Fields and Joe Williams, eager for gossip from land and pelting her with questions about the *Prize*. Cat answered evasively, and finally the two gave way, for it was bad manners to question your fellow about his past—even yesterday's past.

Cat spent the afternoon dicing with them and trying not to look over her shoulder for the captain. From all appearances, the man had drunk enough to keep him abed for some time, but Cat did not trust to the liquor. Ransom was not like other men, she thought ruefully, and he was just as likely to show up suddenly at her elbow, bright-eyed and full of questions.

By the time they anchored off Windlay, she was nervous as a cat and had deserted her friends to skulk in the bowels of the ship where she would not soon be discovered. She emerged only after the ship was bathed in darkness, slipping among the crew on deck like a shadow and amazed at her good fortune in avoiding the captain. She managed her escape with an ease that made her regret her day of anxiety, for she simply joined a group bound for shore, blending in among the men as she always had.

On the beach a pig was roasting over the fire, while men from the *Reckless* and several women were drinking their fill of rum. Cat was surprised by the darkness that surrounded the camp, for no telltale lights denoted the bustling port of Addington, and she cursed her luck to realize they were anchored off a different part of the island. The ground rose gently behind the fire into a ridge dark with trees, while the beach ran evenly in either direction into darkness and silence. To Cat, nothing looked familiar.

Spotting Tom dancing a little jig by himself, she asked him where the closest settlement lay. After some confusion, the seaman, who'd probably had his fill of alcohol for the evening, pointed along the beach. Although none too certain of Tom's accuracy, Cat had no desire to draw attention to herself, so she quietly slipped away into the darkness.

Ransom dragged himself from his bed around nightfall and let Bosun force a meal into him. His movements were stiff and unnatural, as if the very fabric of his being was held together by force of will, and he ate quietly, methodically swallowing the food, though it tasted like dust in his mouth, while his first mate rattled officiously around him. The revelations of the night before returned with his consciousness to wrench at his insides. The love, the loss, and the grief haunted him—along with something else.

"I dreamed about her last night," Ransom said and Bosun cringed, for if the captain began finding her in the bottle, he would return again and again, drowning himself in the drink. "It was so vivid, I could have sworn she was in bed with me, but—" He left the sentence unfinished, tackling the salt beef instead.

"Well, sir," Bosun said lightly, "the only one that was in your bed was you . . . and Cat, of course."

"Cat," Ransom said softly. "Where is he?"

"Can't say for sure," Bosun hedged, loath to tell Ransom that his former cabin boy had probably left him without a word.

"Don't you know?"

"Well, he was in a bit of a hurry, afraid his cousin was worried," Bosun began.

"You let him go?" Ransom, incredulous, raised his voice as though finally shaken from his trance. "I didn't have a chance to question him. He might know something. He might have seen her!"

"No, sir. I asked him, and he was quite certain. There was no woman aboard. In fact, he suggested the lady might be returning home," Bosun said, hurrying on before Ransom could do more than snort in response. "It's a possibility, captain. Why don't we go back to Barbados?"

"Where the hell are we now?"

"Windlay, captain. I thought you might be in need of a little rest. Do you good," Bosun mumbled, his words dying as Ransom burst forth with an oath.

"Christ! I suppose the boy has disappeared into Addington."

"No, sir. We're anchored off the plantation," Bo-sun put in before Ransom could become too riled.

"So he's taken off along the beach?" Ransom asked, but Bosun only shrugged in response. "Well," the captain mused, his voice deep with sus-picion, "his haste seems unwarranted to me. And I happen to be curious as to how our innocent little fellow got aboard Butcher Ben's vessel!"

"He said he was impressed, captain."

"Ha!" Ransom snorted. "That lad weaves more tales than a silkworm makes thread. This time I'm not swallowing his stories. I want the truth, if I have to choke it out of him!" Angrily he rose from the table, determined to find his cabin boy and get some answers.

Chapter 34

The moon was rising brightly over the sea when Cat began to question the wisdom of her decision. The light cast an unearthly glow onto a beach that seemed to stretch into infinity, while the palms swayed gently, the soft rustling of their leaves playing a counterpoint to the crash of the breaking waves.

It was one of the most peaceful and beautiful scenes she had ever witnessed, yet she felt uneasy, as though she were the only human being on the island. Perhaps this seemingly endless shoreline led nowhere, Cat thought, cursing the beach and cursing Windlay itself, for it seemed that disaster struck every time she set foot on the wretched island.

To still these mutterings of doom, Cat waded into the water, which swirled soothingly around her ankles. Comforted by the rhythmic ebb and flow, she was concentrating on the delightful sensation of wet sand between her toes when she heard an eerie tapping noise. It was probably just a leaf hitting the bole of a tree, she assured herself, yet as she strained to listen, she realized the sound was the muffled hoofbeats of a horse running on the sand. Nervously, she glanced about for a hiding place, but there was none, and the moonlight now seemed alarmingly bright.

"Cat!" Her name rang out in the stillness of the night. She recognized Ransom's voice and broke into a run, sure the horse would run her down. But in the end it was Ransom, on foot, who was her downfall. He caught her around the legs, twisting to take the weight of the fall himself, and the two of them rolled over on the sand and into the water.

Intent on capturing his cabin boy, Ransom was slow to realize that the person he was grappling with was not whom he expected. Still, he was not so fogged by grief that he could not tell the wet body pressed against his own belonged to a woman. Soft, yielding breasts pressed against his chest as he rolled through the water, and his hand traced the outline of a slim waist and curving hips.

Whoever it was came up before him sputtering, shaking the water from her hair, and sounding exactly like Cat. "What the hell are you doing?" was her angry question, and Ransom felt disoriented, wondering briefly if his mind and body were playing tricks on him. She certainly resembled Cat, but in the darkness it was difficult to tell . . . With a fierce grunt, Ransom grabbed her by the chin, forcing her face up to catch the moonlight.

It was Cat, and yet it wasn't . . . Ransom had seen this face too many times in his dreams to mistake it, and his eyes roamed searchingly over the features: long, wet lashes over sparkling eyes, gently curving cheeks, and a mouth dainty but delectable. His anger evaporated like mist at the astounding discovery that the face was Catherine's.

For a long moment he simply drank in her visage with the thirst of a parched man. Then, without reasoning or stopping to wonder if he was dreaming again, he lowered his mouth to hers, taking possession of her tender lips with an urgency that could not be denied.

Cat was powerless to stop him, her chin held prisoner by his lean fingers. She thought to slap him away and even raised her hand to his face, but instead her palm gently curved against his cheek, and a tiny sound escaped her throat, for the urgency of the kiss, the desperate yearning of it, took her breath away. Against her will, her lips molded themselves to his, even as she felt a desolate sense of defeat.

Ransom moved his mouth across hers in a fervor of hope and longing and joy such as he had never known before, his fingers caressing her cheek in an unconscious gesture of wonder. Then the warmth that clogged his chest threatened to overwhelm him, and he pressed tiny kisses along the curve of her cheek and her eyelids until he suddenly tasted more salt than the seawater had left behind.

With a jerk, he raised his head to watch her turn her face away, as tears, luminous in the light, welled in the corners of her eyes. "Oh, no," she sobbed. "Can't you just leave me be?"

Ransom took a deep, shaky breath, trying to get his bearings, for this was no dream, no vision, before him, but Catherine. Catherine dressed as . . . No, Catherine *was* Cat! His happiness was momentarily eclipsed by irritation as he realized that the woman in his arms had traipsed about disguised as a boy for God knows how long. She had traveled halfway around the world with a group of grizzled seamen, fooling every one of them, and he grimaced when he thought of his own avuncular behavior. She had probably been laughing up her grimy sleeve at him all along, and now she wanted nothing to do with him.

"No," he said, finally addressing her request. "If there's one thing I *don't* intend to do it is leave you be. I would like some answers, *Cat*, beginning with how the hell you got here."

"Why should I say anything when you won't believe a word?'' she answered, raising her chin defiantly.

"Because I'll throttle it out of you," he said with annoyance.

"Take care, captain," Cat warned. "I may slit your throat as I should have done last time you threatened me." She took a step back, as though preparing for battle, sending the water splashing around them.

"I'll keep that in mind," Ransom said dryly.

Cat frowned at him, considering whether to answer his questions before taking a deep breath and plunging into her tale. "I was sitting on an outcropping below Amelia's gardens when I was struck from behind," she explained, absently raising a hand to her head. "I awoke to the stench of the *Prize* and the warm greetings of a Mr. Blakely, with whom I believe you are acquainted," she threw in snidely.

"So Devlin was behind it?"

"Well, yes," Cat said, her voice registering surprise at his easy acceptance of her words. "Blakely never mentioned him by name, but he kept referring ominously to his 'superior.' He also said my cousin Edward had a hand in it, although how he is tied to Devlin, I have no idea."

"Blakely didn't say?"

"No," Cat answered, suppressing a shiver at the memory of her one-sided speech with Mr. Blakely. "We did not have a lengthy conversation, thank God."

Ransom caught the horror underlying her words, and his annoyance fled. His hand shot out to grasp her arm. "They didn't hurt you?" he whispered, surprised at the fear that overwhelmed him.

"No. You came in time," she said softly, raising her eyes to his. "Thank you for that."

Ransom's relief was so intense that he felt it like a blow to his chest, and his arm dropped limply back to his side. His mouth was dry when he spoke again. "You escaped him when the *Reckless* arrived?"

"Yes. He left me alone, but I had a knife, and I found some clothes that enabled me to turn myself back into Cat."

"God, when I think of you swinging from ship to ship, dodging gunshots . . ." Ransom paused to shake his head, then eyed her intently. "For that matter, when I think of you racing up the ratlines of the *Reckless* as you used to do on a daily basis . . ."

"I enjoyed my work," Cat cut in defiantly, lifting her chin again.

"What in hell made you want to be my cabin boy?"

Cat shrugged. "My cousin Edward was trying to kill me, so I had to run away at once. I could think of nowhere to go but to Amelia's and no way else to get there."

"So you tricked everyone aboard into believing you were a lad," Ransom marveled.

"I wouldn't say tricked."

"Your friend Harry would. And Bosun . . . he'll undoubtedly die of shame when he finds out he befriended a lady," Ransom said, breaking into a chuckle. "And the infamous 'birth scars' that explained your excessive modesty . . . My God, you had an answer for everything." He laughed aloud, and the sound echoed warm and friendly in the stillness.

Ransom recalled more images of his cabin boy, and the more he remembered, the more amused he was that her masquerade had succeeded. He couldn't help feeling some admiration for her ingenuity. Faced with danger enough to send most women into a decline, she had taken her future in both hands, and traveled through innumerable perils, and had voiced not one complaint.

Looking down at the sweet face smiling in re-

sponse to his own laughter, Ransom realized that
the cabin boy he had cared for was the very same
woman he loved, and she was not dead. God, in his
mercy, had granted him one more try for happiness,
and he reached out to take it, heedless of all else.

"Let's go back now," he said softly.

It seemed his words caught her off guard, for she
appeared puzzled and more than a little suspicious.
"Why should I go anywhere with you?" she finally
asked belligerently.

Several answers occurred to him, but he voiced
the one that rose first and most urgently to his lips.
"Because I love you."

Cat felt a lurch in her chest as her heart, along
with time itself, seemed to halt at his words. She
could feel the water, warm and gentle, lapping at
her calves, and she smelled the scent of coconuts
and palms on the breeze, but she herself was caught
in a spell, unable to move or speak, for endless,
timeless moments, until she slowly raised her head
to look at him.

Moonlight dusted his dark hair with stars, and she
could see the sheen of the seawater drying on his
skin, his open shirt revealing the dark, glistening
hair on his chest, only inches from her face. He
seemed so close, closer than he had ever been before. But that was a trick of the stillness, she thought,
as her gaze wandered over the face she loved so
well, afraid to look too closely and test the truth of
his words. Finally, without daring to breathe, her
heart still lodged in her chest, she looked into his
eyes, bright with emotion.

"I love you with every breath in my body," he
said, and Cat felt a frightening thud in her chest
signaling that time was churning back into motion.
Her heart began to compensate for the lost beats,
tripping double-time while she stared in amazement, lost in his dark eyes.

"I love you more than life itself, for when I thought you were dead, I did not see how I could live without you," he whispered, and Cat could hear the catch in his voice. She sobbed aloud, this time in happiness, as she slipped her arms around him and Ransom pulled her tightly to him, burying his face against her neck.

"I'm sorry you thought I was dead," Cat mumbled, ashamed to realize that Bosun had been right. Ransom had mourned her and suffered needlessly while she thought only of herself. "I never dreamed . . . I was certain you hated me," she whispered.

"Even when I thought I hated you, I could not," he said softly. "Cat." He shook his head in wonder. The irony of it all suddenly striking him, he stepped back to look at her, and a warm tenderness filled his chest again as his gaze took in the figure he remembered, the hair somewhat longer, and that absurd jacket, now a soggy mess, sagging from her shoulders. It was Cat, albeit a bit bedraggled, and he wondered how he could have failed to make the connection. The odd feeling of familiarity that had so often plagued him was clear now, and all his doubts and questions fell away, leaving only a fierce and tender love for the child-woman standing before him.

"Cat," he breathed in amazement. He reached up to gently trace a thumb along her cheek, the simple movement causing her to quiver with excitement.

"Let's get you out of those wet clothes," he suggested, misinterpreting her shiver, and his hands slipped the soaking jacket from her shoulders, tossing it carelessly to the sand. What he saw then made him catch his breath, for with the heavy jacket gone, there was no mistaking Cat for a boy. The thin fabric of her wet shirt clung like a skin to her full breasts, while the breeches left no curve of her long, slender legs to the imagination, and Ransom felt desire, long thwarted, hammer in his blood.

He reached for her, his fingertips on her arms sending tremors of anticipation through her body. For a moment they stood thus, both hearts racing as desire rose to a fever pitch, and Cat thought how very different this feeling was from . . . anything . . . before he pulled her close and her thoughts faded into the oblivion his touch invoked.

He kissed her until she was weak with wanting more, his lips insistent upon hers as his hands roamed up her back. Cat strained against him, her arms curled around his neck, her fingers threading through his hair, while his lips traveled along her cheek, her ear, and down her neck to her shoulder, where her shirt clung wetly.

There his fingers pushed at the sodden fabric, slipping it from her shoulder so that his mouth could taste her flesh before he slowly removed the garment, exposing her breasts to his gaze. The moonlight illuminated the alabaster globes, and she felt her nipples hardening in the warm breeze.

"And I thought you were a boy," Ransom breathed in admiration.

"Since then I have . . . filled out."

"And beautifully, my love, beautifully," he said softly while his hands rested on her shoulders, then slid downward, the palms barely touching her skin as they moved over her breasts to rest against her nipples. She arched against him and slowly, gently, his hands closed over her flesh, causing her to sigh in relief. His thumbs caressed her nipples, rubbing them to a peak while her head slipped back and she moaned softly. The uninhibited sensuality of her movements sent desire slamming through his body, and he groaned as he pulled her to him, his mouth rough upon hers.

His hands tangled in her hair and across the silken flesh of her back, while his tongue probed rhythmically in her mouth. Cat strained against him, and he urged her closer, his hand roaming down to cup her buttocks, pressing her against his hardness in a way that robbed her of breath.

"I want you, Cat," he whispered against her lips. "I've wanted you so long . . . Can you feel how much?" His voice was thick with passion.

At first unable to respond, Cat finally tore her mouth from his. "Yes," she gasped.

"What is it, love?"

"I'm having enough trouble breathing," she said. "Don't ask me to talk."

She felt the staccato burst of laughter against her cheek. "Sorry," he answered softly. "No matter what happens, you must not forget to breathe," he advised before swinging her up into his arms.

For a moment her feet dangled in the air, then he set her down on her discarded clothing, the sand giving way beneath her and her hair spilling brightly around her. Cat watched him quickly shed his own clothes, conscious that although she had seen him naked countless times before, he had never looked more beautiful than when touched by moonlight.

When he slipped the wet trousers from her body Cat shivered again at the feel of his lean fingers on her legs. "Are you still cold, my love?" Ransom asked.

"No," Cat answered softly. "It is your touch," she said a little sheepishly.

"Hmmm. I'll keep that in mind," he said, grinning wickedly as he ran his hand along her leg, inducing another tremor in the process. With a gasp, she grasped his wrist to halt his progress and looked up at him. He was leaning over her, his wide shoulders smooth in the moonlight, his smile replaced by intent desire.

"You see, it works both ways, my love," he whispered before his mouth descended. She released his wrist, her playfulness forgotten as she raised her arms to pull him closer, and their mouths and bodies intertwined as passion grew again.

His lips traveled up the slim column of her neck to explore the recesses of her ear, his tongue dancing among the ridges, halting only to nip her earlobe tenderly. Then he pressed kisses along her shoulder blade and under her breasts, and she felt his tongue licking the salt from her skin, teasing a nipple before his mouth closed over it, sucking gently. She arched against him, her hand clutching his silken locks, urging his head closer, and he responded with a long pull that sent a moan escaping from her throat.

"Cat . . . my love," Ransom whispered against her lips as his hand moved along the curve of her waist and traced the smooth skin of her inner thigh, parting her legs. His experienced fingers caressed her gently and rhythmically until she strained against him. Then, suddenly, she needed him, wanted him so that she cried out his name.

Ransom, experienced in the fine art of lovemaking, with a reputation for providing his women boundless pleasure, found himself in danger of losing control as he entered her warm body.

From the first his desire for her had ruled him in a way he could not explain, and tonight all his practiced arts fell by the wayside, replaced by a fantastic joy and all-too-genuine need for her. Still, he held himself back, lavishing his profound love on her body, but when she cried out his name, his last vestiges of restraint vanished, and he could wait no longer.

With a groan, he cupped her buttocks to draw her closer, unable to think, unable to feel anything but the violent pleasure of his body. He was not even aware of the spasms of her release as he whispered, "I love you, I love you, I love you," with each driving motion until, racked with seemingly endless shudders, Ransom Du Prey lost himself . . .

Chapter 35

Ransom kissed the head that lay against his chest and curved his arm protectively around the lithe body intertwined with his, more than a little daunted by the powerful feelings this slender being had brought forth in him. The hardened captain of the *Reckless* considered himself a man of the world, but nothing had prepared him for this beautiful woman—who used to be his cabin boy, he reflected wryly as he ran his fingers absently over her arm.

"What is it?" Cat asked sleepily, feeling him stiffen.

"The scar on your arm. Is it from the knife wound . . . when you saved my life?"

"Now you admit it! At the time I didn't think you were especially grateful," Cat murmured, snuggling against his chest.

"I was grateful," he said, so softly and seriously that she raised her head to look at him, resting her chin on his chest as her hair swirled about her like an aura in the moonlight. "But it showed me I was too attached to you," he explained, running his knuckle along her cheek. "I'm not very good at caring," he whispered. "It comes hard for me, while you . . ." He shook his head in wonder. "Love pours from you like light."

Ransom raised his head, his kiss soft as a butterfly's wing. His tongue traced the delicate outline of her lips, but Cat pulled away, her brow furrowed in sudden worry. "Is it horrible?" she asked.

"What?"

"My scar. Does it bother you, I mean?"

Ransom laughed aloud. "God, no. Why should it?"

"Good," Cat said. "Because I'm sure to have another on my leg. If I keep this up I'll have more marks than Bull Marston!" she complained, rising to her feet to wade into the water.

For a moment, he simply watched the moonlight gleaming on her nude body and glittering in her golden hair as she gracefully moved through the sea. Then he felt the sharp stab of desire, surprising so soon after their explosive union. Lacking the slightest inclination to control it, he followed her into the water, catching her cheek in his hand and gently forcing her to look up at him.

"I love every inch of you, little one, scars and all," he whispered. "It is difficult for me to know that you risked your sweet life for me," he explained. "That's what bothers me, not your scar, not your life as a boy, or anything else about you. I loved you when you lived with me, and now I love you more," he whispered, and was rewarded by a sparkling smile. "Although, I must admit, I do prefer you as a woman, for obvious reasons," he added, grinning wickedly before he claimed her lips in a kiss that destroyed any lingering doubts that Cat might have harbored.

Ransom tightened his arms around the sleeping figure as if to guard her closely. Although the night was warm, he had covered her with his shirt, now dry, to protect her from a chill. He smiled to himself when he thought of the dangers she had been through in her young life, the least of which was baring a thigh on a warm beach, and he swore to himself that he would keep her safe always.

His smile chilled at the memory of her recent escape. He turned his thoughts to her cousin, who had reached halfway around the world to do her harm, and he swore to attend to that one—and Devlin—as soon as possible. If anything were to happen to her, now that he had found her again, now that he knew he loved her . . . Such things did not bear thinking of.

He shook off his fears and thought again how very lucky he was. Even in slumber she looked so appealing that his chest filled with warmth, and he reached over to brush a lock of hair tenderly from her face.

Her lashes fluttering, Cat opened her eyes to a million dazzling stars, her momentary disorientation giving way to the warm flood of memory as she gazed up into her captain's face, a gentle smile curving her lips.

"Idyllic though this spot may be, we should be gone before the sun rises, love," Ransom said softly, his palm caressing her cheek. He smiled, and struck by a surge of love for him, she slipped her arms around his neck to hold him tightly. He ran his fingers through her hair and brushed his lips lightly against her cheek. "Then again, maybe we should remain awhile longer," he suggested in her ear as he felt the pressure of her breasts against his chest, and she laughed, rising from the sand in one fluid motion of long limbs and waving hair.

"Off! Off my clothes," she ordered with a smile, nudging his flat stomach with her toe. "Just look at the state of my wardrobe!" she said when he gracefully rose to his feet, revealing that her clothing, having been slept on, was now imbedded in the sand.

"I've seen you in worse," he said dryly, causing

Cat to turn away indignantly. Ignoring his chuckles, she put the jacket aside and shook the sand from her breeches and shirt before donning them quickly. Then she plopped back down in the sand, sitting back to watch him at her leisure.

It had been a long time since she viewed those broad shoulders shrugging into a shirt, and the moonlight added a sensuality to his movements that sent her pulses racing. Or perhaps it was her more intimate knowledge of that body which made her heart beat faster. "Do you want to know a secret?" she asked softly.

Ransom, in the midst of slipping on his boots, looked horrified. "Good God, don't tell me there are more mysteries lurking in your past, little one!" He seemed unable to look at her without touching her, and he reached over to run a finger along her cheek. "Tell me all your secrets, wildflower," he said, the words husky with emotion.

"I used to love to watch you dress and . . . undress," she confessed, her face reflecting a curious mixture of innocence and passion.

Ransom felt an answering response as desire, hot and immediate, rushed through him again, and he lifted her chin to look into her eyes. "If you're trying to arouse me, my love, you've succeeded," he whispered before capturing her lips in a kiss that was long, lingering, and sweet, and left them both breathless. "You have my permission to indulge in that pastime as often as you desire," he said with a lazy grin. "But for now . . . are you ready to go?"

At her nod, he whistled several times, bringing a handsome black stallion from the trees straight to his side. Swinging Cat up onto the animal's back, Ransom promptly joined her there and gave the powerful steed his head.

The next few moments were a blur, the sand and the stars and the sea all racing by as they galloped

along the beach. Cat had felt the wind in her face
before, but never like this, never at night and never
with Ransom pressed warmly against her back. No
matter what lay ahead, she realized she would always have the sea and the stars and the moonlight,
the memory of her captain's wet body and the wild
ride from the beach where he had held her close,
and clasping the moment to herself, Cat leaned
sleepily against Ransom.

The horse covered the ground quickly, and they
soon saw the dim glow of the bonfire signaling the
privateer camp. But Ransom veered away from the
beach up a gentle slope and into the tall locusts. Not
until she caught a glimpse of a house, larger even
than Lord Claremont's great residence, did Cat remember that Ransom had once said he owned a
plantation here. She stifled a gasp of awe at the
stately brick residence, warmly beckoning in the
moonlight, as they moved onto a wide avenue lined
with trees.

She remained speechless as they rode along the
side of the house to the stables in the rear. Ransom
gave the horse over to the sleepy hands of a young
stable boy and led her along interweaving brick
paths to the kitchen compound. There he announced he must have sustenance or perish, and
Cat finally found her voice, piping up in agreement
to his invitation to eat. Giggling like errant children,
the two were soon were hunting for food.

"Bananas!" shouted Ransom in triumph, emerg-
ing from the buttery, waving a large bunch of the
yellow fruit. Cat leaned back against the brick bake
oven and dissolved in laughter. Dressed in rumpled
clothes and clutching the bananas as though they
were priceless gems, he looked more like a common
thief than the confident captain of the *Reckless*.

Apparently, Cat was not the only person to hold
such a view, for a sturdy woman in a robe and

nightcap appeared in the doorway carrying a lantern in one hand and a rolling pin in the other. She had a decidedly menacing air about her, and Cat's laughter trailed off into silence. "Mrs. Banks!" Ransom said, undaunted by the lady.

"Your grace!" she answered, lowering her rolling pin. "Begging your pardon. I heard the noise and saw the light. Thought it might be one of those lazy bondmen stealing the food from our very mouths."

"We were just searching for a bite to eat," Ransom explained, his winning charm soothing her ruffled feathers.

"Well, well, let me get you something then! It's a sad day when a duke has to rummage among the leavings in his own kitchens," she mumbled. She roused a house boy to fetch some eggs and ham from the smokehouse, placed some cold muffins in front of them, and lighted the huge fireplace in preparation for cooking.

If she was surprised to meet a woman in outrageous-looking trousers, with unruly golden tresses, she did not show it. "Sit, my lady, sit," she ordered Cat and mumbled to herself, "Now maybe we'll see some little ones around here. About time, too."

"What's that, Mrs. Banks?" Ransom raised his eyebrow and grinned widely at Cat.

"Simply mentioned I'd like to live to see your children, your grace," Mrs. Banks answered him without apology or embarrassment.

"So you have said many a time," Ransom noted. "And now I feel your wish may soon be granted, for the beautiful Miss Amberly, whom you see before you, is going to marry me before the week is out."

Cat choked on her muffin.

Mrs. Banks cried, "Oh, happy day!"

Ransom sat back, chuckling.

Cat could only gape in astonishment across the

table as he blithely extolled the virtues of the married state to an astonished Mrs. Banks. Although there was much she wanted to say, Cat dared not speak in front of that lady, so, numb with surprise and confusion, she simply ate her breakfast without actually tasting a bite.

After Mrs. Banks's exit Cat attempted to broach the subject, but all her protestations at this sudden engagement fell on deaf ears. Ransom assured her, in his infuriatingly confident manner, that he would procure the necessary license and make all the appropriate arrangements. To her arguments that her aunt should attend her wedding, he said he would send for her. Amelia, Lord Claremont, Courtney, and anyone else she wished to come to the ceremony could be here in but a few days' time.

"But you can't just drag everyone from their homes," Cat said.

"Why not? This serves as my home when I am in the Caribbean, and I would like to be married here. Besides, you would not want to disappoint Mrs. Banks, would you?" Ransom asked with a grin. "Of course, we could be married at my real home, but I haven't the patience to wait that long, though I would like to take you there someday."

"What home is this? Where?" Cat asked, feeling as if she were climbing the rigging against a strong wind and getting nowhere.

"To my home, Morcester, if you will come," he answered, and suddenly Cat was struck by the reality that he was a duke. The beautiful house and large stables she had assumed were all products of vaguely ill-gotten gains, for she had taken his masquerade for granted, never once accepting his title as real. Yet, she acknowledged, just because he'd shattered her preconceived notions about the nobility did not exclude him from that group. Although a gang of grizzled privateers called him captain, he could hold another, higher title. Stunned, she sat back in her chair, looking at him as though for the first time.

"You truly *are* a duke," she said stupidly.

"You didn't believe me?" He threw back his head, filling the room with the rich sound of his laughter, but for once it was no comfort to her. Things were moving far too swiftly.

"No one aboard the *Reckless* ever addressed you as your grace," Cat sputtered in her defense.

"The men put little enough value in such things," Ransom said, still chuckling. "Captain was the only title I answered to on the ship. But I assure you, my love, that despite all appearances to the contrary, I am truly who I claim to be."

Questions came tumbling to Cat's lips, but before she could speak, the author of their meal returned, dressed for the day, and shooed them out. "Off with you now. The day's beginning, and it wouldn't do any good for the new duchess to be caught eating in the kitchens," Mrs. Banks chided Ransom. She did not have to add that her unorthodox clothing would be even more of an item for gossip.

Ransom led a thoroughly bemused Cat into the cool great house, past louvered galleries still dim in the glow of dawn and along corridors whose mahogany floors were polished to a fine sheen with coconut husks. In the east wing of the house, he threw open a gleaming door to reveal a spacious and well-lighted bedroom furnished with an enormous four-poster bed carved with pineapples. But at that moment Cat was too weary to admire the craftsmanship. She cared only that the bed was comfortable and promptly crawled into it, without a thought for her impending nuptials or anything else.

Chapter 36

Cat was awakened by a timid housemaid who claimed that the dressmaker was there, and his grace sent his compliments. Did the mistress want a bath? She did. Cat luxuriated in the deep brass tub for so long the poor maid practically had to drag her out of it.

Finally dressed in undergarments of unknown origin—she vowed to ask Ransom about them later—and fortified with a cup of chocolate, she met the dressmaker, a no-nonsense lady who poked, pinned, and prodded her while saying little. Cat bore it all in good humor, feeling just a shade guilty that the poor woman and her staff would be bleary-eyed from producing a wedding gown in less than a week. When she tried to commiserate with the woman, however, she was haughtily informed that it was an honor to work for his grace. Rank had its privileges, Cat discovered, for a lovely cream day dress was presented to her that very afternoon.

Dressed once again as a lady, Cat hurried into the main rooms, eager to greet Ransom, who obviously had not changed his mind about the wedding ceremony. With the memory of their night on the beach still fresh in her mind, her lips curved into a unconsciously seductive smile as she searched for him. Her alluring expression fell, however, for when she

310

found him in one of the main salons of the huge house, he was not alone.

Cat smiled politely, a completely different smile from her previous one, as she was introduced to Lady Pontager, an enormous woman dressed in the most outrageous purple cape and matching turban.

"Lady Pontager has kindly consented to stay with us until the wedding," Ransom said, grinning wickedly behind the lady's back.

A chaperon! Cat's lips twitched as she struggled with her mirth. After she and Ransom had spent months living together in the cabin of the *Reckless*, and after the way they had made love last night, it certainly seemed too late for a chaperon. If Cat could still blush, she would have. Instead, she greeted Lady Pontager warmly and took a seat as the lady began complaining of the dull season.

"Thank God you're getting married," she huffed as she eased her huge bulk onto a couch. "A wedding is just what this island needs, although you might wait a bit to do it up right," she accused, her dark eyes reproving the groom-to-be who sat across from her.

Ransom shook his head with a smile. "We want a small wedding here in the chapel, not an enormous event."

Lady Pontager snorted in disgust. "A duke wanting a small wedding! Where is your social responsibility?" Without waiting for an answer, she prattled on. "Well, at least it's something! I swear I have never been more bored on this godforsaken piece of dirt. I was hoping the Frenchies would attack, just to provide some excitement!"

"Some like the quiet of island life," Ransom began.

"Don't talk to me of quiet, your grace! Hmmph! Little enough you would know of quiet, racing off in your ships to rescue beautiful young ladies." She looked at Cat, then loudly called for a servant to bring her some lemonade—and a few cakes.

"When do you serve tea around here, your grace?" she complained, a grin spreading from ear to ear, and both Cat and Ransom had to laugh. It was apparent that Lady Pontager, used to running the social life of Addington, would make herself quite at home.

Lady Pontager, although abrasive, had a sense of humor, and Cat found her more entertaining than annoying. She could not help glancing toward Ransom, however, and eager for a moment alone with him, she could easily have wished her chaperon to disappear from the face of the earth. But this was not to be, Cat soon discovered, as Lady Pontager made her presence felt throughout supper and made no move to retire until Cat, still tired from the night before, slipped off to her room.

Although exhausted, Cat lay sleepless for a long while, her eyes wide upon the ceiling as she listened hopefully for Ransom. But all was silent and, still longing for his arms around her, she finally drifted off to sleep, disappointed that after everything that had happened between them she should have to sleep alone.

The next few days were maddeningly similar. Cat was unable to snatch a private moment with her captain: either he disappeared into town, or she was surrounded by fitters and milliners, trotting out materials of every description until she was certain she would need an entire ship to cart around her future wardrobe. If she did, perchance, see Ransom, then it always seemed that Lady Pontager would soon appear to drag her off to meet with cooks and bakers and flower arrangers, all frantic about the approaching ceremony, and Cat could not, in all good conscience, shirk her duties.

And each night as she lay lonely and disgruntled

in her bed, Cat could not decide whether she was glad that Ransom had set the date so soon, so she would suffer less, or if she was so annoyed with the state of affairs that she should call the whole ceremony off simply to get his attention. Just as she thought she would surely go mad, she was summoned peremptorily to his grace's study, and she could not help worrying that perhaps he wanted to do the same.

She was finishing up a late breakfast, by her standards, when the summons came. Lady Pontager was still abed, so presumably no flower arrangers or musicians required her attention as yet. Cat looked over her shoulder, expecting at any moment to be overcome by hordes of seamstresses, but the halls were delightfully quiet as the footman led her to the study. At the door, Cat felt a tiny stab of uncertainty, as though the whirlwind proposal and marriage plans were all a dream, and when she stepped into the study a stranger would greet her.

"Hello, stranger." The familiarity of that deep, rich voice sent all her worries fleeing as she found herself, for once, alone with Ransom. The bright island sun shone through the long windows onto his shoulders and created a soft sheen on his dark hair. He was grinning warmly, and whether he raised a beckoning hand, or she simply felt his desire from across the room, a few quick paces propelled her into his arms. She pressed her face against his waistcoat, enjoying the warm, comforting presence of his arms around her.

"Miss me?" he whispered against her hair, and she laughed softly before raising her eyes to his. A flippant remark was on the tip of her tongue, but when she looked up into those intent dark eyes, she answered differently.

"Yes," she said huskily.

"I've missed you, too, my little Cat," he whispered against her ear as he placed tiny kisses along her hairline that made her breath come in soft gasps.

"The servants!" Cat managed as his hands traveled down the back of her thin gown to press her against him.

"To hell with them!" Ransom said softly but with feeling as he molded her body to his and captured her lips with his own. Cat responded with all the desire that she had kept tightly in check the past few days, and she slipped her arms around his neck, pulling his head closer to her own. She moaned softly to feel him hard against her. The intensity of her response surprised even Ransom, as evidenced by his quickly indrawn breath.

His hands moved to the top of her gown, and soon it was falling free about her waist while he slipped the chemise, too, down along her shoulders to reveal her pale breasts. In the bright light of day, Cat found the sight almost embarrassing, and she gasped, partly in pleasure and partly in shock to watch him place his palms gently on the creamy globes. She was soon aware only of his touch, however, and closed her eyes in ecstasy as his hands moved over her. His lips again found hers while his fingers caressed her breasts until she wanted him so much that she was pulling him closer, opening his waistcoat and slipping her hands underneath his shirt to feel the skin that lay taut across his chest.

When his lips left hers to burn a trail along her neck and down to her shoulder, Cat opened her eyes again, but when she saw him move his mouth to her nipple, the sun brightening those dark locks, she squirmed against him. "It's so . . . light!" she breathed.

"The better to see your beautiful body," Ransom whispered against her breast.

"But . . . the servants," she said again, weakly as

his mouth closed over her nipple, and a jolt of pleasure shot through her.

"They have strict instructions not to disturb us,"
Ransom said softly, raising his head to look at her.
With a sigh of admiration for her young body, he
put her gently from him. "But I will make sure they
don't." With that, he walked to the door and firmly
locked it, tossing aside his shirt in the process.

"There," he said, grinning wickedly, "now no
one can get in . . . or out." Cat smiled at his words,
spoken as he moved purposely away from the door.
"But I refuse to pull the drapes!" he warned, making Cat laugh at her own embarrassment.

He halted a few steps from her on the thick Au-
busson carpet in front of the desk, his face suddenly
serious. "Come, my love," he said thickly, holding
out his hand. "I want to see you, all of you, in the
light of day." Unable to resist, Cat took his hand,
halting in front of him. In one swift movement, he
removed her dress and placed it neatly on the desk.
Then Ransom himself stood naked before her, and
the sun slid over their shoulders as they moved into
a loving embrace before sinking onto the deep carpet. Thoughts of the brightness and the servants fled
as Ransom moved over her, his hands, his mouth,
and, finally, his body working their magic upon her.

Soon she was arching against him, gasping for
breath as they moved in unison, slowly at first and
then with a fierce and urgent need. Her fingers dug
into the muscles of his back and her frantic whispers
urged him on until neither of them could wait one
moment longer, and, together they found a pounding release.

In the aftermath, Cat was curling, catlike, into his
arms when a knock disturbed their idyll.

"Catherine? Are you in there? Your grace?" Lady
Pontager's high-pitched voice was unmistakable as
it drifted through the door. Cat jumped, but Ran-

som, tightening his arm around her, held a finger gently to her lips. When the door rattled loudly, he only grinned mischievously, and Cat was reminded of the boy he must have been when he had pelted his tutor with plums.

With a loud "Hmmph!" Lady Pontager padded away along the hallway. Cat pressed her hand firmly over her mouth to contain her mirth. Finally, she sat up and sighed.

"I suppose I ought not to hide from her; it might be something important," Cat said reluctantly.

"Ha!" Ransom grunted, running a hand through her thick hair. "Whatever it is, Lady Pontager can take care of it. Today, you and I are going into town," he said firmly. His tone brooked no argument, and Cat nearly clapped her hands together with surprised pleasure.

They were soon up and dressed, Cat's qualms over the bright sunlight streaming through the windows having all but disappeared as they lingered now and then over a kiss or a tender touch.

"Oh, the real reason I called you in here," Ransom said wryly as he reached for a case on the desk, "is this." With a smile, he presented the box to her. Finely wrought of silver, it resembled a jewel case, but was far more elegant than any Cat had ever seen. Silently, she moved the clasp that released the lid to reveal the contents. There, lying on a bed of black velvet, was a necklace of gold and emeralds that seemed to glow with a life of its own. Cat gasped aloud at the magnificence, for surrounding the necklace was a bracelet, earrings, and, tucked into a corner, a ring.

Stunned, she simply looked up at Ransom, who was grinning widely. "Here," he said softly as he took the ring and slipped it on her finger. His hands were warm and sure upon hers, and the familiar face of her captain looked down at her. Why, then, did she feel as though her heart would break? Because this ring represented something tangible between them, something more than a fleeting morning of stolen lovemaking? Cat could only shake her head. "They're beautiful," she said as he kissed her hand, now glowing with a bright emerald surrounded by diamonds.

Holding her hand up higher, toward the light, Ransom looked at the ring with a critical eye. "I bought emeralds to match your eyes," he said softly. "But now I see that your eyes far outshine any jewels."

Cat smiled tremulously at his words and closed the case reverently. "I will cherish these even more than the first gift you gave me," she said softly.

For a moment he looked puzzled, but then, as understanding dawned, the lazy grin appeared. "Although I never expected the blade I gave you to be held at my own throat one day, I'm sure that it was a gift far more useful than these shall ever be," he said dryly.

"Aye," Cat said, her eyes sparkling.

They spent the rest of the day together, dining in town and seeing the sights, oblivious to all else but each other, and Cat began to realize just how wonderful being married might be, for now she had the best of both worlds: the warm friendship they had shared on the *Reckless* coupled with the attraction that sparked between them as man and woman.

When they finally returned to the plantation house, Lady Pontager's complaints were brushed away, and loudly bemoaning the lack of appreciation for her efforts, she went off to bed in high dudgeon. She was placated the next day, however, by the arrival of the houseguests, "the new blood" as she ghoulishly referred to them. Amelia, Lord Claremont, and Courtney, looking bewildered but happy, were rushed from Ransom's ship to the plantation, where Cat welcomed them with open arms.

Lord Claremont immediately expressed his amazement at the wedding invitation. "Good God, I thought you two were on the outs," he said, shaking Ransom's hand in congratulation. Nodding to Amelia, he shook his head. "I suppose she always knew what she was doing, as usual, confound the woman!

"First, she pesters me to find out about Du Prey, and nothing would do but that I must get him here on any pretense. Then, I must always be throwing the two of you together, though you seemed to despise each other. It was getting so I hardly knew what she would have me doing next. Well, I for one thank God it's over!" Seeing the disconcerted looks on the faces around him, he added, "And a happy ending at that!"

"Aunt!" Cat gasped as Lord Claremont's words sunk in.

"Now, Catherine, it was just a little matchmaking." Amelia smiled slyly, gratified that her efforts had finally reached fruition, but not surprised in the slightest. For she had known from the first time her niece mentioned Ransom's name that the two were destined to be together.

Chapter 37

Cat still could not quite believe it. A group of maids flocked about her for the occasion, a beautiful gown was laid out for her, and Amelia and Courtney were there to remind her today was her wedding day, but it all felt as ephemeral as a dream. It seemed ages since she had first fallen in love with her captain, and the time had often been spent in unrequited yearning and more than a little misery, yet now all her wishes were being fulfilled as though a fairy godmother had waved her magic wand.

The dream continued as Cat was dressed in a gorgeous pale pink gown and a diaphanous overdress shot with silver. The seamstress's haughtiness was apparently justified, for the dress was more beautiful than Cat had ever imagined, and she turned this way and that in front of the mirror, feeling like a princess while Amelia and Courtney expressed their admiration.

Always more interested in horses and ships, Cat had never really imagined her wedding, but even had she envisioned the day, she could never have pictured such a setting. The house was bedecked with so many flowers that Cat wondered if every blossom on the island had been brought to fill the rooms with sweet scents, and outside the cloudless blue sky looked down on a balmy island afternoon.

As she stepped from the spacious corridors of the plantation house, Cat lingered on the threshold for a moment, astonished to find her path to the chapel lined with quietly attentive servants eager for a glimpse of the duke and his bride in all their finery. In the face of so many, Cat's first few steps were halting, but she was put at ease by the sight of Mrs. Banks, right up front and grinning widely. Cat smiled in return, and the servants marveled for days about the beautiful, genuine smile the new duchess sent the cook.

The sight of Mrs. Banks seemed to awaken Cat, and she finally began to think of her wedding as reality. If it was more elegant and romantic than she ever expected, the groom certainly was the one she had in mind, and that thought eclipsed all else as she moved to his side in the plantation's tiny, vine-covered chapel.

Cat could see Courtney, beautiful in a pale blue gown, and she smiled at her friend, but when Ransom's long fingers closed about her own, all else faded into the background, and she could see no one but her captain. He looked more than splendid in his black coat, silver waistcoat, and snowy white cravat, and her eyes traveled along his wide shoulders up to his face to watch his lips as he spoke his vows.

Ransom did not falter, his rich voice repeating the words with a warm conviction that all could hear, for as he looked at his bride, he saw not only a beautiful woman but an incredible being, strong and brave yet soft and warm, passionate and desirable, who shared so much with him, who never bored him, and whose love had saved him from himself. Surely, this is what life is meant to be, he thought, clasping her slim hand in his own.

Cat's throat grew thick with emotion as she listened to him pledge his life to her, and she raised her eyes to the dark ones shining down at her. With a mixture of joy and relief, she realized that she no longer had to hold back, to hide herself from him, and, her voice husky with feeling, she repeated the vows that would bind her forever to the man she loved.

What Amelia had seen from the beginning became apparent to all as the newly married couple stood greeting their guests, for the duke and duchess had eyes only for each other. Although more than a few wondered, and whispered, at the urgency of the wedding, no one could deny that they made a beautiful couple.

The hours passed swiftly in a flurry of congratulations and dancing, although by evening Cat began to feel she had been claimed far too often by the guests and too infrequently by her husband. Just when she thought she could not endure one more minute in the arms of Lord Claremont—or anyone else—Ransom suddenly appeared to lead her into a waltz.

By now a blaze of candlelight lit the room, casting its warm glow on Cat's golden hair and the emeralds caressing her skin. Her cheeks were flushed and her eyes sparkled as she smiled up at him, and Ransom felt that familiar thud in his chest at the sight of her. "You are breathtakingly beautiful tonight," he said.

"And so, I might say, are you," Cat replied. Her husband chuckled softly before leading her gracefully out the tall glass doors to the close-cropped grass outside, where a wide lawn extended off into the darkness. The strains of the orchestra's music could still be heard, and light from the tall windows played upon the lawn as they continued dancing, one lone shadow in a twilight world.

"What will the guests think?" Cat laughed softly, breathless at the sheer pleasure of being in his arms.

"We are only dancing," he countered, but then, as though to deny his words, he slowed until they were barely moving, and pulled her close. Cat put her head against his chest as they stepped in and out of the shadows, the music a soft hum on the gentle breeze. After a time, she felt Ransom's hand gently touch her hair, and her head came up reluctantly.

"We should go in, little one. We may be missed," he whispered. Although she nodded, neither made a move until Ransom slowly bent his head to hers. The soft, gentle pressure of his lips on hers sent warmth seeping into her bones, and her hands trembled as they moved to his waistcoat.

"As you said, we should go on . . . I mean, in . . . the house," Cat finished, flustered, and he laughed, pulling her close in a tight embrace before releasing her. With exaggerated formality he then presented his arm, which she took with a delighted laugh, and they slowly walked back into the house, leaving the dreamlike world that only they inhabited, for the bright hubbub of the supper gathering.

The festivities ended not long after supper, presumably so that the wedded couple could retire, yet when the last guest took his leave, and Amelia had shooed Lord Claremont, Courtney, and even the indefatigable Lady Pontager off to bed, Cat, giddy from a surfeit of champagne, was struck with what she regarded as a sudden inspiration. Too exhilarated to go to their rooms, she suggested they join the privateers.

Ransom assented with a laugh, and the two slipped out a rear door and walked hand in hand down to the beach, where they stood in the shadows for a while as they watched their shipmates celebrate the captain's wedding in their own fashion. When they emerged to join the gathering, they were greeted enthusiastically, although there was a moment's pause when it was announced that the captain had married his cabin boy. Ransom, foreseeing such a possibility, had provided enough libations to make the men amenable to this development, however, and they were soon shouting congratulations and bussing the bride.

Bosun, totally flummoxed by the announcement, peered at Cat from under his bushy brows for so long that she finally burst into a peal of husky laughter. "By the saints, it is Cat," he declared. "Lord love you, no wonder he said there was none like you! Here, let me look at you!" he said, taking her hands in his and whistling in approval. "You do seem like a duchess, now, don't you?" he asked loudly before leaning close. "Now, you stick by him, Cat, for you hold him in these dainty hands," he whispered seriously, and Cat silently nodded in agreement before throwing her arms around her old friend. "Here, now," Bosun stammered as she hugged him tightly, and Ransom laughed at his first mate's discomfiture.

Toasts were hoisted until Cat swore she could drink no more, and still they went on without her. Bull swung her high into the air, and Tom Clapper shouted that *he* would have married her, had he known. Only Harry stood back, not ready to accept that the friend he had shared confidences with was not what he appeared. "He's such a trickster himself, he's probably miffed that you pulled off a better one," Ransom said with a laugh. "Give him time."

Suddenly, someone piped a tune, and Joe took the bride's hands in a spirited jig. Tom and Bull, two of the few left standing by this time, followed, and then she was whirling about in Ransom's arms, her heart beating apace. "Can I lure you away to our marriage bed, my love?" he whispered in her ear, and at her breathless nod, they slipped off into the darkness, to the drunken shouts of those sailors still awake.

In the darkened house, Ransom swung her into his arms and carried her to his bed while she giggled delightedly. "Have you had too much champagne, my duchess?" he asked as he removed the pins from her hair and watched it cascade about her shoulders.

"No," she whispered before pressing her lips to his. They undressed each other in the darkness, Ransom with the skilled fingers of a lover, Cat with a delightful wantonness for which the champagne could only partially be blamed. They moved together to the middle of the huge canopied bed, clothes scattered about them, and explored each other with deft fingers and gentle mouths.

"Your skin is so soft, so smooth, my Cat," Ransom said against the tiny hairs at her cheekbone as his fingertips lightly traced her back. His hands and mouth moved along her skin in delicious rhythms, inducing soft moans, but he would not be rushed, even at her urging. He gently kneaded her tender instep, while his lips touched her ankle, and she sighed as his hands and mouth moved up her legs, trailing hot kisses along her inner thigh. Then his hands cupped her buttocks as his mouth found the warmth between her thighs, his tongue seeking her secrets, and she gasped in surprise and pleasure.

Cat's hands found his hair, and she arched against him, murmuring his name as her body shivered in ecstasy. Just as she felt she could bear the exquisite torture no longer, he moved over her, and she tasted herself on his lips as he buried himself inside her. "Ransom, I love you," she gasped as the rhythm built, her hands clinging to his smooth muscles until they both cried out.

Chapter 38

Cat awoke to feel a hand gently caressing her thigh and sighed sleepily, rolling onto her back to view her husband's devastatingly handsome face. He was lying on his side, his mouth turned up in a ghost of a smile and his eyes shining with appreciation as he watched her. After yawning and stretching in a manner befitting her nickname, Cat gazed lovingly up at him. "I love your eyes," she said seriously.

"God, it's good to have you here," he answered before taking her in his arms. Ransom could not remember the last time he had awakened beside one of his lovers, for there never seemed to be the need to stay the night, yet holding Cat's body next to his in the darkness and waking to feel her smooth skin under his hand filled him with awe. He pulled back to look at her and grinned. By heaven, she was beautiful, he thought, and the sight of her gloriously naked body, golden hair spilling about her face, sent desire flowing again through him.

"Our guests," Cat reminded him softly as he took her in his arms, and he groaned to look at the time, while Cat giggled and slipped from the bed.

They spent the next few days entertaining. Cat enjoyed the warmth that her aunt and friends lent to the large plantation house. Although Amelia claimed all were eager to return to Barbados and leave the new couple to themselves, neither Courtney nor Lord Claremont seemed anxious to go, and Lady Pontager was more than happy to arrange amusements for the household.

Finally, however, Amelia insisted, and despite Cat's sincere protestations and Ransom's half-hearted invitations, the trio from Barbados packed their trunks, while Lady Pontager left in search of new diversions.

Reluctant to say good-bye, Courtney comforted herself with the notion of seeing her friend often, but she was dismayed when she learned that Cat might be returning to England. "Oh, that is so far away," she moaned. Her disappointment was short-lived, however, for a new idea struck her. "But I could still visit you!" she gasped. "I've never been to England. Oh, Catherine, say you will invite me!"

"Of course." Cat laughed.

"And introduce me to all the eligible, titled friends of your husband?"

"I don't know if he has any!"

"Pooh! A duke must know everyone who is any-one," Courtney said, with a smile. "In that case, but only if you invite me soon, I forgive you for abandoning me," she declared, giving her friend a quick hug.

Cat could not part so easily with her aunt. The trunks were packed, the carriage waiting, and still Cat could not find a way to say good-bye. Finally, she invited her aunt for a walk around the grounds, a pale imitation of Amelia's own garden. She led her through the trees where the sun dappled and danced. Ducking a branch, then pushing some leaves aside with her hand, she finally forced herself to speak. "Aunt, how can I say good-bye?"

"Don't. Just say you'll be back to visit." Amelia smiled serenely.

"I am indebted to you for so much, not least for letting a scruffy waif like me into your home!" Cat said while Amelia paused to examine a lilac bush.

"Needs pruning," Amelia advised, fingering the bush. "Tell that husband of yours to light a fire under his gardeners!"

Cat smiled gently at her aunt's words, then raised her eyes to gaze off into the blue sky above the trees. "Aunt," she said softly, "do you ever miss the great house? Miss living there, I mean?"

"Good heavens no!" Amelia laughed.

"I was just wondering. It seems to me that Lord Claremont . . . well, has a tendre for you."

"Catherine Du Prey!" Amelia said, her hands dropping to her sides in surprise. "My, how I like the sound of that! Oh, excuse me, your grace, I should say: her grace, Catherine Elizabeth Amberly Du Prey, duchess of Morcester! Gracious, that has a lovely ring to it, doesn't it?"

Cat laughed softly with pure delight. "Yes, it is a lovely name. Thank you for that, too," she said seriously. "But what about you? Can't I do a little matchmaking?"

Amelia took Cat's hands in her own. "My dear girl, I know that William would marry me in a moment, if only to legitimize our illicit liaison!" she said, laughing at the surprise on Cat's face. "You see, Isaac is discreet! But I have no wish to be Lady Claremont. I would have to live in the great house and entertain, and Snuffy wouldn't let me garden! Why, that would be no life for me. You see, I'm so used to doing things my way."

Cat groped for words, but could find none.

"Don't worry about me, Catherine!" the little lady said. "I will get along just fine. I always have. I just want to see you back at the cottage for a visit in a few years, and with some babies for me to spoil, too!"

That night, Cat lay awake in Ransom's arms, watching the breeze gently stir the white lace curtains of their room. In the darkness she thought of how often she had lain in bed, dreaming of her captain; then, her heart overflowing with the need to tell him, she rained tiny kisses along his chest until his dark lashes fluttered open.

"Hmmm, what's this?" he whispered, drawing her closer.

"I love you, Ransom Du Prey," she said, lightly tracing the line of his jaw with her fingertip. "Did I ever tell you about what I learned at the Cock and Bull?"

"Good Lord, I'd forgotten those idiots dragged you there! Remind me to kill both Fields and Williams." His voice was deep and thick in the darkness. Cat leaned across his chest so that her breasts barely brushed against him and felt his body tense in response. "What happened?"

"I met a girl who imparted some interesting information to me," Cat whispered, pressing delicate kisses along his neck and up under his silken hair. "But I've never had the opportunity to make use of it . . ." Her voice, husky with desire, trailed off as her tongue traveled lightly along his neck to his finely muscled shoulder.

"Please, do go on," Ransom urged hoarsely, his voice showing the strain of his control.

Cat lifted her head from his chest, where her mouth had wandered, and smiled up at him seductively. "Actually, instead of telling you, I thought I might demonstrate." She felt the hammer of his heart in his chest, and her own raced in response. As her mouth moved lower, he buried his hands in her hair and she could hear his sharp intake of breath. "Just one thing," she whispered through her own haze of desire. "Don't forget to breathe."

* * *

The days that followed were idyllic as the lovers spent most of their time in the huge mahogany bed, draped in white gauze, that graced the master bedroom. They ate their breakfasts of ripe melons and crisp rolls, with honey and jams, in bed, Cat giggling as something was inevitably spilled on the sheets, and she developed a new appreciation for the warm climate. "In England I would have frozen to death spending this much time without my clothes!"

It was not as though they didn't do anything else, Cat told herself when she began to wonder if the servants were scandalized. After all, Ransom did show her the plantation and the beauties of the island. It was just that, well, he would press his leg against hers under a table when they were dining out, or she would reach out to tousle his hair when they were walking on the estate, and suddenly they were back in bed.

Even now, Cat was attempting to avoid the look Ransom sent her from across the table. As she tipped her wineglass, she sneaked a peek at him, only to catch him winking suggestively. She barely swallowed before dissolving into giggles, then made a desperate effort to regain her dignity. Lifting her chin, she said, "I'm sorry, your grace, but I refuse to retire immediately after dinner again. We haven't remained downstairs past dessert for a week!"

Cat's proper facade was quickly crumbling in the face of her husband, who had placed his elbows on the table, his fingers together against his chin, and was sending a positively smoldering gaze her way. Cat felt her body respond from the tips of her toes to the crown of her head and was on the verge of surrendering when Ransom's manservant announced a guest. The words were barely out of the servant's mouth when a figure breezed in behind him.

"Aha! Here you are, little one," he said, brushing past the manservant and taking Cat's hand. Astonished, she looked into the bluest eyes this side of heaven, covered with the longest, thickest, blackest lashes she had ever seen. "Miss Cat, I presume?" he asked, and pressed a kiss against her hand.

"You are not addressing Miss Cat, but the duchess of Morcester, so don't forget yourself, René," Ransom warned from across the table.

"No!" The gentleman looked astonished and pulled up a seat at the table.

"Another plate, please," Ransom signaled to his servant. "You bastard," he directed at René when the servant exited. "I should slit your throat right now for not telling me the truth!"

"But I told you the truth, my friend. I just omitted the minor detail that the woman you sought with such fierce determination was the same being that you called Cat, your cabin boy!" René declaimed, laughing at the grim expression on Ransom's face.

"This, my love, is a living example of the kind of dissolute profligate to avoid at all costs," Ransom explained, introducing his friend.

"We go back a long way, Ransom and I," René said, inclining his head toward her husband and gazing at her soberly. Just as Cat began to relax, the Frenchman burst out laughing again. "Ah! But it is incredible! To think you had this little beauty under your nose for . . . how long? Sometimes I wonder if your brains are in your posterior, my friend!"

René ate with gusto, flirting outrageously with Cat throughout the meal. Later, when the group retired from the dining hall, he continued showering her with compliments while Ransom watched, unperturbed. For her part, the duchess had the Frenchman in stitches with a few well-chosen stories of shipboard life.

"How much do you want for her?" René suddenly asked Ransom.

"I beg your pardon?" Cat said.

"What makes you think she's for sale?" Ransom asked.

"Ha! It is obvious as the nose on your face, my friend, that your sailing days are over. You have something else . . ." For a moment René looked serious, but then he snapped his fingers and named a sum.

"You're selling the *Reckless*?" Cat cried as understanding dawned.

"Not for that paltry amount."

Cat sat back and gaped in disbelief while the two haggled over a price and finally shook hands when the deal was struck.

"She is yours then, after I sail her back to England."

"*Oui*, my friend," René said, slapping Ransom on the back. "I will take good care of the lady!"

Cat found that the night flew rapidly in the company of the two handsome and charming men, and it was so late when they retired that Cat laughed at the time. "How fortunate that we did not go to bed at our usual hour," she said with a wink at her husband once they were alone.

"So what do you think of René?" Ransom asked.

Although his voice was light, she could tell there was more to the question than there seemed. "Very gay and charming. And so handsome," Cat said, smiling provocatively at her husband. "But," she added seriously, "he seemed so . . . unreliable. Oh, I don't know. Sometimes he seemed so outrageous, a trifle mad, actually." Ransom chuckled softly, drawing her to him and resting his chin upon her head.

"I'm sure of one thing: I'm glad I didn't end up on *his* ship!" Cat laughed. Ransom's arms tightened around her at the thought and at the precarious twist of fate that brought her to him. "I can't believe you sold the *Reckless*," Cat said softly, her arms crossing over his as she leaned into his chest.

"I have no intention of leaving your side, my love. You have a tendency to, shall we say, get yourself in trouble?"

Ignoring his jibe, Cat turned in his arms and searched his face intently. "Are you certain you wish to sell her?"

"My dearest Cat, I would feel much safer knowing you are right under my nose, just in case you decide to dress up as a man and join the gypsies or take a notion to explore the mountain regions of Tibet, disguised as a monk. Also, I would discourage any more of René's ilk from making propositions."

"You are the only man who has made me an indecent proposal!" Cat interrupted.

"Or from flirting too enthusiastically," he amended, and Cat smiled against his chest. "I could also prevent any pirates from kidnapping you." At his last words, she saw his features harden for an instant before he smiled down at her. "So, my Cat, you will just have to get used to seeing a lot of me." He took her face in his hands and kissed her tenderly. "Besides, this is better . . ."

"What?"

"This, my love, is better than sailing." And with that he lifted her off her feet and carried her to the bed.

René left the following day, despite the urging of both Ransom and his wife. "No, I have what I came for," he said, smiling wickedly as he made his farewells on the steps of the plantation house.

"The *Reckless*," said Cat.

"No! A look at you, wildflower! Now, if you could promise me more than a look . . ." He raised his brows and eyed her suggestively as he bowed low over her hand, but Cat only shook her head, smiling at his antics.

"Off with you then, René!" Ransom laughed, putting an arm around his wife to pull her close as the Frenchman mounted his horse.

Watching the interchange, René reined in his prancing horse, turned in the saddle, and laughed. "What a picture of domestic bliss you make, my friend!" he shouted before riding down the avenue.

Ransom shook his head at the Frenchman and turned to admire his wife's upturned face. "René never lights in one place for long. He's always moving, perhaps in search of something he doesn't even know he's looking for," he mused. Then, grinning at Cat, Ransom bent to steal a kiss.

The two made their way about the grounds, Cat picking flowers and Ransom admiring her graceful form as she bent to pluck them. They came to rest under a huge old locust, Ransom dropping to lie on his side while Cat rested on her heels beside him, arranging her flowers into a bouquet.

"I have been thinking of leaving soon," Ransom said, looking up at her and receiving the full glow of her dazzling smile. "I have this idiotic desire to show you Morcester," he added somewhat sheepishly, plucking a flower from her hands.

"Why idiotic?"

"Because I haven't lived there in over ten years! Oh, I've kept it maintained and fully staffed. The estates are in excellent condition. But I never felt any ties with the place until now."

"Have you happy memories of it?"

"Oh, yes," Ransom chuckled, rolling onto his back. "When I was little. I had a wonderful nurse, Mrs. Cubbins. Everyone called her Cubby. If my mother forbade me something, I could always wheedle it out of Cubby, and if Cubby said I wasn't to toss pine cones out of the third-story nursery window onto the target beneath, mother could be persuaded.''

''You sound like a hideously spoiled boy!''

''Oh, I was. Dreadfully. But whenever father discovered one of my plots I was given a sound thrashing. Like the time he caught the cook's boy and me playing ninepins in the long gallery.''

''No!''

''Well, it wouldn't have been so bad, but that we were using his giant chess pieces as pins . . . God, I had forgotten that!''

Cat dropped the flowers in her lap and looked at Ransom, who was staring at the sky overhead. ''What happened to Cubby?''

''She died from some sort of fever when I was fourteen. Of course, I was too old for a nurse by then, but mother kept her on because she was like one of the family. Mother kept saying she might have another child and would need Cubby. I had a brother who died in infancy, but there were never any others.'' He sighed.

''And your parents?''

''They were killed in a fire not long after that,'' he said, focusing on the clouds but seeing into the past. ''They were visiting father's brother. It was an inferno. Wiped out the Du Preys in a single night, except for me. I refused to go. Some childish spat over my cousins.'' He shrugged. ''I can't even remember now, but I know my father and I had quite a row, and then they just took off. I can still see my mother leaning out of the coach, whispering to me to be good and she would make things right with father by the time they got back.'' He turned on his side again, his eyes on the flower between his fingers, as Cat watched him intently.

''I was so devastated. I was afraid to care for anyone—neighbors, friends—for fear they would die, too, and I would be hurt again,'' he said softly. ''Childish notion, but one that became so ingrained I could not easily shake it. Bosun understood that. That's why he was so surprised when I developed a fondness for my cabin boy,'' he said wryly, tapping her nose with the daisy in his hand.

''Ransom,'' she whispered tenderly, her heart in her throat as her fingers reached over to trace the smooth line of his jaw. ''I am glad you did, for I was already hopelessly in love with you.''

''I wish you would have let me know!'' he said with a rakish grin.

''Ha!'' Cat whooped. ''I wasn't stupid! The man I loved said, and I quote: 'Women on the whole are boring creatures,' '' she accused.

''I said that?'' His brow rose incredulously. ''Obviously some foolish patter suited for curious young cabin boys,'' he said with the lazy grin Cat loved so well.

''Pooh!'' She scowled, then peeped at him from under her lashes. ''Am I boring?''

''Ha!'' Ransom laughed. ''Anything but, my love. Anything but,'' he assured her as he took her in his arms.

Chapter 39

They left for England soon after René's visit, for Ransom was suddenly impatient to return, so much so that Cat wondered if René had said something to hurry his plans. No matter, she thought, for she was also eager to see her new home, where Ransom had spent his childhood and where, she hoped, they would raise children of their own.

Cat boarded her old ship in high spirits. She soon found, however, that her voyage on the *Reckless* was not as delightful as when she served as its cabin boy, the sense of adventure and belonging she had once felt having disappeared with her breeches.

Of course, her skirts would have hampered any climbs into the rigging, but that was just as well because Bosun vetoed such activities immediately, saying he would lose several years of his life if she "crawled about up there again."

She found, too, that her sensitivities had altered; the food, the water, and the *smell* seemed more objectionable than before. She had developed a new appreciation for personal hygiene, and her tolerance for certain members of the crew who did not share her enthusiasm became sorely strained. "Now I understand why Amelia never travels," she grumbled. "After living in a garden, the shock would kill her."

Still, Cat fell into her old relationship with Bosun

and some of her other friends among the crew, including Harry, who finally unbent after initially avoiding her, and she had to admit the sleeping arrangements were vastly improved over those on her last trip, for she infinitely preferred sharing the captain's bed to sleeping on her old hammock. More importantly, it was a relief to be able to love Ransom openly, no longer a prisoner of her disguise or her desire, and to bask in the warmth of his love.

As she stood beneath the stars, listening to the ship sounds that had once meant home to her, Cat knew that there came a time when one must let go of the past, that there was no going back, and that each step of life must be forward.

She thought of Wellshire, no longer feeling an urgent pull to return there, and realized that she'd all but forgotten Edward in the bliss of the past months. And that was as it should be, she decided, although she still wanted to see justice served. That part of her life was over, Cat knew, just as surely as her cabin boy days, and her life ahead with Ransom was all that held her interest now.

As if in answer to her thoughts, she felt his presence in the darkness beside her, filling her with a familiar warmth.

"What are you thinking about?" his deep voice asked in the stillness.

"Revenge," Cat answered with a chuckle, well imagining that mobile eyebrow raised in question. "I was thinking how pointless it is."

"Ah." Ransom breathed softly, his voice betraying no surprise at the odd turn of her thoughts.

"Do you still seek Devlin?"

"Yes," he answered, and this time there was a nearly imperceptible change in his voice. "I would not describe my quest as revenge, however," Ransom said. "Let us call it a score that needs to be settled, for the sake of all involved. I was looking for him, but now I find my mission more urgent—since he is the one who ordered your kidnapping."

"What of Edward?" Cat asked.

"I'm sure your cousin was involved in some way, but Devlin took it upon himself to set the scheme in motion," Ransom said. He paused, and she felt a sudden chill. "I cannot allow him to repeat the attempt."

"You know where he is?"

"I have a general idea," Ransom answered, offering no further explanation.

Cat was silent as she looked out over the ocean, hugging her arms tightly around herself in an effort to ward off a sense of foreboding. Although she had no desire to face further threats, she did not like the idea of Ransom pursuing this Devlin, especially if he were as coldly fiendish as his man Blakely. Remembering all too well the evil lurking under Richard's mild exterior, she shivered in the darkness.

"Of course, we must deal with Edward, too," Ransom said, breaking into her thoughts. "Or do you imagine he will wish you well?"

"I would think that now that I am the wife of a prominent nobleman," she said with a smile, "Edward would be wise enough to leave me alone."

"Hmmm." Although Ransom only grunted in response, his tone revealed his disagreement. "You are willing, then, to let his crimes go unpunished?"

"You yourself said it would be difficult to prove he murdered my stepfather," Cat said. "If you think he can be held responsible, then let us do so. Otherwise I wish to forget him," she said firmly.

"I want to make sure he has no further plans for your demise before I dismiss him so easily," Ransom said. "I don't imagine he's the trustworthy type," he added dryly before lapsing into silence. For a few moments nothing broke the stillness but the flapping of the sails and the creaking of the ship while each seemed lost in private thoughts. For her part, Cat was trying to think of some way to dissuade Ransom from his course.

As though he knew her state of mind and had no desire to argue, Ransom suddenly changed his tone. "But enough of this," he said briskly. "It is too beautiful a night for talk of revenge." He pulled her into his arms, and Cat pressed her cheek against his chest, unable to be rid of her own disquiet as easily. She felt as though there was much left unsaid and that Ransom was bent upon endangering himself in pursuit of the two villains who plagued them. She opened her mouth to protest, but his lips on her hair were reassuring, and soon the warmth of his body chased away her lingering chill.

Once again buoyant when they reached England, Cat was eager to begin her new life at her new home—until she actually saw it. To Cat, familiar with Aunt Amelia's comfortable cottage and the spacious country manor of Wellshire, the plantation houses on the islands were enormous and grand. But Ransom's great house on Windlay had in no way prepared her for her first sight of Morcester Hall, the ancestral home of the Du Preys.

Crafted of a pale rose brick, its many-windowed facade rose more than three stories to a high roof where brick chimneys towered still higher. As they drew closer she observed innumerable gabled windows jutting from the roof on what must have been the interior's third floor, and before the stately mansion, lining the steps that fell from either side of the huge front doors, a staff the size of a small village waited to greet the black-sheep duke and his new bride.

Cat was agape. "This is where we are to live?"

Ransom laughed. "It's not so bad once you get used to it."

"I'm sure it's not as forbidding when you grow up playing ninepins in the hallways," Cat said wryly.

"If it will put you at ease, I'll be happy to join you in a game. We can even use the same chess set that I did as a boy, though I believe Father locked it in a glass case after such ill usage."

Cat nearly assented. She quickly found that a month of joking and dicing with a group of grizzled sailors had not prepared her for the deference of Morcester's countless servants. Ransom's servants took her position seriously, and Cat tried to become accustomed to responding to the endless "your graces" and curtsies that were addressed to her.

She claimed she needed a map to find her way around the house, and when Ransom laughed, she didn't have the heart to tell him she wasn't joking. As she walked up the grand staircase with its carved balusters, glancing at the family portraits lining the walls, Cat told herself firmly that she only needed to locate the bedroom and the dining hall. All else was superfluous.

Finding her bedroom was easy enough, as it opened onto the master bedroom and off the infamous long gallery. With a sigh, she admired the French gilt furniture glowing in the candlelight, hardly able to believe that the beautiful room was hers. It was hung in pink silk, with a whimsical collection of drawings and paintings decorating its walls, and she leaned over the edge of the bed to gaze at an entrancing tapestry of a unicorn when she felt Ransom's breath warm upon her neck.

"Mother had a fanciful bend," he said. "You can change the room, or the whole place, for that matter," he whispered against her ear as he slipped his arms around her.

"No, this is lovely . . . Oh!" Cat gasped as she felt his lips against her neck and his hands cupping her breasts. Her gasp turned to soft sighs as her dress fell to her waist, and she felt his warm hands caress her naked breasts, his thumbs running over her nipples, while his mouth sent shivers up and down her neck.

She tried to reach him, but hampered by the bed and his body, she could only press back against him, drawing a low sound from his throat.

"Oh, Cat, my love, careful now, or I can't be held responsible," he whispered thickly against her throat. But Cat, her blood racing to pool and throb in the lower portion of her body, could only press closer against him. His mouth moved along each notch of her spine while his hands continued to knead her breasts.

"Ransom, please," she pleaded, her hands moving over him with a will of their own.

"Cat, have patience," he urged as his hand slipped under her skirts. At his touch, she reared against him, and he felt a surge of wetness in his hand. His request for patience was forgotten in an onslaught of desire.

"Ransom, please," she repeated, more urgently now, and he moaned low before lifting her onto the bed and throwing up her skirts to bare her thighs.

"Cat, Cat," he breathed as he cupped her breasts and moved against the silken softness of her. Lacking the will to deny her any longer, he leaned against her and entered to the sound of her soft cries, the pounding rhythms of her release shaking them both again and again.

Cat wandered along a heavily laden sideboard, choosing from an array of breakfast dishes, including eggs cooked any number of ways, thinly sliced beef, boiled ham, herring, tongue, custards, rolls, butter, jams, jellies, tarts, and pastries. "This is ridiculous!" she said finally, throwing down her fork.

"There is enough food here for the entire crew of the *Reckless*! What happens to what we don't eat?"

"I haven't the slightest notion, my love. Perhaps you should look into it," Ransom answered mildly.

"Well, you can be sure I will! And unless it is going to feed the needy, I am going to order less food for breakfast."

Ransom saw the determined set to her chin and smiled to himself. He knew Morcester would not intimidate her for long. With a sigh, he thought that now was as good a time as any to tell her of his plans. "Cat, I have some business that I must attend to immediately. I hate to leave you here alone, but it's most urgent."

At the word "leave" Cat's gaze flew to her husband's. Although she saw only warm concern in those beautiful brown eyes, she was struck with an ominous foreboding as she remembered his schemes to pursue Devlin. "What sort of business are we talking about?" she asked suspiciously.

"Well, the sale of the *Reckless* for one thing," he answered. "It shouldn't take long."

Cat felt a measure of relief, for how could he chase Devlin around the globe with no vessel? She associated her husband's enemy with the West Indies, so it never occurred to her that the man might now be but a few days away.

Edward, however, was another matter. Ransom could, after all, be intent upon a confrontation with her cousin. Although Cat did not fear Edward as she did Devlin, she still did not want Ransom going off alone, without her knowledge, into a threatening situation. Surely, though, he would tell her . . . or should she ask him outright if he planned to see Edward? She eyed him closely, but seeing nothing amiss in his features, she felt a small measure of guilt at her mistrust.

She looked down at her plate, trying not to frown.

Cat knew now that Ransom held a real title, and wealth along with it, and somewhere in the back of her mind she knew he had to run his businesses. After all, there would be investments and properties here in England to check on. Yet somehow she'd thought any traveling would include her. "Can't I come along?" she asked, annoyed at how piteous her question sounded.

Ransom smiled lovingly and reached for her hand. "Not this time, love, but every other. I promise."

Cat refused to beg and sent him on his way with good grace, but as she watched him ride away, her heart lurched in her chest.

Although he hated to leave his bride, Ransom wanted to make certain that she had a long and happy life with him, and to that end, he sought her cousin. He had already set some of his men to the task of discovering Devlin's exact whereabouts, with the hope of taking care of his enemy once and for all, but in the meantime he intended to make damn sure there would be no further trouble from the current baron of Wellshire.

Ransom did not tell his wife the main purpose of his trip, for he knew she would stubbornly insist on coming with him. And he had no intention of taking her anywhere near either villain when both seemed intent upon doing her harm. Nor did he see the need to alarm her needlessly. Although confident of his ability to deal with both men, he thought it better not to worry her.

His trip to Wellshire yielded nothing, for he was politely informed by the staff that his lordship was in London. Although no one could say exactly where Edward stayed when in the city, Ransom had his own ideas about possible locations, and he finally ran Edward down a few nights later at the Blue Ruin, a rather unsavory gaming hell. His waistcoat unbuttoned and his cravat askew, Edward was slouched over a chair at the faro table, where he had amassed quite a few losses. Sunk rather low, our dear cousin, Ransom thought.

"Moore, aren't you?" Ransom asked, seating himself beside Edward.

"*Lord* Moore, baron of Wellshire. Who are you?"

"Ransom Du Prey, duke of Morcester," Ransom answered coolly. "I have a matter of some importance to discuss with you."

"I'm busy," Edward drawled.

"I'm afraid it cannot wait," Ransom said mildly. He leaned toward Edward, who was ignoring him to watch the turn of the cards. "If you wish to talk here, that is your choice, but listen carefully. You will kindly leave your cousin alone."

"I don't know what you're talking about, you drunk," Edward mumbled, starting to rise from his chair. Ransom's lips curved into a smile that did not reach his eyes and he grasped the younger man's wrist in a deadly grip, forcing him back down into his seat.

"I do not have the desire to end your wretched existence as yet, but I can be persuaded." He spoke softly, without the heat of anger, but with cool conviction. "Ah, I see I have captured your interest. Good. You may forget whatever agreement you have with Devlin, for he is not long for this world, and you will not be either if you persist in pursuing an unwise course."

Ransom's words finally penetrated Edward's opium-dulled thoughts, and he started in surprise, raising his heavy-lidded eyes to look at the man threatening him.

"Yes, the game is up, Edward," Ransom said. "I would advise you to crawl back into whatever hole you came from, for your days as baron are numbered. You see, we frown on those who murder for their title.''

"You can't prove a thing," Edward said.

"Perhaps not." Ransom shrugged. "But I can still ruin you. Don't think I don't have the power," he said softly, waiting for the words to sink in. "Make no mistake, though—if you seek her out, you will see no courtroom or prison," he warned simply, "for I will kill you." The menace in his voice and bearing were unmistakable, chilling even Cat's reckless cousin.

"What the hell is she to you?" Edward finally managed to croak.

"She's my wife," Ransom said lightly as he rose from his chair, leaving Edward gaping after him.

Ransom exited the gambling den feeling confident that he would have no further trouble from that quarter. Although surly, Cat's cousin appeared to be little more than a drunken bully, a formidable foe for an old man and a young girl, perhaps, but a coward underneath his bravado.

Without wasting another thought on Edward, Ransom set his attention to Devlin, a far more clever and dangerous enemy. Hopefully, his sources had discovered Devlin's hiding place by now, so that Ransom could complete his business in London without further delay.

Devlin. Ransom's words to Edward had not been idle, for he had spent a lot of time considering what course to follow with his old enemy. He certainly had enough accusations—and even some hard evidence gathered over the years—to turn the man over to the authorities. If Devlin did not swing from a rope for his crimes, he would certainly spend the rest of his days in prison.

But would that effectively eliminate the threat Devlin had become? Although Ransom had no care for himself, he was concerned about Cat and the family they hoped to raise. Many a foul plot could be hatched from inside prison walls, and there were always men willing to carry out the deeds. Ransom could not imagine Devlin, already obsessed with revenge, losing interest in the Du Preys.

No, Ransom had been over and over this ground, and he always reached the same conclusion: Devlin must die.

Chapter 40

Cat braved Simpkins's hauteur and asked him for the third time if any letters had arrived. The look the butler gave her was known to strike terror into the hearts of unwanted callers and impertinent understaff, but Cat only sighed and thanked him. The last few days had stretched on interminably, and today seemed the worst of the lot.

After Ransom's sudden departure, Cat took her pick of the vast stables and rode, discovering with pleasure the beauty of the Morcester lands as she began calling upon her husband's tenants. It was still hard for her to comprehend that the thick forests, lush green hillsides, and farmlands leading down to the Wye all belonged to Ransom, and she smiled to herself as she remembered how she'd once thought him a masquerader with only ill-gotten gains to his credit.

She enjoyed calling on the tenants, who welcomed her with open arms, hopeful of once again having a Du Prey in residence, and she thrilled to ride again, enjoying the freedom to race over the grassy slopes. Her thoughts never seemed to be totally free of Ransom, however, and even though she kept busy, she fretted over his absence. If only he had not left her so abruptly, she thought, and among strangers in a strange house!

Then the rain started, a gloomy, constant drizzling guaranteed to dampen anyone's spirits, especially someone as lonely as Cat. Since the weather kept her indoors, she took the opportunity to meet with the household staff in an effort to take the reins of organization. She met hostile faces with imperturbable graciousness and those who extended friendly greetings with grateful warmth, but she longed for a friend.

Ransom had rarely been in residence since his childhood, so no visitors called, and Cat was loath to charge into the social sphere unattended and uninformed. As the second rainy day came and went, she began to feel abandoned. Above all, she yearned for her captain, and although she beat them away, gnawing doubts began to appear.

With a sigh, Cat wandered into the library, oblivious to its beauty and charm, thinking only that one could play ninepins here, too, or, for that matter, in practically every room she had seen. Wellshire's library would fit three times over into this cavernous room, where bookcases rose from floor to ceiling on one side, tall windows on the other, while above her head, a variety of angels (at least she hoped they were angels, since they were naked) frolicked in painted scenes among the plasterwork, and everywhere there was the glint of gilt. At one time she would have been enthralled, but her husband's absence weighed too heavily on her mind, so she merely walked slowly around the room, trailing her finger along the book bindings. She was idly noting that the books lacked even a speck of dust to collect on her finger when one of the footmen spoke from behind her.

''Mr. Simpkins directed me to bring this to you at once,'' he said, handing her an envelope bearing Ransom's scrawl. Cat could barely wait until the servant had turned to go before tearing open the letter

and eagerly scanning the single page. It was brief
and to the point:

My Catherine,

I regret that business has delayed my return. I am
now in London, where I hope to conclude matters
in a few days.

All my love,
Ransom

That was all? Cat turned the pale vellum over in
disbelief. He had deposited her here like so much
baggage while he traveled all over the countryside,
she thought with annoyance, and this brief missive
was hardly worth troubling Simpkins about. Her
melancholy surged into anger as she stood waving
the sheet back and forth. Well, she did not intend
to cool her heels waiting for him to take an inclination to visit, she thought resolutely. She would go
visiting herself!

If Ransom had seen the determined set of that
dainty chin, he would have known trouble was
brewing. Holding the edge of the letter to her cheek,
she smiled. Yes, that was just the thing. Why, she
could travel anywhere now that she was married and
a duchess to boot! She needed a change of pace, and
what better balm than a visit to her oldest and dearest friend Budd, the workman who had befriended
her throughout her childhood and who had taught
her all his sea lore. With her new plans firmly set
in her mind, Cat went in search of the appropriate
parties to ensure their proper implementation.

She soon discovered the smooth workings of Ransom's staff extended to traveling arrangements as
her trunk was packed and preparations were made
for her departure the following morning. Cat chose

the young maid who had been attending her, Emily, to travel with her, while the head coachman, Ralston, and an assistant would round out the little expedition. She disdained the slew of outriders Ralston suggested accompany them, unknowingly putting the coachman's nose further out of joint, for he already looked askance at the single trunk that would travel with them.

Blissfully unaware of the usual size of a duchess's entourage and the appropriate complement of trunks, Cat settled back in the elaborate coach, looking forward to her upcoming visit. She decided that she would try to persuade Budd to return with her to Morcester. He could even bring his lady friend if he so desired, she thought with a smile as she leaned back into the plush cushions.

As the miles went by, Cat was thankful for the well-sprung conveyance and her choice of traveling companion. A tiny sprite, Emily was even more talkative than Amelia and kept up a steady stream of patter during the long journey. Cat found that her new status made obtaining rooms effortless along the way, but she was dismayed by the fawning her presence elicited from some of the innkeepers.

All things considered, Cat decided that sailing was much preferable to overland travel, for although it was the epitome of luxury, the coach was still a coach, and as such, a confining vehicle. Longing to be able to stretch her legs for more than a few minutes at a time, she was heartily glad when they arrived in Coxley.

A flurry of activity greeted their arrival, and Cat knew that tongues were already wagging as she stepped from the coach with the help of Ralston, who made his opinion of the village's only inn, and indeed, the village itself, quite clear by the strained accents in which he inquired if this was her destination. Trying desperately to return his icy stare,

Cat could only stifle a giggle as she assured him it was and greeted old Mr. Tyber with a smile.

"Miss Amberly! Where have you been keeping yourself, and what's that contraption you're riding in?" Mr. Tyber asked. Squinting at the ducal crest emblazoned in gold on the side of the coach, he was blissfully unaware of Ralston's affronted glare.

"It is my husband's coach, Mr. Tyber," Cat said, putting her hand on his arm to gently but firmly turn him back toward the inn before Ralston could utter a word. Once inside, Cat rented a room while revealing as little as she could about herself, laughing off and deflecting the probing questions that the innkeeper felt his age and position entitled him to ask.

Mr. Tyber expressed surprise that she was not staying at Wellshire and Cat responded vaguely, not quite sure how the land lay at her old home. Word would soon reach the manor that she was back and staying at the inn, but no longer afraid of her cousin, she spared barely a thought for him.

When she finally made her escape from the kindly but curious old innkeeper, Cat returned to the coach, directing Ralston to the home of Budd's lady friend. She was grateful that she could not see the coachman's face as they turned into the tiny lane and stopped before a dilapidated Tudor house, one of many tall, narrow buildings of the period that were packed together not far from an unpleasant-smelling drainage ditch. Cat hardly trusted herself to look Ralston in the eye as he helped her step down.

"Thank you so much," she said, giving him a dazzling smile. Then "bold as you please," as Ralston would later relate to Mabel the undercook, she walked up the steps and knocked on the door. Cat knocked several times before the door finally was opened by a buxom female with such flaming red hair that Ralston swore it could not be her natural color.

"Mrs. Bottoms?" Cat asked.

The woman's eyes narrowed. "Who wants to know?"

"I'm a friend of Budd's," Cat said, smiling.

At the mention of Budd's name, the suspicion left the lady's face, to be replaced by an expression Cat found equally disquieting, but she gestured for Cat to enter, so Cat smiled and stepped into a narrow room. "I'm Mrs. Bottoms," the redhead said, motioning for Cat to take a seat at a small table. "So you're the little lady," she said, eyeing Cat from head to toe. "Some wine?"

"No, thank you," Cat said. "Is he here? I am most anxious to see him."

"No, he's not here, miss," the woman hedged. "Say, he said you were always a right one, and you look like you're doing all right for yourself. Are you?"

"Where is he? Is he ill? In prison?" Cat's voice remained even, but her hands clenched together in her lap.

"No," Mrs. Bottoms said, then with a frown, she heaved a sigh of disgust at the urgency in Cat's voice. "Well, I suppose you might as well know sooner as later. The man passed on about two months back," she announced matter-of-factly. When Cat gasped in shock, the lady assured her, "There was nothing you could do. It was the consumption, plain and simple." Mrs. Bottoms's steady gaze showed that she had seen too much life and death to take it to heart.

Although Mrs. Bottoms appeared to be wholly unaffected by her announcement, Cat was so shocked that she could only stare blindly at the water marks on the wall, unable to move or speak. The redhead waited expectantly, then clicked her tongue and rose from her chair, returning to push a none-too-clean glass of wine toward her guest.

"Here, drink up, my lady," she said, giving Cat a nudge. Obediently, Cat closed her slim fingers about the glass and brought it to her lips. The wine, thick, sweet, and potent, jolted even Cat's hardened palate, and she blinked as it scorched her throat.

"There now, that'll get you going, won't it, my lady?" Mrs. Bottoms asked. When her guest still did not speak, she clicked her tongue again and, hands on her hips, moved to stand in front of Cat. The frown on Mrs. Bottoms's face plainly stated that the interview was not going as she expected, but then her disgust was replaced by a worried look as she was suddenly struck by the notion that this lady might be having some sort of fit right in her room.

"You all right, my lady?" Mrs. Bottoms asked, her concern not for Cat, but for herself. She did not want any trouble, not her! She urged Cat from her seat. "Come on, miss. Let's get you some air," she said, helping Cat to the door with as much speed as was possible under the circumstances.

On the threshold Cat finally remembered herself and, groping in her reticule for a moment, she pressed some coins into the woman's hand. "Thank you, missy! I knew you was a decent sort," Mrs. Bottoms said, and fingering the coins, she shut the door, leaving Cat standing in the wind on the steps.

Ralston could see the duchess was as white as a sheet, and he rushed to help her into the coach. He was so alarmed by her pallor and by her glazed and unfocused eyes that he went so far as to ask if she wanted a doctor summoned, but she only shook her head.

Cat said not a word to Ralston or Emily when she alighted at the inn and slipped like a wraith past old Mr. Tyber. She went directly to her room, and there she remained well into the evening hours, an untouched tray of food before her, as she alternately watched the activity on the street below and brooded on Budd's death.

Somehow, Cat thought—when she could think—somehow, she should have been able to prevent his death. Budd should have been taken care of in his illness, and she should have seen to it! She spent a sleepless night, tossing and turning on the narrow bed, while going over what she could have done differently. If only she had taken him with her when she left England, she thought miserably, although she knew that Budd never would have approved her scheme to sail the seas.

Morning found her puffy-eyed and, although she finally roused herself after dinner, she was still pale and listless. She stood by the window, staring unseeing at the yard below while her trunk was taken from the room. Emily bustled about, chatting mostly to herself.

"Your grace, all is ready," the maid said.

"You go ahead, Emily. I'll be along in a moment," Cat said. Shaking her head sadly, Emily left, passing Jenny, the inn's serving girl, on her way out.

"Miss Cat—um, beg pardon—your grace."

Cat turned to smile weakly. "Yes, Jenny, what is it?"

"Well, I just wanted to tell you, miss—your grace," Jenny said with a conspiratorial gleam in her eye, "how handsome I thought your husband was."

"My husband?" Cat questioned blankly.

"Why, yes," Jenny said, looking confused. "You are the duchess of Morcester now?"

"Yes."

"Well, the duke was here a few days ago, and—I mean, beg pardon, your grace—but he was a lovely one and not so high-handed as some of that sort, neither," Jenny said, nodding her head for emphasis.

It was Cat's turn to look baffled. Ransom here? Why would business bring him here unless that business was with . . . Edward! "When was he here?" Cat asked.

Startled at the sharp tone in her voice, Jenny looked bewildered again. "Why, I'm not sure. Not more than a week ago."

"Why didn't Mr. Tyber say anything to me?"

"Well, I don't think he understands . . ." Jenny trailed off, and Cat realized that poor old Mr. Tyber would probably never connect her to the duke unless they appeared together.

"Did he stay long?" Cat asked, her mind frantically turning over the possibilities of a confrontation with Edward gone awry.

"No, your grace. Just for a bite. Said he was off to the manor, he did."

Cat's heart lurched at the words Jenny spoke so casually. Had Ransom seen Edward and left again, or was he still at Wellshire? Although her cousin no longer inspired the fear he once had, Cat knew he was not above some trickery—or shooting someone in the back . . .

"Thank you, Jenny," Cat said, rushing past the maid and down the stairs to her waiting carriage. "There has been a change of plans," she told Ralston curtly as he handed her into her seat. "We are not going to Morcester, but to Wellshire Manor."

Although Ralston scowled at her words, his displeasure went unnoticed by Cat, who had thoughts only for Ransom.

"Your grace?" Emily had to repeat her words twice before she finally drew her mistress's attention.

"Yes, Emily?"

"Aren't we going home?"

"We are to visit my cousin," Cat said absently, her face even paler than before. She rebuffed further questions from her inquisitive maid, however, for Cat could spare no energy on the girl. She was too busy praying fervently that her husband still lived.

Chapter 41

Ransom was on someone else's mind, too, but the thoughts were not as kind. Edward was still smarting over the cavalier treatment he'd received at the Blue Ruin and had slunk home to Wellshire, where he could at least bully the rest of the household.

The life of power and ease Edward had envisioned acquiring with his title had turned out rather differently than he expected; he had gained no influence and it seemed that, of late, he garnered little respect as well. Certainly, his newfound wealth should have brought him ease, but his worries had not ended and the money bought him no peace. The gambling gave him little pleasure anymore, while now he brooded constantly over his cousin, who seemed to be the source of most of his troubles.

Damn the little chit! Why all the sudden interest in her, anyway? He had barely given her a thought until Devlin had forced him to recall her existence. Edward winced at the memory of Devlin's contempt, blaming his cousin for it. If not for her, he might never have been dragged into Devlin's presence again. And it seemed that he had barely recovered from that ordeal when the mysterious duke had descended upon him, threatening him as though he were nobody. It was all too much, and he turned to his closest friend of late—the bottle—sorely depleting the cellars before passing out on a couch in the blue drawing room.

The older servants could only shake their heads in disbelief to see the state of things at the manor now. The housemaids ventured out to clean in the morning, but gave the blue drawing room a wide berth after discreetly closing its doors. They had discovered, along with the rest of the household, that the best course was to keep out of the young master's way.

"Good Lord, what is it now?" groaned Bentley, the butler, upon hearing the arrival of a coach. Such a breach of etiquette, which he would never have committed in James Pembroke's day, was little noticed by the other servants, all of whom were feeling too sorely put-upon by Edward's presence to care.

"Why, it's Cat, sir," squealed one of the housemaids, peeking out from behind the draperies to see a well-dressed woman alight from an elegant coach.

Bentley, a wide grin on his face, held the door open as word spread with amazing speed throughout the manor that little Cat was home and stepping out of a fancy coach with a huge golden crest.

Cat swept through the entrance of Wellshire with the grace and style worthy of her new position, but once inside she nearly broke down as she realized that each and every member of the staff lined the entrance hall. Bentley shut the door behind her, intoning, "Welcome home, Miss Catherine," and she felt a lump in her throat as she saw his hearty grin.

With eyes misting, Cat walked along the entrance hall, holding out her gloved hand and speaking in turn to each of her former servants, many as close to her as family. There was Bertha, the cook, and Charlotte, an upstairs maid, and Charlie, the head gardener. "How's little Harry?" Cat asked of Clara, a kitchen maid.

"Taller than I am now, my lady, and stronger than an ox!"

They were still filing in silently from the back of the house when Edward appeared, dressed in the same clothes in which he had arrived from London the night before. "What the hell?" he croaked as he came upon the scene.

For long moments he stared at the poised, well-dressed woman standing before him, unable to see in her the young girl he had tried to murder, but recognition finally came, and with it a sudden paling of his face.

"Get back to your duties," he choked at the servants, but his voice lacked its old bite, and although some fled abruptly, others, Bertha among them, moved so slowly as to seem insolent. Bentley appeared not to have heard at all and still stood stiffly by the entrance as if to watch over Cat.

"Cousin," Cat said softly, surprising herself with the venom in her tone. "Would you care to speak privately?"

Edward nodded, scowling, and the two moved to the main drawing room. Once inside, the door shut behind them, he walked to a side table where a decanter of sherry stood and poured himself a liberal portion, while Cat stripped the gloves from her hands and threw them on a nearby table. Then Edward, who earnestly desired stronger liquor but did not want to call a servant, took a healthy swallow of the sherry and turned to face an adversary he had never thought to see again.

Despite Devlin's promises, Cat had returned, and not as a friendless young thing to be intimidated, but as a fiery woman whose eyes blazed fearlessly. Still, thought Edward, she was no match for him, and he sneered in her direction. "Well, well, if it isn't little Catherine, all grown up, and dressed up, too."

Cat regarded her cousin closely. His handsome face was marred by two days of dark stubble, and his shirt, hanging open, could only be described as slept in. He certainly did not look capable of besting Ransom. "Where is my husband?" Cat asked, emboldened by her new assessment of Edward.

"What?"

Edward truly appeared puzzled by the question, and Cat allowed herself to savor a small measure of relief before questioning him further.

"Don't fence with me, Edward," she said scornfully. "I know he was here. When did he leave, and where did he go?"

Edward shrugged. "How should I know? Perhaps you should keep a tighter rein on him . . . or is he already bored with your charms?"

Cat only smiled coldly at the remark. "Shall I be blunt, Edward? So far I have kept your past misdeeds quiet, but that situation can easily change," she warned. "Prove to me that he left in good health, and I will not send for the authorities."

For a moment Edward stared in amazement, then anger darkened his features. "Why, you little bitch," he snarled, and his arm shot out to grasp hers in a deadly grip, pulling her toward him.

The changes Edward had noted in his cousin were more than superficial, however, for since their last meeting she had battled storms at sea, brawled with sailors, escaped from a pirate ship, and cheated death more than once. Accustomed to taking care of herself very efficiently, she was a far cry from the child whom Edward had once threatened, and she had faced opponents that made him look like the sneaky little weakling he was.

With a grunt, she slammed her foot down on his, then raised her knee where she knew it would do the most damage. Edward fell back against the side table with a cry while Cat dusted herself off and walked to the door.

"Bitch! I'll kill you!" Edward growled. Roused from his lethargy, he stumbled after her, but just then the door was flung open, stopping both parties in their tracks. In stepped a small but rotund man with dark eyes and a dark pointed beard. He moved smoothly despite his girth, and quickly too, apparently, for Bentley followed him, breathlessly mouthing apologies for the intrusion.

"It's all right, Bentley. Leave us," Edward said. When the butler looked questioningly at Cat, he repeated his order with more force. "Get out!" Bentley left the room with as good a grace as he could muster.

The exchange was lost on Cat, whose attention was focused on the stranger leaning over her hand with a smile. "Duchess! It is such a pleasure!" he said, and Cat caught the faint scent of spices before he straightened. "You can't imagine how anxious I have been to meet you," he continued, motioning for her to take a seat. Nonplussed, Cat sat on the edge of her chair, uncertain to whom she was talking.

"When my sources told me you were heading south, I did so hope you would stop at your former home, for the baron here is an old friend of mine," the man said, smiling tightly at Edward for the first time.

For his part, Edward looked even paler than before as he sank into a chair near his cousin. As Cat glanced from one man to the other, she suddenly was struck with the certainty that, although she had never seen him before, she recognized the man before her. With a surprising clarity, she realized that she was speaking to none other than Devlin himself.

He must have caught the flicker of surprise in her eyes, for his thin lips tightened into a mean smile.

"I gather you know me, my dear. How clever of you! But then, I knew you were gifted. I am Tremayne Devlin," he said. Then, his eyes never leaving hers, he spoke over his shoulder to her cousin. "Lock the door, Edward," he instructed. When Edward did not move, he repeated softly, "Edward." This time Edward roused himself and rose to do Devlin's bidding while Cat watched.

"Just a precaution, my dear. I don't want you going anywhere," Devlin said. "You see, I have plans for you."

"Do you?" Cat asked, her voice laced with sarcasm.

"Yes, I do," and the tone of his voice again changed, to a more menacing level. That tone and the look he sent her made Cat suppress a shiver. He was not as cold as Richard Blakely, but he was just as evil, and she shrugged off a tingle of fear.

"I'm afraid your husband is pursuing me quite aggressively, and I need something to hold him up a bit—just until I can leave the vicinity," Devlin said bitterly. "I think ransoming you to your husband . . . no pun intended," he noted with a thin smile, "should fend him off temporarily."

"And do you imagine that I'll sit still for this? That you can take me prisoner in my former home, filled with servants who are loyal to me?" Cat asked, incredulous.

"Oh yes," Devlin said, pulling a small gun from his coat and training it on her heart. "Naturally, you may scream all you like, but by the time your idiotic servants break down the door, you will be long dead."

"You see, it is just a matter of time," he explained. "The more you cooperate now, the longer you will live, yet the chances of your ultimate survival are quite remote. Your loving cousin longs for your demise," he said, inclining his head in Edward's direction, "but, more importantly, *I* want you dead. It will serve both as revenge upon Du Prey and retribution for poor Richard, who died by your devices. So, my dear, you might as well go gracefully."

"I think not," said a voice behind her, and Cat nearly jumped from her seat as she recognized her husband's rich tones. She turned to see him, tall and handsome and calm, as he stepped from behind the curtains covering the French doors. He, too, held a gun, and it was pointed directly at Devlin.

"Did you really think I had lost your trail in London?" Ransom asked coldly. "This time I have been very thorough, and you, Devlin, are through."

Devlin's scowl was filled with hatred, but he did not move or flinch. "Shoot me if you like," he invited, smirking, "but your dear wife will most certainly die, too." He spoke the words with a conviction that Cat did not doubt, for they were at a standoff.

Devlin did not take her into account, however, and Cat could see that all his attention was trained on Ransom, the loathing he felt for her husband seeming to fill the room. Ransom was speaking again, warning Devlin to put down his weapon, and while he talked Cat slipped her hand under her skirts for her precious silver blade.

It sang through the air with deadly accuracy to lodge in the fat flesh of Devlin's shoulder, but it did not stop him. He still held the gun, and his finger pulled the trigger, causing it to discharge directly toward the spot where Cat had been sitting. She had moved, of course, when she threw the knife, but the bullet was still close enough to give her pause even as it cracked harmlessly into the chair. Then another shot broke the stillness and Devlin toppled forward, his features altered by an uncharacteristic look of surprise.

"Was that satisfactory, your grace?" another voice asked from behind Devlin, and Cat was utterly astonished to see her own coachman climb through a window.

"Done to perfection, Ralston," Ransom answered quietly. He, too, moved toward the fallen man, then Bentley's voice could be heard along with loud knocking, and Cat rose to unlock the door.

Edward stood slowly, staring dully at Devlin's lifeless body. Then the enormity of his predicament hit him, and he spun to face Cat. "You witch! *You* are to blame for all this!" he spat venomously.

Ransom quickly stepped to Cat's side. "Careful, Moore. I could easily kill you where you stand, but I prefer not to distress my wife further; nor do I wish to trouble myself to see that you are brought to justice. However, I fear I would find it difficult to relax, knowing you still reside in this country. Perhaps a long trip to, say, Borneo, would suffice. I'm sure there are many 'opportunities' for such as you there, or in the Americas. But there *is* this little matter of your title and claim to Wellshire . . ."

Wellshire was thus left without its baron, and Cat, too, had no plans to remain, for she intended to return as soon as possible to Morcester.

As she lay in her childhood bed the night before their departure, Cat banished any old ghosts that lingered in her rooms of the mother and father she'd never known, the stepfather who'd done his best for her, and the lonely old sailor who'd befriended her one stormy night. She sent a special blessing out to Budd, for without him her life would have taken a very different turn. The thought made her press a light kiss upon the hand that rested on her shoulder.

"Hmmm?"

"I thought you were asleep," Cat said, nuzzling her husband's neck.

"No," Ransom answered, "I was just thinking about the little girl who grew up here. You know, my love, this room reflects you, with its odd combination of lace and wooden ships, books and birds' nests." He laughed softly, then more seriously he added, "We can stay here, if you wish."

"Oh, no. I will be glad to go home," Cat said, leaning against his chest.

Ransom chuckled in the darkness. "To the monstrously huge place full of strangers, as you put it?" he asked.

"Yes. I find the place grows on you, like a canker." Cat smiled against his hand, drawing a laugh from him. "Just as long as you have no future travel plans that exclude me," she warned.

"Hmmm, let me think . . ." Ransom rubbed his chin as if in thought, then yelped as Cat's dainty teeth closed over his finger.

"No, I have no travel plans," Ransom said, and Cat released his finger to press tiny kisses along his palm. "But what of you, my little Cat, have you any surprise trips in the offing?"

"No," she answered, having the good grace to hang her head guiltily even as she giggled.

"No more masquerades or outlandish adventures?"

"No, captain," Cat whispered with a smile. "I see nothing ahead but smooth sailing."